Three Words

by
Matt Turner

T-Mac,
I hope this brings you a smile. I have many memories of you: In class, or on the court, but ill never forget your kindness the day of grad. You helped me with my nerves, and this world is all about small kindnesses.
            Never Change.
                Matt Turner
                2012

Copyright © 2012 by Matt Turner
First Edition – September 2012

Illustrator: Rory Card

ISBN
978-1-4602-0459-7 (Hardcover)
978-1-4602-0457-3 (Paperback)
978-1-4602-0458-0 (eBook)

All rights reserved.

This is a work of fiction. Names, characters, businesses, organizations, places, events and incidents either are the product of the author's imagination or are used fictitiously. Any resemblance to actual persons, living or dead, events, or locales is entirely coincidental.

No part of this publication may be reproduced in any form, or by any means, electronic or mechanical, including photocopying, recording, or any information browsing, storage, or retrieval system, without permission in writing from the publisher.

Produced by:

FriesenPress
Suite 300 – 852 Fort Street
Victoria, BC, Canada V8W 1H8

www.friesenpress.com

Distributed to the trade by The Ingram Book Company

To Those I Love
Have Loved
And Have Lost

The First Three Words

Chapter One

Tristan loved gym class. He had an insatiable appetite for showing his prowess when it came to anything athletic. As he walked down the dimly lit hallway, he took note of all the different faces he saw. *High school is just so strange* he thought. There were faces he feared, faces he respected, faces he pitied, and faces he wished he could see more of. The hallways were not that crowded at his small country school, but to him, it seemed like the biggest place on earth. Tristan was constantly thinking about his image and his social status—like any other teenager—but unlike some, he was perfectly willing to play the teenage game.

Tristan had two years under his belt. He was now a proud ninth grader. He knew exactly how life worked, especially at Sageview High School. Make friends with everyone. Don't burn bridges. Play sports, and become popular. Date pretty girls. If you climbed the social ladder intelligently enough, eventually, *eventually*, you could become Tyrone Randall. The sun at Sageview rose and set on Tyrone, and Tristan knew it. Phase one of becoming Tyrone's successor was being a gym class all-star.

Tristan rounded the corner and headed for the gym. He looked left and right, trying to locate Ryan. He wondered how hard it could be to find his gigantic friend and frowned as it became increasingly difficult. He thought the world of Ryan but was easily annoyed when his friend did not stick to game plans. The two of them together were an amazing team. They were loved by the entirety of the junior high. Ryan was the Robin to Tristan's Batman, the Pippen to his Jordan. Although secretly, Tristan wondered who was the more valuable of the two. Ryan was his best friend, but he was also his competition for high school supremacy.

"Ryan!" *Where is he?* "Goddammit..." Tristan muttered as he turned back toward the gym.

"Watch your mouth, Cage!" Mr. Ferguson hollered.

Ahhh Ferguson, he thought, *always trying to be the hero of the teaching world. Friggin' loser.*

Tristan paid no attention to the robust annoyance and turned back to his immediate concern.

"Ryan!"

Tristan started to panic. Inside the gym doors awaited the most beautiful girl on the planet. She was dark-skinned and dark featured and *exactly* the princess Tristan needed at his side. Ryan knew the plan; they had gone over it ten times in Math. *Where the hell is he? There's no way I'm going in there without him.*

Tristan had laid the groundwork all last year for this moment. Today was the day Rachel Smith would be his.

Tristan spent the entire summer agonizing over how he could get Rachel to fall madly in love with him. He watched *Titanic* at least five times. Read poetry—even wrote some poetry—studied a few chick flicks, and even talked to his grandmother about how to treat women. The long and short of it was that Tristan was obsessed with making Rachel love him, and was hell-bent on succeeding.

The problem was he had a few obstacles he needed to overcome, after an epic failure his first try. Being himself—the guy who listened, the guy who cared, the guy who was genuine—failed miserably. It simply wasn't good enough. Rachel liked senior high boys, older, more *mature*. She liked rock'n'roll, not light rock, and she was interested in much more than kissing—which Tristan had never even done. So what happened was pretty catastrophic;

Tristan ended up in 'the friend zone,' and Rachel developed a crush on a tenth grader, nicknamed 'Guns,' for his massive biceps.

Tristan could not comprehend what made Guns so attractive. He smoked—the rumour was he smoked weed—was always in trouble at school, and he drove a beat-up excuse for a car that resembled a NASA project gone bad. Guns swore incessantly and had brutal grades.

Maddeningly, Rachel didn't seem to notice the flaws in his personality, though it probably helped that he was built like a Greek god. He seemed to always have a tan, even in the winter. He had sandy blonde hair and blue eyes. And the worst part of all was that Rachel loved every little bit of it. Tristan knew he was essentially competing with Sageview's Brad Pitt, and it scared the hell out of him.

It was not Guns that scared him, but the competition. He could very well lose. He was afraid of how it would *feel*. Tristan had a problem with his damned stubborn feelings getting in the way. But that was all going to change this year, when he began his quest to become king of Sageview. When he was King, Rachel would be his Queen.

Tristan knew he was well equipped for the challenge. He was very good looking, at least as far as fourteen-year-olds went. He had naturally curly, dark brown hair—almost black—that was currently worn rather long. He was tall, dressed well, and he was told he had a killer smile. Perhaps his greatest asset though, was his deep green eyes that always seemed to reflect kindness and sincerity.

Tristan muttered a curse to his parents, who had obviously raised him to be emotionally undesirable to the opposite sex, and attempted to regain his focus. Ryan was still AWOL.

The sounds of gym class were just about all he could hear: mats being thrown to the floor, Mr. Gibbs directing traffic in his commanding voice, and someone, *someone* calling his name.

Rachel? Nope.

Tristan turned and smiled as his friend Deanna rushed to his side.

"I was just in the locker room," Deanna said with an evil grin, "and you should see what Rachel is wearing today. She's going to have *all* your attention today, Tristan."

"Oh God," Tristan said. He could feel the blood rushing to his face. "Could you please keep your voice down D?"

It was no secret that Tristan was head over heels for Rachel, but he only talked openly about it to Deanna and Ryan. He had to keep his calm, cool exterior to the rest of the world. Tyrone Randall was cool as ice, and he ran the joint.

Deanna laughed. "Sorry, Tristan," she said, "but you are just so cute when you are flustered." She blew Tristan a quick kiss and ran to help some other kids set up the wrestling mats.

Tristan turned and continued toward the locker room. He pushed his way through the locker room door, hoping and praying that Ryan would appear so they could go over the plan one last time. After a quick, somewhat desperate scan of the small locker room, he sighed and promised himself to kill Ryan—*painfully*—if he screwed this up. Tristan walked to his locker and kicked off his shoes. For a moment he paused. He put both hands against the lockers and he rested his forehead lightly on his own. He said a silent prayer.

Please God, let my love life work out for once.

He took a deep breath and finished changing. Tristan gathered himself and walked toward the locker room door. Then he heard it: the unmistakable laugh of Ryan Carlyle. Ryan's laugh was high pitched, frantic, and deafening all at the same time. It was as disturbing as it was contagious. Anyone who heard Ryan laughing would undoubtedly begin laughing as well. Ryan entered the locker room backwards still laughing at whatever was going on in the gym. He turned to see Tristan scowling at him.

"Awww c'mon man," Ryan said, "It's not my fault! My girl hauled me into the book room for a make-out session after Math."

He stared at Tristan, looking like a six year old who had just spilled his milk.

Tristan could no longer hold back a grin. "You're an idiot. Hurry up and get changed."

Ryan moved quickly to his locker. As he was changing he got right to the point: "Ok, let's make sure we have this straight. We are scheduled to wrestle today in class. We wrestle, we put on a show, and then I say you pulled on my shorts and call you a cheater. We get into each other's face and Mr. Gibbs breaks us up. You look like a badass, and Rachel falls in love with you. How am I doing?"

"Better than I expected," Tristan said, pleasantly surprised. "Let's get out of here before Mr. Gibbs snaps on us."

The boys left the locker room and took a seat on the wrestling mat. One of the other boys, Matt, tapped Tristan on the shoulder and flicked his eyes towards the girls' locker room. Tristan looked up and felt his jaw drop. Rachel had just come into the gym wearing tight athletic shorts and a basketball jersey over her white t-shirt. Tristan had a thing for girls in athletic gear, and Rachel, well, Rachel was something else.

He started to panic. "Ryan," he whispered, "Ryan! Don't beat up on me. Make me look good!"

Ryan patted him on the back to let him know all was well, but they both knew it would be hard to make the scam believable. Ryan had an overwhelming size and strength advantage. On paper, Tristan was screwed. Ryan stood six foot three, and his strength was already legendary. Carlyle should mop the floor with him. At fourteen, Ryan had already maxed out the weight on the universal gym set—a whopping 300 pounds. Growing up on a farm had its advantages. Ryan was a freak of nature in all the right ways, and the girls loved him; luckily he was off the market.

Rachel took her seat, and Mr. Gibbs followed behind her and went to stand in front of the class. "Good afternoon, ladies and gentlemen. We have a special treat for you today. As you know, we are finishing up our wrestling unit and our in-class tournament is almost at an end. Today is our championship match. Ryan Carlyle, with a record of 4-0 will face Tristan Cage, with a record of 3-1. Good luck to both of you."

Tristan and Ryan rose simultaneously and walked to the middle of the mat. Mr. Gibbs went over the rules as a formality, and the boys shook hands. They attempted to make it seem like they were serious about winning, and it must have been believable, because the entire class erupted into cheers for both boys. Tristan was pleased. Their enthusiasm was an unexpected, but welcome, addition to the plan.

The bell rang and the boys grappled hard. Their classmates cheered even louder. Tristan quickly realized how lucky he was that Ryan wasn't trying. He was no match for Ryan's strength. Ryan allowed him to keep up for the first round—for dramatic purposes—and all was going perfectly. All the other students were cheering loudly, and Rachel was obviously into the action. Maybe she winked at him—maybe it was his imagination.

Who cares, he thought, *soon she will be mine.*

Mr. Gibbs rang the bell for the second round. They met at the centre of the ring and started rolling around on the mat. After a matter of moments Ryan broke free, stood up, and started ranting about how Tristan had pulled on his shorts for leverage. Tristan was beaming inside, but forced himself to be furious on the outside.

Ryan was a great actor. "I thought you were my friend! I can't believe you tried to cheat!"

Tristan fought back, "You were losing and are making excuses! I can't help it that you are a sore loser!"

The class went silent when the argument began, and they were all waiting in anticipation.

Tristan was ecstatic.

Soon Mr. Gibbs would break them up and he could act like a wild man trying to get to Ryan. The only problem was he couldn't see Mr. Gibbs anywhere. He tried to hide the panic on his face; the plan was going to fail! He would be in the friend zone forever, and Guns would be making sweet love to—

DAMMIT!

At that moment he caught a glimpse of Ryan moving his lips ever so slightly. Tristan was furious, and desperate enough to actually hold some contempt for his counterpart for being so ridiculous at such an important moment. What could he possibly be—

And then he realized what Ryan was mouthing ever so subtly: *hit me.*

Tristan closed his eyes and swung.

Chapter Two

All hell broke loose. Tristan felt himself engulfed in man-sized arms as Mr. Gibbs reappeared as if by magic. Tristan hit the mat hard, with Mr. Gibbs on top of him. His mind was racing. Had he just punched his best friend in the face? Ryan definitely told him to, *or had he?* A million thoughts were fighting for the right to be heard as he tried hard to assess the severity of the situation. He had made solid contact; his hand felt like it had collided with the man of steel. He chuckled at the thought. At the moment, Ryan was his hero, and if he would ever speak to him again, he would be sure to tell him so.

Focus, Tristan!

God he was bad at that. Who was this person screaming in his ear?

"Cage, have you lost your senses!? What in God's name were you thinking?"

Tristan pried his face off the mat to look, as best he could, at an irate Mr. Gibbs. Gibbs had Tristan's face shoved hard into the mat. Tristan peered over his shoulder to see that his teacher's face was contorted in a way that reflected his genuine surprise and anger. Tristan could feel the breath of Mr. Gibbs on the back of his neck, and it was making him very uncomfortable.

"Uhhh, Mr. Gibbs, I think I'm ok now. Can uhhh, you let me up?"

"Shut up, Cage. You can stay down here until the end of time for all I care." Mr. Gibbs pulled himself roughly off of Tristan's back and bent over to check on Ryan. Tristan held his breath. He hoped he hadn't hurt the big lug, but at the same time he didn't want to look like a weakling in front of Rachel. So, hopefully he had left some sort of mark. He sat up slowly. Tristan observed what he could through a tangled web of limbs that had crowded around the fallen martyr. Ryan was flat on his back holding his mouth.

Tristan quickly examined his throbbing hand. There were no cuts, so hopefully he hadn't hit Ryan in the teeth.

"Carlyle, you ok?" Mr. Gibbs was bent over, one hand on his knee, the other on Ryan's shoulder. Ryan nodded slowly, and Mr. Gibbs beckoned a couple other guys to come help Ryan to his feet. For the first time, Tristan was aware that there were many sets of eyes on him, most did not seem friendly. Apparently his classmates did not appreciate his new found aggression, especially against someone as well-liked as Ryan.

Oh well, Tristan thought, *let them think what they want, as long as Rachel got a front row seat.*

His eyeballs were scanning frantically—*where is she?* Then he spotted her. She was staring directly at him. She was shaking her head.

Wait, NO! Shaking her head? This was not right. She was not smiling, in fact, she was scowling. Tristan quickly did some mental math and concluded that shaking of the head plus scowl did not mean love. It did not mean lust. It did not even mean infatuation. She was disgusted! How could this be! Rachel loved bad boys! Oh, this was just excellent. He had punched his best friend in the mouth, faced a likely suspension, and his hand hurt like hell.

Tristan stood up quickly, with every intention of explaining himself to Rachel, but before he got a single step Mr. Gibbs had him by the sleeve dragging him to the office.

Tristan sat waiting in the principal's office hunched over and miserable. *How could I be so stupid?* He was confused and angry.

Girls are evil, he thought. She sent mixed signals all the time. She told him what she liked in a guy, and when he tried to be that guy, she was disgusted. All he wanted was for her to like him. *What do I have to do?* He talked to her on the phone until 2AM about how Guns was so wonderful. He listened. He never complained about it. He let her copy his math homework almost daily. He always gave her his green skittles because she liked them best. He walked her to class. He walked her home. She told him he's the most wonderful guy, but none of that seemed to interest her when it came to a relationship. Tristan shook his head; he was on the verge of tears. He had ruined his life for someone who didn't even give a shit.

The office door opened and Ryan walked in. He had an ice pack pressed to his mouth with his right hand, his left hand held the yellow office referral. He slumped down in the chair next to Tristan.

"Did it work?" Ryan said almost inaudibly. It was very hard to hear him through the mass of ice pressed to his face.

"I don't think so," Tristan said. "She did not look very happy at all."

"Well—"

Tristan cut him off. "I'm so sorry, man. I really thought you told me to hit you. I totally get it if you are pissed. I'm sorry." The last part was uttered rather weakly, for Tristan felt weird apologizing so earnestly to another boy.

Behind Ryan's ice pack the right side of his mouth twitched into a grin.

"I *did* tell you to hit me. And you bloody listened. Didn't hold anything back, did you?"

Tristan could not believe his friend's good humour.

"Well, I had to make it look real."

Ryan chuckled. "I'd say you definitely did that. Oh well, just a fat lip. Mrs. Anderson says the ice will take the swelling right down."

Tristan could feel himself smirking now. "I didn't actually knock you down, did I?"

Ryan started to backpedal. "Uhhh no, I just, uhhh, lost my balance is all."

Both boys started to laugh hysterically. The last words spoken before the principal entered the room were from Ryan's maimed mouth: "You owe me."

Luckily, Tristan did not get suspended, but Mrs. Anderson sentenced him to work in the cafeteria at lunch for the entire week. He hated it there. It smelled bad—like burnt oil and fried fish—and he had to wear that stupid hair net. Not to mention, he had to endure the 'slave status' he had taken on as his friends became accustomed to ordering as much as possible from the deep fryer where he was stationed. He was sure the guys had never eaten as many chicken fingers and fries as they had that week.

Tristan and Ryan decided that they shouldn't talk for a week in order to give the impression that they were still mending fences. It seemed a lot easier than explaining the entire conspiracy to everyone who asked. They wrestled, they were competitive, and things got out of hand. The End. Luckily, everyone seemed to accept this version of the events.

Rachel hadn't spoken to him since the event. He didn't understand. What had he done to her? He had heard through the grapevine—Deanna, Matt, Eric and some of the others—that Rachel was friends with *both* Ryan and Tristan and refused to take sides in such an immature matter. *Immature. Sure, if Guns*—he was so tired of calling Marvin 'Guns' his real name was much less intimidating—*if Marvin had punched out someone she would be ranting about how manly and brave he was.* The entire fiasco was just plain ridiculous.

Tristan, slaving at the deep fryer on the last day of his sentence, was loathing himself for stooping to such a juvenile level to get some attention, when Rachel appeared at the counter to order. She smiled at him and blew him a kiss.

Dammit!

He shook his head to clear the imaginative demons from his mind and resumed his punishment.

Chapter Three

The bus ride home on Friday was blissful. The day was relatively warm, and the windows on the bus were open. The wind whipped through the aisle like tiny tornadoes wreaking havoc on any loose papers or hairdos it could find. Tristan found it relaxing. He dreamed it blew away the events of his horrible week. He imagined his memories turning to dust and disappearing behind him with the wind. He closed his eyes and rested his head on the seat. It was a forty-five minute bus ride, through a winding series of farms and forest.

He had taken the trip so many times that he could almost see his surroundings with his eyes shut based on the movements of the bus. He knew which kids got off at which stops, and he knew which landmarks were on which turns. Most kids hated the bus ride, but Tristan used the time to relax. He allowed his relaxation to reach a point where he was almost asleep when he was rudely interrupted by his perennial seat mate:

"Awww come on, Trist, let it *go*," she said. "You'll always have me."

They had been friends since second grade. They lived a kilometre apart and took daily walks to the local Ultramar to placate their mutual love of candy. Their orders never varied: Tristan would get three licorice pipes, a bag of skittles—the original red package—and chocolate milk. Deanna always got Barq's cream soda, an assortment of penny candy, and Cool Ranch Doritos. They would sit outside on the gas station steps until dusk and then walk home. They were the best of friends.

"Not now D," Tristan said. "I just want to sleep—or die, whichever comes first."

"I know you had a rough week, Trist, but it could have all been avoided if you had just let me in on your little scheme. I could have told you it wouldn't work."

"Huh?" Tristan said, half dumbfounded and half hurt. *What was wrong with the plan?*

"Of course, I'm amazed you couldn't see the flaws in it yourself. You know Rachel as well as I do, and there's no way a little stunt like that would impress her. She values your soft side for a reason."

Tristan rolled his eyes. "Yeah." he said sarcastically, "values it for sure."

"She does," Deanna said, showing some frustration. "You are one of her closest friends, and she adores you. She just doesn't see you as any more than that."

"Well D, this has been uplifting." Tristan sank gloomily back into sleeping position.

"That's not what I meant, Tristan. She just likes older guys; I don't know why, but she does. There's nothing you can do about your age."

There was nothing that drove Tristan crazier than things he could not comprehend. What was the allure of older guys? He really didn't get it. Besides, there was only two years between him and Marvin. Sure, Tristan didn't have a car or big muscles or facial hair or sexual experience, but he had, well *Jesus,* what *did* he have?

Deanna knew him well. "Tristan don't." She threw her arms around him and gave him a big kiss on the cheek. Tristan made a face like he had just swallowed a can of sardines and wiped off the kiss. He scowled at the playful grin on D's face. She was obviously thrilled about the reaction she had gotten from him.

She has a very pretty smile.

Tristan curled up and fell asleep to the sounds of D's laughter and slept the rest of the way home.

When Deanna woke him up again it was their stop. He grumbled something even he didn't understand, said goodbye to his other friends on the bus, and followed D down the stairs and onto the random driveway that took them to and from school. They made plans to meet up for the gas station, same as they always did, and went their separate ways.

It was a beautiful October afternoon. The summer lasted much longer than usual this year. Tristan was scuffing his Nike high tops across the pavement as he walked. He still hadn't fully recovered from his nap. He valued his walk from the bus stop—at least until winter—because it was one of the only times he was alone and could enjoy that fact. Tristan did not dread going home. He had a younger sister named Emma, in sixth grade, and his relationship with his parents was what he assumed typical for a teenager: rocky with a chance of landslide. But there was no real animosity. In all likelihood he would shoot hoops before dinner in the back yard, play video games with Ryan, Matt, and Eric until seven or so, then meet D for their walk to the Ultramar. It would be a pretty normal Friday night. He welcomed normal.

His driveway was quite long, but normal for his small town. They lived just outside Sageview in Milton. The nearest city, Plymouth, was about an hour away, thus making the little gas station the most exciting thing in Milton. Not even Sageview had much except for farms and a Co-Op. He admired the changing leaves on the way up his driveway and was tempted to pluck a nice apple red maple leaf for Rachel, but he stopped himself.

No way, he thought, *just get your ass in the house, and stop thinking about Rachel!*

His mom, Patty, welcomed him home by hitting him in the face with a drying towel.

"A little help please"

"Mom," he said, dragging out the word, "can Emma do it please? I've had a long week, and I just wanna shoot hoops and blow off some steam."

"You've had a long week?" His mom chuckled. Patty was a great mom, but she was a stay at home mom, and it was a fact that she seemed to resent more and more. Tristan understood this to a point. His mom struck him as a very independent spirit. He knew she planned to go back to work once both he and Emma were able to look after themselves. Since Emma was only eleven, his mom planned to stay home for a few more years.

"Long week Tristan? Try working nine hours a day without leaving the house." She said a few more things under her breath and went back to scrubbing a casserole dish.

Tristan could feel the tension mounting and knew, if he refused to help his mother, it would result in a new addition to his week from hell. He walked begrudgingly to the sink and began to dry dishes. His mother thanked him when they finished and he went out into the yard to play basketball before supper.

He had lost track of time when his mother called him in for dinner. His father was absent, working late, and Emma was at her friend's house. Just Tristan and Mom. He actually enjoyed the prospect. He and his mother got along considerably better when it was just the two of them. He was most like his mother; they were both patient—at least in comparison to his father—preferred to avoid conflict, had similar senses of humour, and were generally laid back. His sister was like his father; she was fun loving and full of energy, but quick to anger and unpredictable.

Supper passed with table talk and a few laughs. Tristan offered to help clean up, but his mother let him off the hook this time. He secretly thanked God for the small blessing and got on the phone with his friends to play some video games.

The other two boys seemed to have no problem with how quickly Tristan and Ryan had gotten their 'friendship train' back on the tracks. Perhaps they just assumed that guys didn't hold grudges—which was the general feeling with most guys. Regardless, it was nice to have some normalcy back in his life. Tristan felt good as he parted ways with the guys and met with Deanna for their daily walk.

The October evenings were cooling off quickly and Tristan had thrown on his black "Iron Knights" sweater. He was proud of his involvement with the basketball team and wore his team colours of black and gold with honour. Somehow he just felt *bigger*, more inflated, when wearing his basketball gear.

Deanna saw him waiting at the end of his driveway and started to trot toward him. Tristan loved how she dressed outside of school. Deanna had on black sweats and a red hoodie. Tristan enjoyed seeing girls in guys clothing. It made them less intimidating. D's shoulder length brown hair bounced as she jogged along. She had a big smile on her face, as per usual, and she slowed to walk beside Tristan towards their Mecca, the Milton Ultramar.

They each got their usual and plopped down on the cool concrete steps to enjoy their snacks. Tristan adjusted his jeans as they started to ride up a little as he sat down. When he was comfortable, he started munching on a black licorice pipe. D was sitting next to him chatting away happily about how Jessica Randall had flipped backwards in her chair in science class. Blah blah blah.

It was as if sound ceased to exist. Tristan could not hear anything. He was staring at D's face like he had seen it for the first time. She was actually really pretty. She had dark eyes, brownish green, full red lips, and tiny dimples that were always on display due to her pleasant demeanour. Tristan began to imagine her at his side instead of—

Whoa! Brakes! Snap out of it, Cage!

Tristan shook his head and took a nice long drink of chocolate milk, much like he had seen his father do once or twice with "The Captain". Deanna stopped her story and chuckled.

"Thirsty?"

Tristan could feel himself blushing, but he wasn't sure why. "Yeah, uhhh yeah."

"Sometimes Trist, you are just so weird. Gosh, it got really cold."

Tristan hadn't realized, but it was almost dark and had cooled off quite a bit. As he was about to stand up, Deanna snuggled up to his arm. Tristan was not used to this type of invasion into his personal space by D. If she got close to him it was normally to give him a big bear hug or a punch on the arm. At first he was taken aback; he may have spasmed a bit. Slowly he relaxed and allowed her head to fall gently on his shoulder. His heart was racing. *What is happening?*

He looked straight ahead. He was afraid to look down at her. His hands gripped his chocolate milk like a life preserver. He dared not move. Suddenly, he could feel Deanna's eyes on him.

"Trist," she said softly, "look at me."

Oh my God. This is not happening. They were best friends. She liked him. Did he like her? Tristan had gone back into panic mode. Why did he not have a life advisor in his pocket? How did he get into these situations? What the hell was he going to do?

She spoke again, still gently.

"Trist?"

He took a deep breath and allowed himself to look down at her. Their eyes met. The last beam of sunlight over the horizon caught her face.

"Yeah?"

She smirked.

"Your fly is down."

Chapter Four

Tristan slumped down on the edge of his bed. He stared into his closet like it was a deep, dark void. His face was numb. It hung limp and lifeless, his countenance all together hollow. He could not function. His stupidity was too much for him to comprehend. How arrogant was he to simply assume that D would have fallen in love with him at some point? He twisted the events in a way that would benefit his sudden obsession with having a female companion.

I feel sick.

The walk home had been awkward, but mostly just for him. He didn't say a word the entire trip home. He had simply stood up, zipped up his fly, and walked lifelessly next to Deanna. Luckily for him, Deanna continued gabbing about the day's events after laughing hysterically at his expense. She must have assumed that he was quiet due to his embarrassment or she was simply too caught up in her own story to notice. Either way, it was yet another small blessing.

It was dark in Tristan's room. The only light spilling in came from the kitchen which was right around the corner. He heard his mom and dad discussing something, finances maybe, he didn't really care. He envisioned a meteor burning through the atmosphere hurtling toward his house, more specifically, his window. Just when his imagination was going to allow him to be put out of his misery he was snapped back to reality by a familiar, but annoying sound.

"Trissstaaan," his sister yelled, her voice like a laser beam, "telephooone!"

Tristan rolled back onto his bed and reached for the phone.

"Hello," he said miserably.

"Tristan, you sound terrible. Are you ok?"

Oh my sweet lord Jesus, Rachel is on the phone. Composure. Breathe.

"Yeah uhhh, I'm fine. I was just asleep. What's up?"

His heart was racing.

"Well, we had a rough week, and I think I was too hard on you. I know how competitive you are, and it probably got the best of you. I was hoping we could hang out tomorrow, maybe watch a movie?"

Don't answer too fast and do NOT use your high-pitched excited voice!

"Uhhh that should be ok, I have to go for a run first." *Yeah that was good. Good, quick thinking.* "After that I should be ok at any time. When you wanna come over?"

"I was thinking I'd get my brother to drop me off on his way to the city. Maybe four or so?"

"Sounds great. See you then—wait, what movie should we watch?"

"I'll leave that to you Mr. Cage." She sounded amused as she hung up the phone.

The emotional highs and lows of his week had been enough to destroy a person's nervous system, but this last turn of events was worth it. *Time alone with Rachel. Oh yesss.* Wait a second, were his parents going to be home? What was his sister going to be doing? Did he have to babysit? More importantly, what movie were they going to watch? The stress was mounting.

He couldn't choose a guy movie—that would make him seem selfish. Action/adventure was out. He loved fantasy films like

Legend and *Willow,* but he couldn't be seen as a nerd. *Hell no.* Maybe a good horror move: *Chucky* or *Alien*? If she got scared she'd have nowhere to go but right into his lap. But what if she didn't like horror. She may simply refuse to watch it if she were too afraid.

Dammit!

What was left? Dramas are too boring. Can't watch an immature cartoon, certainly not with maturity obsessed Rachel. A chick flick? He'd seem charming, he'd seem understanding!

Oh my God, I'd seem gay.

Chick flick was out.

What was left? Way too stressful. Did every guy go through this? Wait a sec—Comedy. Comedy was good. Everyone loved to laugh. It was general, both sexes liked comedies. Laughter would lighten the mood and make for a very positive environment. *Perfect*. He had lots of comedies. Now which one to watch? *Wait, not that simple.* There are action comedies, romantic comedies, and general comedies. He was definitely over-thinking, but it was necessary. He had to repair the damage he had done on Monday. It had to be a generic comedy, just a plain comedy with no desperate romantic twists. He had it.

They would watch *Dumb and Dumber.*

Tristan walked into the kitchen, under the guise of being thirsty, to pump his parents for information on where they would be the next day. Tristan's mom was staring at him with a weird grin on her face. When they made eye contact, she slyly went back to examining the documents in front of her. His father didn't even look up.

"So what are you guys up to?" Tristan opted for the direct approach for information. Small talk was not his thing. Besides, the faster he went to sleep, the faster it would be Saturday at 4PM.

"Nothing of your concern, son," his father said bluntly. "Who was on the phone?"

"Just a friend." The fact that wasn't a lie made Tristan die a little inside.

"Mmhmm," his mother said still smirking. "Your father and I were 'just friends' once too."

"Patty, our son doesn't have time for girls. Or at least he shouldn't be concerned with them yet. At this age, they only bring trouble."

Tristan rolled his eyes. Why did everything have to be so difficult with this man? He could remember a time when they got along incredibly well. He and his father used to do everything together, but a few years ago they had drifted apart. Tristan did not know why, or how it had happened. He was just praying that it did not come between him and his date. *Date, yeah that was a good word.*

"Cam, we don't even know if it was a girl. I was just razzing Tristan a little."

"Well?" Cam questioned. "Guy or girl, son?"

"Female." Tristan took a more scientific approach, hoping it would lessen the blow.

"What did she want?" his father asked half-heartedly.

Tristan knew that this was going to be more difficult than he had planned. "I invited her over to watch a movie tomorrow afternoon."

"Oh you did?" His father's eyebrows perked up. "You didn't ask permission yet."

Tristan could feel his blood pressure rising. His mother gave him a warning glance as if to say, *Let it go, it's not worth it.* Tristan bit his lip and gave in to his father's wish. "Ok Dad, may I *please* have a friend over to watch a movie?"

"Without the attitude, please"

"What attitude? Dad what are you talking about? I'm just asking." Tristan *knew* this was going to happen. He always dealt with his father as patiently as possible, but no matter what he tried, the result was the same: disaster. He had not been angry before, but his father's constant prodding was *making* him angry. He didn't know if the old man did this on purpose, or if they were just *that* different.

"Dad, all I want is to have Rachel over to watch a movie. That's it. Please?"

Cam leaned back in his chair and let out a long sigh. "I'm not sure, Tristan. We're not going to be home tomorrow."

Tristan didn't know whether to leap into the air like Peter Pan or fall to his knees and beg like a kid in a candy store. His parents weren't going to be home! But they may not let him have Rachel over. *Dear lord this would be the perfect time for an intervention.*

"Three rules, son."

Thank you, Jesus. "Sure Dad."

"One, she is gone by midnight. Two, she has her own way home because we won't be here to take her; and three, you have to watch the movie in the family room *not* your bedroom."

He could live with that. "Deal."

His mother was smiling again. "We are going on a trip with some friends to Greenfield. We'll be home on Sunday. Emma will be at Stacey's house."

"I, uhhh, I'll be here alone?" He couldn't help but stammer. As excited as he was, he was getting scared too. Rachel was more 'experienced' than he was. *Yeah, probably jumping the gun a little.*

"Yeah, but don't get any ideas," his father said coolly. "I have your uncle checking on the house periodically. So make sure you stick to our deal."

"Will do! G'nite!"

Tristan did not want the conversation to last a second longer. The longer it went on, the likelier it was that his good fortune would run out. He grabbed a glass of water and hit the sack.

The next morning Tristan rolled out of bed at 11AM. He walked groggily to the kitchen and opened the patio blinds. Rain. Oh well, all his plans were happening inside. He went to the fridge for some milk but stopped to stare at the note held by a magnet at exactly his height:

> *See you tomorrow. We left 20 dollars for snacks and dropped your sister off at Stacey's. Have Fun.*
>
> PS. Remember the Deal.
>
> Love Mom, Dad and Emma xo

Oh happy day. Family room, bedroom, bathroom, front lawn didn't matter! He was going to be *alone* with Rachel. He grabbed the milk and took a swig right from the carton, just because he could.

It was amazing how much thought went into the meeting. He desperately wanted to call it a date, but he knew Rachel wouldn't see it that way. He got up off his bed and stared into his closet. What was he going to wear? He needed something that said, *I'm hot, but not desperately trying to win your affection.* That wasn't the sweater his grandmother gave him last Christmas; and why the hell was it visible? After shoving the sweater into a deep dark corner, he resumed his assessment of his wardrobe. He thought brown looked good on him, but the brown he had was mud stained white. Red was too flamboyant, and most of his school clothes were too casual. He needed something a little nicer. He decided to wear a white dress shirt he had worn to a wedding last year, without the tie, un-tucked, with his dark blue jeans. Oh and boxers—*definitely boxers.*

After he showered he spent a long time messing with his hair. He didn't know if he wanted to comb it, or let it dry curly. Deanna told him he looked best when his hair was curliest, but Rachel wasn't Deanna.

In the end he wore his hair uncombed, in its curliest form. He also decided to wear his baseball cap. He *always* wore his hat when he was able, and it would seem weird if he didn't have it on—at least that's what he thought. He wore his hat tilted slightly to the right. Not to seem tough or to fit with some late '90s fad, but because he liked to be different as much as he could. As far as he was concerned, he looked as good as he was able, and with four minutes to spare.

4:01PM. She's not coming. End of life. Please God, allow a quick and easy passing. Perhaps a snake bite, or a heart attack—the doorbell rang. He shot off his bed like Superman to a bank robbery. This was it. *Breathe, killer. Breathe.* He adjusted his hat and walked to the door. He put his hand on the doorknob to open the door, and as he did his overactive imagination decided, once again, to scare him half to death. He imagined that when he opened the door Marvin would standing next to Rachel. She had brought Marvin to the movie date!?

Damn Brain.

He blinked twice to clear his mind and opened the door. All was well. Rachel was standing waiting for him on the door step. The only other boy in a kilometre was her brother driving back down his driveway.

"Hey Rach, come on in".

Rachel had been there before, but they had never been alone. Luckily it didn't feel awkward. Was his hand shaking? She plopped down on the couch and asked playfully, "So what movie did you choose? I'm dying of curiosity"

"Well, curiosity killed the cat, Rachel..." *What? That didn't even make sense you idiot! For a pretty funny guy you definitely boned yourself on that one! For the love of God, recover. Too much pressure.*

"...and I need you alive for what I had in mind." *Risky, very risky.*
Silence.

Rachel burst out laughing. "Oh Tristan, are you nervous? That is so cute!"

Cute. Cute? He is cute? Babies are cute. Puppies are cute. Was Guns cute? No, Guns was hot as balls with a side of dead sexy.

He wanted to throw the remote through the window, but he composed himself.

"I have my moments," he said through clenched teeth. "Want anything before we put the movie on?"

"Just for you sit down and relax. I have never seen you so uptight! It's me, Tristan. Just Relax."

Tristan sighed and put the tape in the VCR. He sat down next to Rachel, strategically. He sat close enough that they could touch at some point if he got daring, but not so close that he made her uncomfortable. He was encouraged when she didn't move away.

The movie was a hit. Rachel had never seen it before and laughed her ass off. Tristan always laughed at the movie as well. His favourite part was when Harry threw the snowball at Mary from about three feet away. Classic slapstick comedy moment.

After the movie Tristan used the twenty dollars his parents had left to order them pizza. It took a while for it to get to them as the closest pizza joint was fifteen minutes away. They ended up getting the works because that was Rachel's favourite. Tristan had simply agreed to all of the toppings—even though he hated onions, mushrooms, tomatoes and peppers. He could choke them down.

While they were waiting for the pizza, they decided to watch another movie. This time it was Rachel's turn to choose—according to her at least. She looked long and hard at their extensive movie collection before choosing *Armageddon*. *You have got to be kidding me*, Tristan thought, *I need to leave the room when Bruce Willis dies so she doesn't see me cry, that damn scene gets me every time!*

Tristan's strategic bathroom break saved him at the end of the movie, but it didn't save Rachel. She was sobbing when he got back. He sat back down, slightly closer this time, and left the rest to fate. Sure enough, Rachel's hand found his as Ben Affleck and company returned to Earth unscathed. The ending drew more tears from Rachel, and before he knew it, she was practically in his arms. Tristan tried to mask his shaking hands, but it was really difficult. He was so nervous! He had never kissed a girl before. He didn't know how. He had no idea which way to turn his head or how long he should keep his lips pressed to hers. All he knew was that he was going to try.

As the credits rolled, and Aerosmith played in the background, he got his chance. Rachel put her hand around his waist and looked him in the eye. "I saw you picking off your toppings. You are such a sweet guy Tristan Cage."

There was no setting better than this. If you wanted something you had to go get it. Tristan closed his eyes and went in for his first kiss.

God hated him.

Catastrophe. Absolute disaster. The brim of his hat hit her square in the face. He sat, stunned. Rachel tried to mask her laughter with her hand pressed to her mouth. "Tristan, did you try to kiss me?"

"Nuhhh, no." I was just getting more comfortable. It was an accident." *Jesus, Sweet Jesus.* This wasn't happening. Why did he wear the damn hat? Marvin didn't wear hats, this wouldn't have happened to him! *Nooo!*

The door swung open. *You have got to be kidding me. Why me, God?* His parents walked through the front door. It was only 8 o'clock. It was not Sunday morning. He had time to fix this! No, his parents had come home early for whatever reason. Camping; they had planned on camping—they went camping every year in Greenfield to see the leaves. *But it's raining.* They had to come home because of the rain. This was a nightmare.

Tristan's father walked in and greeted the both with a very jolly hello.

"Hi kids! Lots of time left for one more movie. The night is young. What do you say to watching one with your Mom and me, Trist?"

Tristan's jaw dropped. This wasn't happening.

Oh, but it was. Cam went to the shelf, grabbed a movie and shoved it in the VCR. He then walked over to the couch and sat down directly between Rachel and Tristan. Rachel giggled and gave Cam a shove. Tristan laid his head back and found himself, once again, praying for that meteor.

Chapter Five

The latest blunder in the attempt to win Rachel's heart hit Tristan hard. He was embarrassed and lost all confidence in his ability to do anything remotely competent. He needed some time to recover his manhood. He spent the next couple of weeks distancing himself romantically from Rachel. He didn't ignore her in fact, they were getting along great—he just stopped pursuing her so aggressively. He was very aware of the fact that this maneuver could allow Marvin to seal the deal, but he honestly needed to recuperate.

Although Ryan laughed hysterically when Tristan told him what had happened, it was his advice that set Tristan straight; he was just trying too hard, and it was getting him into trouble. Plain and simple. Basketball season was starting, midterms were approaching, and winter was just around the corner. Tristan had a lot more chores in the winter, namely; snow removal. He had lots to keep him busy and, for once, he embraced that fact.

The Sageview Iron Knights had a notoriously strong basketball program. Their colours of black and gold were feared across the province. Tristan was one of the best players on the Junior Boys squad. This year he would be a veteran, and felt he shouldered a lot of the coach's expectations. Tristan was the starting small forward and last season's most improved player, an honour voted on by coaches and teammates. He didn't know what it was, but ever since he started playing the game, it lit a fire deep inside him.

Tristan was quite tall for a 9th grader, almost six feet, and quite agile. He wasn't naturally athletic, but had a work ethic that was second to none. He was the best shooter on the team, and many thought he was the most intelligent player as well. Ryan was the team's centre (that was a no brainer) and Matt and Eric played as well. Eric was the coach's son and was league MVP last season (almost unheard of for an 8th grader).

The first team tryout was scheduled for Wednesday. Most ninth graders were shoe-ins for the team, but they still had to participate in tryouts. It was a good way to break into the intense basketball season Tristan knew was coming, so he didn't mind. They all had to be in top form to make sure they maintained their standard of excellence.

It has been three weeks since the 'hat horror'. Rachel didn't play basketball, and that would allow for further romantic rehab. Deanna was quite a good basketball player, however, and he looked forward to spending more time with her. In his attempt at healing, he had inadvertently distanced himself from her as well— an unfortunate side effect as a result of her evil sex. They would have lots of time to chat and catch up at practices and on road trips. The junior teams always travelled together, and their practices were one after the other. No doubt they would be car-pooling back and forth again this year as well. He would have plenty of time to make up for lost time with D.

It was the first week of November when Marvin Guns McGee and Rachel Smith officially started dating. Tristan knew it was coming; he had braced himself, and if he was going to be angry, he'd have to direct some of it at himself, and that would be counterproductive. He simply sucked it up and accepted reality. He was Rachel's friend. Nothing more. Now all he had to do was get rid of that nagging ache inside his chest. It was no big deal really, just a constant feeling of nausea that, when paid attention to, felt like someone had poured gasoline down his throat and lit his heart on fire. Just a minor setback.

Tristan did his best to hide how much it hurt to see Rachel with someone else. He was doing a great job of it too. He listened to Rachel's stories about how strong Marvin was, about the deer he had shot, about how much he could drink—that's right, *drink*—and about how they always went on back roads to make out in his 'sweet ride'. Tristan listened to all of this in order to be a good friend. It had been his decision, after all, to stop chasing after Rachel, so he had no right to be angry. Every now and then he would catch Ryan shaking his head at him from a distance as if to say, *Why are you doing this to yourself?* But Tristan soldiered on.

Tristan endured until the last week of November. It was a Thursday, one he would always remember as 'Black Thursday'. Tristan sat with Rachel every class they had together. This particular day they were in science class, second to last period of the day. Rachel had been acting weird all day long. She was smiling all the time and laughing at things that weren't even close to funny. Tristan could have told her the sky was falling, and she would have shrugged it off. Unfortunately for Tristan, things were about to start making more sense. Tristan was working away on his assignment when a note slid onto his desk. They were seated in pairs, so he knew it came from Rachel. He opened the note:

Guns and I Did It last night. ☺

Smiley Face? Tristan threw up in his mouth but swallowed it back down. He looked up slowly and gave her a smile that looked more like a grimace and a nod that looked more like an epileptic seizure. *What could she possibly be thinking? Why the hell would I want to know this?* He could feel the anger welling up inside him. He clenched his fists and gritted his teeth. *Smiley face?* That was it. Tristan snapped.

"Are you fucking retarded?!" he screamed. The whole class stopped. Ryan's jaw dropped and his hands went limp, causing his pen to fall to the floor. Nobody had heard Tristan angry before. He was the 'calm one'. Mr. Ferguson leapt up from his desk. His face was crimson. He opened his mouth to chastise Tristan, but it was too late. Tristan beat him to the punch.

"I am *not* your friend. I have been much more than that for over a year! I carry your books, I help you with homework, I listen to all your stories, I give you advice, I sit with you every class! You lead me on *every single* day! If you could not see the way I felt about you, then you are the dumbest person I have ever met, and if you *did* know, you are a heartless bitch."

Rachel's eyes were filling with tears, but Tristan really did not care. He could not remember a time he had been so angry—or jealous. He wheeled around and stormed out of the classroom. If he didn't get out of there it was going to get a lot worse. He marched straight to the guy's bathroom and up to the sink. He placed his hands on the counter and leaned toward the mirror. He stared at himself. *Oh Tristan, what have you done?*

He knew Ferguson was behind him and he heard the door open. "Caaage!"

Tristan raised his hand in Ferguson's direction. He didn't look at him when he spoke. "Mr. Ferguson, I know I am in trouble. I swear to you I will go right to the office just as soon as I calm down."

Tristan took the silence as agreement, and he heard the bathroom door close. His mind was moving a hundred miles a minute. Guilt set in. There was a time and place for everything, and that certainly wasn't it. He just couldn't believe her! All he could see in his mind was their bodies pressed against each other; so many times he had imagined it, except he had been the boy involved, *not* Marvin. He felt sick again. He was going to be suspended for sure. This was the second major rules violation this year. He wouldn't be able to play basketball for the duration of his suspension and he would be grounded for sure. Girls were the devil.

Tristan took a deep breath and walked to the principal's office with no more outbursts. He walked right past the secretary and into Mrs. Anderson's office because he knew what was coming. He accepted his imminent doom.

Mrs. Anderson must have sensed that Tristan knew he had done wrong. It did not lessen his suspension—three days for swearing and defiance—but she did not yell or lecture, she simply asked if he was alright, passed her judgment, and informed him he would have to work in the office until the end of the day.

On the bus ride home, Deanna was abnormally stoic. She didn't say a word until halfway through the trip home.

"Tristan, why do you care enough about Rachel to explode like that? There are lots of girls who would kill for you to be that passionate about them. I just don't get you."

This was unexpected. Tristan didn't really know how to respond. He tried to say something back to her three times and all he achieved was uttering the first syllable of unfinished thoughts.

Deanna didn't talk either. She just sat there shaking her head. Tristan had expected her to go up one side of him and down the other on how mean he had been. This response was, well, unbelievable.

He looked out the window—then back at D. He repeated this process until he was dizzy but still couldn't find anything to say. He was tired of talking, tired of being serious, tired of explaining himself. He had to save all the emotional energy he had left to deal with his parents when he got home. Neither he nor D spoke a single word the rest of the way home.

His parents took the news of his suspension exactly how he thought they would. He was grounded for a week, on *top* of his suspension. Also, while he was home from school, he would have to scrub and clean every inch of his house. His mother had done most of the talking, which was a good thing. His father was furious, but kept his cool for the duration of the conversation.

After supper Tristan turned over all the electronics in his room. He did so without a complaint. Complaining at that point would get him nowhere. He shut his door, after his parents were satisfied that all non-educational material was gone from his room, and sat down to read. He put the book down after thirty seconds. He simply couldn't focus. His mind was too occupied with how Rachel was doing and why Deanna had acted so weird. One thing was certain; he'd have a few days to think about it while he did his best Cinderfella impression.

Chapter Six

Tristan survived his suspension, and his grounding, without any further mishaps. When he went back to school everything was relatively normal, except that Rachel wasn't talking to him, which was expected. He did not pursue her or even attempt to contact her; they both needed the space. It was almost Christmas time, and he hoped they could bury the hatchet after vacation.

Deanna was happy to see him when he got back. She was no longer acting strange, and she never again mentioned the bizarre conversation on the bus, or what had happened between Tristan and Rachel. She was her happy-go-lucky self, and she and Tristan became seat mates in class as well as on the bus. Deanna joked constantly about how lucky she was to be allowed to sit in Princess Rachel's seat each class. Tristan let the teasing go uncontested. Deanna was so refreshing! She was more fun than he thought, and that was saying something. Tristan didn't think it was possible, but by Christmas, he and D had grown closer than they'd ever been before.

Tristan spent a lot of time wondering what it all meant. He and Deanna had been best friends for years, but he had never missed her over vacations. He was always more concerned with other girls. Deanna was one of the guys. This was a strange new development, and Tristan felt uneasy about it. He knew he usually read too much into things—he had learned his lesson the night his fly malfunctioned—and decided to just let things be. If anything was going to happen with Deanna, Rachel, or any other girl, forcing the issue was obviously the wrong way to achieve your goals.

School resumed January 4th. A new year. It was going to be girl-free and, as a result, trouble-free. His resolve was strengthened when he returned to school and spoke to Ryan, who had broken up with his girlfriend only to reunite with her two days later. They were once again on the rocks. Ryan was simply too nice. He didn't have it in him to hurt Sydney, even though that's what had to be done. Tristan told him so, but he already knew what would happen. Ryan might as well just marry the girl.

Tristan was an interesting contradiction. He could see the flaws and pitfalls of everyone's relationships but his own. The advice he gave was always well thought out and sincere. He generally got it right too. For example: he knew that Sydney's primary motivation for dating Ryan was the status that came with it. She loved being 'Ryan's girl'. She loved being envied by others. She loved popularity, and attention. To Sydney, Ryan was a means to an end. Tristan wondered how long it would be before Ryan allowed himself to accept this and make the decision to end things with her stick. Tristan wondered this often, but knew it wasn't going to be anytime soon. Tristan made many mistakes in his own life, but he was an excellent friend. He would take on the role his friends needed of him, and right now, Ryan just needed support. So that's what Ryan got.

Ryan did not enjoy awkward conversations. He was very good at keeping things that bothered him to himself. Not long after he explained his recent relationship woes he changed the subject:

"Big dance next week, Tristan. You going?"

Tristan accepted that his friend did not want to dwell on his issues with Sydney, so he took the bait. "I think so, yeah. Although I'm not sure I'm ready to see Marvin and Rachel all over each other."

"Understood man. That whole situation was messed up. You really gave it to her in Ferguson's class though." Ryan chuckled. "That was classic."

"Glad you enjoyed it," Tristan said. "I'll just make sure I stay at the other end of the gym. In a dimly lit corner. With a blindfold on. With—"

"Jesus! Enough." Ryan said, laughing. "We'll make sure you have a good time. Besides, if Rachel sees you sulking it will only make her happier."

"This is true." Tristan knew he could not show any interest in Rachel. He had the separation he needed and could not be sucked back into that death trap. *Yeah, that describes her nicely. Rachel the Death Trap. Lure in victims with sweet scents and beauty only to snap shut to entrap her prey in misery.*

Yep. That was much better. The dance was a go.

The junior boys varsity basketball team had practice before the dance. They had practice Thursdays. Period. The coach did not care what was going on outside of the basketball team. Your athletic commitments came second *only* to school—and death. The coach worked them hard that day. They must have run a million suicides, at least that was how it felt. Their friend Eric was the coach's son, and his family lived very close to the school, so Eric offered to let Tristan and Ryan stop by and shower before the dance. The boys gladly accepted and got a home cooked meal out of it too.

Eric's mom made them pizza for supper. *Homemade pizza,* Tristan thought, *was much better than the rush job they did at pizza joints.* Tristan's observant personality took control once again as they were eating. Eric looked a lot like his father. They both had sandy blonde hair and strong jaw lines. They were both ruggedly handsome, the quintessential farm boys, and they both shared broad shoulders with slim builds.

Tristan had his head tilted to the side while he was taking in the Childs' genetic similarities. He was still chewing on his pizza when Ryan chuckled and waved his hand in front of Tristan's eyes.

"Snap out of it, dude," he said. "You been starin' at Eric for a whole minute. You got a little man crush?"

Eric smirked and gave Tristan a wink. Tristan cursed his habit of spacing out at any given moment and went back to eating. He would get Ryan back for that little comment later.

Tristan got ready for the dance in ten short minutes. He enjoyed the fact that he didn't have to agonize over his appearance. There was no one to impress. He simply showered and shook out his hair like a dog. He threw on a blue polo with horizontal white stripes over his customary pair of dark blue jeans and was ready to go.

Ryan, on the other hand, was taking forever. Tristan and Eric hollered up to the second floor bathroom for him to hurry up.

"Come on man it's time to go!" Eric yelled. "What's taking so long?"

Ryan yelled back, "Uhhh nothing. I just can't get my hair right."

Tristan and Eric looked at each other like Ryan had lost his mind. "Who cares, dude? You *are* a dude right?" *Ha. Vengeance.* Tristan patted himself on the back for a job well done.

When Ryan finally pulled himself away from the mirror, the boys were ready to go. They headed out on foot. The walk to the school was only five minutes. Soon they were walking up the long driveway to Sageview High, which was located high on a hill that overlooked their soccer field. The driveway was actually quite steep, and all the boys were starting to feel the sting of the cool wind as well as the burn in their calf muscles. Even though it was January, and the temperature was close to zero, the boys were all too macho to wear jackets.

The three of them met up with Matt—the missing part of their quartet—at the front doors. He had to go home to do chores before the dance; he still smelt a little like barn, but nobody had the heart to tell him. The foursome walked coolly into the school as a single unit. It didn't take long for the guys to get separated though. As soon as Sydney laid her eyes on Ryan, she dragged him away not be seen again. The boy was whipped.

When Tristan finally made his way up the stairs to the gym, he couldn't help but notice the job the decorators had done. Their aging school had been turned into a very attractive party scene. The hallway was lined with white Christmas lights, and there were strategically placed streamers running wall to wall. The gym itself was very dark. The only thing clearly visible was the shiny disco ball hanging from the ceiling. It was throwing light that fell to the floor like flakes of snow.

Tristan walked to the side wall, past the eleventh graders bumping and grinding to Notorious B.I.G's *Mo Money Mo Problems*. He sat down next to Eric and took in some more sights. The girls looked good! God, he loved how 'Dance' equaled 'scantily clad'. There was a lot of skin on the dance floor, mostly because guys didn't dance until slow songs. Dancing was for gays—really they were just too self-conscious and didn't want to look bad.

The guys stayed sidelined reminiscing about the basketball season until the first slow song of the night. As soon as the slow music started the guys dispersed like geese in a flying V. It was almost like it had been rehearsed because each guy had already scoped out and discussed—in some situations played rock/paper/scissors for—the girl they would dance with first. This song was especially important, *November Rain*, which meant the dance would last a blissful nine minutes with the partner chosen. You just needed to get there fast.

Tristan headed straight for Lacey, a good friend who looked damn good in her low cut silver halter top. He did not mind staring at *that* for nine minutes. He and Lacey attempted to talk over the music, but eventually gave up. It was just too loud. Two minutes of talking, seven minutes spinning in a circle and staring at each other. Fine by Tristan.

As per usual, the DJ played two slow songs in a row. Tristan's heart sunk when he recognized the familiar electric guitar rift. *Lightning Crashes*. He and Rachel had danced to this song every time it came on for over two years. He suddenly felt trapped. He kept his eyes on the floor. He did not want to look up and see Rachel dancing with someone else to this song; especially Guns. He walked as if he were visually impaired, holding his hands out feeling for bodies to guide him back to the solace of the sidelines. As he was walking he bumped into someone: dead on.

"Oh sorry I was just—"

"Just dance with me," Rachel said.

Tristan's head snapped up instantly. His eyes lit up like light bulbs in a dark room. Tristan took her by the hand and led her to an open spot on the floor. She wrapped her hands around his neck and he ran his hands down the back of her dark blue dress to rest on her lower back. Tristan was afraid to look down at her, but he didn't have a choice. Rachel let her fingers slip to the top of his neck and pulled his head down. It was hard to hear her, but she made sure that he understood.

"Tristan, I'm sorry."

"Wha, what?" He stammered.

"I'm sorry for everything. The truth is I loved having the best of both worlds. I enjoyed all the perks I had with you and got to be with Marvin at the same time. It was stupid and selfish, and I'm sorry."

Nooo!

Just when he was starting to move on—she was so beautiful tonight and so sincere. This song. This moment. He wanted to kiss her.

What?

Kiss her. Was he insane? Her boyfriend was probably watching like a hawk. He hesitated. He could not kiss Rachel. It was happening all over again. Death Trap.

He looked her in the eye.

"I'm sorry too."

Seemed fitting. He didn't know what else to say. He was panicking. She took a hold of his wrist and slid it down, gently, to rest on the top of her ass. She spoke softly in his ear. "It should have been you. I should have chosen you."

Her lips glided from his ear across his cheek. They were so soft and so warm. They were about an inch from his own when he grabbed her hard by the shoulder's and pushed her an arm's length away.

"What are you doing, Rachel?" he asked. "What about Marvin?"

Her eyes filled with tears. "Don't you want me, Tristan?"

What was going on? Was he dreaming? Was the world ending? His frown was hurting his eyes it was so intense. He simply could not make sense of this.

"Oh forget it!" she said and with a sob she turned and ran from the gym.

Tristan took two steps after her and stopped. Something was wrong. If she wanted to talk she would come back and explain. The fast music had started again and no one had seemed to notice the drama taking place on his part of the dance floor. He went to his chair and sat down next to Matt. He must have looked distressed because Matt picked up on it right away.

"Tristan, I take it you found out?"

This was getting ridiculous.

"Matt, what the hell are you talking about?"

"Guns cheated on Rachel. He's over there with Jessica Marsh." Matt used his chin to point at the new couple making out on the other side of the gym.

"Figures," was all Tristan could manage. He didn't know whether to chase after Rachel and drown her in her own tears, or comfort her. What was that stunt she tried to pull? She must be in a ton of pain, but why would she do that to him? She couldn't be thinking straight. He was going after her.

Tristan stood up and jogged out of the gym. He looked up and down the hallway trying to figure out which way Rachel had gone. What he saw was more than he could comprehend. Rachel was standing toe to toe, arguing with Deanna.

"You had no right to do that to him, no matter what happened to you! You use him constantly, and you can't bear the thought that you lost both guys in your life. You could have had Tristan and avoided all of this, but you chose Marvin. Now you have to live with the consequences. I won't let you hurt Tristan anymore. The next time you talk to him, it better not be to fuck with his head, or you will have bigger problems than Marvin the man-whore."

She left Rachel slumped against the wall, balling. Tristan was dumbfounded. He was both honoured, and appalled. D had been extremely hard on Rachel. Who did he go with? Did he turn and walk away with D, or did he go and comfort Rachel? Once again his mind was made up for him. Deanna grabbed him by the arm and dragged him back into the gym. "Let's dance."

Tristan was being dragged like a dog on a leash. The slow songs had started again. Deanna's fury subsided, and she had her head resting gently on Tristan's chest. Her dark hair was pulled up in a bun and she was wearing a gorgeous red dress. She looked up at him, and he attempted to speak his mind, ask some questions, but she beat him to the punch. "Shut up and listen"

Tristan stood with her, interlocked, the romantic words spilling over them. He lost himself in the moment. A tear rolled down D's cheek. It was the first time he had seen her cry.

He was speechless. Utterly Speechless. So he did the only thing he could. He bent over and kissed her. It was his very first kiss.

Chapter Seven

The next couple of months were spectacular. Tristan and Deanna spent every minute they could together. Tristan made it a priority to make sure he always had a flower for her on Thursdays, commemorating their first night together. Tristan's favourite part of the whole experience, thus far, was asking Deanna questions about her feelings 'pre-relationship.' Apparently, Deanna had always liked him, and he was just too oblivious—or stupid—to notice. She always felt inadequate because all the girls he fell for were the prettiest and most popular. She never had the confidence to approach him for fear of rejection. Tristan wanted to tell her that wasn't the case, but in truth, he was blinded by his feelings for Rachel for a long time. Deanna had probably made the right decision.

Tristan enjoyed putting the pieces of their journey together in his mind, sort of like a puzzle. All of the hugs and kisses, the commitment to see him daily for summer strolls to the Ultramar, and especially that one strange night where they got so close only to discover his 'barn door' was open. Everything seemed to make so much sense, for the first two months.

This was Tristan's first relationship. Deanna's too. Tristan did not consider himself young, he was fifteen now. He definitely had a grasp on how relationships were supposed to work. Besides, he had seen all those movies and read all those books. With his incredible knowledge on the subject, what could possibly go wrong?

It was March, two weeks until basketball provincials. The Iron Knights were sitting on an undefeated season. They were the number one seed in the tournament—ranked 1 of 8—and they only had one real challenge on paper, a team from another district who was known to run a very aggressive pressure defence, which was something the Iron Knights were not used to facing. Coach was meticulous as usual. He would prepare for every possible situation. He added an extra practice each week to prepare specifically for Barlington's pesky defence.

These extra practices was scheduled on Sundays. Sundays were Tristan's day with Deanna. Even though they spent every moment at school together, he didn't feel that was enough. Besides, they were supervised at school. This coming Sunday was especially important because his parents were going to be gone all afternoon. They were taking his sister and one of her friends to see a movie in town. Tristan had plans; he was going to show Deanna just how romantic he could be.

Sunday rolled around and Tristan started preparing for his day of romance. His parents left at 1PM and Deanna was supposed to show up at 2. Tristan used this time to set up his CD player and light some candles. He was going to give Deanna a wonderful massage to make sure she knew how important she was to him—plus, that was how they did it in the movies.

The physical aspect of their relationship had progressed rapidly. He would never have guessed how sexual she was. He was shocked at first, but it didn't take him long to accept it. Tristan had gone from very inexperienced—never having kissed a girl before—to third base in two months. He assumed this was normal, for a relationship as perfect as theirs, and enjoyed the attention.

He got showered and dressed fairly nice—nothing extravagant because his clothes wouldn't be on long anyways—and sat down to wait for Deanna. *Everything needed to be perfect for his perfect girl.* He chuckled at his mushy thoughts. The doorbell rang.

Tristan leaped up and opened the front door. He felt his expression deaden. Matt and Ryan were standing in front of him. Ryan spoke first: "Tristan, we are here to stop you from being an idiot. We have practice in half an hour. You better get your ass in gear."

Tristan was amused, but he knew what was important.

"Guys I'm not coming to practice today. I already told you that. I have plans."

Matt spoke next, not as patiently as Ryan had before.

"Listen, Tristan. We have hardly seen you since you started dating Deanna. We are cool with that because we know how much you wanted something like this, but it is getting a little retarded. You love basketball remember? If not basketball, come hang out with us."

Tristan was angry. "I thought you guys were going to cover for me."

"We were but," Ryan hesitated, "We are offering you a way out here. Just come with us, and we won't have to tell coach why you are not at practice."

Tristan was furious. "This is just great coming from you, Carlyle." Tristan oozed bitterness. "You are the most whipped guy in history. All I have ever done is support you when it came to Sydney, and she's a bitch."

Ryan clenched his jaw and his eyes glazed over. "If you were anyone else, Tristan Cage, I'd kill you."

Tristan didn't back down. The two boys were toe to toe on Tristan's door step. Matt intervened.

"Come on, Ryan, he's lost his senses. Let's go."

Ryan shook his head and waited a moment, perhaps hoping his friend would see reason, but it would not be so. Ryan and Matt left Tristan fuming on the porch.

Who did they think they were? Tristan was smart—the smartest of them—and he knew right from wrong. He had saved their asses numerous times, and this is how he is repaid? *Let them go.*

He went back inside and waited for the one person who understood him: Deanna.

When D arrived, he threw his arms around her, and she giggled. She noticed something was wrong right away and listened to his story without interrupting. She shook her head, "Ryan should know better. He's missed practice for Sydney before."

"Yeah I know! That's what I told him."

The two smiled, appreciating their mutual feelings on the matter and continued kissing on the couch. Eventually, Tristan covered her eyes and led her to the bedroom. He lit the candles and turned up the music. He and Deanna were extremely intimate, but there was an undeniable power in the air, more so than usual. An uncontrollable passion gripped Tristan's mind and body. His hands were shaking, as were hers. They were both nervous, but both of them knew what was to come.

They were about to make love.

Tristan had read about sex, he had seen it in movies. It would be no problem. The scene was set. It was perfection. He had gotten some protection from the teen health nurse at school. He searched for it now it the relative darkness of his bedroom. Once he found it, things would take care of themselves.

Tristan's hands were shaking as he attempted to open the package. No luck. He decided to use his teeth. His nerves would not allow him to do anything that required fine motor skills. He eventually got frustrated and jerked his head down violently with the condom package in his mouth. *Wow, that tasted bad.* In his impatience he had destroyed the first condom. *Ok, let's try that again.* Tristan was mortified, but he moved on as smoothly as possible. This time he got the package open and he felt triumphant—but now what?

He tried to remember everything he had learned in sex ed. How exactly does this thing work? He quickly scanned the box for instructions…

"Come on Tristan, just put it on." Deanna sounded impatient, perhaps she was embarrassed too.

Tristan bagged it as best he could—might as well have used saran wrap—and took a deep breath.

Fifty-six seconds later he was no longer a virgin. Excitement, fear, and apprehension consumed the next twenty minutes of his life. Was that it? Did that count? Did he prepare properly? Was she happy? Was it perfect? Was he good at it? Was he horrible? *Oh God, hopefully I wasn't horrible.* Did he hide the evidence? *No—must do that. Flushy Flushy.* His mind was moving faster than it ever had before.

Deanna seemed content. She was smiling and asking just as many questions as he was. They were ecstatic. They agreed to only tell one person each, and they had to agree on who was to be told. Deanna chose her best friend Amy, and Tristan was fine with that—Amy was a nice girl, weird, but nice. Tristan felt a pang of guilt as he realized who he wanted to tell right away. Ryan. He wanted to know what Ryan thought of all this. Deanna said she was fine with his choice.

They spent the rest of the day lying on his bed exploring what they had done. Was it good? Was it bad? Did it change things? Neither of them thought it was bad, and they both agreed that nothing would change. They were just as in love as they had been an hour ago.

Deanna had plans with Amy that night, so she was preparing to leave by six. She gave Tristan an enthusiastic kiss, promised to call later that night, and bounced out the door and down the driveway. Tristan let out a large sigh as he closed the door. Everything was perfect.

His parents were due back anytime, so he cleaned up the candles and flushed the condom down the toilet. All evidence of his taboo behaviour was wiped out. He perched himself on the couch with his book to appear as inconspicuous as possible when his parents walked through the door. He found himself feeling content, but also a little guilty for missing practice. Coach would not be happy.

Tristan called Ryan that night. Ryan was angry, but he was a notoriously nice guy. He heard Tristan's apology without interruption. Tristan promised to make more time for his friends and not miss anymore practices. Ryan seemed satisfied and Tristan, unable to contain his excitement, cut right to the chase.

"Ryan, I am no longer a Virgin."

"What!?" Tristan heard a loud crash and some minor commotion.

Tristan was laughing. "Everything ok?"

"Yeah, " Ryan said. "I just dropped my plate. You aren't joking are you?"

"Nope. Not kidding. Happened today."

"Oh my god, what was it like?" Ryan sounded like a child who had just met his sports hero.

"Well," Tristan said, but then he realized that, truth be told, he didn't know how it was. It was short, rushed, and chaotic, but he didn't want to admit that. He'd rather keep his distorted vision of it being perfect. "It was awesome man, totally perfect."

"That is really weird, dude. I have trouble getting Sydney to third base."

Both boys spent the rest of the conversation discussion their developing sex lives.

Deanna called while he was talking to Ryan. He answered the beep and told her he just had to let Ryan go. After he said goodbye to Ryan, he began his conversation with D. He was worried that she would act weird—would *he* act weird? He reminded himself to act normal, completely normal.

He tried to banish the worries from his mind: that the day had meant less to her than it had to him, or that she found she regretted the decision she had made. Tristan was unsuccessful, it was like a vault of emotion, and possibilities, had been opened inside of him.

After a few moments talking to Deanna, he was happy to realize that nothing seemed out of place. Her voice was normal, and she had lots to say. Everything was fine.

Tristan had been on the phone for about fifteen minutes when his mother poked her head through his bedroom door. "Tristan, I need to talk to you. Please don't make me wait."

Tristan could feel the anxiety rising. Had he forgotten something? She couldn't know. It must be something else.

"D, I'm really sorry. I gotta go. Talk tomorrow, ok?"

As soon as the phone was down Tristan's mom came in and closed the door. Patty looked concerned more than angry. Tristan took solace in the tiny detail.

Patty began, "Tristan, I was doing a load of laundry before bed…"

Tristan knew exactly what was going to come out of his mother's mouth next. He had picked the condom wrapper off of the floor and told himself he would throw it out.

"… and I found this in your pocket" Patty held the open wrapper in front of her. "Explain."

Tristan felt the blood drain from his face. He went pale. He lowered his eyes. He wanted to die. He couldn't face his mother. "Have you," he said. "Have you told—"

"No," Patty said, "I haven't told your father, *yet*. Start talking."

Tristan was wringing his hands together like he was trying to wash off a disease. He couldn't focus. This was bad, really bad.

"I uhh." Tristan tried to think. "I made a decision, Mom. It was mine to make."

Wrong.

"What?" His mother didn't yell. She appreciated how important it was to keep this private, at least for now. If Tristan's father found out about his 'exploits' it would be worse than bad—*catastrophic* most likely. "You are fifteen, Tristan! Fifteen! Do you have any idea what type of commitment, rather, responsibility you have taken on?"

Tristan had thought about it. Or had he? He wasn't sure at the moment.

Patty continued her interrogation. "Is she using protection as well? Or was it just this?"

"Wh… what?" Tristan didn't understand.

"Is she on the pill?"

"No." Tristan was starting to feel remorse for the decision he had made. He didn't want to feel this way. It was all supposed to be happy and easy. It wasn't supposed to be hard.

"Tristan, honey, how could you support a child? What if, Son? What if? You have done something very serious today. I am not going to tell you it was wrong, because it can be beautiful, but it was definitely serious."

Patty sat beside her son. Tristan had his head in his hands. Both fists were filled with balls of hair. "Listen to me," she spoke softly, "I love you, Tristan, and we will keep this between us. I know you are getting older, but you are still in our house ,which means you must respect my wishes as well."

Tristan nodded slowly in agreement.

"You and Deanna will not be alone again in this house. You lost that privilege. I cannot supervise you always, and if you choose to make this decision again, at least be *extremely* careful, although I choose to believe you will be smarter next time."

Tristan was not angry. He was surprised. His mother was extremely understanding. Although the guilt trip was awful, he felt that he would escape the disaster relatively unscathed.

"Oh, by the way," Patty said as she gave her son a hug, "you are grounded. I'll leave you to come up with an excuse of your choosing, but you are grounded."

Tristan nodded again. The whole sex thing was much more complicated than he thought.

Chapter Eight

Tristan spent the next practice doing suicides while the team did other things. To add insult to injury, he had to sit on the bench for the entirety of the regular season's last game. Lesson learned. He was starting to realize, the hard way, that he made some bad decisions when it came to his priorities. He had been dating Deanna for three months, they got along great, but he ticked off some of the most important people in his life. Eric still wasn't speaking to him. He couldn't believe that Tristan missed practice for a girl.

Luckily for Tristan, Coach was more forgiving. Feeling that Tristan had been punished enough; he was inserted back into the starting lineup for the provincial tournament.

The Sageview Iron Knights won provincials. They completed their undefeated season. Eric, Tristan and Ryan earned team MVPs, and a huge celebration was held at Eric's house. The party was a parent supervised celebration, so the team was kept in check when it came to potential shenanigans. The REAL party would be held at Tyrone Randall's house the following weekend. Tyrone was the captain of the senior boys team who had also won provincials. He decided to hold one of his legendary parties in dual recognition of the school's accomplishments. Tyrone lifted his usual "no juniors allowed" rule this one time. All the boys were honoured to be invited, especially Tristan, who idolized Tyrone.

When Tristan got home from the Eric's, he wasn't in the door ten minutes when the phone rang. It was Deanna, and she was *not* happy.

"Pretty late, Tristan. I thought you were going to call me," she said flatly.

"I know, D. I'm sorry, I thought it would be too late. I didn't want to wake up you or your parents."

Tristan held his breath. He didn't know why, but the situation was starting to feel very tense. There was no reason for D to be angry, but he could *feel* her bitterness.

It had just been him and the guys at coach's for a celebration!

"I heard that your party was pretty interesting," she said.

"What? D, seriously it wasn't a party. We mostly ate and played video games."

"That's not what I heard." D's voice was cold. "I heard that Eric's sister had friends over late as well. What a coincidence that you are late getting home. Ryan too, I suppose. I wonder if Sydney knows."

It was more of a threat than a question. Tristan hadn't even thought of Tara and her friends. Tara was nineteen and was in university. It was true she had friends there, but they stayed far away from the junior high boys. Tristan figured that would be obvious. He hadn't seen them more than once the entire time.

"D, really," Tristan was distraught. He didn't know what to say. "We didn't even see them."

"Sure, Tristan. You guys were probably chatting away with them until the time you came home. I can only imagine the topic of conversation too. You guys must love experienced college girls."

Things were getting carried away. It was Tristan's first experience with jealousy. He had never pictured D as they jealous type; she was normally very reasonable. This was plain crazy.

"D, why would college girls want anything to do with us? We are just kids to them."

"Oh, so you would have *liked* their attention if they wanted to give it then?"

"That's not what I said," Tristan stammered. "You're twisting my words."

"Whatever, Tristan. It is obvious to me that you had a great time. That's all I needed to know. Goodnight."

Tristan stayed sitting on the coach with the dial tone playing in his ear. What the hell just happened? Why was she acting this way? How did she know there were college girls at the house? Why did it matter? Tristan was spellbound. He had no idea what to say, or what to do. He laid on his bed and tried to read, to escape, but he couldn't. D wasn't answering her phone. He didn't want to keep calling. It was midnight for God's sake. He was replaying his conversation with D over and over again—it made no sense.

Tristan woke up on top of his covers with his book on his lap. Sunday. He was supposed to hang out with D before practice, if she stilled planned on coming over. Tristan crawled out of bed and found his way to the kitchen for some breakfast. He sat at the table and chewed on his Lucky Charms like a cow would chew on grass. Mindless and numb. He was trying to figure out why D had been so angry. Maybe having sex, taking the next step, had affected her. Maybe it had changed something.

Impossible. He still felt the same. It must be something else, she must have been having a bad day.

Lunch time rolled around and still Tristan hadn't heard from Deanna. He didn't know whether he should call or not. He didn't want to seem obsessive or needy. But he didn't want to make it seem like he didn't care either. Impossible situations felt like being stranded at sea with no life jacket. One way or the other, you were going to drown.

At one o'clock Tristan picked up the phone. The phone rang three times before Deanna answered.

"Hello?"

"Hi D. ummm you are supposed to be here. Are you coming?"

"Well, I was waiting for you to call. I am going to be a little late, but I am still coming. We have some things to discuss. I'll be there in fifteen minutes."

"Ok. Bye D."

Things to discuss? Tristan had a nauseous feeling in the pit of his stomach. He did not want to deal with a fictional situation. He had done nothing wrong! What could there possibly be to talk about? Maybe she meant she had good things to discuss, D was always positive. Yeah, she was probably over whatever mood she was in the night before.

Tristan hung onto his hope right until Deanna came to the door. There was no hug, no kiss. His hope of an easy reconciliation faded quickly. Deanna walked straight to his room. She plopped down on the bed without a smile. She beckoned for him to join her.

"Tristan, we need to talk."

"Ok." He said. He felt impending doom. He hoped that was just his dramatic nature rearing its ugly head.

"Last night you should have wanted to be with me after your big victory. I had plans for you. I waited all day to see you. Instead, you chose your friends. I don't mind if you have friends, but on special occasions I should be your first priority."

Nothing like cutting to the chase.

Who was this person? D's countenance, her entire aura had changed. She was not emitting the positive light he was so used to getting from her. Sunny Deanna had turned dark and cold.

"D, I'm sorry. I didn't think of it like that. I thought you would understand. It would have been rude of me to skip out on the coach's invitation. I—"

Deanna cut him off. "Oh my god Tristan. I cannot believe you."

What? This is insane.

"You are constantly making the wrong choices. I have thought long and hard about this, and it just seems like I have more invested in this relationship than you."

"D, that's not true!" Tristan's heart was racing. He didn't know what he could say to convince her otherwise. It felt like no matter what he did the situation got worse. He felt hopeless, trapped.

"Deanna you are the best thing that's ever happened to me. It may have taken me a while to see it, but now that I have, I want to hold onto you forever. Please. I'm sorry I upset you, I really didn't think you would be waiting around for me."

"Tristan, I know you care about me, just not as much as I care about you. I want to have sex, Tristan. We haven't done it since that day. Why won't you show me how much you care?"

Tristan knew that was a fact. He was worried about when it would come up. It wasn't that he didn't want to. He was just scared. His mother had done her job well.

Tricky. Proceed with caution, Cage.

"I'm scared ok? That's just honest, I'm scared."

"I'm scared too, Tristan," she replied smoothly, "but my feelings for you override that fear. Being with you, I've realized that I'm a very physical person, and I want that in a relationship."

Tristan was feeling even more trapped. He felt pressure. Pressure to do things he didn't necessarily feel comfortable doing and making decisions he didn't feel comfortable making.

Tristan was silent. Speechless. He shook his head slowly with downcast eyes. This was not the Deanna he had known for years. She was different. But he cared about her, almost more than he could handle.

"Deanna. I said all I can say. I'm not angry, just really confused. I don't know where all this is coming from. Everything was fine— then boom. I get hit with this."

"I'm sorry you feel that way, Tristan." She was patronizing him. He hated that. "I guess we just need some time to ourselves. To think about what we want from all of this."

Tristan couldn't help but compare this new mood of D's to Rachel. It felt the same. The atmosphere, the pace of his heartbeat, the impending doom. There was no way they could break up.

They were soul mates, together forever. He had the letters from D that agreed with him.

"Whoa D! What the hell? Are you saying we need to break up?"

"No Tristan, just less time together. That's what you want isn't it?"

At what point had he given her that impression? All because of one goddamn gathering with his friends?

"No, that is *not* what I want. I want to be with you. I love you."

He said it before he knew what he was saying. He had wanted to say it for some time. He had been waiting to say it to someone since he figured out what love was. He knew the word was overused, he knew the word got thrown around, but he meant it. Every word.

D's facial expression changed. She softened. "You what?"

"I… I love you Deanna."

Her eyes welled with tears. She gave him a playful shove in the arm. "I love you too."

D's mood changed as if by magic. She was herself again, almost as if the new sides of her were opposite sides of a coin. Tristan just hoped the powers that be didn't decide to gamble again anytime soon. He sometimes felt that he was the object of entertainment for higher powers.

He and Deanna spent the rest of the time in his room in each other's arms. By the time she had to leave, he felt like things were back on track. He and Deanna parted happily and he was able to enjoy some time with the guys—without guilt.

When Tristan was alone again he thought hard about what Deanna had said to him. He did not want her to feel like she had more invested in the relationship than he did. It took some time, but he devised a plan for the next day that should make her realize how much he cared. He got up from his bed and went to the kitchen to prepare.

Chapter Nine

Tristan concealed his instant picnic in his backpack. He planned everything to a tee. He was lucky enough to get a nice April day. He packed strawberries with whip cream, peanut butter and jam sandwiches—a favourite of D's—Oreo cookies, and apple juice. He had a bright red blanket he borrowed from his mom, and he brought his portable CD player with miniature speakers for music. He was rather confident that Deanna would be swept off her feet with his romantic gesture.

Tristan kept his plan a secret, even from Ryan. The picnic lay hidden in his locker until lunch. When the lunch bell rang he immediately grabbed Deanna and took her, and his backpack, to the front of the school. High on the hill overlooking the soccer field was a large stone slab that had been put there years earlier by one of the graduating classes. Spring thaw was in full swing, so the slab was the perfect place to drop his blanket for the picnic because it was dry. Deanna seemed amused, but asked no questions. She allowed Tristan to do his thing. When all was prepared she was beaming. Tristan was very proud of his charming plan.

The little CD player he brought played all kinds of romantic music. They ate and fed one another playfully missing each other's mouths on purpose. Both Tristan and Deanna had whip cream all over their faces by the time the bell rang to end lunch hour. There had been plenty of fun and laughter, and Tristan had gone the extra mile to show how much he cared. Tristan felt like he had his best friend again, as well as his girlfriend.

The rest of the day was fabulous. He and Deanna showed no traces of their rough patch. They sat together on the bus, as usual, and Deanna talked and talked about how amazing it had been that Tristan brought a picnic to school. She said it was the sweetest thing she'd ever seen. When they got off the bus, she gave him a huge kiss before they parted ways.

The next day at school was a little different. In fact, it was a lot different. As they were waiting for morning classes to start, a familiar face walked over to Tristan and asked if she could talk to him. He looked to his left, if looks could kill, Deanna's fury would have torn Rachel to shreds. To his right, Rachel was undaunted. She asked again, "Tristan can I talk to you please? It is totally innocent, and has nothing to do with you and me, other than the fact that I want my friend back."

Tristan attempted to move, but Deanna had a death grip on his arm. He turned his head and said softly, "I'll just go over there. You can watch everything that happens."

Deanna let up, but Tristan still had to pry his arm from her proverbial bear trap. He walked a few steps away and looked at Rachel. She seemed very calm and controlled, a good thing. He knew talking to her was like ignoring the "Don't feed the Animals" sign, but if he didn't, he would be ignoring the moral conscience he took so much pride in.

"Tristan, I have put you through a lot this year, and I just wanted to say that I'm glad you are happy. I miss the time we spent together, and I would love if we could hang out again, if only from time to time. I would rather that than nothing at all."

Tristan did not know how to respond. He didn't want to take too long to think about it as he didn't want to offend Rachel. His first instinct was to say, *sure I'd love that*, and give her a *friendly* hug, but he hesitated because he was afraid of Deanna's reaction. That unsettled him more than anything else. He was shaping his decisions based on the fear of Deanna's reaction. Was that normal? Was that healthy?

He looked tentatively at Rachel, "You bet Rach. I'm sorry too." He gave her a quick hug and walked back to sit with Deanna. He felt her eyes on him before he even looked over at her. He had gambled and lost.

"What was that, Tristan?"

"What was *what*, D? She was just apologizing. You saw what happened, it was totally innocent."

"Did you need to hug her?"

The answer was of course, no, but if you were in a secure relationship a hug wouldn't matter much, would it? Tristan didn't know if his decision to hug Rachel meant anything or not, but he knew D's decision to be angry about it spoke volumes.

"I was just being nice, D."

Deanna's reply was venomous, "Yeah, well, you always are, *especially* to Rachel."

With that, she stood up and stormed away. Ryan took Deanna's spot and threw his arm around Tristan.

"Welcome to the wonderful world of dating, my friend. Now we can suffer together."

Tristan beat his head against the wall until the bell rang.

Ryan and Tristan sat together for the rest of the day. Deanna refused to sit with him. Tristan understood why Rachel was a sensitive subject, but he had chosen D. Maybe D felt she was chosen by default? Tristan wasn't sure. He just hoped they could patch things up, yet again, before Tyrone's big party.

Tristan managed to convince D to talk to him on the way home. He didn't like the response that he got. Deanna wanted some space, a break. According to her, Tristan made too many bad decisions and it was making her doubt her feelings for him. She was unsure of how he felt about Rachel, and she was unsure about his feelings for her. She was a mess, and needed time to think. She would not be going to the party with him, and she would not be speaking with him for the rest of the week. No matter how hard Tristan tried, she would not acknowledge him for the rest of the bus ride home.

When Tristan got home he went straight to his room and shut the door. He just wanted to sleep. When you slept, you felt no pain, and he didn't want to hurt anymore. It felt like his heart had clubbed his brain with a mallet. When he made it to his bed he had every intention of sleeping, but the emotional roller coaster he had been on recently finally caught up with him. He broke down and cried. His body shook with the force of his emotion, and he didn't want to talk to anyone. He curled up in a ball and toughed it out. All on his own.

—

The next three days felt like he was living a different life. He avoided Rachel—being seen with her could only make things worse—and tried to give Deanna the space she wanted. He said good morning to her, and although it was really hard, he let her go off with her friends. Tristan couldn't explain it, but seeing her smile and laugh with her other friends hurt him deeply. It was as if she was *enjoying* the time without him, while he was a ball of agony.

Tristan tried approaching her again on Friday in a last ditch attempt to get her to go to the party with him, but she said she was hanging out with Amy and would talk to him on Monday. She was so nonchalant dealing with him that he doubted he would even hear from her at all. His heart was breaking.

Ryan stayed at his house Friday night and all day Saturday. They talked about boy things—sports and supermodels—and discussed, briefly, their girl troubles. Deanna was still not speaking to him and Sydney was still a controlling bitch. Enough had been said about relationships. The boys played video games and watched movies. Almost, for an instant, Tristan forgot how bad things were.

Tristan and Ryan got ready for the party together. As much as Tristan needed Ryan's presence to feel confident, Ryan needed Tristan as well. The boys were a team in everything they did. The party would be their first grown up bash. They would be tempted by things, offered others, but as long as they had each other, they could not be corrupted.

Tristan was up front with his parents. He and Ryan were going to a party and would need to be picked up. Tristan was honest about everything he expected to see at Tyrone's and was surprised—very surprised as a matter of fact—that his father was proud of him. Cam agreed to drop them off and pick them up, but not without the threat of a painful death if they came home smelling like anything but cologne.

Tyrone's blue bungalow was quite literally bumping. It was vibrating with the volume of music being played, and there were people everywhere. Half of Sageview must have been at his party. Most were holding drinks, and there were others—in a circle on the back deck—passing around a joint. Tristan was intimidated, but not afraid. He and Ryan walked into the house and found Matt on the couch next to Lacey and Sean. The boys plopped down and made themselves comfortable. Again, Tristan thought about Deanna. He was sad, but it had been her choice not to come.

Matt offered Tristan a beer, and Tristan respectfully declined. He was content watching the NBA playoffs on TV. The music was loud, but it was good, a mix of everything and all of it recent. Sydney found Ryan and was soon sitting on his lap. Ryan looked at Tristan as if to say, *Sorry, man*. But Tristan understood. If Deanna had been there, he'd be making out too.

About an hour after Tristan sat down, his friends had dispersed. Ryan had gone off to find a room with Sydney, Matt left with Lacey to mingle, and Tristan was left on the couch alone, but only momentarily.

Rachel came storming into the room, her face drenched with tears. As soon as she saw Tristan she latched onto him and soaked his chest. She was sobbing so violently that her convulsions were moving him back and forth. Tristan put one arm around her and tried to calm her down.

"Shhh Rach. It's ok," he said a little stunned. "Shhh..."

Finally Rachel finally stopped crying.

"It's" and for a second she almost said Marvin, "It's Guns," she said, sniffling. "He He's such an asshole."

"Rachel, it's ok, tell me what happened."

The music was so loud, and Tristan genuinely wanted to help, so he took Rachel by the hand and led her to a room. The door was shut. Tristan knocked. No answer. Tristan opened the door a crack and peeked in. It was a bedroom, an empty one it appeared. The music was so loud! It was very disorienting. Tristan stepped into the room and froze.

Locked in a passionate embrace were two half naked souls. One of them was Deanna.

"Deanna, what the fuck!?" Tristan caught fire. He let go of Rachel and strode into the room.

Deanna jumped up and covered herself. She was shocked, but didn't look embarrassed. Her movement allowed Tristan to see who her new lover was. Rage caused Tristan to see red. Lying, three-quarters naked and grinning back at him, was Eric Childs. Tristan's jaw was clenched shut. All rational thought left his mind. He knew the music was loud, but he couldn't hear it. He knew people were talking to him, but he couldn't hear them. His fists were molded into weapons. He hurtled his annoying conscience deep into the depths of his psyche. It would not be needed.

Deanna had put her shirt back on and her mouth was moving. Tristan's anger was making him crazy, for he found it funny that her mouth was trying to console him after it had done all of the damage. He even smirked. The tension in the room was unbearable. He shifted his gaze from Deanna to his 'friend.' Eric did not look concerned. Perhaps he thought this was Deanna's problem. If that was what he thought, he was wrong.

"Get up Eric. Now."

Eric didn't move. He just stared back at Tristan. "Eric, get up or I will drag you out of the goddamn bed."

Eric laughed. Laughed! *What the hell is he laughing at? Has the entire planet lost their minds?* Tristan was shaking. Adrenaline pumped through his veins.

"Tristan," Eric said with a smirk. "What are you going to do about it?"

What the…

Eric was his friend! They had known each other for years! Deanna could wait. The way Eric dealt with the situation just pissed Tristan off more. He started moving toward the bed. Eric swung his feet over the side and stood up, but before he could comprehend what was happening, Tristan swung as hard as his body would let him. He imagined his fist as a wrecking ball and Eric's face as the building that needed to be torn down. He made solid contact. Eric hit the floor like a ton of bricks. Tristan could feel the throbbing pain in his hand. Physical pain was all he could feel at the moment. Emotionally, he was numb.

Tristan looked down at Eric who was holding onto his face. Eric spit a bloody piece of flesh onto the carpet. Tristan hoped it was life threatening, but he was sure it was only a tooth. Eric was breathing hard and looked up at Tristan.

"You're dead."

"Bring it," was all Tristan cared to say.

Eric charged him and Tristan was driven back into the dresser. The girls were screaming for help, for them to stop, but the boys were too busy trying to kill each other. Eric was strong, but at that moment, Tristan's fury gave him an uncanny power. Tristan bounced off of the dresser and spun around, it hurt, but he didn't care. As he rebounded off of the dresser he and Eric became separated for a moment. Tristan, with impressive speed, used the space to entrap Eric in a choke hold. He felt his forearm dig deep into Eric's throat. He was trapped, and Tristan felt nothing but vengeance. He was going to kill the prick. Eric struggled, but Tristan just squeezed harder.

Before Tristan could finish the job, he was hit—by what felt like a freight train—and tackled to the floor. He got up fast and immediately looked for Eric so he could pummel him some more, but between him and his victim stood a six foot three wall of muscle. Ryan looked as though he was in the twilight zone. He was so confused. He had his hands held out holding back the two combatants.

"Ryan," Tristan said in an eerie voice, "move."

"Tristan," Ryan gasped, "are you crazy? What's wrong?" He was bent over trying to catch his breath; he must have run from the other end of the house.

"That piece of shit was in this bed with Deanna." Tristan said bitterly.

Ryan's confusion doubled as he turned to look at Eric. "Is that *true*?"

Eric nodded. "She said they weren't together. And besides, today, she wanted me. I don't know why he's so mad. Bros before hoes."

Ryan looked at Eric like he too was seeing him for the first time. Tristan couldn't believe that he had been so naïve as to think that Eric was his friend. They all knew what Eric was like: egotistical, selfish, headstrong. Tristan thought that friendship would shelter him from that part of Eric's personality, but that had obviously been a critical error in judgment.

Ryan looked at Tristan, then back at Eric. He turned toward Tristan for an instant, then, in the blink of an eye, he spun and punched Eric square in the face. The sound his fist made in conjunction with the cartilage of Eric's nose was disgusting. It sounded like dropping a rock into a tub of jello, a sickening *spluck*.

Three Words

Eric's nose was definitely broken, and he was out cold. Ryan turned to Tristan and gave him a nod. They were a team, and Eric had wounded his teammate. For that, he'd been punished. Ryan grabbed him by the arm and dragged him forcibly out of the room and through the crowd of people who had gathered at the door. Tristan looked over his shoulder only to see Deanna kneeling at Eric's side. The commotion was unbelievable, and in moments, the wave of people hid Deanna, and her fallen lover, from his sight.

Tristan was starting his return to reality. His hand hurt like hell. He looked down, there was a lot of blood. Ryan had probably noticed the gaping gash in his hand and was dragging him somewhere to get help. He definitely needed stitches. Much more noticeable was the pain in his chest. His heart was broken. What happened to Deanna? Why had she done this to him? Why had she said she wasn't going to be there? She knew Tristan was going—it didn't make any sense. It was obvious Eric just wanted a piece of ass, but D?

Ryan hauled Tristan outside. Tristan could hear Sydney chirping away demanding to know what was going on. He heard Ryan tell her to shut up and try to be more helpful. He gave her Tristan's number and told her to find a phone and call Cameron. Sydney looked surprised at Ryan's new found independence, and did as he asked. Ryan stood over Tristan like a father protecting his fallen son. If Eric, or anyone loyal to him, thought about coming after Tristan they would have to deal with Ryan first.

Tristan felt a new affection for his friend and finally gave into the physical and emotional pain. He just put his head down and tried to shut off his brain. Twenty minutes later Cameron arrived. They put Tristan in the back seat and sped off to the medical clinic. Tristan could vaguely hear Ryan telling Cameron what happened. Tristan passed out shortly after. He hated blood.

Tristan needed five stitches to seal the cut on the knuckle of his right hand. The needle did not feel good. He had an extremely weak stomach, the only thing that had saved him from passing out at Tyrone's was blinding rage and adrenaline. There had been a couple of times when Tristan had passed out from nasty hang-nails.

By the time they got home it was after 1AM. Tristan didn't want to talk about anything that happened, and those around him understood. He knew that the next day he had some explaining to do, but he had a newfound appreciation for his parents, and his best friend, all of whom played a part in saving his ass that night.

Chapter Ten

Much to his disappointment, Tristan woke up the next day. His hand was bandaged but his heart was not. He felt like he was going to throw up. His mind replayed what he had seen with Deanna and Eric like some sort of sadistic film. He had to see Deanna. His anger turned to despair. He didn't know whether to get up, or try and go back to sleep. Sleep, as before, was a sweet release from reality. Tristan started to cry. He didn't care if he sobbed loud enough for anyone to hear, he didn't care about much of anything. It was another cosmic joke to realize that today was Sunday, usually his day with Deanna.

His mother knocked softly on his door. He didn't say a word. She came in and sat next to him. She placed her hand on his thigh and said nothing. After a few minutes she gave him a warm hug, and left him alone. His mother's silent comfort was helpful. Tristan realized that there were some people who knew what he needed, and who actually cared about him.

When he calmed down he came out to the kitchen. His father was making breakfast. Cameron nodded to his son and informed him that Ryan had gone home earlier in the morning to do chores, but would come back later. Tristan accepted the pancakes his father had made and started eating. By the time he finished he was flanked by his parents sitting on either side of him. It was time to spill the beans.

He told them everything. It was a relief to let go of all the pain he was feeling. His parents did not interrupt him, they let him talk. Cam looked more frustrated than anything else, and Patty looked plain sad. When he was finished speaking, his father spoke.

"Tristan, this girl did not love you, and you did not love her. This is not love."

It was not what Tristan wanted to hear. He loved Deanna. He knew he did. His heart beat faster when she was around. He imagined things with her he had never dreamed of with anyone else. She made him smile. She was always there for him. Tristan would do anything for her; he would have died for her. Tristan figured it was easy to think all of these things while he was so emotional, but couldn't stop himself. He held his anger in check. He knew it was common for adults to doubt the feelings of teenagers. Tristan knew that teens were often more dramatic and chaotic, but feelings were feelings, regardless of age.

Patty just squeezed his hand and smiled at him. He and his mom had grown closer over the course of his ups and downs with Deanna. And after last night, he felt closer to his father too. Although he had not liked Cam's last comment, he was extremely grateful for what his father had done for him in the last 24 hours.

Ryan came back later that day. He brought Matt with him. Their quartet was down to three. They agreed to exile Eric from their group until the end of time. Tristan tried to explain how grateful he was to Ryan for being such an amazing friend, but Ryan would have none of it. "You'd have done the same for me," was all he said with his big goofy grin occupying most of his face.

Tristan ran through many scenarios in his mind. Perhaps something happened to Deanna that he didn't know about. A death in her family, an illness, perhaps she was ill herself? Had sex changed her? Made her hormones gone crazy? Had she simply changed her mind about him and made the wrong decisions about how to end things? Regardless, he was unsure if her actions were forgivable. According to Ryan, if Tristan even thought about speaking to Deanna again, he would kill him.

Tristan dreaded school on Monday, and for good reason. Seeing Deanna made things much, much worse. It could have been the fact that she was walking with Eric, although the surgical tape holding Eric's nose together was mildly comforting, or it could have been the fact that she was smiling, either way, seeing her was immensely painful. He noticed every little nuance that had been his before. The way she flipped her hair, the way she bit her thumb when she was concentrating, the dimples that defined her pretty smile—regardless of what she had done, Tristan still loved her.

He watched miserably as Eric released her hand. She walked toward her locker. Tristan waited until she was alone and gathered courage. He approached her much like he would approach a dangerous animal. She had already shown the ability to wound him deeper than physical pain was capable of. It was his heart he was protecting. When he said her name, his voice shook. "Deanna."

She did not turn around. She paused for a moment. Her head tilted sideways for an instant, and then she kept on with what she was doing. Tristan felt like a ghost, like a figment of her imagination she was trying to ignore. She looked like Deanna, but she acted like someone under an evil spell.

"Deanna, for the love of god you have to talk to me. You owe me that much."

She turned and looked at him. The way her eyes used to sparkle was replaced with a mindless vacancy. There was only the dull green of her iris looking back at him. "What do you want Tristan? I think you said enough when you and your behemoth hurt Eric."

Hurt Eric? A week ago they had been in love, telling each other they were in love. She had kissed him passionately, he felt it. They had made love, only once, but that was enough to bond them together forever. They were each other's first. For Tristan, she was the first kiss, first partner, and first love. How could that have changed in a week?

"Deanna we are together, you cheated on me. How can you be so cold?" Tristan pleaded with her. He was trying to bring the good Deanna back from the dead.

"We weren't together Tristan. I told you, I needed space. During my time alone, I realized that Eric was the right guy for me. He takes care of my needs."

Tristan's face resembled an unfinished quilt. There were so many emotions running through him that the different pieces had warped his visage in a way that felt unnatural. He ran his hand through his hair and sighed. It was so painful!

"Eric is an asshole. He was my friend, and look what he did to me. You are just an object to him Deanna. Why can't you see that?"

"Typical Tristan, always the good guy. Look what you did to him. You knocked out his front tooth." She eyed the bandage on his hand, "You were choking him half to death. Then you let Ryan break his nose. What kind of friend are you?"

Tristan felt the tables turning on him. He had lost his temper, yes, but for good reason! How could she not see how wrong she was? It felt like Deanna was the creator of the atom bomb, and instead of Japan, she dropped it on Tristan.

There was no emotion in her, Tristan wished for answers. He wished he knew what had happened to her. She was once the most perfect person he knew. But now, now she was a monster.

He felt weak. Despite his anger, he said the only three words that mattered to him.

"I love you."

She squinted her eyes like she was talking to a pet she no longer wanted. "I don't want your love, Tristan. It would be best if we didn't talk. Please don't call me or bother me again."

She turned coldly. Her hair cascaded down her back as she let it out of her ponytail. She marched down the hallway to meet Eric who had been waiting for her. Eric grinned back at him as the two walked away, hand in hand.

The Second Three Words
(3 years Later)

Chapter Eleven

The crowd was loud, but Tristan couldn't hear them. His focus was unwavering. He had tunnel vision, and this was the game of his life. He had carried the Iron Knights on his back since the season started, and this game was no different. With the university scouts in attendance, more than just an upset hung in the balance, his future did too. The Falcons had just scored a basket to tie the game at 68. Ryan Carlyle took the ball behind the baseline and passed it in to Tristan.

Tristan had been punishing the Sunnyvale defence all night long. His decision-making skills were second to none. If the double team came, he found the open man. If they played him single coverage, he went one on one to the basket. If they played off of him, he drilled the three pointer. Tonight, he was unguardable. Tristan looked at the clock. 28 seconds to play.

He dribbled the ball up the court. The Sunnyvale fans were jeering him, but he did not notice. The only thing he saw was the hoop at the other end of the gym. He glanced at the coach to get the play call. He passed the ball to Matt on the left wing, turned, and cut hard down the key.

20 seconds to play.

The Sunnyvale coach was screaming, "Get 11! Get Cage!" Tristan loved that he was feared.

Ryan set a hard screen on the baseline as Tristan curled toward the corner. Tristan's man got hung up on Ryan's massive body, and Tristan was free. He sprinted for the corner. The Sunnyvale coach fuelled his confidence. "Don't let him shoot! Get the shooter!"

But it was too late. Matt made a pinpoint pass right into Tristan's midsection. Right in his wheelhouse. As soon as the ball hit his hands, it was gone.

Time slowed.

Everyone in the gym watched the ball's perfect rotation through the air.

Swish.

Tristan's teammates flew off the bench and smothered him in hugs and high fives. The Iron Knights had beaten the number one ranked Sunnyvale Falcons, something that hadn't been done since Tyrone Randall led them to victory, three years earlier. Tristan glanced up and saw his mother and father hugging. His kid sister, Emma, was cheering and calling his name. They were the only ones. The disgruntled Sunnyvale fans were quickly making their way out of the gym.

The Knights lined up and shook hands. Their win would be talked about all year, and Tristan was glad he would be at the centre of it. The scouts were impressed with his performance but wanted to see more of his games. That was fine with Tristan. There was plenty more greatness to be seen.

Tristan was the last person onto the bus, right behind Ryan. One of the grade tens congratulated him on his way by, "You played awesome, Tristan."

Tristan smirked at him. "Thanks rookie. Hope you were taking notes." Tristan didn't need confirmation of his greatness from a tenth grader, or anyone else for that matter. He had earned it. He had worked his ass off for three years. He practiced every day. The only people he gave the time of day to were his family and Ryan. Basketball kept him focused on what was important. Basketball made him invincible.

Three Words

Tristan sat down next to Ryan and put his headphones on. Music was his saving grace. It pumped him up as well as calmed him down. Ryan didn't bother talking to him; he knew Tristan would just gaze out the window for the duration of the trip. Tristan didn't talk much at all anymore.

The bus dropped Tristan off outside his house on the way back to the school. Any students located on the bus's main drag were let off to aid parents with travel. Tristan gave a quick wave to Ryan and walked up his long driveway. He said a quick hello to his parents before sealing himself in his room. He spent hours there. It was his sanctuary. It held his books, his movies, his computer, and his weights. He had everything he needed.

Tristan read some of his history textbook before bed. He was just as focused on school as he was on basketball. If he was going to get a scholarship his marks needed to be great. He did not want his parents to shoulder the burden of his education costs.

Tristan woke up at 6AM to get on the treadmill. He drank his full glass of water before heading downstairs. *Had to stay hydrated.* Tristan put his headphones on and ran for forty-five minutes. When he felt he had sweated enough, he showered and shaved. He didn't have to do much to his short black hair. The natural curls kept it relatively neat and tidy. He had felt liberated when he cut his long hair off a year before. Short hair was much easier. He didn't let it grow more than a couple inches long.

After he ate his fruit salad—Thursday's were natural fruit days—he called for his sister, and they waited at the bus stop together. They were the only two at their particular stop, the only other person who had boarded at their stop moved into Sageview a year earlier. Tristan blocked the memories from his mind and forced himself to think about the game the night before.

Tristan sat by himself in the back seat of the bus. Everyone knew not to sit with him. The last person who had tried left with a bruised ego. Tristan was not to be disobeyed. He was both feared and respected, a goal he had worked very hard to achieve.

When he got to school he accepted the praise he received from students and staff with open arms. He was the man. He was the best, *he sure was*. He played fantastic, *he sure did*. He would play basketball for a living, *nah, but thanks anyways*.

Tristan went straight to the gym to shoot hoops before class. He did not bother looking for Ryan in the mornings because he spent that time making out with Sydney. Tristan hated Sydney and hated the fact that Ryan didn't have the balls to kick that bitch to the curb. He also hated affection. Affection led to feelings, which led to people thinking they were in love, which was, in fact, impossible. Love was a fictitious feeling created to make married people less miserable.

When Tristan stepped onto the court, those who were there moved to another net. The last time Tristan had been hit with a stray basketball he had kicked it to the other end of the gym. Nobody wanted to piss him off. He loved having all the space to himself. He practiced until the first bell rang and went promptly to home room. He broke no rules, he wasn't late for a single class since he got to senior high. A clean record was imperative to securing the best scholarships. Tristan knew that students in a rural school had to work much harder than kids in a city school due to numbers; city schools had higher population and more exposure. Tristan had to play it smart.

Tristan passed Sydney in the hall as he went to homeroom. She must have just 'dropped Ryan off'. Sydney batted her big blue eyes at him and gave him a smooth, "hello". Tristan rolled his eyes in return. He reminded himself to inform Ryan that he was an idiot for allowing this girl to leech off of him. She had almost broken up with him numerous times until he got his big Scholarship to Winchester University.

Ryan was recruited an entire year before most people. He was picked up for track, not basketball. His incredible athleticism only grew as he got older, and his physique was godly. He had placed first in discus, javelin, 100 meter, and high jump at provincials that year, blowing all his senior competitors out of the water. It was such an impressive performance that scouts who had never heard of him offered anything he wanted to attend their school. Luckily for Winchester, that was exactly the place Sydney planned to go.

Tristan enjoyed his walks to class. There was a lot of eye candy at Sageview. The senior high girls were represented well. A lot of them were extremely good looking, and luckily for Tristan, most loved attention from him. He didn't sleep around, but he would make out left right and centre. A boy needed his playtime. Commitment was overrated, and he made sure girls knew that up front. Tristan only had two rules: no home wrecking—he refused to get with a girl who was in a relationship—and no sex. Unfortunately for him, his moral conscience had been shoved to the side, but not obliterated.

He made sure Adrienne Axley saw him look her up and down before he entered the classroom. Adrienne and her perfect breasts were high on Tristan's priority list. He strolled to the back of class and sat down next to Ryan. Thank god he had decided to take as many classes without Sydney as possible. Tristan convinced him that it would be hard for him to focus with his girlfriend in the room. Tristan was sure Sydney wouldn't mind, that left her free to get her flirt-on with the rest of Sageview.

If only she would contract a fatal disease…

The bell rang for first period: History. It was ironic. Tristan loved that class, it was probably his favourite, but the one face in the school he never wanted to look at was in that class as well—they had *History* together in more ways than one. Tristan hadn't spoken to her since she shattered his heart into a million pieces three years ago. He hated her. He loathed her. What she had done made Satan look like the Easter Bunny. It was because of her that Tristan no longer believed in love, shunned emotional connections, and viewed all girls as a means to an end. Girls were only as faithful as their options.

This was the one and only class they shared in two years. Tristan made sure of that. He would have been able to avoid this too if he had been able to take Calculus first semester. Naturally, the teacher was on maternity leave until January, so the course was not offered until then. Thus, he had to take history first semester and endure being in the room with hell spawn. No matter, it was almost Christmas break, and after Christmas, it would be one short month until he was free of her evil presence.

Mrs. Wiley started the class with a lecture on the Persian Wars. Tristan loved ancient history, especially war history. He was fascinated with strategy and tactics, probably why he loved the game *Risk* so much. After her brief lecture she announced there would be a project assigned. Tristan's pen, which was moving smoothly across his page, stopped.

A project that's fine, just don't tell me that—

"This project will be done in pairs."

Tristan almost laughed. It would be too much of a coincidence if she were to say—

"I will be choosing those pairs."

Tristan closed his hand around his pen like he was strangling it. What were the chances? He looked at Ryan and Ryan's eyes were wide as saucers. He understood the implications. World war three could be started if—

"Ryan Carlyle and Adrienne Axley"

Ryan gave a small fist pump and couldn't help but grin. Tristan shot him a fierce glance. Ryan shrugged his shoulders, "What? She's hot."

"Matt Staunton and Lacey Connor."

Ok. That was two less options to save him.

"Tristan Cage and…"

Fuck. He knew it before she said it.

"…Deanna Greene."

The whole class murmured. Mrs. Wiley quieted them quickly.

"Oh hush now! I am perfectly aware of the mutual dislike between the two. This is senior year, and you are all adults. I expect you to conduct yourselves maturely."

The class was quiet. Tristan's eyes were burning a hole in Mrs. Wiley's forehead. She sure picked a good time to test his citizenship. He couldn't do this. He would talk to her after class.

Ryan didn't dare say a word, he was perhaps the only one who knew how bad this could get. Nobody infuriated Tristan like Deanna. Nobody had ever hurt him worse. Tristan had changed his entire way of life to protect himself from the pain she had caused him. Tristan had taken every possible step to insulate himself against *feelings*. The way he was now, he felt sorry for Deanna. No matter how she may have changed, her bitterness was no match for Tristan's.

Mrs. Wiley continued, "The project will be on the effects of war. One of you will be a famous leader from the past, the other will be a citizen, or soldier, effected by the wars that leader has started. One will interview the other and vice versa. The questions asked should reflect the values important to each specific party at the time. The Q and A will be held here in class on Tuesday, December 16th, last day before break. Please rehearse beforehand and make sure you know what questions you will be asking each other."

Tristan turned his head and looked directly at Deanna for the first time in years. Almost instantly his mind flashed back three years ago. He saw the remorseless look on her face as they stood next to her locker. Tristan had told her he loved her, and she had chosen the guy she cheated on him with. *Eric Fucking Childs*. Tristan had stood there for an hour without movement. He felt...

NO!

NO! He felt nothing! This is exactly what he had been afraid of. He had spent years recovering from what she had done to him! Years! One look at her and every emotion came crashing down upon him. He would not allow it. He forced himself to think of something much more appealing: Vengeance.

Chapter Twelve

Tristan and Deanna spoke briefly, as briefly as possible, to determine when they were going to meet and work on their project. They were both free the next day after school, so it was decided they would just stay until it was finished.

3PM Friday afternoon came very fast. Too fast. Tristan felt like he was moving in slow motion as he walked towards the library. Maybe it was because he *was* moving slowly. He was walking as slow as humanly possible. He was not looking forward to the day's prospects. He and Deanna had not had a real conversation in years. Their relationship was limited to avoidance and the odd emotional outburst, usually from Tristan, attempting to inflict as much verbal damage as possible.

Tristan muttered curses against Mrs. Wiley as he pushed through the library doors. The first thing he saw was Deanna's shoulder length brown hair seated at the first available table. Tristan decided that fear was an emotion he wasn't going to let her have the privilege of seeing. He put on his best "I hate your guts" face and sat down across from her.

Tristan stared. He was attempting to light her on fire with his mind—it wasn't working. *Maybe she would spontaneously combust. No, wait, spirits from hell were probably immune to fire.* He would need crosses and holy water.

Deanna looked up from her work, "So…" she said shyly.

"So…" Tristan responded.

They sat in silence for ten minutes. Tristan was tapping the end on his pencil on his paper trying to keep busy. Deanna was biting her thumb. He used to think it was cute, now he wished it would explode taking her head with it.

Fifteen minutes passed and neither had said more than a single probing word. Something had to give. The last thing Tristan wanted to do was sit there longer than he had to. He manned up. "Look, we need to get this thing done. I don't like it any more than you do, but it is what it is."

She looked at him. Her eyes were still green, but there was no spark.

"Ok Tristan, whatever you say."

That's right. Whatever *he* wanted. He was glad she saw reason. Tristan had an idea.

"Why don't we do Julius Caesar and a Roman soldier? Caesar fought many battles and expected a lot from his troops. It should make for a relatively easy Q and A."

"Hm." Deanna looked thoughtful. "Sounds good to me. Which one am I going to be?"

Tristan wanted to say, *whichever one dies first*, but he held his tongue. He had to let Deanna think he actually cared about this assignment, when, in fact, he had a much bigger score to settle.

"Ummm whichever one you like," Tristan said as genuinely as possible. "Why don't you be Caesar? Everyone would expect me to be because I'm the boy. It may get us some brownie points to do a role reversal here."

Deanna seemed satisfied with the idea. "Sounds good, Tristan, let's get to work."

The partners only talked when absolutely necessary. Otherwise, they researched and worked on their own. They had been at the library two hours when they were content they had enough material to finish at home. They agreed to meet the day before the presentation to polish things up.

Three Words

Deanna left first, and Tristan thought to himself as she left, *I'm going to enjoy this.* As soon as she was gone Tristan packed up his things and went to see Mrs. Wiley. Tristan had known what he was going to do since he sat at the table with Deanna. All that awkward time had allowed him to formulate his plan. Tristan knew Mrs. Wiley was always the last teacher to leave the school, she was hardcore. He made his way to her room and knocked.

"Come in," said Mrs. Wiley.

Tristan walked over to her desk and sat down. He knew how to talk to adults. He was very well respected by all the teachers at the school for his excellent grades and work ethic.

"Tristan, I was very glad to see how well you handled things with Deanna. I know you two don't get along. I saw you two working at the library and was very impressed. Things seem to be going well."

"Oh they are Mrs. Wiley. We got a lot done, but we have a problem. My parents scheduled a doctor's appointment for me in the city on Tuesday. Since it is the last day of school they didn't think I would be missing anything." Tristan considered his next set of lies very carefully; they were crucial. "I assume we have to get this done before break, or else Deanna and I would have two extra weeks over everyone else."

Mrs. Wiley eyed him suspiciously.

Tristan continued. "I talked about it with Deanna and we both think we should switch partners. If you put me with Ryan, I can work with him all weekend and present on Monday. Adrienne could then work with Deanna and present on Tuesday."

Tristan anticipated Mrs. Wiley's skepticism, and was ready for it. "I know this is short notice Miss, but I only just realized it while we were working. That is why we spent so long in the library; we researched two sets of scenarios so that we would both be prepared. Look, I did Julius Caesar. Ryan would make the perfect Roman soldier. Deanna researched Adolf Hitler."

Mrs. Wiley was thoughtful. Tristan held his breath. The plan was perfect. He would present on Monday with a different partner and Deanna would watch as he used all their research to present the only thing she had prepared for. He would simply skip school on Tuesday to support his Doctor's appointment cover and Deanna would be screwed. She would only have one night to re-plan everything with a new partner. Sure, Adrienne would get stuck in the crossfire, but this was war, and in war, there was always collateral damage.

Tristan was so busy daydreaming that he barely noticed Mrs. Wiley had started talking again.

"No, I don't think so Tristan. It is too short of notice for Miss Axely. Although I'm sure Ryan would be willing to help out, it would not be fair to Adrienne. You will just have to present on Monday with Deanna, or change your doctor's appointment. Have a good night."

Tristan glared at his teacher and through clenched teeth managed a feeble, "Good night."

Tristan's genius plan was not so genius after all. Oh well, plan B. Tristan left the room having lost the battle, but he would win the war.

He and Deanna ended up presenting, as planned, on Tuesday. They had met the day before and went over the questions they were going to ask each other. It was a shame really; if Tristan didn't hate the girl with a fiery passion, the presentation could have been pretty good.

Tristan and Deanna were the second group to present after Matt and Lacey. It was a tough act to follow too, they had done a great job on Franklin Roosevelt and the second world war. It had been funny and informative, always a good educational combo.

They assumed their positions at the front of the class. Tristan introduced the premise of the presentation, Caesar and his soldier, and the presentation began. Little did Deanna know, Tristan had swapped out the questions she expected him to ask, with questions he was *going* to ask. The fireworks were about to begin.

Tristan was set to ask questions first. He looked up and caught Ryan's eye. He gave Ryan a little wink and Ryan's eyes grew wider. He knew Tristan was up to something.

"Almighty Caesar, we the soldiers, your greatest servants, honour you." Tristan saluted. "We have some questions to ask, if of course, your greatness is willing to answer."

Tristan's character was convincing, so Deanna played along: "Yes soldier. You may ask your questions."

Tristan looked down at his cue cards. He looked at the witty questions he had devised last night to slowly extract revenge on Deanna. Suddenly though, he felt an old nemesis creeping up on him: Memories. He saw her body pressed against Eric's. He felt his heart break all over again. He had invested so much of himself in her. She destroyed every ounce of his being. A shadow came over Tristan's face. He brought his eyes up slowly from the cue cards, they smoldered.

Ryan saw the change and stood up to stop what he knew was coming, but it was too late. Tristan's fury was in the driver's seat.

"So Caesar, you still fucking Eric Childs?"

Jaws dropped around the room. Everyone stared in dumbfounded awe of what had just happened. Mrs. Wiley jumped up from her chair. "What!? What did you say Mr. Cage?"

Tristan turned some of his bitterness on the teacher, "I asked the whore in the chair if she was still fucking Eric. It is not a very difficult question."

Mrs. Wiley did not know what to do. She had never seen such open defiance, such anger. Tristan turned his head to Deanna who was sitting mortified in front of the class.

"Well?" he asked again. "Well?"

Tristan could feel that Deanna was very uncomfortable. He expected her to lash out at him with harsh words, but none came. She just sat there. It was unacceptable. A few moments passed in awkward silence. Tristan was about to lose his mind some more, but before his verbal onslaught could continue, Mrs. Anderson was standing at the door. *Mrs. Wiley must have paged the office,* he thought, *how clever.*

Tristan's classmates were still in shock. Some of them had never heard him speak a word outside the classroom. He was calm, cool, and collected. He was especially cool under pressure. Look how he performed on the court. None of them could understand where he was coming from. Tristan found the looks he was getting amusing. Nobody cared about others, not really, only when people had something invested in you did they become genuine. Tristan figured half the people in the room didn't even care what Deanna had done to him. *If they even remembered, if they ever knew at all.*

Mrs. Anderson tried to grab Tristan's arm to guide him down the hall, but he shook her hand off violently. He wasn't going to bother explaining himself to her. She would just attribute his anger to teenage angst anyway. Adults chose to forget the emotions of their youth. For as they got older, they realized that their first love was the only true, untainted, uncorrupted love they'd ever felt. He doubted if Mrs. Anderson was even married. He doubted she even liked men.

Tristan was suspended. Big surprise. It was like Déjà vu. The last suspension he had suffered was because of a girl too. Every time he got in trouble it was because of girl. As Tristan sat in the office and waited for instructions on what to do next, his revolve cracked. Tristan looked away and wiped a tear from his eye with the back of his hand. For as he sat there he realized the truth: all the time he had spent trying to change himself had failed.

He still cared.

Chapter Thirteen

It was Sunday, the first Sunday of Christmas break. Tristan loved Sundays. It was the only day he could be himself, the only day he *allowed* himself to be himself. He spent Sunday's writing and watching movies. He wrote poetry and watched movies that inspired him. Nobody knew about that side of him, not even Ryan. He kept his activities on Sundays a secret. They showed his vulnerability.

After he and Deanna broke up he wrote a letter to *Chicken Soup for the Teenage Soul* explaining what had happened and how he felt. He wanted to reach out to other people who had been hurt so badly, and let them know they were not alone. Tristan had never heard back, he didn't even know if they got the letter, and if they did, they obviously didn't care about Tristan Cage from Sageview. Who even knew how they picked the stories that made it into those books? He didn't care anymore. He obviously wasn't cut out to be a writer.

His poetry took on many forms. They started out reflecting his deepest desires: to love and be loved. Eventually, however, they took on his anger and cynicism about love. Today's poem was different, and when he was done writing, he read it over a few times because he could not believe he wrote it.

We hurt Others
Because we hurt ourselves

We hurt ourselves
Because we've been hurt by others
You are in pain
I am in pain
We must break the cycle

Tristan stared at the paper. He often discovered things about himself through his writing, things he didn't realize were there. When he wrote he allowed himself to be free. Free of bias, free of opinions and free of corruption. Unfortunately for him, it appeared that he felt guilty.

Tristan's pain had been allowed to fester. He had to let it go, but in order to do so, he would have to confront the person he feared the most: Deanna. He allowed his fear to become hate because it was easier. It was so much easier to hate her than fear her. His hate allowed him to hold onto the past, his fear made him *deal* with it. Apparently he was not ready to do so until now.

Tristan turned off the movie he was watching, *Titanic*, and stared at the telephone. He was about to make a call he hadn't made in years. It was time to end this.

Tristan's palm was sweaty as he picked up the receiver. It took him three tries to dial her entire number. He prayed that she answered so he didn't have to talk with her parents, they must have heard about his colossal meltdown. The phone rang once—*Please God.* The phone rang twice. *What am I doing?* Three times. *Hang up you Idiot!*

"Hello?"

Shit! No turning back now.

"Hello Deanna."

The phone went silent. There was a long pause.

"What do you want?" she asked cautiously.

"I want to apologize. I want to more than apologize. We need to talk, I need to talk. There are a lot of things I have to say that I have kept inside for a long time. I don't expect you to understand,

I don't expect you to listen, but I would really appreciate it if you gave me the chance to know why you did what you did. It has taken me three years to get up the courage to do this. At least respect that."

Another long pause. "I do Tristan. I do. I respect what you are saying now. A lot has changed, you know."

"Maybe it has Deanna, maybe it has, but I am extremely angry, and the only way I can ever forgive you, or myself, is to understand why it happened. Are you busy tonight?"

"Tonight? Listen Tristan this is all pretty out of the blue—"

"Not for me. I have thought about it every day for three years. Please Deanna."

"Fine. Ok. Where do you want to talk?" Her voice was not unkind.

"I'll borrow my parent's car and pick you up. Say seven?"

"See you then."

Tristan hung up the phone and swallowed hard. That had been really difficult. It would be even more difficult to keep his calm and be nice all night long. He knew once they started talking about *the incident* that he would get defensive and impatient. He just hoped that he could keep calm long enough to get the answers he needed and give himself some peace of mind.

His parents had no problem with letting him borrow the car, he rarely asked for it. His relationship with his parents had been quite good for some time. There had been no girls to screw with his head, and he was so dedicated to school and sports that there was no other trouble to get into. He spent the majority of his time at home.

Tristan lied and said he was meeting Ryan. He knew his parents would object to him seeing Deanna. They were no longer her biggest fans. Tristan stepped outside. It snowed lightly and the way his porch light made the flakes of snow shine reminded him of the disco ball the night he and Deanna had their first kiss.

Tristan adjusted his white, mesh back, baseball cap to ensure it was sitting at its signature tilted angle, and walked to the car. Deanna's new house was very near the school so it would take him thirty to forty minutes to get there. That was a lot of time to change his mind and turn around.

He did, in fact, almost turn around a number of times. In all honesty, his decision to meet Deanna was probably a bad idea, but he needed to do it for his own sanity. Thus, he soldiered on. He thought of an interesting analogy. He had a lot in common with a soldier at that point in time. He was going to battle, possibly war. It might kill him, but he was obligated to go.

The closer he got to Deanna's, the more nervous he got. He hadn't been nervous in a while. Part of him wondered if she would even meet him. For all he knew Eric would be there waiting for him. That wouldn't be so bad though, he relished the thought of handing Eric his own ass *again*. He calmed his imagination down. It was highly unlikely that Eric would be there. He had moved to Cedar Ridge, a city two hours from Sageview, for basketball exposure. The scouts paid much closer attention to city schools. Meeting Cedar Ridge in the provincials was definitely on Tristan's wish list.

He pulled into Deanna's driveway a little after 7PM. He didn't go to the door, or honk the horn. Instead, he waited patiently. He needed to compose himself for their meeting.

He didn't have to wait long. Maybe a minute or two, and Deanna came out to meet him. She opened the passenger side door and hopped in the car. They didn't say hello. Tristan drove to the school parking lot and there they sat, in silence, for quite some time. To Tristan's surprise, it was Deanna who broke the stalemate.

"Eric and I broke up two months ago. I'm surprised you hadn't heard, or maybe you did and just wanted to make things worse for me."

The truth was, he hadn't known. Everyone close enough to Tristan who could have given him the information knew better than to talk about Deanna. She was a no fly zone.

"I didn't know. Really I didn't, but I'm not really sorry."

He told himself that he would be calm, and as nice as possible, but that was already proving difficult. The entire meeting would be pointless if he didn't get things out in the open.

"I know you're not," she said flatly. "I wouldn't be sorry either if I were you." She sighed. "Look Tristan, I know you are here looking for answers from me, but I don't have any. I know what I did to you was horrible, worse than horrible, but it's almost like I became a different person when I was with you. For whatever reason, you brought out the worst in me."

"I brought out the worst in you?" Tristan was speechless, he thought he treated her well.

"Oh Tristan, still so hard on yourself." She said, a hint of kindness behind her exasperation.

He hated that she could still read him. She didn't have any right, but he kept those thoughts to himself and let her continue.

"It wasn't anything you did, you were amazing to me. I wasn't ready for you, and that is the truth. I couldn't match your readiness, your commitment. It scared me, and to this day I don't know why, but I think about it a lot. Eric hated how much I talked about you."

That was ironic.

"You talked about me huh?" Tristan tried to hide the contempt in his voice, "Why's that?"

"Because Tristan, the more I learned about Eric, the more I missed you. Instead of doing the right thing and breaking up with you outright, I panicked and sabotaged the relationship so that you would hate me. It was easier that way. I knew if I pushed you hard enough, you would hate me for what I'd done."

"Whoa, can you hear yourself? You put me through hell on purpose to make things easier for you? Then you went on to miss me?"

Tristan's words were more out of guilt than anger. He had done the exact same thing in order to deal with her. Resorting to hate *was* easier.

"Yes. That's what happened. I have no excuses Tristan. I was young and very *very* stupid. There were so many things I wanted to try: pot and booze, sex and rebellion. I knew you were too good to allow that to happen. I felt pressured to be something I couldn't. At least not at that time."

Tristan was touched by her honesty, but he was still the casualty of her emotional anomaly. He could find some respect for her again, but forgiveness may be out of the question.

"Why did you agree to come with me? I have been pretty awful to you—for a long time."

"Yes you have Tristan," she laughed.

Tristan couldn't believe she was laughing.

"Don't forget," she began, "I knew you better than anyone. I knew exactly what would happen if I pushed you far enough. Not even Rachel had done near what I did."

Rachel. Another person Tristan had severed contact with for his sanity.

Tristan shook his head. It did seem like she had put a lot of thought into her words, they sounded sincere. He searched his mind—and his heart—for something genuine of his own to say, but all he could find was criticism and anger. So he said nothing at all.

"Tristan, I came here so that you could see that I've changed. I am not that girl anymore. I am truly sorry for hurting you."

Tristan Froze. What was that?

What was *that*?

He felt something warm on his hand. It was her hand. She was *touching* him.

Red Alert!

Her lips, the lips he remembered tasting so good, were still so appealing. He looked away. Her hand moved to his forearm. He heard her seatbelt unclasp. –*Click*– He gazed out the windshield to look down onto the soccer field which was covered in a thin layer of snow. Her hand went up under his sleeve onto his shoulder. He could sense her body moving across the seat towards him.

His anger fuelled his desire and he suddenly felt the urge to take her right then and there. *No. This can't happen.* He was falling for it again. He could not, *would not*, be the victim. He trained himself to show no emotion, to be a dick, to shut out anyone who could care about him, *especially* Deanna Greene. Her other hand touched his face. His heart beat like a hammer against his rib cage. Her hand gently turned his head. He could feel her breath on his face. Her lips brushed his.

No!

Tristan jerked back in the seat and raised his arm to push her away, but as he did he lifted his foot off the brake. Deanna's backside inadvertently knocked the car into neutral. Tristan panicked and tried to turn the car on to go in reverse, but it was too late. The car had already rocked ever so slightly over the edge of the pavement. The momentum of the car picked up and down they went. The car bounced hard three or four times on its journey down the hill. Deanna was screaming and she flipped upside down in the passenger seat. Tristan still had his belt on so he was locked in. They hit the soccer field and things levelled out. Tristan tried turning the car on again. No dice. He pulled the emergency brake while pressing in the clutch and brake as hard as he could. The car slowed, but not fast enough. The snow made it just slick enough that he couldn't quite stop the car before the little Civic lurched over the soccer field side line and went vertical.

The nose of the car hit the bottom of the ditch like a hammer hitting an anvil. The car moved forward and Tristan thought it was going to roll. He threw his weight backward and the car stiffened momentarily before it crashed back down, right side up. They were on two wheels and tilted forward, but they were stopped. The front of the car looked like an accordion.

Tristan jerked his head to the right. Deanna was sobbing, but she was alright. She had a small cut on her forehead, but other than that, looked no worse for wear. Tristan gave himself a quick checkup and was totally fine. He undid his seat belt and opened the door. It was a four foot drop to the ground. Tristan hopped out carefully and made sure the car was stable. He climbed the ditch and got to the other side of the car. He yelled to Deanna to open the door.

"Can you get out?"

"I think so. I'm pretty dizzy." She replied groggily.

"Ok just open your door, and I'll help you down. We'll get you to the clinic to get checked out."

The door popped open and Deanna stood ready to drop. Instead, she lost her balance and fell. Tristan moved to catch her but the footing was slippery and she was falling from a decent height. He absorbed the impact, but couldn't stay standing. They crashed to the ground with Tristan on bottom, and Deanna on top of him.

"Ouch." Was all Tristan could mutter. There was a large rock, or something of similar size and density digging into his back.

Deanna rolled over and swung her legs around to straddle him. "My hero."

He reached up and grabbed her firmly by the shoulders. He pushed her aside. "We need to get your head looked at. Come on."

With that, he started his climb up out of the ditch.

Chapter Fourteen

Tristan had difficulty explaining to his parents why their car was written off in the school ditch when he was supposed to be five minutes down the road at Ryan's. Tristan came clean, and his father was furious. Tristan would be helping to pay for a new vehicle.

Once again Tristan had set out with good intentions, only to be boned by fate. He must have been an awful person in a former life. What were the chances of rolling down the hill at your school in a Honda Civic? He swore to himself that the world would be a better person without females. At least females who preyed on your senses like a ninja. Women were mind ninja's.

Tristan hadn't spoken to Deanna since the accident. He was unsure what to make of it all. *Feelings. Here we go again.* Tristan felt the sudden urge to kick something. It was two days before Christmas. *'Tis the season to be merry*? When was that part going to kick in? Tristan still had some shopping to do, and he had practice, so there was plenty to do to keep his mind busy. He had an idea. He would invite Adrienne shopping. Perhaps trying to focus his attention on some new girl would work. Reverse sexual psychology.

Adrienne accepted his offer without hesitation. *Christmas might come a few days early.* She even offered to drive. Most traffic had to pass by Tristan's to get to Plymouth anyway, so he didn't feel ungentlemanly accepting her offer. Besides, her family had money, and it would mean riding in luxury. Adrienne arrived in her parent's purple Cadillac at 11AM. This gave Tristan a few hours to shop, and flirt, before practice at 4.

They had an hour long drive to the city to make small talk. As it turned out, that wasn't difficult at all. The two actually had a lot in common. They both loved sports, and although Adrienne was not a basketball player, she was very impressive at volleyball, and they both loved movies. Adrienne suggested that they see one, but Tristan reminded her that he had practice. He would not be making that mistake again.

The mall was jam-packed, and Tristan hated crowds. He despised feeling like a sardine. The stores were shoulder to shoulder, and he couldn't move without bumping into a stranger. Adrienne, however, was right at home. Nothing stopped that girl from getting where she needed to go. If there was a rack of clothes she wanted to see, it was like a defensive linemen try to get at the quarterback. Bodies flew.

Tristan was both intimidated by her resolve and impressed. He realized that it benefitted him as well, as she was very interested in what he needed to pick up. Once he let her know, it was a much easier shopping trip. Tristan picked up art supplies for his mom and Arnold Schwarzenegger movies for his dad. He got picture frames for his sister—she was fifteen now, and girls at that age seemed to want to snap pictures of everything—and by that time it was two o'clock. Almost time to start the journey home.

He and Adrienne were making their way back to the main entrance when Adrienne informed him she had one last stop to make, and with a wink, she grabbed him by the arm and hauled him into La Senza.

"I need some new *undergarments*, Tristan. She said with a playful smile. "Care to help out?"

The truth was, there wasn't a man on the planet who could say no. Adrienne was a regular man-eater. She was voluptuous, not thin, but certainly not overweight. She had dark auburn hair that was cut to frame her face. She was always well kept and well dressed. She had dark brown eyes that always stood out due to her choice of eye make-up, which was usually black, but not gothic or EMO. Adrienne was always put together to make men drool. Tristan found the combination of dark hair and dark eyes particularly mouthwatering.

Adrienne knew she had Tristan's attention. She took him by the hand into the centre of the store. Tristan had never been in a La Senza before.

"Well Tristan, where do you want to start? Bras or panties?"

Wow, this chick gets down to business.

It was more of a demand than a question. Tristan honestly couldn't answer her. He had never been in the presence of someone so *open*. Adrienne cocked an eyebrow and put on a seductive grin.

"Well? Maybe I was wrong, maybe I don't need this stuff. Shall we go?"

Hell no. Say something! "Bras first."

She smiled. "Ohhh my favourite." She whirled and walked right to the wall where the bras hung freely. As she was looking, Tristan swallowed dryly. He must have drooled away the majority of his saliva. Adrienne was reaching a little higher than her five foot five frame would allow her to go. She seemed to be aiming for a baby blue bra. Tristan took in every ounce of her hour-glass figure as she stretched.

Tristan was slightly disappointed when she finally asked for his assistance. He was enjoying the show. At six foot two Tristan had no trouble accommodating her. Once she had it, she put on her naughty smile once more.

"I like blue, Tristan, and pink. What colours do you like?"

She held the blue bra up over her breasts. They were enormous. Tristan blinked a few times to make sure he wasn't dreaming. "Black is good. Try a black one too."

"Ohhh good choice. Lacey or Solid?"

Lace was see through. *Go with the lace!* His brain was screaming at him.

"Lace is nice."

"Lace *is* nice. Who knew you were so into women's fashion?" She gave him a wink. "Ok, Tristan, I have a bunch of bras to try. Let's move onto underwear."

Tristan knew there were other people in the store, most of whom were female, but he didn't care. He was having the time of his life.

"Hmmm. I usually wear thongs, Tristan. I hope you won't be too shy looking at those."

Sweet jesus. This girl was sexy.

"Uhhh nope. I uhhh, I should be fine. I have a lot at home."

What the hell! No.

"I mean I have seen a lot at home."

Yes because seeing your fifteen year old sister's thongs in the laundry is the perfect reference right now you tool. Fix it!

He didn't have to. Adrienne knew he was flustered, and she loved it. She dove into the bin of underwear and invited Tristan to join her. Tristan did not feel comfortable rooting through women's underwear with so many other girls in the store. He sort of picked around like a person picks up garbage off the ground. Index finger and thumb like the fabric carried a disease. Adrienne didn't need him anyway. She knew exactly what she wanted.

She picked out a few pairs, all solid colours, that would match her bras. She hailed a sales lady and informed her she was ready to try on her items. Tristan got a smirk from Brenda—the clerks had very noticeable name tags—and he blushed. His face was on fire.

Tristan moved to sit on one of the in-store benches when Adrienne shot him an icy glare.

"What do you think you're doing, mister?"

Tristan was confused. His heart gained momentum. "I was just going to sit—"

"Oh no you don't. Get in here so I can model for you. I need your opinions with them *on*."

Tristan felt his heart stop. He had trouble getting it going again. He asked God to restart his heart, for at least the next twenty minutes or so, then his life could be taken. Shortly after, he felt his heart start pumping blood again. *Phew.* This was the best day of his life!

Tristan took a seat on one of the change room benches. Adrienne went into the stall assigned to her by Brenda, and Tristan saw clothes start hitting the floor through the small space at the bottom of the change room door.

"Which colour first, Tristan?" she asked from behind the closed door.

Tristan was gaining confidence fast. "Blue."

"Ohhh, my favourite." There was some swishing and clasping, and unclasping, and the door swung open. She had one hand on the door frame and the other on her hip. Adrienne made habanera peppers seem mild. Tristan tried to catch his breath.

"What do you think of this one?"

Adrienne really knew how to choose colours for herself. The blue of bra/thong combo was a daring contrast to her dark features. She was stunning.

Tristan honestly couldn't talk so he just made rapid jerking movements with his head that he hoped resembled nods instead of seizures. She smiled a truly evil smile, and he loved every second of it. "What colour next, sir?"

""Black. The uhhh lace one."

She twirled and shut the door. Thirty seconds later she resumed her position in the doorway wearing her black lace bra complete with matching thong. That combo was the winner. *Holy shit.* Tristan tried desperately to see through the lace, but it was patterned well enough to distort anything he tried to see.

"Ohhh, I see you like this one," She giggled. He hoped it had been the look on his face that gave it away, and not something else. He glanced down quickly and turned his body sideways.

She glanced left, then back to her right. When she was satisfied nobody was looking she quickly skipped out of the change room and grabbed Tristan by both wrists. She pulled hard, but not that hard; she had a willing partner. He allowed himself to be taken into the stall. She clasped the door and kissed him hard on the lips. He picked her up by the ass and spun her around. He pushed her into the wall for leverage. He felt her legs lock around his back.

Somebody was pounding on the door. Brenda did not think it was cute anymore.

"Get out of there! What are you two doing! This is a public place! Get out or I am calling security!"

Tristan stopped kissing her and attempted to put her down. She looked at him, much as the devil would look at a soul within his grasp, "We have at least 5 minutes before security gets here."

Tristan didn't care if he went to prison. He pushed her back against the wall and kissed her. She put her fingers up his shirt and dug her nails into his back.

Yep.

His soul belonged to her.

Chapter Fifteen

Tristan was late for practice. *Oh well.* The extra running was definitely worth it. The car ride home wasn't even awkward. Adrienne just laughed at his constant *wows* at how hot and adventurous she was. She freely admitted that she liked the attention. Tristan learned, recently, how important giving healthy attention to girls was. Healthy, he supposed, depended on your definition. Adrienne was already a very *healthy* girl.

Tristan would be lying if he said he wasn't interested in Adrienne after his introduction to La Senza. He wasn't stupid though. He made a lot of very dumb decisions when it came to females in the past. He did not want Adrienne to be another one. He questioned the loyalty of a girl—he already had serious trust issues thanks to Deanna—who would make out with a guy on the first date—*was* it even a *date*, more of an excursion really. He definitely had his concerns, so he wasn't going to get too attached to Miss Adrienne Axley.

The best part of the entire experience was Ryan's reaction to his retelling of the day's events. They were alone in the locker room after practice, and Tristan exiled the other players early so he could watch Ryan turn green with envy. As soon as Tristan got to the part where Adrienne had asked him to watch her model, Ryan started shaking his head.

"You are such a lucky bastard," Ryan said. "I have been staring at the same girl since eighth grade, and I'm not even sure I like her half of the time."

"Oh just wait," Tristan said. "I haven't even got to the best part yet."

Ryan sat gaping at him while he finished his tale.

"That is so hot," Ryan said finally. "God, I would have paid for something like that."

Tristan laughed. It felt good.

"I'm not surprised though," Ryan said. "All she talked about, while we were working on our history together, was you. I love you, man, but I was almost sick of hearing about you by the end of it. I told her you were a prick and that she should date me, but she seems to believe you are a nice guy, *beneath it all*."

Tristan smiled. "We both know you were a very good boy. Sydney probably threatened to cut your balls off when she found out you were paired with Adrienne."

Ryan grimaced. "She did too. God, that girl is so uptight. But we already know how Syd can be. What are you going to do about Adrienne?"

"I dunno, I—"

"Look Tristan, I know you got burned, burned *bad*, but that was three years ago! You were fifteen for God's sake. You cannot keep using girls like this to make yourself feel better. Eventually you are going to end up hurting someone, if you haven't already. Besides, I think it's time you gave relationships another go. I know how much you want to something romantic. The real Tristan is a hopeless romantic, and we both know it." Ryan paused for a second. "Never tell anyone we had this conversation. We sound married."

The advice seemed funny coming from Ryan, but he had a point. Tristan often worried that he had hurt some of the ladies he fooled around with and didn't know it. His popularity had soared to a level where any girl would probably be afraid to give him grief because of the social ramifications. Also, he had not told

Ryan everything that had happened in the car with Deanna. He left out the part where he had felt something too. He decided to come clean.

"Tristan, are you retarded?" Ryan said. "That girl fucked one of your closest friends while you were in the *same house* . I said let it go, but that doesn't mean you date the bitch again."

Ryan had more trouble forgiving Deanna than he did.

"I know, and I know it's corny, but I can't help my feelings can I? You are still with Sydney, and I hate her."

"Sydney didn't bang you in Tyrone's bedroom."

So true. *God, he's right. How can I still have feelings for Deanna?* He looked down at the scar on his right hand. It was his constant reminder of the power girls once had over his emotions. He did not want to give it back to them. He nodded in silent agreement with Ryan's argument. Ryan seemed satisfied.

"Enough of that," Ryan said with renewed energy. "Let's go watch my parents get wasted while they play scrabble."

Christmas was pretty basic that year. Tristan spent Christmas Eve and Christmas Day with family, and the rest of vacation was eaten up with basketball. The Iron Knights went to the New Year's invitational at Carlson High as was the annual tradition. They won easily and were moved up in the provincial rankings from fifth to third. The only two teams ahead of them were Sunnyvale, whom they had already beaten, and Cedar Ridge, the team Eric Childs played for. Tristan had another stellar performance, and two scouts approached him after the game. They informed Tristan that they would be at the provincials, and if he was still in top form, that he would have a full ride to any University.

The conversation with the scouts helped him re-focus on what was truly important: basketball and school. He put thoughts of Deanna behind him—to the best of his ability—but he had been talking to Adrienne quite a bit. He made sure she knew that he was in no position to start a relationship yet but that he enjoyed hanging out with her. She was fine with that, but she said the make-out sessions were over because she didn't like to share. Adrienne was actually a pretty classy chick.

Tristan missed the first day back from break to finish the rest of his suspension, but that was fine with him. He used the day to study for upcoming exams. He was back at it on Tuesday, and it felt good. Tristan learned to love routines. They kept things simple.

January passed with very few notable events. The Iron Knights continued to win games with Tristan leading the charge. He breezed through exams and hung out with Adrienne once or twice a week. Sundays he kept for himself.

February started much like January did, uneventfully, until the sixth. Tristan went to history and noted that Deanna was not there. Although he was attempting to move on, he didn't harbour the same resentment he had before. Deanna had been absent a lot lately. Tristan wondered if the incident in the car had affected her more than he thought. Maybe she transferred out of the class? He made a mental note to check up on that later in the day.

He was walking Adrienne to their next class when the fire bell rang. He rolled his eyes. So predictable. It was freezing cold that day, and Principal Anderson loved to give fire drills in the worst of conditions. She would always say, "If your procedures work at the worst of times, you know you are doing them right." Tristan turned to head down the stairs to the emergency exit, but Adrienne grabbed his wrist. He hadn't seen that smile in a while.

She shoved him into the storage room and slammed the door. "I'm sick of waiting Tristan. A girl has needs." She pressed into him and he felt himself going backwards. He slammed into a bookshelf and a copy of Shakespeare's *Hamlet* landed at his feet. *To be or not to be,* he thought.

Well, he was going with *be*. He wrapped his arms around Adrienne and picked her up. He dropped her down on a work table. He had one arm around her waist and the other on the back of her head, underneath her hair, pressing her lips firmly against his own.

Three Words

"Be with me," she whispered.

Tristan froze. Part of him knew this would happen, but he still wasn't ready. He stopped kissing her and hung his head. She used her hand to lift his chin up gently. "Be with me," she said, softer and with more feeling.

"I can't," he said quietly.

"I'll help you."

"I can't." He wrapped his hand affectionately around the hand that still touched his face. "I'm sorry. I'm not myself."

There was disappointment in her eyes, but her face remained strong as it always was. "I will be here for you, Tristan. Whenever you decide you want me."

She kissed his cheek and left the room. Tristan stood there alone for a long time trying to will his feet to move. They were not listening. It had been hard to refuse Adrienne. Despite the misgivings he had about her in the beginning, she had shown genuine feeling when it came to him. He suddenly felt as if he were back in the situation with Rachel. Except this time, it was him that was screwed up. Tristan looked out the window at the students gathering for the fire drill. He took note of all the faces that he respected: most of the staff, the basketball team, especially Matt and Ryan, and Rachel. There were the faces he pitied, the druggies and misfits. And then there was the face he wished he could see more of—Adrienne's. Finally, he looked for the *one* face he feared, but Deanna was nowhere to be found.

Tristan used his alone time in storage room to try and make some sense of his life. Really, all he had succeeded in doing to this point was hurt or alienate people. No amount of basketball—and no success in school—could erase the fact. He was not the person he wanted to be. He had always envisioned himself as the hero, the good guy. He always assumed the role was his, but now he realized he had yet to earn it. He always either tried too hard, or gave up too easy. There was no happy medium for Tristan Cage.

Perhaps Tristan's biggest roadblock was love. He thought he knew what it was, but he had lost all faith in it. People got tired of each other, or grew too familiar. People changed, and that changed the dynamic of their relationship. Tristan was so afraid of finding something wonderful and losing it the way he had lost Deanna. Fear was ruling his life.

Tristan opened the book room door, and as he stepped out into the hallway, it felt as if he was waking from a very long dream. He looked up and down the halls for Adrienne. He needed to talk to her. He had changed his mind. He thought he caught a glimpse of her rounding the corner at the end of the hall. He took two long strides to catch up to her, when someone else rounded the corner. He couldn't stop. He ran into her, and books flew everywhere. Tristan bent over quickly and picked up all the books he could lay his hands on.

"I'm so sorry," he said. "I guess that's why you aren't supposed to run in the halls huh?"

"Not that the rules apply to you, Tristan Cage." Came the bitter reply.

Tristan knew who he had run into before he turned around.

"Amy. How nice to bump into you."

Deanna's best friend, Amy, had been a casualty in his quest for justice. The two of them went toe to toe many times. Amy was a good friend. She always defended Deanna's honour, no matter how hard Tristan tried to sully it.

"I'm not in the mood, Tristan. Just give me my books, please."

Tristan obliged. They were about to part ways when Tristan stopped her.

"Amy, wait. I noticed Deanna wasn't in History today. I haven't seen her in a while it seems. Do you know where she is?"

"What do you care, Tristan?"

"Wait. Whoa, I'm not being a dick, I swear. We had a talk before Christmas. We agreed to let bygones be bygones. She didn't tell you?"

"No, she *did*. I don't agree. I told her she should have severed ties with you long ago, but she cares about you."

Tristan felt the tug on his heartstrings.

"Well, is she on vacation or something?"

"No Tristan. She—" Amy looked distraught for a moment. "Maybe you should talk to her, Tristan. She'll be in school tomorrow."

Tristan was confused. "Come on, Amy, I'm just curious."

"I know Tristan, but it's just complex."

Tristan started to worry. Amy did not look comfortable at all.

"Is she back with Eric or something? Visiting? Because if she is I could care less. I just—"

"No Tristan, it's not that."

"Then what?" Tristan was desperate now. "Is she ok?"

Amy's eyes filled with tears. "She's sick, Tristan."

Chapter Sixteen

Tristan walked to Deanna's house as soon as school ended. He didn't care if her parents liked him or not. He didn't care if she wanted to see him or not, and he didn't care that he would be stranded in Sageview. He needed to hear it from her lips. Why hadn't she told him? Was their friendship that far gone? How long had it been going on? He had so many questions. He stopped walking. Tristan felt ill. Almost his entire motivation for going to see Deanna was to satisfy his nagging curiosity. *No.* It wasn't that. He was afraid that she had been sick a long time, and if she had, he had been brutally unkind to her during her struggle. He had to know that he was not that awful, that he was not the evil one. He didn't care that he hadn't known. The hero always made the right decisions with limited knowledge.

Tristan's inner war would have to wait. It was snowing, and he was starting to feel the icy February cold through his minimal layers of winter clothing. He took a deep breath and walked the last quarter mile to Deanna's house. Her new place was a classic farm dwelling. A two story white house, old fashioned, with a walk in porch. Tristan thought it was an upgrade from her last, very ordinary, house in Milton.

He stood at the door with his hand in the air ready to knock for what felt like an eternity. He dreaded the reception he would receive, but the issue was too serious to allow fear of acceptance to hold him back. He would be there for his friend, if she needed him to be.

Tristan's arm felt like a stone slab as he brought his knuckles into the front door. The knock seemed to echo forever. Tristan's body was rebelling on him as he waited for someone to answer the door. Physically, he wanted to turn and run before the door had a chance to open, but his willpower held him still. He forced himself to wait.

Moments later, the door opened a crack. Deanna's Mom, Maggie, opened the door. The look on her face reflected surprise more than anger. "Tristan, this is unexpected. We haven't seen you in a long time."

"I know Mrs. Greene. I just—is Deanna home?"

Tristan could not handle small talk; his mind was in fast forward. It may have seemed rude, but he figured he may as well just come out with it.

"She is, Tristan, but she is sleeping. You will have to come back another time. It was good to see you."

Maggie closed the door, and Tristan hung his head. He sort of expected the response. He would just walk back to the school and try to find a drive home. His parents would not appreciate having to come get him in the quickly accumulating snow. As he moved away from the door, it opened again. This time, Deanna's father stood where Maggie had.

Karl spoke sternly, but not maliciously. "Why are you here, Tristan? As far as we know, you and Deanna haven't spoken in years."

Tristan felt a pang of resentment for his past deeds and forced himself to enter into conversation.

"Deanna and I have had our issues with one another Mr. Greene, but I heard something at school today that couldn't be ignored. No matter what our recent history has been, Deanna and I were extremely close once. I need to know if she is ok."

Karl softened, but he was not totally convinced. "I understand your past with my daughter, Tristan, but what she needs now is a friend, no more, no less. Every instinct in my body tells me if I let you in this door it will only make things worse, but my daughter has asked us to allow it. Before you decide to step in here or not, know this: if you hurt her now on top of everything else, I'll kill you."

Tristan was shocked at the bluntness of Karl's words, but he believed him. The family had obviously been through a lot lately. Tristan could see the wear in their faces. They looked much older since Tristan had seen them last. *Heroes do not shy away from adversity,* Tristan told himself.

"Mr. Greene, I promise if at any moment I feel I am making things worse for your family, I will leave. I swear."

Karl nodded his head and slowly opened the door allowing Tristan to enter. "She's on the couch in the living room. Around the corner to the left. She's had a long day. Please keep your visit short this time."

Tristan took his boots off and Karl took his coat. His body started to shake, not violently, but subtly with the mix of adrenaline and emotion. He saw the back of her head first, everything seemed normal, he made his way parallel to the coach. Her face was deathly pale and she had dark circles under closed eyes. As he looked down at her she woke and smiled at him. Despite her weakened state he saw something he hadn't seen in years, a twinkle in her eyes.

"Tristan," she said, "to what do I owe the honour?"

"I umm," Tristan was truly speechless. He was overcome with emotion, he didn't know how he'd react, but it was almost too much. "You're sick, D." *No shit you moron.* That's all he could think of to say? No wonder she ended things with him.

She smiled a sad smile, "Yes, Tristan, I am. I have been for a year now."

A year. Tristan was afraid of that. An entire year she had suffered while he was on his selfish quest for personal glory. God, people could be so misguided by foolish pride and emotional pain.

"I'm so sorry for everything, D. I didn't know."

"I know Tristan." She put her hand on his arm. "I didn't want you to, because I didn't want your sympathy. I was so happy when you called to see me before Christmas, we moved on together without your knowledge of this." She coughed, it sounded exhausting. "I'm sorry about trying to push things further though, I was just feeling really good that day and felt somewhat normal again. You have power over me still, Tristan Cage."

Tristan could not believe what he was hearing. The tears were streaming freely down his face, but he was in control of it for the most part, he could still talk. "Forget about that, D. Please, forget about everything. I'm here now, and I'll never turn my back on you again. He kissed her forehead and squeezed her hand, which had found his, only moments earlier.

For the next half hour Tristan listened to her story. It was both excruciating and commendable. She found out she had leukaemia a year ago. The doctors caught it early and tried to control it with oral medication, but it didn't work. They had moved closer to the school so she could attend more easily. The forty-five minute bus ride took too much out of her. She had started chemotherapy three weeks prior. She told him how awful it made her feel, physically, but gave her strength emotionally because the doctors said it was working. She had to go for treatment once a week, but it wiped her out for a couple days after. Eric had broken up with her just after school began. He was a big star at Cedar Ridge and felt like she was holding him back. He pretended that her illness wasn't as serious as she said it was. He was a real asshole. But of everything that happened to her, she was most upset about losing her hair. It just started to fall out due to the radiation. Tristan told her that he couldn't notice it, and he really couldn't, but she told him that it would fall out quickly now, and she would need to wear a wig in a week or two.

It seemed like Deanna had more to say, but she was fading fast. Tristan kept his promise to Mr. Greene and forced Deanna to let him go. He promised to be back every day after school, and any days she needed him.

Karl offered to drive Tristan home, but he would have none of it. He told Karl to stay with his daughter and that he would find his own way home. Tristan walked back to the school. He hoped that there was still someone there so that he could get in. He looked at the snow covered road and accepted the fact that he wasn't leaving Sageview that night. He walked up the hill to the school with visions of sleeping on the school wrestling mats.

Chapter Seventeen

For the next month, Tristan spent a lot of time at the Greene house. He was there after school, after basketball, and on weekends. Tristan would have willingly sacrificed basketball, but Deanna wouldn't hear of it. She was adamant that, without basketball, Tristan would be worse company. He was not willing to argue with a cancer patient.

Tristan helped out around the house, doing chores that would normally have been Deanna's. He cleaned, he took care of the pets, he even did small carpentry jobs on doors or flooring. He did whatever needed to be done. Deanna's father worked long hours on their small farm, and her mother was a nurse, who also worked weird hours. During these times various family members would check on Deanna: aunts, uncles, grandparents, and cousins. Tristan got to know the family quite well, and they respected what Tristan was trying to do.

School was a challenge. Word was out that Deanna had cancer. He would hear things like: "Tristan is only helping out so much so people will think he's a nice guy." Or, "Tristan thinks he's some sort of saint." What was wrong with everybody? Was he a part of that world? What was so wrong with trying to do the right thing? How could that possibly make people jealous? He assumed it was jealousy that made people say the things they did, he couldn't attribute it to anything else. He refused to believe that people were that ignorant.

Regardless, he was a very confident person, especially in his high school. He was encouraged by the fact that nobody ever said anything to his face, although he got some funny looks at times. The only people who seemed to show him any support were teachers and Ryan. Ryan was a given though, he was always Tristan's rock. Tristan could ask him to walk into a live volcano with him and Ryan would do so willingly, without a question. He trusted Tristan's judgment, and Tristan was truly grateful.

In spite of social challenges, the only thing that mattered to Tristan was Deanna's condition. She was much stronger than he would have guessed. She always stayed positive despite the pain or discomfort. In just over a month she had gone from being a large question mark in his life to an inspiration. When he looked at her now, an inexplicable feeling come over him, it was different than what he felt for her earlier in his life, but just as powerful.

Deanna didn't like talking about her illness, in fact, she would talk about anything but. Tristan understood. If he were sick, the last thing he'd want to do is deal with the fact every time he had a conversation. Everyone needed a chance to escape. As a result, most of their conversations ended up being about him. What school he was going to next year, how basketball was going, what girls he was interested in—he found this one rather awkward, but it was one of Deanna's favourite topics—and how things were going at home. Tristan constantly told white lies on the final point. He did not want Deanna forcing him to go home when he was perfectly content doing what he was doing.

It was the first week of March, and Deanna started attending school regularly again. She was very nervous. Not because of her health, the work she had to catch up on, or the questions she would face. She was afraid her wig was too noticeable. Tristan reassured her many times that the wig was very realistic, but she would not listen to him. He felt a sudden dislike towards his own hair, since her lack of it was what bothered her most.

D's first week passed smoothly and without incident. She was calm, cool, and collected dealing with all questions—and she got some interesting ones—about her condition. She planned to do her chemo on Fridays so as to miss the least amount of school, and she stayed with teachers for an extra hour Monday to Thursday to get caught up. A system was in place to help her move forward, and Tristan was content.

Her second week back was a much bigger challenge. It was a winter day, but warmer than it had been. Many students took advantage of the warmer air and went outside for lunch. Since Deanna was cooped up so much of the time, she wanted to be outside as well. Tristan had a basketball meeting so he told her he'd see her later. Amy took her outside to eat, and Tristan went to the gym.

Lunch came and went and Tristan did not see Deanna. He had no classes with her, save history, therefore did not think much of it. He was sitting in biology when he overheard two girls talking. He was not eavesdropping, simply passing by, when he heard Deanna's name. He frowned and slowed his passing to hear what they had to say. He was immediately on the defensive and ready to pounce on anyone who dared be disrespectful. One of the girls, Becky, was giggling. "…and then it just flew off. Can you imagine eating and having that land in your lap? I would just die."

Tristan's nails dug into his palms. His fists here balled up so tightly that his fingers ached. He knew what they were talking about. How could he have been so stupid? He had forgotten about the wind. He made a mental note earlier in the day to remind Deanna to make sure her wig was secured before going outside. He was embarrassed for D; he knew how scared she was when it came to her baldness, but these girls would pay for their indiscretion.

"Die? She very well *could* die you insensitive bitch. At this moment in time I would give my own life to transfer every bit of her pain into you. Then maybe you would keep your fucking mouth shut."

Becky dared not challenge Tristan. He was still at the top of the social food chain. He may have been losing momentum, but nobody had the balls to call him on it just yet.

"Don't ever speak of her again unless you have something good to say."

Once Tristan made his point he told the teacher he had to use the washroom and promptly ran to Deanna's house. No answer.

"D, open the door!"

Nothing. Tristan pounded harder. "Open up, Deanna!"

"Go away, Tristan! I don't want to talk. I don't want to see anyone. Just go away!"

Tristan figured something like this would happen. It was a good thing, for all his stupid decisions, he did not completely lack foresight. He took out the key Karl had given him in case of emergencies and put it in the lock. Tristan reassured himself that although it was not a matter of life and death, it was definitely a crisis.

The door swung open.

"Tristan! How dare you walk in here. I told you to leave!"

Deanna was on the couch with her head in her hands. Her head was cleanly shaven as it made the patches of hair that remained less visible. Tristan's heart ached. He was afraid to move towards her. He did not understand her hostility towards him, but then again, he couldn't really understand what she was going through at all.

He took a hesitant step. Success. One more step. Success. His heart must have gotten an upgrade because it was pumping faster than he thought possible. All those free throws he had made with seconds to go and the clutch plays he had made with the game on the line, none of them compared to the tension he felt at that moment.

He lifted his foot for the third step. Too close.

"Tristan," Her voice was cold as ice. "I am not fucking around. Get out of my fucking house!"

She looked at him. Rage turned her pretty face into a monstrosity. "I am sick and tired of your game Tristan. Stop pretending like you actually care. Stop helping me to make yourself feel better, and get the fuck out."

That hurt. It hurt a lot, but he wasn't moving. He took another step.

"Deanna…"

Her face changed from monstrosity to small child. The tears came freely.

"I was normal, Tristan. I was normal for a week. As long as I look normal everyone treats me normal. The cancer is on the inside, nobody can see it. All I had to do was look normal."

Tristan understood now. Her baldness was the only external symptom she showed. By hiding it, she felt better than she actually was. But now that everyone had seen how sick she was, she had no choice but to accept it herself.

Tristan reached out his hand. He half expected it to get severed from his arm, but no such blow came. He reached a little further to touch her. She shook her head like he was forcing her to go to bed when she didn't want to. He worked his hand up her arm to rest around her neck. She shook, but she didn't push him away. He sat down next to her. He felt a surge of confidence having gotten that far. It felt as if he had just navigated through a mine field.

He hugged her, and she let him. She held onto Tristan until her mother got home from work, two hours later.

When Tristan got home late that night he went straight to his father's rum stash in the freezer. Cam thought it was an ingenious hiding spot, but Tristan thought him a little naïve to think that his eighteen year old son wouldn't know where to find some booze.

He took out a quart of white Captain Morgan and went to his room. He knew what had to be done. He didn't care what people thought. He didn't care what people would say about him or who he would be compared to. He was ready to do the right thing. He grabbed his disposable camera and took a picture of himself for his mother, she had always loved his curly hair. He took the rum and his razor into the bathroom. He took a shot from the bottle and looked in the mirror.

He said goodbye to his curls, and shaved his head bald.

Chapter Eighteen

There were many bald people in the world, but none at Sageview High. Tristan could not allow Deanna to stand out like that—not now. Tristan thought he looked pretty good bald. He looked better with hair, but he looked fine bald. He looked tougher, more rugged. He could accept that. It was a small sacrifice for what it would achieve. He didn't know if Deanna would be at school or not, but he would see her eventually. He hoped she would be as thrilled as he imagined.

Tristan wore a touque to school. He found it really cold his first hairless morning. Sageview had a 'no hats' policy, so Tristan knew the cat would be out of the bag as soon as he stepped inside the school. He waited for Deanna until the bell rang for home room. He figured she wouldn't show up due to her embarrassment the day before, so he turned to head to class. He was taking off his shoes when a familiar voice spoke his name: "Tristan?"

He grinned as he looked up to see her. His grin faded to a look of amazement. Deanna had come to school, but without her wig. Her bravery brought tears to his eyes, but he refused to cry at such a happy moment. He laughed instead. She was beautiful. Her baldness did not take away from her at all. Her green eyes shone with a new light, and there was no hair to take away from her trademark smile. She was smiling coyly at him with her hands in her pockets swaying back and forth.

"I figured I may as well learn to like it."

"I hope so," Tristan said still laughing. "There will be more of it to love." And he pulled off his black touque.

Deanna stood open mouthed. Her shock and awe overwhelmed her. She put her hand over her mouth but her smile could be seen despite the barrier. Her eyes misted and she blinked to clear them. She could contain her joy no longer. She threw her arms around him and they laughed together. Tristan lifted her off the ground and spun her round and round. They walked to class looking like a couple of fuzzy peaches.

Ryan almost pissed himself laughing when he saw Tristan. It was though he was seeing him for the first time. He slapped his leg with his paw like hand and his contagious cackle filled the air. "You crazy bastard!" And he laughed some more. He got up and gave Tristan a giant man-hug.

Tristan was both intrigued and surprised that the talk of the day was not the new bald kids, but whether or not the two bald kids were dating again. Tristan assured everyone who asked him that they were just friends. Dating had not worked out before, and they were much more content as friends. Adrienne seemed skeptical, but pleased with his answer. Tristan noticed something disconcerting, however, as he was explaining his relationship with Deanna. The strangest feeling of dishonesty came over him when he was describing their plutonic status. He was lying to himself. He and D had talked many times about, "What they were," and they both agreed that their past and her illness were a recipe for disaster. But the truth was, Tristan cared for her more than he ever had before.

The lunch bell rang, and Tristan met up with Deanna. There was an interesting foursome at the table that day. Tristan and D were joined by Ryan and Amy. Amy wasn't usually found in the same area code as Tristan, and Ryan ate lunch with Sydney unless she said otherwise. Ryan and Tristan joked together as they always did, and Amy spoke to Deanna in whispers, untrusting of the two she had detested for so long. Apparently Tristan's self-sacrificial behaviour had not redeemed him enough in Amy's eyes.

Tristan was making fun of Ryan about his musical preferences when the first intermingling occurred.

"You like '60s rock?" Amy asked Ryan as if he had no right. "I thought meat skulls only listened to metal."

Ryan blinked a couple of times to process the unwarranted onslaught. "Yeah I do. I didn't think emo kids were so concerned with others opinions."

"I am not emo you ignorant asshole." Amy was definitely flustered, and Ryan was enjoying the fact.

"Oh no? I'm sorry. I meant emotionally unstable."

"Ohhh," Amy fumed. "I wouldn't expect any sensitivity from a pussy whipped redneck anyway."

Tristan and Deanna were trying to muffle their laughter, but it wasn't working very well. They huddled together to isolate themselves from the angst of their closest friends.

"Oh please girl, this redneck could straighten you out pretty fast. You just need a good roll in my hay."

"Rolling in your hay would be like trying to find a needle in that haystack, if you get my drift."

Tristan almost choked on his french fry. The two of them were in each other's faces to the point where they were both leaning over the table. Amy was quite attractive when she was angry.

"If by needle, you mean jackhammer, you would have no trouble at all." Ryan came back.

Amy smiled sarcastically. "Sure big fella. That's not the word in the locker room."

Ryan's eyes were big as saucers. They were nose to nose now. Tristan was about to intervene when Ryan reached both hands across the table and grabbed Amy's wrist. He dragged her over the table onto his lap where he promptly cupped her hand onto his package.

"Now my little gothic princess, you tell me how big it is."

Deanna was squeezing Tristan's arm, and she looked as if she was going to have a heart attack. Amy's face was burning with anger. Her breaths resembled those of a bull before it charges the matador. She quickly freed her arm and smacked Ryan hard across the face. She hit him so hard it spun his head round. When he brought his head back her face had changed. She no longer looked angry *exactly*.

"I had to do that on principal."

With that, she kissed Ryan hard on the lips. Tristan could not believe his eyes. Sydney was going to go ballistic! This was *awesome*! Tristan expected Ryan to throw her off, but instead, he wrapped both arms around her and kissed her back. The two were making out in the dead centre of the cafeteria. The teacher on duty hollered for them to get a room; they had lost their grip on reality. Tristan and Deanna left in bewilderment, but laughing all the while.

Later that day, Ryan and Sydney broke up. Tristan would never have believed it if he hadn't seen it. Sydney was not upset, only angry. She ranted and raved about how Ryan would never find anyone like her and that he was making a mistake. She stormed away, leaving Ryan standing alone. Ryan had done a complete one eighty all in one day. Tristan didn't understand how he changed his mind about things so quickly—he hadn't mentioned anything to Tristan—but somehow, for whatever reason, Ryan found the strength to end his five and a half year relationship on the heels of a random make out session in the school cafeteria.

After practice that night, Ryan explained himself to Tristan.

"I wanted to break up with her for years. I was just afraid of hurting her. She was always mean and making excuses for things. She never wanted to spend time at my house or with my family. We were always fighting about the stupidest things. I just started to feel as though I was spending all my time miserable. When I see you and Deanna enjoying yourselves, and how important it is for her, I realized life is too short for all that crap. Something snapped inside me today at lunch. I had to break loose, I had to be free."

Tristan found Ryan's honesty refreshing. He smiled openly now. Ryan knew it wasn't going to be easy getting over Sydney. They had been together too long, it was more habit than anything else. At least he took the first step, and Tristan would support him the rest of the way. Tristan changed the subject to ease Ryan's discomfort. He asked about Amy, and Ryan just chuckled.

"I dunno man. She's a crazy one. That whole thing was just random and foolish. I needed something like that."

"Yeah well, you definitely did. Everyone in the school saw you. Was Sydney upset about that at least?"

"She never said a word about it. She must have known, she's the biggest gossip queen in our school. I think she was just as happy to be free as me, but afraid to admit it.

"Yeah, sounds like Syd. Too proud to admit she was wrong. Too proud to admit she was involved with you for the wrong reasons."

"Yep." Ryan shook his head. "At least I'll be able to enjoy the last half of the year here. I haven't really enjoyed school for a while. I was always too busy trying to fit Sydney's vision of a relationship. Who knows, maybe I'll give Amy a call." He smiled and gave Tristan a playful shot in the arm with his massive fist. "I can't get used to you as a bald man."

Tristan ran his hand over his bald head. "Yeah it is weird for sure." He laughed. "But Deanna's reaction was worth it. She was so happy."

"You know Tristan, you guys look like a married couple, not just because you are both bald, but you seem so together, so effortless."

"C'mon Ryan." Tristan was exhausted from explaining his relationship status. "You know how that turned out last time. We can't trust ourselves in a relationship together based on our past. People change when their status changes, and we aren't willing to mess with emotions right now. Especially with her being sick and all…" Tristan trailed off, hoping Ryan would get the point.

"I know, Tristan. I was just saying. I know it must be hard for you. Lord knows how it must feel to be in your situation. Just know, I always got your back."

"I know you do, big fella. But right now both of us have to get our minds off the girls and keep them on the court. Provincials next week."

Ryan sucked in air through clenched teeth. "Ohhhh yeahhh."

The Iron Knights had their highest ranking in three years and were going in as the second seed. Only eight teams made the provincial tournament. Teams were ranked based on their performance throughout the season. The tournament was single elimination, lose and you were out. The first ranked team would play the eighth ranked, the second would play seventh, so on and so forth. Rankings were a big deal.

Tristan nodded his head in agreement, but he couldn't help but see the face of his nemesis as he did so. The Iron Knight were the second seed, but the Cedar Ridge Raiders were ranked first—led by Eric Childs. Tristan sobered quickly at the thought of his enemy.

The attitude in the locker room was suddenly very solemn. Tristan put his game face on. He hoped Eric was ready for round two, because the gloves were coming off.

Chapter Nineteen

Tristan sat in the locker room at Sunnyvale High school. His coach was talking, but he wasn't listening. The coach didn't care, he knew Tristan was in his own world. None of the team spoke to him, they knew better. Even Ryan, Tristan's closest friend, kept his distance. It was his ritual. Before every game, when Tristan donned that jersey, he was no longer himself. He was a machine; focused and relentless.

It was five minutes before the provincial finals. Sageview won their first two games rather easily. The seventh ranked Oilers in the first round were no match. The Iron Knights shredded their defence like it was non-existent.

The second round versus Sunnyvale was more interesting, but had the same result: an Iron Knights victory. Tristan had been unstoppable. He and his team earned the respect of the crowd. Tristan had tournament MVP written all over him if they beat Cedar Ridge. He was in total control. He commanded his team on the floor with unwavering vigilance. He scored at will, and his defence was impeccable. He stuck fear into the hearts of his opponents and didn't allow himself the luxury of celebrating.

Now, for the first time in the tournament, the Iron Knights were underdogs. Cedar Ridge had won both of their games easily as well, due in large part to the stellar play of Eric Childs. If Tristan was playing great, Eric matched his greatness. Eric was stronger, faster and an all-around better athlete, but Tristan was smart, patient, and skilled. Both young men knew how to take full advantage of their attributes, but there could only be one winner. It would be Eric's pride versus Tristan's vengeance.

When the Iron Knights left the locker room, the crowd erupted. Everyone loved the underdog. The colours of Black and Gold were visible from one end of the bleachers to the other. Many of the fans Tristan recognized, as many had made the trip from Sageview to support the team, but there were also many new fans recently won over. The Iron Knights, led by Tristan, went into their structured and impressive warm up. Everything was clockwork, nothing out of place.

When Tristan wasn't actively involved in part of the warm up, he was scoping out his opponents. Eric was much bigger than he remembered, and he had some help. There were at least two players that matched Ryan's height, but none of them were going to be able to match his strength.

During one of his assessments of the opposition, Eric caught his eye. It was the first time the two had made eye contact since Eric moved. Eric smirked in his patented arrogant way, and Tristan just stared at him.

This is war.

When the referees called for captains, Tristan and Ryan made their way to centre court. Eric and another Cedar Ridge player came for the Raiders. Tristan and Ryan wore the look of stone cold killers. Eric was smirking like he had already won.

"What's the matter ladies? You look afraid." Eric jeered.

The referee scolded him quickly and informed both sets of captains that he planned on a clean game with no unsportsman-like behaviour. Eric apologized to the ref, passively, and resumed smirking at Tristan. The referees were making some last minute suggestions to the players when Tristan glanced into the stands. His family and friends were seated alongside Deanna. Adrienne, and even Amy, also made the trip. They were all holding an enormous banner: Go Iron Knights Go! It pried the first smile from Tristan's stingy lips.

Eric followed Tristan's gaze and smiled wider. "Deanna huh Tristan? Back Together? Hope you like sloppy seconds."

Tristan lost it.

He cocked his fist, but it was caught with the Jaws of Life. Ryan grabbed onto him and started dragging him toward the bench.

"Childs you son of a bitch I'm going to kill you!"

Eric just smiled as he walked back his own bench.

"Tristan. TRISTAN!" Mr. Gibbs screamed at him. "Calm the hell down! We need you. Don't let him throw you off!"

Ryan was staring at Eric as he walked back to his bench. Tristan wasn't the only one who hated him. Tristan took another look into the bleachers and saw Deanna smiling at him. She mouthed the words, "I'm amazed by you." The gesture snapped him back to reality. He thought to himself, *it's time to end this.*

Tristan joined the team in the huddle to lead their renowned cheer. Tristan called out at the top of his lungs. They would drown out the pathetic cheer of the Raiders. The strength of their voices was almost deafening. The huddle of boys rocked back and forth in a wave of precise movements.

"Iron Knights"

The rest of the team followed.

"Hooo Rah Hoo Rah"

"What's our creed!"

And the knights followed him again.

"Fight together, Play Together Win Together!"

"Iron Knights why do we bleed?"

"For Victory Hooo Rah, For Victory"

"One Two Three. Victory!"

The crowd exploded into cheers at the power and enthusiasm of the Iron Knights. Tristan looked down at the number 11 he had worn so proudly for the last three years. Tristan looked around at the scene in the gym and soaked it all up. It was his last high school game, and he planned to leave it all on the floor.

Ryan crouched in the centre circle ready for the jump ball. Tristan took his position in the back court and waited for the tip he knew was coming. Ryan didn't lose jump balls.

The ref tossed the ball into the air.

Game on.

Tristan caught the ball and surged forward. The Iron Knights broke up the court. Ryan's speed surprised many of the opposing players and he was wide open. Tristan tossed the ball into the air and watching his friend soar toward the basket. Ryan caught the ball with both hands and dunked the ball hard. He let out a roar as he swung on the rim. The crowd went ballistic. Chants of "Go Sageview Go" filled the air. Tristan winked at his mighty friend and cheered on his teammates.

Defence.

It was Tristan's job to guard Eric, and it was no easy task. Eric was powerful and fast, a deadly combo. He would shoot if Tristan gave him too much space, and drive past him if he got too close. Tristan had to be smart, and patient.

Eric backed Tristan down, punishing Tristan's chest with blows from his shoulder. He spun quickly and scored, but not before he and Tristan engaged in a nose to nose stare down.

Ryan passed the ball into Tristan who pushed the ball up the floor to with his famed intensity. They would hit hard and fast all game long. Tristan passed the ball to the wing only to get it back a moment later. Eric was hung up on a screen and Tristan was open. He heard the yells from his old coach, now enemy, Coach Childs, "Get to the shooter!" Tristan smiled. He loved inducing panic.

As soon as he caught the ball, he let it fly. Three points for Sageview. Deanna stood up and cheered. She jumped up so fast that she ripped part of their banner, but nobody cared. Tristan's eyes flicked quickly to the scoreboard. 5-2 Iron Knights.

Eric and Tristan fought for position. Eric got the advantage and Tristan was pinned behind him. Tristan realized Cedar's game plan: Either tire Tristan out by forcing him to play physical, or foul him out. Either one was good for them. Once Eric had the ball Tristan had no choice but to let him score. Getting into foul trouble would not help matters. Eric flexed his bicep after his basket and made sure Tristan saw it.

Back to the attack.

Tristan tossed the ball into Ryan under the basket. Ryan kicked the ball back out to the wing for Matt who was open for a jump shot. Matt pulled the trigger but missed, the ball popped into the air. Ryan flew above all others to grab the rebound.

A new shot clock.

Ryan whipped a pass to an open Tristan on the three point line. Eric jumped at him to avoid Tristan's deadly three pointer.

Tristan anticipated the move and put the ball on the floor. He drove to the basket hard. He jumped with every intention of slamming the ball into the basket when he got blindsided by a hard foul. In mid-air, Tristan could not regain his balance. He looked up to see the lights of the roof above him before he landed hard on his back.

He could hear whistles, but all the air was gone from his lungs. He fought for breath. He rolled back and forth gasping for air. Ryan had Eric by the throat and both teams were off their benches. Ref's were attempting to break things up. Two Raiders tried to pull Ryan off of Eric but were not having much luck. More whistles. Tristan turned onto his side and looked at the crowd. His family and friends were fighting to see him through the mass of people. They looked worried. Mr. Gibbs was crouched over him asking if he was alright. His voice was panic stricken.

Tristan's back hurt like hell, he tried to stand but couldn't. The crowd was in a frenzy due to the small brawl that had broken out on the court. Tristan knew he had to get up. He took a moment, braced himself for agony, and forced himself to stand. The crowd cheered, Tristan's section leading the way. He cringed. He was hurt, but he could play.

Ryan had been peeled off of Eric by three referees. He stood at Tristan's side ready to defend him against all who dared try and hurt him. Both teams stood staring at one another with the referees in the middle. The head ref, exasperated, finally made his call. "Flagrant foul. Two shots, and the ball."

The entire Raiders team was outraged. There were many cries of "bullshit", "cheaters!" and many less pleasant opinions.

Tristan limped to the free throw line, but as he walked, he smirked at Eric who glared back at him.

The game went back and forth until halftime. Tristan fought through the pain, but it was difficult. He was nowhere near as explosive, so he had to rely heavily on his teammates. They had not let him down. Unfortunately for Tristan, Eric played even more physical than he had before, but Tristan expected no less. Again, he relied on his teammates to help him on defence as well.

By halftime, the score sat Iron Knights 41, Raiders 45.

Tristan took some meds at half time for the pain, and coach Gibbs looked at his back. It was swelling. Tristan figured he had bruised his tailbone at the very least. Despite his obvious discomfort, nobody suggested that he sit out. Nobody dared. Tristan's face spoke volumes.

The second half was just as even as the first. The teams traded baskets back and forth. Any lingering Raider fans were now behind the Knights. Eric's dirty play hadn't won him any supporters. Every basket Sageview made the crowd cheered with renewed hope and enthusiasm. Every basket for the raiders was met with boos and jeers.

Tristan found it harder to breathe as the game went on. He spent most of the time during time outs guzzling water and taking pain killers. Ryan watched him suspiciously, but never said a word. If at any point he felt Tristan was damaging himself too badly, he would be the one to put a stop to it.

Three Words

The score was 78-76 Raiders with 2 minutes to play. Every basket against them now was a dagger. The Iron Knights dug in. Eric pounded Tristan again and again under the basket. Tristan was doing his best to stay in front of him, but he was too weak. Eric caught the ball and spun to the basket. Tristan hung his head instantly, but lifted it when he heard the all too familiar rallying cry of Ryan's roar. Tristan heard the loud smack of skin meeting leather as Eric's shot attempt was swatted off the backboard and out of the key. Tristan sprinted toward the loose ball. He corralled it successfully and the crowd cheered. The Knights were off to the races once more. Tristan found Matt with a pass for a wide open layup.

78-78 with one minute to go.

Eric was tired, Tristan could tell. If he could force him away from the basket and force a jump shot Eric would probably miss. He didn't have the energy to make a long range shot. Getting him out there would be the problem. Eric fought to push Tristan under the net. Tristan would not give in. He shoved his forearm into Eric's back and pushed. He had to get Eric at least 15 feet from the basket. He dug his back foot into the floor and pushed. *Success!* Eric caught the ball and had no choice but to shoot.

Eric made it look so easy.

Swish.

Tristan hung his head…he had done everything he could to stop him. He looked up, shaken. 30 seconds to play.

The Iron Knights were out of time outs, they had used them up giving Tristan the breaks he needed to continue. The ball was literally in his court. His injury fought to hold him back, but he wouldn't let it. The game was about more than his feud with Eric, more than his desire to please the scouts. It was about triumph. He needed Deanna to see him succeed in case…

NO.

Focus.

Tristan felt the beads of sweat trickle off his nose. Time ticked away. 27...26...25.

He didn't panic. He was cool as ice. He blew by the first defender who challenged him, and spun past the next. 24...23...22...He passed the ball to Matt on the wing and the Knights ran their patented game ending play: Tristan sprinted down the centre of the key. Eric was right on his heels. Ryan set a hard screen with a little extra oomph that rocked Eric backward. Tristan was free. He made for the corner. His legs were jello, his back screamed at him to quit.

No way.

Tristan caught the ball and set his sights on the rim. He heard the frightful cries of the Cedar Ridge coaches: "The shooter! Get Cage!" It was like a replay of the Sunnyvale game earlier that season. Same time, same place.

Same Result.

Tristan rose up and catapulted the ball into the air. The crowd went silent.

Swish.

Tristan fell to his knees. He couldn't believe he had made it! His silent reverie lasted only for a moment. His entire team jumped on top of him. The roar of the crowd was deafening. Ryan pulled him up and gave him a hug. "Way to go boy...Wooo! Hell yeah!"

Ryan was pulled off of Tristan by an aggressive Amy. "Good game, you redneck."

He smiled. "Thanks, bitch."

She leaped into his arms. Tristan left the new lovers in a sea of bodies. He wanted to see Deanna. He passed the scouts who were waiting for him, they could wait. His family was still together in the stands.

"We couldn't get to you son," Cam smiled. "We are so proud of you." Tristan felt the tears coming, but he suppressed them. He hugged his family members and made his way down the line.

Deanna was hopping up and down like a kid at Christmas. "You were so amazing, Tristan! Come here!"

She jumped into his arms and his back gave out. He just couldn't support the weight. It hurt so bad! They fell, crashing backward into the next row of seats. Deanna was laughing up a storm. "You were supposed to catch me!"

They must have looked funny, the two bald heads sprawled all over one another, but they didn't care. It was just one of those moments.

Tristan wrapped his arms around her and squeezed. Life was much better bald.

Chapter Twenty

The scouts were in love with Tristan. He was promised a full ride to any school he chose. He was most concerned with the local universities though, due to Deanna's situation. He had time, and the universities would come to him. For the next few months he would help Deanna catch up for graduation. *Wow, graduation.* He hadn't really imagined life after high school until recently. He had adapted so well to what it was like at Sageview. The world beyond excited him, but scared him a little too.

Deanna got stronger through April and May. Her treatments were going well, so the doctors said. Tristan had been to a few of Deanna's sessions; he did not enjoy seeing D hooked up to needles and machines. It made his stomach lurch. Deanna would shoot him a brave smile before every procedure. Tristan knew it hurt her, but she was more concerned with his comfort level than her own pain.

It had been four months since Tristan was reunited with D, and their relationship was truly bizarre. They acted like they were dating, but they weren't. He slept over at her house from time to time in a separate room; he accompanied her to doctor's appointments; they looked at universities together, but that was the extent of it. There was nothing physical between them, and they rarely if ever talked about upgrading their status. They were both content with the way things were. Like D had said to him once before, "If it ain't broke, don't fix it."

Tristan drifted apart from other girls in his life, unfortunately, this included Adrienne. She informed Tristan that she held no hard feelings for what he was doing with D. She actually thought it was incredibly sweet, but her feelings for him were too strong to hang around. She made the decision, for herself, to put some space between them. Tristan was disappointed, but she was right. His commitment to Deanna made it impossible to have a relationship.

Deanna was officially caught up on her courses on June 5th. If she continued with regular attendance and passed her exams, she would graduate with the rest of the class. Her family threw her a party in honour of her achievement, and all were invited. Tristan's parents even showed up to show their support. Tristan was very proud of them for this open display of affection. Perhaps they too were getting over their concerns about his new relationship with Deanna.

The party was a huge success. Many kids from school showed up, and though they were disappointed when nobody was serving liquor, they stayed anyway to enjoy the various opportunities to socialize and play games. Ryan and Amy were inseparable for the majority of the night, proving the theory that opposites attract. Tristan was concerned that Ryan was just rebounding and Amy would get hurt, but Deanna informed him that Amy was just recently out a long distance relationship herself. The additional information put Tristan at ease. The two would help each other through their tough times, and if something came of it, so be it.

The weeks leading up to graduation were hectic to say the least. It was one school event after another. The grads had finished their last fundraiser the Friday after D's party. They auctioned themselves off as slaves in the community. It was no surprise that Tristan was bought by his longtime nemesis, Mr. Ferguson. Ferguson had him shingling his house the next day in a sizzling 27 degrees. While Tristan was doing shingles, Ferguson sat on the front lawn in a recliner and drank beer. Every once in a while he would ask Tristan if he was thirsty, only to laugh at his predicament. Tristan endured the punishment humbly. After all, he had made 450 dollars for his grad class.

Ryan spent the day doing a half-naked carwash. He was purchased by the local gas station and they told him he had to put on a car-wash that day. He put on his bathing suit and every girl in Sageview got their car washed that day—*twice*. Amy ended up at the library, no surprise there, helping to organize and re-shelve books. Deanna lucked out too, she was bought by Tristan's sister Emma, who took her to the movies. Tristan was convinced he got shitty end of the stick.

When the four got back together to discuss their day as slaves, it was apparent Tristan was the only slave of them all. Ryan got a tan, Amy got potential work experience, Deanna got to watch *Spiderman,* and Tristan got the worst sunburn of his life. He didn't realize that you could burn your head—it was unpleasant. The four sat at Deanna's kitchen table. D rubbed lotion on Tristan's burned head. She giggled, "Tristan, you should have worn a hat."

"Thanks D," Tristan growled. "I was too busy shingling Fatty's roof to realize I was burning alive."

"Awww," Ryan said. "It's alright little fella. You just pissed off Ferguson one too many times."

Tristan chuckled, "Yeah you are probably right, but it was worth every second."

The recently formed foursome spent the rest of the night recounting their day and discussing their uncertain futures. University was a hot topic, as were relationships—specifically Ryan and Amy's— exams, and graduation. Each graduating student had to choose a fellow grad to walk in and out of the gym with. This person was supposed to be someone special who you shared memories with. It was decided that the best friends should not be separated. Tristan would walk with Ryan, and Deanna would walk with Amy.

Graduation scared Tristan. He felt as though he had turned a corner in his life this past year, and was afraid to tackle the unknown. He hated that he and Ryan would be separated. Ryan's scholarship was to Winchester University, and they had a very weak basketball program. Tristan was most likely headed to Saint Agnus, which was only an hour from his parents. Saint Agnus had notoriously strong athletic programs and was the closest option to Deanna. The decision was more strategic for Tristan than it may have seemed. By choosing a school with a strong basketball team, he could justify his decision to Deanna for staying close to home. She would not have accepted him making a decision based on her.

Deanna was doing university through distance education, over the computer and through the mail, she would be at home most of the time, and it would take her longer, but it was what she had to do until she was better. Tristan understood, and was determined to stay as close to her as possible: for moral support. He told himself she needed him. He needed to believe that because he needed her just as bad.

Tristan spent the week before graduation glued to the people he cared about. He had gained such an appreciation for time and how precious it was and was soaking up all of the memories he could. Deanna knew what he was up to, but she never asked him about it. She allowed him to obsess in silence because she knew how important it was to him.

When graduation day came, it was bittersweet for Tristan. Normal people were elated when the time came to leave high school. Tristan was convinced it was doomsday. Nothing would ever be the same, and he had trouble thinking positive. Usually change in Tristan's life was for the worse. He was moping around before the ceremony and was sitting alone in the cafeteria. He had just picked up his gown and thrown it on cursing and swearing. It didn't take long for his friends to find him, and they were all wearing smiles.

Three Words

"Come on, buddy," Ryan said with his giant grin. "I'll always be there for you, you know that. Don't be so crazy. No matter where I am next year, you'll always be my best man."

Tristan was embarrassed. He scowled at Deanna who just shrugged. Amy came over and gave Tristan a hug. "Who would have thought Tristan Cage was such a softy. It looks good on you Tristan, but don't wear it out. Come on."

She kissed him on the cheek and took Ryan by the hand. They walked out of the Cafeteria leaving Deanna alone with Tristan. Deanna sat down next to him and put her head on his shoulder. Tristan shifted his eyes over to peer at the top of her head. He rolled his eyes. It was impossible to be cranky around these people.

"Deanna, I told you not to tell him I was going to miss him. That sounds so lame coming from a guy."

"I know Tristan, but he had a right to know. He has never let you down, and I don't think he ever will."

"Not like you, huh cheater?" Tristan said with a smirk.

"Ohhh do not go there, Tristan Cage!" She shot up and punched him hard in the arm. "That was a low blow!"

"Speaking of low blows…"

"Tristan!" She hit him again, harder. "Come on you fool."

She grabbed him by the hand and hauled him out of his self-pity.

Tristan and Deanna hugged their families and prepared to line up for their entrance. Tristan felt the pesky anxiousness threaten to return, so he decided to focus on something more productive: possible ways to commit suicide. Tristan grinned at Deanna—she would never know.

Their families went to sit down for the ceremony, and Tristan took his place beside Ryan. Deanna and Amy were right behind them. The friends took one last look at each other as high school classmates, and began their walk towards one of life's greatest milestones.

It was hot as hell in the gym. Their already smaller than standard sized gym was packed. Tristan was sweating up a storm, and his thoughts wandered to a glass of ice water instead of getting his diploma. The heat had a funny way of making you not give a damn about reality.

Mrs. Anderson did awards first. A special award was given to Deanna for her accomplishment. Her family had donated a yearly bursary to a student who showed great determination in the face of adversity. She received a standing ovation.

Ryan received special mention for his scholarship the next year, and he also received athlete of the year honours. He had been a member of the provincial champion basketball team, and had placed first in the province in three track events: discus, javelin and high jump.

Amy had top marks in chemistry, math, and physics as well as the highest overall average for graduating females—a stunning 94%. Mrs. Anderson announced that Amy had received a full academic scholarship to Western University. Ryan glanced at Tristan. Neither had known. They looked at Deanna who pretended to wave at someone in the crowd. Western was three provinces away, at least a sixteen hour drive. Ryan looked a little hurt.

Tristan's accomplishments were impressive as well. He received the highest overall grades in english, history, sociology and physical education. He had the highest overall average among graduation males, 93%. He was also awarded the Scholar Athlete award for his achievements in sports and academics. The crowd cheered when it was announced he would be attending Saint Agnus, the local university, on a basketball scholarship. He looked out into the crowd. His sister was standing screaming at the top of her lungs, and his mother and father were locked in a tearful embrace. Tristan fought back tears himself. He was very proud of what he had done.

Deanna squeezed his hand when he sat back down. She was misty-eyed too. When all awards had been given and diplomas handed out, everyone on stage was ready to go. The graduating class of seventy-four students switched from grad mode to party mode. The grad party was to be held in Matt Staunton's field that night. It wouldn't be proper to celebrate graduating from Sageview high without drunken debauchery in a cow pasture.

Tristan agreed to be the designated driver. He didn't care much for drinking and the others were raring to go. He told himself that Deanna's enjoyment was the first priority that night. She had been through so much and worked so hard to graduate that she deserved a night to let loose. She donned a wig for the party and was dressed to the nines. She assured him that she was alright to drink and that it wouldn't conflict with her treatments or medication. Tristan was skeptical, but she wanted it so bad that he let his reservations slide.

It was a beautiful night for the party. The stars were out, and the music was loud. Tristan had to refuse free booze on numerous occasions. He had become even more of a celebrity since his game winner at provincials. Anything he refused, Ryan gained, as he was holding nothing back. He and Amy were plastered by 9PM. With the night still young, Ryan and Amy went to find a tent.

Deanna took it much slower but the eventual result was the same. She too inherited much free liquor from classmates who had grown to respect her as a role model. Tristan wore a sheepish look as he ushered his drunken companion around to mingle with fellow grads. Deanna was actually quite an entertaining drunk. She had lots of funny stories to tell, mostly at Tristan's expense, and kept poking her own face to see if it was numb. Apparently that was her cut off point. When she could no longer feel her face, she would drink no more.

Tristan thought the final poke would never come, but at half past midnight, Deanna cut herself off. It could have been the poke, or the fact that she tripped over a fire pit and almost dragged Tristan to his death. Either way, he was glad she had seen reason. Tristan dragged her laughing and singing to a rock by the river nearby. He took a blanket with him to keep her warm. They sat together, and the first fifteen minutes was consumed with trying to rid Deanna of her hiccups.

They tried everything. Tristan even hid behind the rock and popped up trying to scare her, but to no avail. Finally, Tristan suggested a trick he developed himself that almost always worked. There was no bed handy so he had to improvise. He got Deanna to straddle him and bend backwards. Deanna was quite amused by this and it took Tristan a few tries to get her to stop dry humping him while cackling with insane laughter. She was never drinking again. Once he had her situated and leaned backwards he told her to hold her breath. Thirty seconds into the procedure another couple came over the hill.

"Oh sorry!" They called out. "Go, Tristan!"

Oh god. "It's not what it looks like!" Tristan called back, but they had already gone back the way they came.

Jesus.

Deanna was still holding her breath. When she finally sat up, she smiled. "They're gone! You are such a genius, Tristan," she said. "A bald, sexy, caring, sensitive genius."

She ran her hand over his bald head to rest on the back of his neck. The look in her eyes changed from drunken oblivion to sober awareness. She looked into his dark green eyes. "Kiss me, Tristan. It won't mean anything tomorrow. Just help me finish this incredible day right. Kiss me."

Tristan felt like he was fifteen again. Deanna's beauty was an aphrodisiac all on its own. He hesitated. Deanna was drunk, he was sober. Would he be taking advantage of her? Did she know what she was doing? Tristan suddenly wished he had been drinking too. The decision would have been much easier.

"D..." It's like she could read his mind.

"Shut up, Tristan. Turn off your sweet switch for now please. Kiss me."

Tristan did as she asked. He closed his eyes and went in for the kiss.

It would have been one of the most romantic moments of his life, if D hadn't thrown up all over him.

Chapter Twenty-One

Deanna spent the next week trying to apologize to Tristan. She didn't really remember exactly what happened, but Tristan explained, only once, and that was all he was willing to do. Tristan wasn't angry, he just didn't feel like reliving the love life blunders he thought he left behind him. Tristan washed himself off in the river after Deanna's Barf-Fest, then he took her to a tent and put her to bed. He stayed up a while chatting with Adrienne, who seemed very excited to have some alone time with him, then went to bed himself.

Tristan reassured Deanna over and over that it was alright. He even laughed at her a few times. She cried when he told her. She was afraid he would think she was the 'Old Deanna' again and stop hanging out with her. That fear had pissed Tristan off more than having her puke all over him. Had he not demonstrated his unwavering loyalty by this point? He thought it better to just keep reassuring her. She would get the point eventually.

Tristan spent the majority of the summer at Deanna's house. He got a job working at a local farm so he could maximize his time with her. He stayed at the Greene house through the week and went home on weekends. It was a wonderful system. He wouldn't miss farming as a summer job, but looked forward to expanding part-time job options when he moved to Plymouth. Smelling like cow shit everyday had lost its luster.

July was a great month, one of the best in his life as far as he could remember. D was doing well and they were getting along wonderfully. The time they spent together was never a burden and they never got tired of one another. They went to carnivals and watched tons of movies. They swam in the river and took long walks around town. Tristan's favourite activity though, was every night at 7PM when they would walk to the Sageview Ultramar.

August rolled around, and Tristan realized the clock was ticking. It was only two weeks until he had to start basketball practice, and three weeks until he moved into his new apartment. For some reason it felt like he was moving into a whole new world, another universe. Apartment hunting had been stressful, but Deanna and his parents were very helpful. They found something affordable and really close to campus. Living on campus did not appeal to him. He was aware of the party scene that never slept in university, and he wasn't sure he wanted to be a part of it.

He had met many of his new teammates already at various meetings and gatherings over the course of the summer. They were pretty cool guys, and most of them were from other parts of the country. The thing he noticed most was the size of them, they were much bigger than the average high school player. Tristan hoped he would be able to keep up athletically.

He said his goodbyes to Ryan and Amy the week before. Amy had to go early because she was headed so far from home. She and Ryan were officially dating—that boy wasted no time—and he agreed to go with her to help her get settled. When he got back, he would have to get moving himself.

Tristan was on the ropes at home—same old story, Tristan should be spending more time with his family before he moved away. The only one who seemed to be understanding was his sister Emma, and that was only because she would get to take his room. Deanna seemed to be feeling better for the past while and they thought he didn't need to be there. The truth was, he *wanted* to be there. He hadn't come out and told them that, but they should have been able to assess some of what he was feeling and be more supportive. He wasn't a child anymore.

The day before tryouts started, Deanna was working on her scrapbook. She had started scrapbooking after graduation. She took pictures of everything! She was sitting next to Tristan on the couch and she was cutting around a picture of them at grad. She had the page all planned out with chunks of lyrics from their song. The page was Iron Knight Gold and Black, and there was glitter everywhere. Tristan smiled and went back to playing his video game. Deanna was abnormally quiet, but he figured she was just concentrating. Once Tristan realized, however, that she hadn't said a word to him in almost an hour he gave her a shove in the leg and smiled to try and get her attention. As he did, he noticed a splash on the page that had not been made by any scrap booking tool. The splashes became more frequent, like raindrops in a pool, and Tristan started to panic.

"D? D, what's wrong?"

He put his hand on her shoulder and tried to turn her head. She was resisting.

"Tristan, it's nothing really. Just the memories in this book, they get to me sometimes."

It was a reasonable answer, but Tristan knew Deanna better than that. She was always sunshiny and bubbly when it came to everyday activities and memories. They didn't make her sad.

"Nice try, D," Tristan said suspiciously. "What's going on? This isn't like you."

She started to shake. It wasn't normal. Tristan gripped her with both hands "D, what is wrong!"

"Leave it alone, Tristan!" she cried. Her outburst was an explosion of his insides. She was crying openly now. They sat on the couch staring at each other. She softened quickly.

"Tristan, I'm so sorry." She touched his face and then moved to embrace him. He allowed her to pull him close in an affectionate hug. "You have been so amazing, Tristan. You are the best boy I have ever known, and will ever have known."

Past tense. What?

"D, you are scaring me."

She paused, and took his hands. She took a moment to compose herself and looked him in the eye. Her emerald green eyes were sad, but her strength returned.

"I'm dying, Tristan. I have been dying since February. They caught it too late."

No. This isn't funny.

"I couldn't tell you. I had to enjoy the time I had left. Tristan, please understand. I was afraid of how you would react. Tristan listen…"

No.

"…the treatments are prolonging my life, but they won't for much longer. The cancer is spreading."

It was so sudden! This couldn't be happening! He was the hero, he had saved her. They were going to grow old together and take walks together every night. They would get married and have children. They would make love. They would…

Too many thoughts! Too much emotion. Tristan couldn't take it. He started shaking his head. Deanna reached out and grabbed his hands.

"Don't do this, Tristan. Don't do this. Come back to me. I know what you are doing, and it is no one's fault." She was pleading with Tristan to calm down, but he couldn't.

He shook her off and stood up. She stood with him. He was still shaking his head.

No.

Tears were boiling over. He had to get out of there.

"Tristan! Don't, please!.."

"NO!!!" Tristan screamed and ran out of the house. Deanna was calling after him as well as her grief stricken voice would allow. He just ran. He ran as far as he could as fast as he could. It had all been for nothing. Everything he had done and all he had hoped for…

He ran until he couldn't breathe, then he ran further. He ran until he was dizzy, then he ran further. He ran until he couldn't run anymore. He collapsed next to the river. He had run a long way. He blinked for a moment. He wished for death. He hated everything. He looked to the sky and envisioned God looking down at him, and he said the first three words that came to his lips.

"I hate you."

Then it all went black.

—

Tristan was being shaken by strong hands. It felt like he was being beaten.

"Tristan? Tristan, are you alright?" Karl sounded worried.

Tristan moaned and rolled onto his back. He stared at the sky. It was twilight, it would be dark soon.

"Get up, son. C'mon, get up." Karl helped him to his feet and got him to the car.

"It took us forever to find you. Deanna is worried sick. She called us as soon as you left."

Tristan muttered something like, *I'm sorry*, but the words were inaudible. Karl passed him a bottle of water.

"We told her to tell you before, Tristan. We warned her it would kill you, but she swore us to secrecy."

Tristan looked up at Karl for the first time since he had been discovered.

"Somebody should have told me." The world was spinning again. He leaned out the door and threw up. Karl put his hand on his back.

When he was sure Tristan was alright, Karl spoke again:

"We need you, Tristan. We all do, especially Deanna. Put yourself in her shoes. She needed to feel normal, be *treated* normal, before that was no longer an option."

Tristan felt sick again. *So much for this being a dream.* He let his head drop onto the dash. He lifted his head up and let it drop. Over and Over. The pain was relieving. Physical pain was much easier to deal with than what was happening inside of him.

Karl grabbed hold of him. "Tristan! Stop this!"

Tristan stared at him blankly as Karl threw his arms around him and held him close. Tristan felt like a child, but he didn't care. He let himself break down. He let himself cry. Karl Greene dealt with Tristan like he was his own son and held him until the sun went down.

Chapter Twenty-Two

They said bad things happened in threes.

Tristan looked forward to basketball practice the next day. He *needed* it. It was where all his frustration went, his anger. When Tristan got the entire story from Deanna, it wasn't pretty. Once treatments stopped working, she would cease to have them. After that, she had a maximum of six months to live. She figured her treatments would end sometime in September. Deanna's parents watched him learn what they already knew with painful anticipation. They wept with Tristan, and Deanna had to stop many times to finish the truth. In the end, the entire group was exhausted. Tristan got up that morning and left immediately. He needed his game.

Practice was going incredibly for Tristan. He was impressing coaches and players alike. His fury kindled his passion, and he was truly unstoppable. He made fourth year veterans look like rookies. He was weaving around defenders like they were merely pylons. He was making almost every shot he took. He was on fire.

Tristan was carrying his scrimmage team single handedly. They were blowing out their opposition. Two points to victory. Tristan pushed the ball up the floor at top speed, he was faster than he thought, or in better shape than he thought because nobody could keep up with him. *One defender left.* Tristan stopped on a dime just inside the three point line. He shot the ball. The defender had moved underneath him to stop him from getting a potential rebound, but Tristan had yet to land. When he did, he landed on the defender's foot.

The pain was instantaneous. The ligaments in his ankle snapped and crackled like breaking spaghetti. As soon as his foot hit the ground he doubled over in pain. It hurt so bad! Was it broken? How long would he be out? Would he lose his spot on the team? Many thoughts flew through Tristan's mind at warp speed. The pain wasn't enough to drown them out.

Coaches and players formed a circle around him. He could hear people whispering their concerns but he tried to ignore them. Speculation would only fuel his overactive imagination that had a knack for the negative. He held his ankle but refused to look at it. Coach Reynolds asked him if he was ok. He could not speak. When they got Tristan vertical, the pain worsened. It was nauseating. He dared not look down. He knew he was headed to the hospital, but he would rather them take him to the vet and put him down. Without basketball, he could not survive what was coming.

Tristan waited in emergency for only twenty minutes. *A little luck*, he thought sarcastically. It was not possible to find anymore more bitter and angry than Tristan Cage. The doctor made a face when he looked at Tristan's ankle. This face was not encouraging. Doctor's should be made to take acting classes to reduce the shock factor for patients.

Tristan had broken his ankle and torn many of the ligaments that held things together. He would be out the entire season and would have to rehab for another six months. He wouldn't be able to walk for at least four to six weeks. The news was not taken well.

When Tristan called home to inform his family that he couldn't drive and needed pick-up, he was in for another bomb. Emma answered the phone after three rings. Tristan could tell right away that something was wrong. Emma's voice was shaky like she had been crying.

"Hello."

"Hey Em, it's me. I got hurt pretty bad at practice today and can't drive."

"Oh my God Tristan, are you ok? This day has been just horrible..." Emma started to cry. Tristan could hear her sobs over the phone. What now? Emma was a fifteen year old girl, and quite a drama queen, but she sounded genuinely upset.

"What's wrong Em? Don't tell me something has gone wrong at home, or I'll shoot myself. This day has been bad enough so—"

"It's Dad," Emma said. "He had a heart attack."

Tristan was stunned. His father was only 48 years old. A heart attack? Impossible.

"Emma this is not time for jokes."

"I'm not kidding, Tristan." More sobs. "He is ok they think, but he and Mom are at the hospital in Plymouth, they are not far from you. I had to stay home in case you called."

Bad things really did happen in threes. Perhaps more eerily than that, his father was in the same building he was sitting in now. "Em, I'm *at* the hospital."

"What?" Emma was not the type to handle family members in a hospital, let alone two at the same time.

"I told you, I got hurt. It's just my ankle, but it hurts real bad and I can't walk. I'm going to try and find Mom and Dad. Ok? Hang tight."

Tristan hung up the pay phone and wheeled his chair to the nearest reception desk. Sure enough, his father had been admitted three hours prior. He got the information he needed and was off, as fast as he could muster, to check on his family.

His father was in intensive care which was on the fourth floor. Tristan was a little buzzed from the pain killers they had given him, so he hailed a nurse down to get him up there. Tristan had many conflicting emotions as he was being pushed by the nurse. Deanna was dying, she had maybe eight more months, his father had *almost* died as far as he knew. He had not been there when his family needed him, and now they would need him at home a lot more. But he couldn't leave D now. He had to spend as much time with her as possible. The decisions ahead were not very appealing. It seemed no matter what he chose, he would be making a bad decision somehow. All of this with no basketball for the entire duration of the struggle. The one constant he had in his life was gone when he needed it most.

Fuck.

He saw his mother sitting on a bench outside his father's room. When she saw him, she looked angry, but when she realized he was in a wheelchair she softened a bit.

"Tristan! What are you doing here? I mean, what are you doing here like this?"

Tristan quickly told his mother what had happened, but he was not concerned. He wanted to know about his father. Patty told him that Cameron had been having chest pains for a while, a fact everyone had failed to mention to Tristan, and he was working that day clearing brush from the back yard. Cam just collapsed. The heart attack had been mild, but Cameron was going to need to make a lot of changes to his diet. He would also need surgery to open up the arteries around his heart that were clogged due to high cholesterol.

Tristan rested his forehead on the palm of his hand. It was too much. All of it. He had not enjoyed the matter of fact way his mother explained things to him either. She had been through a lot that day, but Tristan knew that she would need someone to blame, to help the pain she felt. That was the way she worked, Tristan had inherited it somewhat. Today he was blaming God, but he knew that his mother blamed him.

"Tristan, we needed you today, we've needed you around home a lot of days. Your father is getting older. He can't handle what he used to."

"Mom I don't think this is the time or place. I think—"

"I don't care, Tristan. I really don't. You are hurt, and I'm sorry for that. Deanna is sick, and I'm sorry for that too, but you need to get your God damned priorities straight."

The conversation, being held in the middle of the Memorial Hospital, was going nowhere fast. Tristan didn't know whether to turn and wheel away, or stay and weather the storm.

"Nothing to say Tristan? I wouldn't expect you to anyway. You are like a stranger to us these days. Do you even care what happened to your father?"

That stung.

"Mom, for God's sake listen to what you are saying! Of course I care, I love you guys."

"Do you? Do you?" His mother was getting more agitated. "You sure love Deanna. We can see that. You show her that, and her family too." This last part oozed jealousy.

"Mom, she has cancer! How can you—"

"How can I *what*? Wish that my own son would care as much about his own family as he did for someone else's? I'm sorry Tristan, but sometimes I wish Deanna didn't even exist."

That was crossing the line. Patty did not know what he knew—she did not know Deanna was terminal—but she knew how much he cared about her. She was hurt, scared, and angry, but people needed to project their feelings onto someone else for a change. Tristan would not say another word. The fury burned so strongly that he forgot entirely about the painful throb in his foot and the day's events. He wheeled his chair to a respectful distance, and said no more to his mother. He stared into space and awaited word on his father.

Cameron needed to be in the hospital for a couple days, but he was stable. The doctor recommended that Tristan be taken home so he could rest and elevate his ankle. The cast sucked. It was uncomfortable, heavy, and itchy. His mother drove him home, but they had to leave one of their cars in the city until someone could drive it back for them. Neither Tristan, nor his mother, spoke a single word to each other the entire way home. The tension was thick, but Tristan didn't care. He felt guilty about what happened to his father, that he hadn't been there, but what his mom said about D had been too much.

When Tristan got home he got Emma to help him to the basement. There he would stay, on the couch, until the end of time. He didn't want to move. He didn't want to think, honestly, he didn't want to breathe. He would stare mindlessly at the television until the pain inside went away. The best option at the moment was to feel nothing. Feelings were what caused pain in the first place.

Deanna was the only one brave enough to try and talk to Tristan the next couple days. Emma had tried, but unfortunately, Tristan had bitten her head off. Little sisters were made to release anger upon. When Deanna first saw Tristan he knew he looked like he had died. She knew how much he needed basketball, and she alone knew how much its absence would be felt over the next few months. Tristan told her about his dad and Deanna put her hand over her mouth.

It was dark in his basement, and the only light was coming from the television. It shed a ghostly flame on Deanna's face.

"Tristan, you can talk to me. I know my situation is adding to what you are going through right now, but you can't keep it all inside of you. It is too much for one person to carry around."

Tristan desperately wanted to take her up on her offer, but he couldn't. He was most upset about the fact the she was going to die. How could he talk to her about that? He missed Ryan now more than ever, another absence that was sorely needed. Tristan just adjusted the pillow holding up his lame ankle and said nothing.

"Tristan, *please*." Her voice cracked. He could see she genuinely felt for him. She reached her hand out to touch him. He allowed it. She rested her hand on his chest and spoke very softly.

"You cannot do this to yourself, Tristan. More than anything I need to know that you will be ok when I'm gone." Tristan opened his mouth to protest, he didn't want to talk about this now, but Deanna talked over him with surprising authority.

"Listen to me. Don't interrupt." Tristan decided to humour her. "I need to know that you are ok when I'm gone. You will get better, you will play basketball, you will patch things up here at home. I need to know these things, Tristan, because I am leaving."

Tristan's eyes burned. Reality was so harsh, but Deanna remained calm. "I have accepted it, Tristan, and I know you are angry. You are angry with me, with your mom, and with destiny or fate, whatever you want to call it, you are angry. It is ok Tristan. I understand. I have been there. When the doctors told me I was terminal I was so mad *at everything*. I was scared too, probably more than I was angry, but then I found something to hold onto, something that meant more than living or dying. I found you, Tristan Cage. And I will not let you destroy yourself."

Tristan couldn't help the tears. He buried his head in his hands.

She hugged him tight. "I will always be with you. Know that. I will watch over you, and I will protect you like you have protected me. Believe that Tristan, believe that I will guide you. Use that knowledge to get you through."

"I'm going to miss you so much." Tristan could hardly get the words out. His body was convulsing with the force of his emotion. Deanna was still quite calm.

"I'm going to miss you too, Tristan."

He grabbed ahold of her. He could not help himself. The pain in his foot subsided, or he just forgot about it, either way, he kissed her. He kissed her as passionately as he could. He tried to breathe life into her, to give her some of his life force, to keep her longer. Tristan squeezed her as if she were a life preserver, the only thing keeping him afloat in his sea of despair.

Chapter Twenty-Three

Deanna stopped receiving treatments in Tristan's second week of University. She had no more than six months to live. Her hair would come back once the radiation left her system, but she figured her hair wouldn't have time to get very long.

Tristan went to and from class as quickly as possible for a person on crutches. His ankle was healing *slowly*, but it was in bad shape. His leg looked like an eggplant from the knee down. The swelling was still quite bad, but Tristan felt he couldn't be missing class, especially in first year. His rush was for one purpose only, so he could get home to see Deanna.

His father was doing well. He was still rather weak, but otherwise back to normal. He and his family had a long discussion about the state of things. Once they found out that Deanna was terminal, his mother had turned a pasty white colour. They were now very supportive of Tristan's time with Deanna. In return, he promised to be much more aware of the time and effort he was putting in at home.

It was a huge relief to patch things up, even temporarily, with his parents. It gave him some much needed breathing room in the realm of decision making. He was staying at Deanna's for the next few months, until she was hospitalized. Tristan made the almost two hour drive to and from class every day, with a bum ankle, in order to maximize the time he and Deanna had left.

Deanna's spirit never dwindled. Her resolve never faded. She worked every second on her scrapbook when Tristan wasn't around. She was determined to leave as many good memories behind for her loved ones as possible. Tristan helped out as much as he could. They no longer took walks, he simply couldn't, so they spent their time watching movies and reminiscing.

Tristan couldn't imagine what it was like for Deanna. She spent every second knowing her time was almost up, yet she never complained. Everyone who knew her knew she would soon be gone. What thoughts ran through her head? It must have been so scary for her, but she would rather die scared than spend her remaining days unhappy with those she loved. Tristan had to follow suit. He could, at no time, drop his guard and get depressed. He had to be as strong for her as she was for everyone else.

In October Tristan noticed a change in Deanna's energy levels. She had to work much harder to stay awake, and she slept two or three times a day. He brought her meals and helped her scrapbook. He helped with as much around the house as he could while she slept so that her parents could spend time with her. He even attempted helping Karl with mechanical issues on the vehicles, but that was a waste of time. Tristan was as useful in a garage as a knife was in a gun fight.

Karl and Tristan had grown extremely close. They did almost everything together when Deanna was resting. Karl, more so than Maggie, needed to talk about his feelings. He and Tristan bounced thoughts of one another freely. It was more than male bonding. They were more than friends.

At the end of November Deanna could no longer live at home. She was too weak. The cancer had progressed faster than the doctor's anticipated. At first, the hospital staff took exception to how much time Tristan spent there, especially after visiting hours, but after so many nights sneaking in and sleeping on a chair, they finally turned a blind eye. Someone had even *misplaced* a cot in her room for him to sleep on.

Three Words

Deanna's condition was bad. Tristan knew it. She attempted to keep her sunny disposition at all times, but the sickness was changing her by force. She lost a lot of weight, and it started to affect her personality. She had mood swings, sometimes nasty ones, but could remember what she had said. She was always sorry, and felt horrible. Knowing she had said hurtful things was harder on her than the cancer.

Perhaps the strangest, and most difficult thing for Tristan was when it started to affect her memory. She sometimes forgot who people were, or called them different names. She called Tristan "Will" a couple of times. It stung so bad, but he would never let her know it. He never once corrected her when she called him a different name. Karl and Maggie noticed the pain each time she slipped, and someone would reach out and squeeze his hand.

Tristan had never experienced someone dying before. He wasn't prepared for what is was actually like. It was not easy, it was not swift. She did not look like herself. She did not act like herself. She was fading away like the images on a fogged up mirror. She suffered. Everyone around her suffered. Tristan found himself praying that God would release her from this nightmare, but Tristan also found himself doubting God's existence.

Hours were spent holding a hand that seemed lifeless. Tristan could see Deanna's chest moving up and down. Sometimes it seemed like it took all the energy in her body just to draw a breath. Tristan would read her *Lord of the Rings* while she slept. It was his favourite book. He hoped that it's incredible story of perseverance in the face of impossible odds would keep her strong, and follow her wherever she was going.

On the 23rd of December, the doctors told the Greene family, and the Cage family, that Deanna had very little time left. It was ironic, D told Tristan many times the only thing she didn't want to do was die at Christmas. Tristan cursed God for adding this insult to injury. He was the last one to leave the room after the news had been broken. He thought Deanna had fallen asleep, but she took his hand.

Her grip was so feeble, so weak, but somehow it emanated a warmth, a power.

"Tristan." She spoke, almost in a whisper. It was the first time she had gotten his name right in a week. Tristan looked at her. Her stunning beauty was battered by the illness, but not beaten. Somehow her eyes, though diminished, still shone when she looked at him.

"I want you to leave, Tristan." She was not mean, quite the opposite. Her voice quivered. It hurt her to say the words.

"I need you to go. You need to go. Her eyes pleaded with him. "You cannot watch me die."

Tristan shook his head violently. "No, I'm staying."

Deanna smiled. It may have been mistaken for a grimace if Tristan had not spent so much time by her side the last couple months. "You are everything to me, Tristan Cage. So many times I saw us getting married. So many times I saw our children. You are the perfect man, I have known it my whole life. I love you with all my heart and soul, but you have to go."

Tristan swallowed hard. His resolve vanished. Tears cascaded over his twisted expression. "I'm not leaving you," he sobbed. He bent over and kissed her lips. "I told you I'd never leave your side."

"You never have." Her voice was fading. She was getting weak fast, and wouldn't be able to talk much longer. "You have done things people only dream of doing, Tristan. You are, and always will be, my hero."

Her word choice crushed what was left of Tristan's strength. He fell to his knees by her bed. Tears trickled down her face as well. This would be the last time they ever spoke.

"Go Tristan. Go." She squeezed his hand one last time. Her words were barely a whisper. She shut her eyes. As she was drifting off, she used the last of her energy to wave him closer.

He shut his eyes hard in an attempt to compose himself as he leaned over her bed. He cupped her face gently, and brushed her lips with his.

They kissed their last kiss.

After moments, precious moments, of resting his forehead on hers, Tristan forced himself to leave. It was as if he was driving a sword into his stomach inch by inch, but he turned and shut his eyes. The last of his tears ran down his cheeks and he left Deanna Greene to die.

He felt the eyes on him as he walked past the rest of Deanna's family and friends. He felt their sympathy, their pity, but he kept on walking. He would not look back.

Tristan sat at the kitchen table all night long. He didn't move. The phone sat in front of him. He knew the next time it rang that Deanna would be gone. His parents flanked him on either side, each held one of Tristan's hands. They felt his violent anticipation in the strength of his grip. The phone rang at 8:30AM Christmas Eve. Tristan did not answer. He stood up and went to his room and willed himself to sleep.

The funeral was boxing day. Tristan was invited to pray with the family and sit with Maggie and Karl. He was treated like a son, and he would act like one. He gripped in his hands the scrapbook that he had been given for Christmas. It was wrapped and placed under the tree in green wrapping paper. He hadn't written in months, but pinched between the scrapbook and his sweaty palm was a speech that he had been asked to read. It would not make sense, maybe not to anyone, but Deanna had kept it close to her until her death. In her mind, it had been the blessing that brought Tristan back to her.

Tristan stood at the podium. Ryan held a distraught Amy close to him. His parents nodded at him for encouragement. Karl and Maggie were both looking at the floor, fighting for composure. Adrienne, always so supportive of him, sat near the back. She looked utterly heart broken. She put her hand over her heart to show he support.

Tristan shed no tears. He was calm, he was a rock. He would continue Deanna's strength. She would protect him, and watch over him. He unfolded the lined paper.

"This is a piece of writing that Deanna valued. I was asked to read it here."

> *We hurt Others*
> *Because we hurt ourselves*
> *We hurt ourselves*
> *Because we've been hurt by others*
> *You are in pain*
> *I am in pain*
> *We must break the cycle*

"Goodbye D. We will miss you."

At the grave site it was pouring rain. It was warm for a December day, but the rain was cold. Tristan's black pea coat hung open. The rain lashed his face and body, but he didn't care. He was the last one left. He didn't know how long he stood staring at the tombstone, but it was a good while. Adrienne had stood holding his hand without saying a word for as long as she could bear. She had kissed him on the cheek and left long ago.

Tristan held the scrapbook D had given him tight against his body protected by his coat. The rain ran freely onto his face from his bald head. He didn't know what to do, he didn't know how to move. He felt anchored in place. He felt like if he left, hope would go with him.

But he couldn't stand there forever. D had told him so. She told him she needed him to be ok. She told him she'd be watching. He looked up at the sky and allowed the rain to wash over his face. He allowed it to cleanse his body of the hatred he held for the one dropping it on him.

Three Words

He rested his hand on the tombstone and spoke the only three words his lips would form.

"I love you."

The Next Three Words
(3 years later)

Chapter Twenty-Four

"Chug! Chug! Chug!" came a chorus of encouragement for Tristan Cage. Tristan slammed his empty glass onto the table. He was seated with a fellow university student. They were surrounded by onlookers at the local pub. Tristan figured he would win; his opponent was already three sheets to the wind. Six glasses of Keith's finest later, he thought otherwise. His opponent was still going strong.

Nine beer was nothing for Tristan, not at this point. A couple years ago two beer would have been enough, but he had spent the last while *training*. Tenth beer down. He felt his own resolve cracking. His opponent's hand shook as he guided the yellowish liquid to his lips. Tristan watched with blurry apprehension. His opponent started chugging and the crowd cheered. As he slammed his glass to the table, he quivered. Tristan raised an eyebrow. The fellow turned green. Tristan raised both eyebrows.

Game over.

Tristan grimaced as his unknown adversary turned to the side and puked all over the floor. The crowd cheered and jeered. Tristan put down his eleventh and final beer for show and grabbed the money on the table. Two hundred bucks, that might pay his bar tab. Tristan made his way through the crowd to the bar where he paid his bill. He left the pub with many pats on the back and invitations to come back soon. Tristan competed every Saturday night and hadn't lost in a month.

Tristan stumbled to the curb and raised his hand to hail a cab. He smiled drunkenly at himself. Cabs were not picking him up. His state must have been too apparent. He had to get it together and act sober.

After what seemed like an eternity, a cab finally pulled over for him. He gladly accepted the gesture and hopped in the back seat.

"1411 South Towers Please." Tristan slurred.

"Alright kid, but don't you dare puke in my Buick."

Apparently, Tristan had not sobered up as much as he thought. Tristan thanked the cabbie and tipped him well before teetering his way into his apartment building. The elevator was down, *of course it was*, which meant he had to take the stairs eighteen flights to his door. The chances of making it were slim. He considered passing out on the lobby couch, but the last time he had done so they called the police. Up the stairs he went.

Tristan had to pause every second or third floor to make sure he didn't get sick, or pass out. Either would have been disastrous at this point. His cell phone read 3:30AM. He had lots of time. He sat down for a moment to text Callie, a girl who loved to take advantage of his drunken state. When he had sent the text—Meet me at my place in 20—he continued his ascension.

By the sixteenth floor Tristan was hurting. He regretted his text. There was no way he was getting laid tonight. Even if Callie showed up, he was in no shape to perform. With two floors to go, Tristan dug deep and soldiered on.

It took a half hour to get up the stairs. He got to his door at exactly 4AM. He reached into his pocket for his keys to open the door. *Hm. That's not good.* He reached into his other pocket. No dice. His keys were nowhere to be found in his jacket or his dark blue jeans. He laughed, he was not surprised. *Just another day in the life of Tristan Cage.* He slouched down and rested his back against the door of his bachelor apartment. He told himself to keep his eyes open, but the insanely high concentration of alcohol in his blood had different ideas. Tristan passed out.

When he awoke, he was in his bed. He had no clue how he got there. He rolled over at the sound of clanging dishes to see Callie wearing one of his basketball jersey's, and *nothing else*, making breakfast. He thought, *now I remember why I gave her the spare key.* He rolled over to sit up, but it was not that easy. His head felt like it had been ran over by a dump truck. He put his hand on his forehead and slumped back onto his mattress.

"Long night?" Callie asked in her sweetest, most mocking, tone.

"You could say that," Tristan grumbled.

"You really shouldn't drink so much. I expected *more* than what I got from you last night. You will have to make up for it, double, now that I'm making breakfast."

Tristan planned on it, even though she was breaking the rules by staying overnight, but he would make an exception since she saved his ass—yet again. Tristan didn't know why she kept coming back. For all intents and purposes, Tristan just used her. She was a nice girl, actually she was a great girl, but Tristan didn't do relationships. He glanced up from his bed a second time. Her long blonde hair hung down to the numbers on the jersey. She swept the hair from one shoulder over to the other and kept on cooking. Smelt like pancakes.

Tristan looked down. Callie had left him the decency of underpants. The rest of his clothes were in a heap on the floor. He scanned his apartment, she had cleaned again. The computer sat in the corner, free of dust. The couch's cover was neatly reset, and the video games that had been happily strewn across the floor were now settled neatly on the TV stand. The sneakers he kept in the corner by the dresser were missing, presumably in the closet, and the stain on the carpet under the two stairs to the kitchen had disappeared.

"What time is it?" Tristan asked. His voice was husky and his throat was dry. He needed water.

"Mmm." Callie looked at the microwave. "It's eleven. Time to rise and shine."

It was Sunday. Tristan kept Sundays for himself. Callie had to be satisfied and out of his apartment by one at the latest. He was already uncomfortable breaking his routine by allowing her to stay. It was, after all, Sunday.

Tristan got out of bed and threw on a pair of black and red basketball shorts. He sauntered up behind Callie and put his hands up the front of the loose hanging jersey. The Toronto Raptors had never looked so good. Callie let out a sigh and tilted her head to the side. Tristan kissed her on the shoulder and started making his way to her neck. When he got there she spun around. Her forest green eyes had only one thing in mind. He lifted her up and dropped her on the counter as she pulled the jersey over her head.

—

Tristan walked Callie to the bus stop. He thanked her for helping him out as in as neutral a tone as possible. She gave him the same sad smile she did every time he said goodbye and told him it was no trouble at all. She kissed him on the cheek and boarded to head back to the university residence. Tristan waved goodbye and began his walk to the gym.

Tristan loved basketball, but recently it hadn't loved him. He had been cut from the university team that he had looked so promising for after high school. He suffered a badly injured ankle in his first year and spent the twelve months healing and rehabbing. After a successful preseason in his second year, he re-injured it worse than before. Surgery was required to fix it the second time around, and the coach, after two entirely botched seasons, let Tristan go despite his talent.

The news crushed Tristan. After Deanna died he invested every ounce of desire and motivation he had left into recovering from his injury. He needed basketball, and if he couldn't play, he needed to focus on something, anything to keep his mind occupied. When he found out he couldn't play for the team, he considered transferring to another school, but no team would pick him up. His injury made him a high risk. Tristan was forced to accept the fact that organized basketball, at least the way he knew it, was over for him. Fortunately, Tristan had found a group of guys that played almost daily. It was recreational, and there wasn't much glory in it, but he no longer cared about glory. When he played basketball the world went away, his brain shut off, his memories disappeared. When he played basketball everything made sense.

The guys he met were all pretty cool. He did not get close to anyone as a rule. The closer you got, the worse it was when you were let down. He had a best friend once, but Ryan had moved to Winchester, which was only two hours from Saint Agnus, and he hadn't heard from him in over a year. Ryan was a big shot varsity athlete and no longer had time for his old friend from Sageview.

It was funny how people changed over time. The process always intrigued Tristan. Ryan had become a complete ass—someone who was once the best guy Tristan knew. Tristan too had become an ass in an attempt to keep the world from fucking him like it had in the past. Tristan cared about very few people. The last of his grandparents had died that past summer, which left even less for him to invest feelings in. He cared about his parents and his sister, Karl Greene, and Amy Lang. Everyone else was expendable.

Tristan always received a warm welcome when he got to the gym. He was instantly respected for his on court abilities, and friendship came easily to those who were respected. The same nine faces he saw almost every day were waiting on him to get started. One of the guys, Alec, gave Tristan a slap on the back.

"Let's do this man."

Tristan nodded and laced up his ankle brace. He stepped on the court not a moment too soon. The memory of Deanna's death surged to the forefront, only to be wiped away, as the basketball hit his hands.

Chapter Twenty-Five

Tristan listened attentively to his Greek History professor. Tristan's love of history had grown since he got to Saint Agnus. He was in his third year, and his grades were stellar. He made the Dean's List all three years. Tristan always sat at the front of class, it was the only place he could stay focused and awake. Today's topic was Alexander the Great. Tristan found it ironic that a disease had been what killed him when he had survived so many brutal battles. It actually made him chuckle. Alexander reminded him of Deanna.

When the professor dismissed the class, Tristan waited, not so patiently for the other eighty students to funnel out. That was the drawback to sitting at the front, the door was at the back. He was leaning against the wall swinging his backpack from side to side when someone spoke his name. The voice sounded familiar. He looked around in the crowd but couldn't make out anyone he really knew. Suddenly, a pair of arms were thrown around him, and dark hair was all he could see.

Amy looked up at him. Tristan was floored. "What the hell are you doing here?"

She looked at him slyly, "What kind of welcome is that? I thought you would be glad to see me."

Tristan gaped at his friend. She was supposed to be at Western, studying chemistry. At least, she had been last week.

"I am. It's just—" Tristan said. "It's a wonderful surprise, but how—"

Amy smiled her patented devilish smile. "I transferred, Tristan. Obviously. I had been planning it for a year, but I didn't tell you. I wanted it to be a surprise."

Tristan and Amy had grown very close since Deanna's death. Amy and Ryan broke up in the second semester of their first year at University. He said it was the long distance, but they both knew better. Ryan went image crazy when he got to Winchester, and part of maintaining your jock status was banging a lot of girls. Tristan knew why they had broken up, and Amy did too.

"Well, where are you staying? On campus?"

She pouted. "I was hoping I could stay with you, if you get rid of the parade of girls going in and out of your apartment."

Tristan bit his lip. He spoke freely of his exploits to Amy, mainly because she was so far away and couldn't actually *see* the life he was living. At that moment, he felt a little ashamed. He was also a little worried that she might be half serious about living with him, you never knew when it came to Amy. She had always been a loose cannon.

"Ummm. Well I, uhhh only have a bachelor and—"

"Oh Tristan," Amy said, laughing, "I'm staying in residence. I almost had you though! You looked so scared." She was beaming.

Tristan scowled. He looked grumpy, but felt relieved to have her so close.

"You'll have to come stay with me the odd night, Trist. But you *know* you are sleeping on the floor. You are a hot boy, but not hot enough for me."

Tristan didn't take the insult personally; he was more than used to her abusive language. She hugged him again, and they went to get lunch.

After a chatty lunch and a brief inspection of Amy's room he left her to mingle with her floor mates. Tristan did not want her new acquaintances to get the wrong idea. He cringed as he began the walk home on the cool October evening. As he walked, he planned his evening. He wanted to show Amy the bar scene in Plymouth. In fact, much to his surprise, he wanted to spend as much time with her as possible. For a brief moment, Tristan regretted leaving the residence in the first place.

After calling Amy, it took her all of thirty seconds to agree to go out with him. It had been almost a week since his last drink, but he was determined to give Amy a good show. Tristan made sure he mentioned nothing about his "competition" as they made small talk walking to the bar.

He got his normal table at the pub and greeted familiar faces with a smile and a wave. The music was loud, but not as loud as it would be later that night. Tristan summoned the waiter and ordered his water. If he was planning on drinking, he was always as safe as possible. He drank water before and after. It was more to satisfy his guilty conscience, that he was actually protecting himself, more than anything else.

Amy's eyes widened. "Same old Tristan, huh?"

Tristan grinned. Poor girl had no idea that she would be keeping him vertical for the walk home.

"Yeah I know Amy. Sad eh? What do you want?"

Amy ordered a White Russian. She always was the classier classless kind of girl—the kind who looked trashy but acted classy. Amy had adopted the souped-up-skater-girl-with-an-attitude look. Tristan liked it, who didn't like being seen in public with hot girls?

Tristan sipped at his water and Amy nursed her drink. They talked about everything under the sun, only passing over their memories of Deanna, they both found that topic far too painful. It was easy to tell when one or the other thought of something that reminded them of D, they would smirk and stare off into space for a moment only to be brought back by a snappy change of subject. Both Tristan and Amy were experts at avoiding what hurt them most.

Tristan's table grew steadily with friends he had made over the years. He introduced everyone to Amy, and she was an instant hit with the guys. She was extremely out going and vocal, a relative homing beacon for horny guys. It was fine, as long as they knew going home with her was impossible. Tristan took on the role Ryan so willingly vacated: Amy's protector.

The pub atmosphere continued gaining momentum. The music was louder and the people were sloppier. Drunken slurs flew left and right followed by alcoholically induced laughter. One of Tristan's nightly companions wandered by and plopped down on his lap. A shadow passed over Amy's face, but only momentarily. She grinned at him and raised her glass in acknowledgment of his new toy. Tristan raised his glass in return.

At eleven o'clock the pub's nightly tradition was prepared. A circle was made around Tristan's table and Amy was gently steered out of her seat to stand at the front of it. She frowned at Tristan, but he simply gave her a wink. Tristan was preparing to show her how a man defended his drinking title. Tristan paused for a moment, suspended in time. For a second, a very brief second, he may have allowed himself to be *proud* of that. Regardless, he didn't have time to worry about what he had become. He needed to focus on the task at hand. He drank the last of his water and made sure his hat had its trademark tilt. He sat back confidently and waited for his opponent.

Someone must have explained to Amy what was going on because he suddenly heard her voice, "Whooo go Tristan!"

With that, the crowd erupted into cheers for him as well. He was the defending champ after all.

He turned around to give Amy a smile and she hopped into the air clapping gleefully. He heard a loud cheer in the other direction and knew his opponent was coming to the table. He was prepared for anyone to sit at that table, A giant, a friend, a foe, a total stranger...

Ok, almost everything.

Three Words

A beautiful young lady plopped herself down at the table. Auburn hair, hazel eyes and lips that had avoided him for so long. She wore the smile of a temptress that he remembered all too well. Things just got interesting.

"Hello Tristan. I hope you aren't afraid to take on a girl."

Tristan matched her playful gaze.

"Not at all Rachel. Not at all"

The eager observers erupted as the two raised their first glass.

Chapter Twenty-Six

Tristan woke with a start. Where was he? He lay on his back staring at a foreign ceiling. He had no clue where he was or how he got there. The whole drinking bit was getting to be a hassle. Tristan rolled onto his side. Lying next to him was a cute brunette. The only problem was that he didn't recognize her and he didn't know her name. He lifted the covers. He was a whole lot of naked. Tristan scanned the small room with his eyes while his body lay still. If he moved, he might wake the stranger next to him, and he wanted to avoid an awkward name guessing scenario.

Tristan attempted to squeeze his body out from under the covers with minimal movement. As he did so the body next to him groaned and rolled over. Her arm swung toward him like indestructible wire. If she got a hold of him he would never get out alive. He decided to gamble. Tristan rolled out of the bed and fell onto the floor. The impact was muffled by the carpet, a small blessing. Tristan crouched, naked and alert. He held his breath waiting for the stranger to speak, but no voice came.

He crawled around looking for his clothes, his underwear, her underwear, anything he could put on. He just needed to get the hell out of there. It wasn't the first time he had been in this situation, he was a master of escape. He found his underwear by the closet door and spotted his jeans by the closed bedroom door. He noticed a trend here. He crawled to his jeans and opened the door.

–Creeeak–

Shit!

Another groan came from the bed. *Red alert.* Tristan crawled at baby warp speed and shut the door behind him. He pressed his back to the door. His head was pounding. He needed aspirin, but he needed the rest of his clothes more. Just as he suspected his socks were by the couch, and his shirt just outside the small kitchenette. He followed the trail of clothing to the door. It was like Hansel and Gretel dropping bread crumbs. His clothes guided him to safety. He picked up his jacket which lay just inside the door.

"Mornin' Sunshine!"

Tristan almost had a heart attack. He jumped up and cupped his private parts. He spun around to see a grinning Rachel with her eyebrow cocked. Tristan was speechless and a little exposed.

"Uhhh Rachel. Hi. I mean uhhh good morning. Do you mind if I…" Tristan used his eyes to gesture to the heap on the floor.

"By all means," Rachel said gesturing with an open palm.

"Could you, uhhh, turn around maybe?"

"Oh! How rude of me." She joked playfully.

She turned her back on him, slowly, as he put his underwear on. Once he got that far he relaxed a little and dressed in a less frenzied fashion.

Once she heard the swish of his jeans being pulled over his thighs she turned around. She leaned against the wall with her arms crossed. Despite the awkwardness—and confusion at least on Tristan's part—he couldn't help but look her up and down. She looked mighty appealing in her tank top and pyjama pants.

"Rachel! Come back to bed. It's just some random that Bex brought home last night."

Tristan's looked left to right as if his head were on a swivel. What now? Could the walls talk in this place? He had been scared shitless twice in the last five minutes. Rachel looked over her shoulder and called back.

"He's not a random, Kyle. We went to high school together, and I'm the one that hooked them up. I'm just saying goodbye."

"Whatever, just get back in here," Kyle shot back.

She said it so nonchalant. Had Rachel graduated high school only to become a pimp? Between the onslaught of puzzling information and the massive headache, not to mention the cottonmouth, Tristan was starting to get agitated. He scowled at Rachel who returned his glare with a sweet smile.

"I'll explain later Tristan. Want to catch up over lunch?"

What the hell?

"Sure?" Tristan wasn't entirely sure of how he should answer, but he wouldn't mind seeing more of Rachel. He would also like to know what the heck happened the night before.

"Ok, see you at noon? We'll meet at Subway down the street."

"Ok. Uh where am I?"

She was laughing openly at him now. "You're on Prichard Street, four blocks from your apartment. You better go now before Bex wakes up. She'll be wicked pissed you didn't say goodbye."

"Right." Tristan put on his shoes and bolted.

Tristan felt naked on the way home, he forgot his hat. His bald head was exposed to the ill-tempered October wind. Leaves flew everywhere as he traipsed back to his apartment. He was avoiding the call to Amy to run damage control. Whatever happened he must have ditched her at some point. He hoped she wasn't too mad at him.

He checked his cell phone as soon as he had left Rachel's, but he couldn't find any evidence of how his night played out, or any information on how Amy felt about the whole thing. He half expected to find a nasty text or voice mail accosting him for his lack of tact. He was happy to find that no such message had been sent, but also afraid that meant she wasn't speaking to him at all.

He suppressed his nagging fear and flipped open his phone. He found Amy on the contact list and pressed the call button—then held his breath. Amy answered after three rings.

"Hello, Mr. Cage." She sounded very pleasant. Tristan hoped this was not one of Amy's little head games.

"Hi Amy. I just woke up in a random apartment. I'm so sorry for leaving you."

"Leaving me? Oh my God Tristan I was in the cab that dropped you off. You really don't remember much, do you?"

Tristan was baffled. Amy was not angry at all. She was laughing at him!

"No I don't remember anything," he said dejectedly. "I was at Rachel's, that's all I know."

"Yeah," she giggled. "After you won the drinking game you hit on her all night long. She seemed to be feeling it too, but for some reason you ended up making out with her roommate. Don't worry though Trist, I was with you most of the night. Rachel and I played catch up and your friends are all super nice. I had a great time. Don't worry so much!"

Tristan was relieved. At least he had some sense, not very much, but *some*, when he was hammered. He informed Amy of his lunch date with Rachel. Amy simply encouraged him to go and told him that she wanted details when he got back. Tristan agreed to call her that evening after he played ball. Once he hung up the phone with her he made his way to his own apartment. He had never been so eager to shower.

Tristan shaved his head after his shower, as he did every day. He embraced his baldness freely. He loved that he was different, and he loved that he could show his everlasting devotion to D's memory by doing so. Most people thought he shaved his head because he was a basketball player. He didn't know where that stereotype came from, but he didn't care. People were generally ignorant anyway.

He checked himself out in the mirror and flexed a bit; he was still in great shape. He prettied himself up, though he was unsure why. He even paused in the middle of his grooming to try and figure out why he was preparing as though this were a date. He

Three Words

cringed as he recalled preparing for dates with Rachel in the past. She was the queen of man eaters.

Pause.

This was *not* a date.

Rachel was waiting for him when he got there. She was wearing a tight yellow hoodie and blue jeans. *Why did she always have to look so damn sexy?* Tristan tried to corral his thoughts into a less sexual corner of his mind, and was still fighting to do so when he sat down. She smiled at him, and he returned the gesture.

"So Tristan," she said. "Where would you like me to start?"

Tristan had an answer ready. "Did I beat you?"

She chuckled. "Oh yes, it wasn't even close. You even drank three extra just to please the crowd. You can really hold your booze, Cage. I definitely didn't expect it." She sounded impressed.

Tristan smirked and played with a napkin on the table. "Yeah, people change Rachel, at least their actions change. You still look the same."

"I am Tristan, I haven't changed much, though we haven't really known each other since junior high school." She took a sip of her water. "My looks haven't changed much, except for a tattoo and a piercing or two."

Tristan didn't know if that comment was meant to free the sexual sensations he tried to trap, but it did. He wanted so badly to know which piercing was where. He tried to hide his wandering thoughts, at least for the moment. Tristan lifted his hat off for a moment. "This is as much as I've changed. Oh, and a pin in my right ankle, holding it together."

Her features softened. "I heard you lost your position on the basketball team, I'm so sorry, Tristan."

He shook his head. "None of that, girl. I have adapted. I still play daily, and it is a lot less stressful without all the expectations." It was a lie, but it sounded good.

She nodded and once again seemed impressed with him. Her bangs hung down over her right eye. She sipped at her water some more. The serious turn in the conversation left them both speechless. Tristan decided to rescue the rendezvous. "So, what exactly happened after I beat your ass?"

She almost choked on her water. "Ha! You tried to get some ass that's what! From me for starters."

"Well obviously I didn't succeed." Tristan made a puppy dog face that Rachel responded to by splashing water on him with her straw.

"I have a boyfriend, Tristan! You heard him this morning. I told you I was dating Kyle, but that didn't seem to stop you." She shook her head like a mother scolding her child. "I am not used to such an *experienced* Tristan. You are quite the charmer."

"You sound impressed," Tristan said.

"Tristan, I have always liked you, and I always wondered things about you. Some of those questions were answered this morning." She winked at him and her eyes dropped to his crotch. Tristan pursed his lips and looked down too.

"Oh, I see." He grinned.

She was definitely flirting with him. She always had been an enigma. She seemed interested, but was always with someone else. It was a very frustrating scenario to find himself in—*yet again.*

"So," he said, "who is Bex, and how did I end up in her bed?"

She smiled. "Becky is my roommate. She was eyeing you up from the moment you won the competition. She was very put out when she saw you wanted me, but eventually you got tired of me shooting you down and moved onto her."

"I'm sorry. I uhhh." Tristan was embarrassed. He hit on her until he could get no further, because she was taken, and arbitrarily moved onto her roommate as the next best thing.

"Tristan it's alright! Besides, you came onto me first, so that will save a girl's esteem, and don't worry about Becky, she isn't mad. She gets around."

She gets around? Tristan wondered if he should go get tested. He couldn't remember if he used protection. He was annoyed with himself. How classy can he expect a girl to be if she sleeps with him the night she meets him? That would never be a girl you took home to meet your mother. Consequently, he was just as pathetic as the other half of the consenting party.

Rachel noted his disgusted expression. "What? Becky is hot, and she has high standards. You should consider yourself lucky mister."

"Well yeah I guess—" he said, :"I dunno, I think I'm just tired of sleeping with nameless people. It's a recent development, but it's losing its luster."

"Uh oh, Tristan. That sounded very sincere. Be careful, you may be losing some of your new bad boy charm."

Tristan waved his hand, "No, No. I just need to make sure I don't get a random STD. Nobody needs that.

Nice recovery.

The rest of the conversation went well, some mild flirting and lots of reminiscing. Rachel only brought Deanna up once, and that was to give her sympathies. It lasted a whole thirty seconds which was fine with Tristan. Rachel filled him in on Kyle. They had been dating just over a year, and he was a construction worker. She was waitressing and going to University part time. She never was a scholar.

Tristan had to end the reunion because he had class at one. He was sad to go, but didn't want to push the envelope too much the first time they hung out. At least he didn't smash her in the face with his hat. Rachel gave him a pretty long hug before he left and made him promise to call soon. He put her number in his phone and was on his way.

Tristan was once again fantasizing about Rachel Smith, and this time it seemed like he had a real shot. He was lost in happy thought on his way to class when he stopped in his tracks. That it didn't matter to him that she had a boyfriend only illustrated how far Tristan Cage had fallen.

Chapter Twenty-Seven

It didn't take Tristan long to start rationalizing his actions. As far as he was concerned, nobody cared what happened to others so long as they had nothing invested in them, and even then, that didn't always stop people from hurting each other. People were driven by whatever motivated them as individuals; it had nothing to do with the feelings of others. People who pretended they were so good hearted were just acting. *Good people* were just putting on a front so that others thought more highly of them. Their image was their motivation, not the betterment of the world. The few people who were inflicted with the delusional disease of caring were not long being brought crashing back to reality by death, deception, or betrayal.

He didn't bother going home. He went straight to the gym. All of the bitterness, uncertainty, and self-loathing had to go away. The only way to do that was to make it all disappear with the magical sphere he relied on so heavily. Tristan skipped his next class and played basketball for four long hours. He pushed his twenty-two year old body to the limits until it almost snapped, but it was not to be. Much to his disappointment, he lived to see another day.

That night Tristan sat alone in his apartment. He didn't answer his phone or turn on the television. He didn't go to the computer. Rather, he stared at a pill bottle for three hours. He wondered if it would be painful to die from an overdose. He wondered if the pain would be worth it. He wondered a lot of things. Regardless of his thoughts, the pill bottle remained full. He was desperate, but not that desperate. He was just going through a phase, he told himself, phases always end. Tristan would just have to find another band aid to cover the pain inside of him, or another bottle to shove it in.

He flipped open his cell.

It was close to midnight when Callie arrived. He met her at the door. If he jumped her right away it would give her no time to talk. Tristan definitely didn't want to talk. He wanted to have sex, meaningless sex, in order to remedy the pathetic depression he couldn't seem to escape. Tristan always thought that depression was a mask, that it was just a figment of people's imaginations. He once believed that positive thoughts bred positive results. Unfortunately, Callie was a victim of that change of heart.

Callie looked fantastic, as always. She would look better without her clothes though. Tristan wasted no time getting down to business, Callie always said she loved a guy who was spontaneous. She was very receptive to his barrage and it was apparent from the varying levels of her moans. The two stumbled backwards toward his bed. Tristan looked for the two steps down into his living room but missed the first one. He and Callie tumbled to the carpet. Carpet was just as good as a bed, and they definitely made it seem so. They were rolling around interlocked in a ball of ecstasy. Tristan could feel his worries fading away until…

"I love you, Tristan."

What? No No that must have been a slip.

She said it again. "I love you *so* much."

Definitely not a slip!

Tristan pushed her away from him. She was shocked, but not yet insulted. He searched frantically for his shirt. "Ok you need to leave, Callie. Now. Get dressed."

"Tristan, what's wrong?"

"You know exactly what's wrong! You broke our rules!"

"Rules are meant to be broken Tristan," It was clear she didn't understand the trauma she had caused.

"This is not fucking funny Callie! Get dressed and get out!"

Callie's eyes flickered around the apartment. She swallowed hard and slowly gathered her clothing from the floor. Tristan waited for her anger, he wanted her to be angry. He needed an excuse not to call her. He needed an excuse to be afraid of her. He pushed her further. "Hurry up, Callie. I'm serious."

She paid no attention to him. He couldn't see any sign of tears, and that was good. She must be furious with him. *She must want to tear my head off*, he thought.

Callie walked right up to Tristan and kissed him on the lips. "I know what you are doing, Tristan. And part of me wants to tell you to go fuck yourself. Part of me wants to slap you in the face for leaving me naked and ashamed while you storm around ordering me to leave. Part of me wants nothing more than to walk out that door and forget about you. I know I'm not the only girl that goes in and out of your door Tristan. I am not stupid. But that part of me is constantly silenced by the other half, who is truthfully in love with you. Underneath all your defences, you are a wonderful guy. But you aren't done hiding yet. I get it. If you are expecting me to storm out of here it is not going to happen. I will leave, but on my terms."

Tristan couldn't believe what he was hearing. He used her and she knew about it. He embarrassed her and made her feel like an idiot for saying words that any other guy would kill to hear from a girl like Callie. He did everything to push her away and there she was, still standing. Well, that was unacceptable. She had no right to make him feel this way. She knew the rules.

"I'm sorry, Callie. But I could never love a slut."

He regretted the words the second the left his mouth. But it was too late. Callie dropped her head.

"Oh Tristan…"

She fought for composure, but she couldn't hide the tears. She kissed him and he felt her lips quiver. "Goodbye."

She turned and walked toward the door. She looked back at him one last time before she left. Tristan Cage mutilated another innocent soul because he was a coward. The apartment was dark and he stood next to the stove. He wanted to be alone, he wanted no attachments, and now he didn't have to worry about Callie any longer. He should have been thrilled, mission accomplished, crisis avoided, but he was not relieved.

There was a knock at the door. Tristan's heart skipped a beat. Callie had come back. He told himself not to be happy about it, but he couldn't help it. Tristan felt a small flame rekindled inside of his darkness. Here was a chance for redemption. Tristan ran to the door. He yanked on the door handle like he was attempting to rip it from the door that held it, but it was not redemption that waited on the other side of the door. It was temptation.

Rachel stood staring at her phone. Tristan heard his phone ring. He looked over his shoulder and looked back at Rachel. She let out a giggle. Tristan knew instantly that she had been drinking.

"Oh there you are." She slurred. "What are you doing here all alone silly? A boy like you needs company."

Tristan sensed her innuendo, but was hesitating. Rachel had a boyfriend. There was no way that he was letting her stay with him. *No way,* he thought, *nothing she could say would—*

"Tristan, I know you want me."

His resolve wavered quickly. Why was she there? They had only reunited days earlier. Something was off about the entire situation. Tristan had almost entirely forgotten that Callie had left minutes earlier.

"Rachel, you're drunk."

"You're right." She pushed her way past him. "Care to take advantage?"

Tristan's male instincts were surging to the forefront. Rachel's knee high boots clicked across his entryway floor. She bent over and unzipped the right one. She looked back at him. "Want to watch a movie Tristan? *Dumb and Dumber* maybe?"

Tristan could not believe she remembered that, especially in the state she was in. Or maybe that was *why* she remembered. Tristan was still standing in the doorway with the door open. Part of him prayed for the strength to ask her to leave. That part was weak. Tristan closed the door and allowed Rachel to use him to steady her balance while she whipped off her other boot. Her green top was very tight, and very low. She had an amazing body. She smiled at him. "Like what you see?"

He wasn't embarrassed. He didn't care that she caught him checking her out. That would make things easier. "I do. I always have, Rachel. You know that."

She took his hand and walked him slowly to his couch. She pushed him lightly, but hard enough to force him to sit. She stepped onto the couch and swung her other leg across his body. She eased herself onto his lap. She moved her head from the right to the left. Her dark hair fell parallel to her body. She kissed him.

This kiss lasted for a moment before she spoke again. "I have always cared about you, Tristan. I wanted you for so long. You were the sweetest guy I ever met. I know you want me too."

Her speech pulled at his heart strings. He recalled how much he had cared about her before he and Deanna got involved, but that was a long time ago. He stared at her, but the thought of Deanna had done something strange to him. He felt his conscience come roaring back.

What would she think of you now?

Tristan tried to speak, but Rachel put her finger gently over her lips. He could make out her silhouette by the moonlight coming in his window. She smelt like perfume. She kissed him again, this time making her intent well known. She pushed Tristan back onto the couch and started working her way from his lips downward.

Chapter Twenty-Eight

Tristan woke the next morning on the couch, fully clothed. Ultimately he had been unable to accept the role of the other guy. He knew far too well how it felt to be said guy, and was unwilling to stoop to that depth. He swung his legs onto the floor and rubbed his eyes. It was still pretty early. He forgot to close the blinds and the sun was just cresting the neighbouring buildings. Tristan was very uncomfortable. His jeans were riding up his crotch and he knew he had slept awkwardly. He couldn't wait until Rachel left, but as he scanned his small bachelor apartment, he realized Rachel was already gone. The bed was made and her boots were no longer in the entry way.

Tristan ran his hand over his bald head. He wanted so badly to be with Rachel. It would have been a crowning achievement in his otherwise disappointing life. He was unsettled by the resurgence of his pesky conscience and told himself that he would need to be careful in the days to come; in case it decided to cause problems again.

Tristan got himself off of the couch and hobbled into the kitchen. His leg was asleep. The pins and needles were a nice change from the guilt he normally woke up with. Tristan opened his box of Lucky Charms and realized he didn't have milk. He walked to his computer crunching handfuls of his favourite cereal and sat down to peruse Facebook. He looked down at the keyboard to find a freshly written note.

Tristan,

I'm so sorry for showing up drunk and stupid. It was a bad day for me, and I dealt with it totally wrong. You did the right thing making me go to bed. You're a great guy.

Rachel.

Tristan shook his head and slid the note off his property. He should have found the note cute, or complimentary, or thoughtful at the very least, but he found it annoying. He couldn't understand why Rachel would come to him, why she would force him to make good decisions. It was blind dumb luck that he had been able to refuse her advances. She had just caught him at a vulnerable moment. Girls were trouble, and he couldn't get wrapped up in Rachel again and all the heartache that came with her. Instead, Tristan decided to head to the University and study.

One of the horrible things about a campus was that you always ended up running into people you don't want to see. It was an amazing phenomena. Tristan would piss off some chick one day and see her the next. His university had ten thousand people, but it never failed. Sure enough, as he rounded the street corner to walk towards the gym, there was Callie. Tristan muttered curses under his breath, but forced himself to walk forward. She already saw him. It was too late to run.

"Tristan," she said sounding surprised.

Hi Callie uhhh. Sorry about yesterday." Tristan's body wanted to sprint away so badly, but he forced himself to stay still. He hoped the jitters that resulted weren't noticeable.

"It's alright Tristan, really. You just aren't ready for a relationship, I guess."

Tristan hated having conversations on street corners. People were coming and going, weaving through them like water through a strainer. There was absolutely no privacy whatsoever, but it didn't seem to faze Callie.

"I hope we can still be friends, Tristan."

What?

Tristan could not understand her. She should hate him. Deep down he was happy that she could still smile at him, but it made him feel incredibly guilty.

"Of course, Callie. Call anytime."

She gave him a quick hug and started off in the other direction. As she was walking away she paused and turned back to face him. "I meant what I said, you know." And she was off again.

Tristan stood alone on the street. He couldn't muster the will to move just yet. Was that really necessary? The damage to Tristan's resolve had already been done, the extra two cents she offered demolished it completely. Tristan could handle hurting girls with no morals, who were using him too. Tristan could handle hurting girls who were bitches, controlling or selfish, but he could not handle hurting someone who obviously cared about him so much. He couldn't believe it. When he had met Callie, she was so willing to let him into her pants that she figured she was just another object, but he had made a mistake. She was wreaking havoc on his senses. He felt *bad*.

Tristan was no longer in the mood to study. Instead, he retreated back to his apartment and called Amy. He hoped that his old friend would be able to banish the guilt he felt about Callie. She sounded happy to hear from him and used her playful tone as she answered. "Well Well, Mr Cage, finally decided to call me huh?"

"Yeah," he replied with a grin, "it has been a wacky few days. Do you wanna hang out tonight?"

"I'd love to. Your place or mine?"

Tristan invited her to his place to watch a couple movies. He hadn't had a good ol' fashion movie night in a while. It was one of his traditions with D, and he wasn't willing to share it with many others. They decided on his place for relative privacy. Since Amy lived at the residence there would be parties going on all night long. Tristan felt like he partied enough that month, and Amy agreed with him. His place would be much safer.

Amy arrived right on time at 8PM. When Tristan let her in he couldn't help but stare. She was dressed, but barely. Her mini skirt earned its name and her strapless halter top left little to the imagination. She wasn't wearing her glasses, revealing her icy blue eyes, and her make-up was done. Amy looked like she was headed for a night on the town rather than a movie session with Tristan.

Amy noticed Tristan's eyes scanning her from head to toe. She smirked at him. She had such devilish features. Her dark hair was put up in a hot mess. There were bobby pins everywhere that forced pieces of her hair up. She looked incredible. Tristan wasn't going to complain, he could look all he wanted. What was happening in his imagination would stay there and nobody would ever know.

"I know what you're thinking Tristan." She winked at him.

No Friggin Way. Things were getting far too weird.

"And there's no way I'm ditching our movie night. I'm going out with the girls after we're done."

Phew. Tristan was relieved. He worried she had gotten all dressed up to see him, that would have added an interesting dynamic to his already thoroughly screwed up love life. He took one last look at her, stored her hotness in his memory, and offered her some popcorn. Thankfully, Amy the seductress was replaced by Amy his goofy friend. They watched their movie in peace and quiet as they both hated when people talked, moved, or even breathed during movies.

Three Words

Amy was lying on the couch with her feet up on Tristan's lap. Tristan held his bowl of popcorn with his arms over her outstretched legs. Tristan did his best not to glance at her hiked up mini skirt. He knew Amy didn't care, for her and Tristan were that close, and they both knew nothing could happen between them, but she was still a girl. A hot one too.

Tristan's brain was playing ping pong with itself. One second he was fantasizing about Amy—he really couldn't help it—and the next minute he was chastising himself for having any sexual thoughts about her at all. He was waging war with himself as he stared blankly at the movie on his television. To the outside world, he was just caught up in the action.

Near the end of the movie Amy must have had an itch on her left ankle. She started scratching it with her right foot, causing friction in his lap. She moved it back and forth and Tristan bit his lip. *Just watch the movie, dumbass.* Amy's foot moved from her ankle into his lap, but it didn't stop moving. Tristan refused to look at her. It seemed like a pretty blatant flirtatious act. He figured she didn't know what she was doing. The only way to tell would be to look at her, but what would he see? He was suddenly, tense, anxious.

Tristan turned his head, slowly, as to not draw her attention if she was indeed distracted. The ghostly flicker of the movie shed just enough light in the dark room that he could see her face. She was looking right at him, her blue eyes like sapphires. She was biting her lip and looking directly at him. Her foot was still moving up and down his thigh. Tristan felt the temperature in the room rising. Her left hand slid across the carpet and gripped the remote. The TV went off and all was dark. Tristan felt the soft skin of her legs slip out under his grip. He could sense the shift in her position. He could feel her lips on his neck. She had him—his neck was his weak spot.

Tristan's hands shook with anticipation. His heart was telling him to push her away, but the rest of his body was locked in a sexual trance. Her lips slid from his neck to his jaw line. The hand that he intended to push her away with grabbed a fist full of bobby pinned hair and pulled her closer. She made her way up his jaw line to his ear lobe. She whispered to him, "I have waited so long for this."

His mind screamed at him to stop. *She's Deanna's best friend! She dated Ryan!*

But it feels so good! He opened his eyes and caught a glimpse of something jutting out from under his bed, barely visible in the moonlight. D's scrapbook. He had to end this.

"Amy, stop." He said through pressed lips.

She wasn't listening, or she was ignoring him.

"Amy, *please*." Tristan gently eased her away from him, far enough that he could speak to her. She looked pained. How could he have been so stupid? The signs were all there. She had moved back home to attend school with him for god sakes.

"Amy this can't happen. You are too important to me, and I am not ready for this. Feelings have destroyed everything I ever cared about. I don't want to hurt you"

She cut him off. "The only person you ever hurt is yourself, Tristan. When are you going to let her go? It wasn't your fault and I hate watching you—"

"Watch me *what*?" Tristan could feel his irrational anger taking over. "I was sure she would live. I asked God to save her. I prayed every night. I watched her suffer. I didn't even cry at her funeral. I haven't cried since."

Amy reached for his hand, but Tristan pulled it away. She tried turning his head to look at her, but he wouldn't allow that either. The emotional force field of Tristan Cage was impenetrable. It had to be that way.

"Tristan, don't do this."

"I bet you dressed like this on purpose, to seduce me. I bet you are not even going out with girlfriends tonight."

Amy's strong independent exterior wavered. "I would never lie to you, Tristan. In fact, I think I'll leave now."

She stood up proudly showing no signs of having been insulted. "You are important to me, Tristan. But this whole self-loathing thing is getting boring. Deanna is dead, she's gone, and if you don't learn to accept that your pain will never leave. You are pushing everyone away, and I am going to get the hell out of here before you push me away too."

In moments, she was true to her word. Tristan heard the door open and close. She was gone and he was left sitting alone in the dark, *again*. Amy was the third girl to leave his apartment in an awkward fashion in two days. Three girls! They were gradually increasing in sentimental value as well. Amy was by far the most troublesome. He was angry with her, but also angry with himself. He expected her to show more respect for D's memory, but she was right about one thing. He was losing people fast. Tristan had a moment of panic as he realized the only people he could call were family members. Ever since Deanna's death he left a wake of destruction no matter where he went.

Tristan flicked on his lamp and pulled out D's scrapbook. He flipped to a picture of D holding his basketball. She had taken this picture just for him. She said he could have both of his loves all in one. Tristan stared at the picture for more than minutes, maybe even hours. He knew that he had to change, that he was wasting a life, and that it wasn't fair. What if Deanna could see him now? Would she be impressed? Would she be proud? Tristan knew the answer. He tried to close the book, but hesitated. He knew once he did, he would finally be letting her go.

After two years and eleven months, Tristan could finally admit to himself that he was sad. He shut the scrapbook and cried.

Chapter Twenty-Nine

Fall turned to winter, and Tristan had a large hill to climb. He started seeing a grief counsellor, and she informed him that his actions were not uncommon, especially for young males. Apparently bottling up your emotions, or ignoring them altogether, was a very popular coping strategy. He met with her twice a week and was making progress. His first step was becoming more comfortable talking about D in casual conversation. She told him he should be able to talk about her life happily at any given moment. That was not an easy concept for him to adjust to.

Tristan went to visit Karl Greene every Sunday. He figured it was fitting considering it was his day with Deanna for so long. Karl loved to play Crib, the number of crib games played in those two months must have numbered in the hundreds. Karl was a man's man, and didn't show much emotion, but it didn't take an expert to tell that he was happy to have Tristan around. Maggie, D's mom, had left Karl a year earlier. Their marriage just wasn't the same after Deanna passed. They talked about his daughter a lot. Tristan had trouble with his openness at first, but in time, it became refreshing. Karl had truly loved her.

Amy forgave Tristan's reaction to her display of affection, but she hadn't shown any signs of liking him in that way again since. In fact, a month later, she started dating Bryan, a football star at Saint Agnus. Tristan was mildly jealous, and surprised at her quick change of love interests, but figured he may have misinterpreted what happened on his couch. Maybe it was just an odd moment for both of them.

Tristan grew closer with Rachel as well. He got to know her boyfriend, Kyle, and liked him well enough. Rachel's relationship was a nightmare, however, and Tristan had to leave their apartment many times because their shouting matches were too much to bear. Tristan didn't think either of them were very happy with the way things were, but both had become dependent on one another, thus they stayed together. Tristan spent many hours comforting her while she cried, but Kyle was by no means the bad guy. Tristan realized that Rachel was rather high maintenance. She needed her own way all of the time, and she needed a ton of attention too. Sometimes Tristan felt sorry for Kyle.

Tristan started writing again that Christmas. He wrote a note to Deanna on scrapbooking paper and shoved it in a small metal thermos. He went to the cemetery and buried the thermos with the letter inside. He vowed he would return with a new letter each Christmas to keep Deanna informed. He had figured out a way to move on with his life and stay loyal to her memory at the same time. He believed that she was looking down on him anyway, but this was for his peace of mind too.

By the time January rolled around Tristan had developed a new outlook on life for the New Year. He felt better about things. He hadn't drank in quite some time, and he didn't feel the need to. He felt more like his old self, confident and in control. He demolished his Christmas exams, earning top marks in Ancient History and Mythology. He also picked up his grades in his English classes due to being reunited with his muse. Things were finally looking up for Tristan, and he didn't feel the need to date, or even *be* with girls. It wasn't to stay safe, and it wasn't to avoid hurting anyone, he simply wasn't interested in dating. Dating and relationships had consumed so much of his young life that he simply needed a vacation. *A chick vacation.*

Three Words

Tristan spent most of January mending fences and rebuilding bridges he had burned—mostly with girls he had humped and dumped. Some offered forgiveness, others never wanted to see him again, either way, he cut down on the awkward street-corner meetings. Alec got a kick out of the different reactions he got from girls. No matter what the result, they all usually got a laugh at Tristan's expense.

February flowed into March. He was at home one weekend and preparing for his weekly visit to Karl's in Sageview. Tristan had worn a hoodie home for the weekend due to the unseasonal warm weather. Sunday though had cooled. He was rooting through his closet for a jacket. He had one, at the back, but that was a last resort. He hadn't worn that coat since the funeral, and he didn't plan on donning it anytime soon.

His mother came in and asked him what he was doing.

"Looking for a coat mom. That's all."

She put her arm around him. "I can get you one of your father's, but that black pea coat has always looked good on you." Her hint was far from subtle.

"I know but—"

"I know you haven't worn it since the funeral, but I think it is time. Besides, I spent two hundred dollars on that jacket."

Tristan stared at the black lump of wool like it had been quarantined. He wondered if it was safe. He gave his mother a squeeze and slipped the coat off its hanger. He took a breath and threw it on. His mother smiled and fixed his collar. "You are such a handsome young man. You have my looks." They shared one last smile before Tristan confiscated his mother's keys and headed out to the car.

Tristan had a nasty habit of misplacing things as soon as he came into contact with them. He was rummaging around in his pockets for the keys when his hand came into contact with a piece of paper. He pulled it out expecting to see a receipt, but as soon as he set eyes on it he remembered. He flashed back to Deanna's grave after the funeral. Adrienne stood with him until she couldn't take the cold rain any longer. She had slipped a piece of paper into his hand that he absent-mindedly put into his pocket. He had never looked at it.

He opened the paper to find an address, email address, and cell phone number. Tristan knew Adrienne went to Winchester. Before he had lost contact with Ryan, he heard that she was doing well there. She always was smart. Tristan couldn't decide how he felt about this piece of his past creeping up on him. He and Adrienne had been very close, almost dated even. He had a real soft spot for her. He looked up for guidance, from D, from God, whoever thought it was necessary to send his memory back in time. He didn't get any answers. He was on his own.

Tristan tucked the paper away hoping he would forget about it as easily as he had before, but the entire forty-five minute drive he was visited by memories of Adrienne Axley. Adrienne had so many qualities that appealed to Tristan. She was spunky, playful, beautiful, and kind just to name a few. He couldn't believe how she had stood by him when Deanna was dying. She wanted more from him than he could give at the time. Maybe he was ready to try relationships again? Maybe he would give Adrienne a call.

His visit with Karl was ordinary. They played cards and talked about old times. They made plans to visit the next week, and Tristan headed for home to repeat the same mental tug of war he had engaged in on the drive over. He was relieved to pull into his own driveway where he could shut his bedroom door and pick up the telephone.

Tristan rubbed the small piece of paper like it was a wishing stone. Traces of the old Tristan were quickly rearing their ugly heads. The operator spoke in his ear, "Please hang up and try your call again, or stay on the line for assistance." The only thing was, he hadn't pushed a button yet. He had picked up the phone and froze. What if she didn't remember him the way he remembered her? What if she resented him for the decisions he had made? What if—

For God's sake, Tristan. Stop being such a retard.

Tristan moved the receiver away from his ear and shook his head. It was a ritual of his to clear the negative thoughts from his mind. Once he had composed himself he slowly dialled the number on the paper. The phone rang once. Tristan hung up the phone like it had a virus. His eyes scanned the room. Thankfully, no one had been there to witness his neurosis. He picked up the phone for the second time. His hand was shaking as his finger approached the redial button. What was he so afraid of?

Tristan, somewhat reluctantly, pressed the button. He could hear the seven beeps that could spell his doom. One ring: *relax, breathe*. Two rings: *Fuck this*. Tristan hammered the phone back onto its base. Maybe he wasn't ready to put his heart out there just yet. He would try again after dinner. Adrienne hadn't heard from him in years anyway, what was another few hours?

Tristan's father drove him back to his apartment after dinner. The weekend was over and he had to be back for class on Monday. He said so long to his father and promised to come home again the following weekend. Tristan opened the door to his apartment and flopped down on the couch. He stared at the ceiling trying to motivate himself to finish an English essay that was due that week. He looked around the empty apartment and found that the solitude he once coveted was now plain lonely. He held his cell up in front of his face. It was time to try his luck with Adrienne again.

Tristan dialled her number and pressed the phone hard against the side of his face. He would not allow himself to freak out and hang up this time. One ring: *so far so good*. Two rings: *still going strong*. Three rings: *uh oh, haven't come this far yet*. Four rings: p*hew, maybe she won't*—

"Hello?"

Shit! Say something.

"Hello," Tristan muttered.

Very original, you moron.

"Can I help you?"

"Adrienne, it's me, Tristan. Hi."

"Who the hell is Adrienne? And who are you?"

Tristan blinked. The voice on the phone wasn't even female. He was so preoccupied with his anxiety that he failed to recognize the sex of the voice that answered his call.

"Ummm. Adrienne Axley? I was given this number to contact her."

"I dunno who that is, mate. But I am not her. Goodnight."

–Dial tone–

Well, that went well, Tristan thought sarcastically. He flicked on his lamp and looked hard at the paper. For the first time he noticed how ambiguous Adrienne's numbers were. He looked at his call history and the number he dialled. Either she had given him the wrong number, or he misread the numbers. They all looked the same! Her twos looked like sevens; hell, her ones could have been sevens for that matter. Maybe all of them were sevens. Tristan rubbed his face with frustration. He knew it was probably a sign to turn back, but he ignored it. Four combinations of two, ones, and sevens later, a familiar voice answered.

"Hello?"

Oh my god that is definitely her voice. Tristan recognized her sultry tone.

"Ummm, hi Adrienne. Do you know who this is?"

Silence.

"Adrienne?"

"I told you before, Randy, don't call me anymore! I'm sick of this shit!"

What? Who the fuck is Randy?

"What? Uhhh, no. It's Tristan. Tristan Cage."

Silence again.

"Tristan?" she said.

"Yes Tristan. Sageview class of oh two. Tristan!"

"Well it has only taken you three years to call."

Uh oh.

"Yeah well I was—"

"Busy fucking every girl at Saint Agnus? I heard. Goodbye, Tristan."

–Click–

Tristan stared at his phone with his mouth agape. He hadn't heard Adrienne angry before, especially with him. Her words were extremely unpleasant, but not entirely undeserved. How and why was there news of him at Winchester? He didn't even play varsity anymore. The only answer Tristan could come up with was that Adrienne had been actively checking in on him, much as he had on her until he lost contact with Ryan. Who would have been giving her information though? Tristan was a little angry. He thought gossip would have ended after high school, but he knew better than that. University was just as rife with gossip as high school ever was. He hadn't slept with *that* many girls anyhow. He had fooled around with a ton—maybe more than a ton—but he had only had sex with a couple. He should have been more discrete. Hindsight was 20/20.

Tristan, brutally defeated, rose from the couch and walked to the fridge. He felt the sudden urge to eat—a phenomena he once equated with being female, but found that it was actually quite comforting. Tristan sat down with a bag of Swedish Berries and started to put a nice dent in it. His phone rang. Tristan frowned and stared at his phone waiting for caller ID to recognize the call. Adrienne's number popped up.

What the…

He picked up the phone. "Hello?"

Adrienne sounded choked up. "I'm sorry Tristan, I had no right to freak out on you like that. You were just in the wrong place at the wrong time. I'm so sorry."

Tristan's amazement was growing.

"It's ok Adrienne. I—"

"No it's not, Ok. I have been waiting three years for you to call me, and when you finally do, I act like a huge bitch." He could definitely tell that she was crying.

"Adrienne, please. It's ok. Calm down. It's my fault I didn't call. I went through a rough patch. And—"

"I'm sorry I commented on your personal life, Tristan. Oh god, I'm such an idiot!"

"Adrienne, I'm not sure what's happening here. I didn't mean to upset you."

"Oh it wasn't you, Tristan! It was Randy." She sobbed. "I never cry Tristan, really. And I'm not normally like this. I just have such bad taste in men."

Warning bells went off in Tristan's head. The last old flame he made contact with almost slept with him over relationship problems. Maybe Randy was her boss or something? *Not likely.* Tristan decided to take the bait, he didn't have the energy to do anything else.

"Who is Randy?"

"My boyfriend. It's my fault really, but, god I'm a mess."

Figures. Worse than the warning bells was the jealousy he felt. He had always thought of Adrienne as his, ever since she expressed feelings for him. She was so steadfast, so loyal. Tristan figured a lot could change in three years. And realistically, he expected her to be angry, but he hadn't prepared himself for the fact that she could have moved on and found a new man.

"Oh yeah…" Tristan tried hard to sound like he cared about Randy, but it was difficult through clenched teeth. "so uhhh, what happened?"

"Oh nothing really, I guess. I dunno. Nothing different than usual. He seems to care about me, but we still manage to fight. God, I'm sorry. This is so embarrassing."

"I don't really know what to say. Maybe you should talk to him about all of this. I really don't know what to say." Tristan hated repeating himself but he was at a loss for words. He felt awkward and wished he had called earlier, or later, whatever time saved him from the awkward scenario.

Adrienne took a breath, he heard it clearly. "You're right, Tristan. Let's say I call you back when I've calmed down. I'd love to have a real conversation with you." She sounded much more like herself.

"Sounds good. And Adrienne?"

"Yes?"

"Don't forget, ok?"

"I won't." She sounded mildly amused. "Bye Tristan."

Tristan hung up and wiped his forehead. If felt as though he'd been in a boxing match. The conversation was one hell of a roller coaster ride. It hadn't matched up with the movie he had created in his mind—the one where Adrienne answered the phone and professed her love, still burning, after all those years. Instead, Tristan heard a new side of her—one that gave him doubts as to whether or not she was stable—and learned she was already in a relationship.

Still, it couldn't have gone much worse.

Chapter Thirty

Adrienne sounded much better the next few times they *talked*, it might have helped that most of them were via Facebook. Tristan loved to type much more than he loved to talk. Things could be difficult to understand sometimes without hearing the persons tone or seeing their expressions, but Tristan was much braver without those variables as well. Things were said over the computer that would never be said in person or even on the phone.

Tristan and Adrienne reminisced a lot about high school. 'What ifs' abounded. Tristan usually dropped hints that he wished they had of dated, and Adrienne agreed. But Tristan would only go so far with his advances. He did not want to be too forward with a girl who was spoken for, even if it was Adrienne. She didn't talk about Randy much, which Tristan thought odd. He figured this was just a sign of her unhappiness. Anyone he had encountered who had a good relationship normally had trouble *not* talking about the person they were with—to the point where it got annoying.

Based on her Facebook photos, Adrienne looked the same. She was so gorgeous. Tristan remembered very clearly the day they shared at La Senza. It was the hottest thing that had ever happened to him. He felt twinges of jealousy every time he imagined the romantic, physical times they had together. He had missed his chance. He tried not to hope for the end of her current relationship, but he couldn't help it. He hoped for it each time they spoke. Unfortunately, it had been a month, and still no news of a break up.

Tristan asked Adrienne about Ryan, and she passed over the question with a smooth deflection. She told him that he was doing well, struggling with his academics a bit, but rumour had it that professors favoured him anyhow. That was the only information he could pry from her on the subject. She sounded cautious and awkward every time he asked about Ryan. He figured she found it uncomfortable being the liaison between friends who had grown apart.

Adrienne agreed to hang out with him the first weekend she was home. They planned to get some coffee and catch up in person. Even though they had been talking daily for over a month, they had yet to see one another. Randy lived out of province and would be gone all summer. Tristan saw this as both a blessing and a curse. He wouldn't be around to piss her off so they probably wouldn't break up, but at least he wouldn't be breathing down Tristan's neck. Tristan could essentially make himself boyfriend *number two* without the physical perks—which was most unfortunate.

The day of the reunion, Tristan made sure he woke up at a decent hour so he could clean his apartment and groom. After hours of work, he realized that Adrienne may not agree to come back with him. She could have had other plans or simply feel uncomfortable being alone with him. Tristan tried to banish these thoughts from his mind as they just made him angry. He turned his attention to grooming and made sure his head was cleanly shaven and hair was trimmed in all the right places, just in case. He had grown out a very short beard that he thought contrasted nicely with his bald head. Tristan thought it made him more ruggedly handsome, a trait most girls seemed to like.

Tristan took one last look in the mirror to ensure he was presentable, tilted his hat to the right, and departed for his rendezvous with Adrienne. He took one step out the door when he saw Amy walking towards him. He smiled at her, and she smiled back. He didn't have time for small talk, he would be late. Whatever Amy wanted would have to wait. He opened his mouth to tell her so when he noticed her holding up her left hand. He was confused at first until he saw the glint of diamond. He felt his jaw drop, and his mind went blank. *It can't be an engagement ring. She and Bryan have only been dating three months.*

She leaped on top of him, "I'm engaged!"

Then again...

She hung off Tristan's lifeless body. He forced himself to lift one arm to embrace her. Was she insane? She hardly knew him! Every pre-emptive engagement cliché he ever heard threatened to spill from his mouth. He settled for a much more conventional approach.

"Wow, Congrats."

"Tristan?" She let him go so she could look at him, "You don't sound very excited."

"You uhhh. You just caught me at a bad time, that's all."

She accepted that answer, reluctantly.

"Oh really? I should have called I guess." Her smile returned. "But I was just so happy! I had to tell you first."

Her flattery didn't change that fact that Tristan thought she was insane.

Maybe she was just really really drunk.

"He just proposed over lunch like..." she looked at her cell, "twenty minutes ago!"

There goes that theory.

If she had just gotten engaged twenty minutes ago what was she doing talking to him? He figured if people were recently engaged they would spend time together, but what did he know? Everything he thought he knew over the years turned out to be completely wrong, so why should this be any different? He put on his best fake smile and hugged her.

"I promise I'll call you as soon as I get back and you can tell me all about it. Ok?"

The classic line seemed to appease her, and she leapt back into his arms for a farewell hug. "Don't you dare forget, Tristan! Or you won't be invited to the wedding!"

What the hell?

"Oh, I won't forget. See you!"

Tristan fought the urge to vomit as they parted ways. He knew jealousy was dominating his emotional feedback, but he didn't want to admit it. A couple of months ago he had almost hooked up with Amy, and now she was engaged? He was not prepared for her to be off the market, he hadn't finished deciding if *he* wanted her or not. He also hated the prospect—no matter how unlikely—that the whole thing could work out for her. Where was *his* happy ending?

Tristan put up a psychological barrier to combat the information he had recently been given. He entered the Starbucks and found Adrienne in no time. She hopped up as soon as she saw him. She was the second girl to hang off of him that day, but her embrace felt much different, warmer, more affectionate. She looked just how Tristan remembered. Her chocolate brown hair was cut sharply and framed her face. Her dark, sultry eyes were the perfect complement to her exotic features and her body was inviting. Tristan had trouble looking away from her chest. She wore a low cut top, it was hard to force his eyes upward.

Tristan was reluctant to let her go, and hoped his cling factor was not too noticeable. She smiled knowingly at him, but pushed him away gently. They took their seats and Tristan was still fighting to catch his breath, for the first time he found her beauty intimidating.

"Tristan, you look amazing." She said with a slight shake of her head.

Their physical attraction hadn't lost any of its potency.

"You do too, truly." He replied honestly.

Three Words

She grinned at him. She had never been shy. She leaned over the small table.

"So, are you going to buy me coffee?"

"You want something with a little more kick to it?" He was impressed with his playful response. Her eyes were almost impossible to look away from.

"Tristan, alcohol this early in the day?" her tone matched his playful intent.

He prayed she would accept his offer even if he was only half serious. Something to take the edge off would be greatly appreciated. He had to play his cards right.

"Just a social drink, of course, to celebrate our little reunion"

She was intentionally overdramatic as she shifted back and forth in her chair considering his offer.

"Alright Tristan. Just one. I don't need you taking advantage of me."

They talked and laughed as they changed venues. When they arrived at the pub Tristan sat them down at his regular table and pulled Adrienne's chair for her. She smiled and accepted the gesture gratefully. Tristan sat down across from her and tried to hide the fear he could feel rising inside of him. He fooled around with both of the waitresses on duty. Tristan suddenly realized it was a huge mistake to bring her to *this* pub, to *his* pub. Sure people knew him, but the majority of the staff was female! *Things were going to get tricky.*

"Tristan!" He moved his hand in front of his face in a lame attempt to disappear.

"Hi Candace, how are you?" Tristan replied as calmly as possible. Candace was a nice girl, but lacked an oral filter. Tristan was gripped with fear.

"So nice to see you back! It's been a while" Tristan shifted his eyes to Adrienne who didn't seem the slightest bit thrown off by the appearance of the busty red head.

"Last time I saw you…"

Oh Shit.

Adrienne was grinning with anticipation. She was enjoying his discomfort.

"...you were asleep beside me." She laughed and slapped him on the back.

Who says that stuff in public? Tristan was mortified.

"Yeah well, I had to get to class the next morning..." Panic gripped every fibre of his being.

"I'm just busting your balls, Trist," Candace said with a grin. "We both knew what it was all about. Who is your friend?"

Tristan introduced the girls and placed their order. When Candace finally showed some mercy and walked away, Adrienne spoke.

"Nice girl." She sipped her beer and peered at Tristan as she drank. Her sarcasm was apparent.

"She uhhh..."

"Oh Tristan, I'm not angry. I have a boyfriend remember?"

Don't remind me. And the hits just keep on comin'.

"Besides, I think it is cute how uncomfortable you were. I always knew you would snap out of your man whore phase. You were one of the good guys."

Her comments made him want to jump for joy and slit his wrists all at the same time. She obviously still thought highly of him, but had to mention her dipshit boyfriend at the same time. Tristan reached for his beer.

"Let's not go there. We must have more interesting things to talk about than my personal struggles." He said, attempting to deflect the conversation somewhere more enjoyable.

She smirked. God he liked her mouth. "I'm sure we can find something, Mr. Cage. Any ideas?"

Tristan had a bunch. Unfortunately they all involved things boyfriends may disapprove of.

"I do, but Randy may take exception."

Daring.

She ran her tongue across her bottom lip.

"Randy's not here, is he?"

Fireworks were going off, and his body was having a party. Had he heard that correctly? Tristan had to stop himself from getting too carried away. The devil on his left shoulder was screaming at him to push the envelope, but the aggravating angel on his right shoulder was louder.

"What's he up to today?"

Cage, you don't deserve a penis.

He expected Adrienne to look insulted, or at least disappointed, but she just shook her head without losing her smile.

"Same old Tristan."

They spent the next hour chatting about any random thing that came to their minds. They laughed and enjoyed each other's company without the aid of intoxication. Tristan soaked up every second of her attention. He hadn't realized how much he missed her, or perhaps subconsciously he knew and wouldn't allow himself to admit it. He simply hadn't been in a place that would allow him to commit.

Tristan invited Adrienne back to his place for a visit and she accepted. There wasn't much to see in Tristan's tiny apartment, and the tour was short lived. Tristan wasn't ready for her to leave so he proposed they watch a movie. She agreed happily almost before he finished the question. Tristan chose *The Girl Next Door*, it was one of his favourites. The two sat next to one another on Tristan's couch, but not too close; they were a friendly distance apart. Adrienne had never seen the movie before and suffered fits of laughter throughout. It may have been the body rocking humour of the film, or just her excuse, but she gradually made her way closer to Tristan. He noticed increasing proximity and did his best to accommodate her by not moving away. The resolve he showed earlier was fading fast.

By the end of the movie her hand found its way up the back of his shirt. Her nails were lightly scratching his back. It felt sensational. He tried to get rid of the images of her scratching him more passionately on his bed, but it wasn't going well. His blood was boiling. As soon as the credits rolled, he turned in her direction. Tristan's heart beat convincingly against his chest. Passion threatened to rule the moment.

The fingernails on his back dug deeper. Adrienne's dark eyes lost none of their potency in the dimly lit room. She searched his face for a sign of what he was feeling, but he figured it spoke for itself. The urge to kiss her was taking over his motor control. He tried to move his left hand up towards her face, but it found her breast instead. He paused, he never hesitated, but he did then. He pulled his hand away but she put it right back.

"It has always been you, Tristan." she said.

She moved to kiss him, but he turned his head to the side. Tristan felt something tear inside of him.

Fuck my life. What was stopping him?

She had a boyfriend, and Tristan didn't know how he felt about Amy's engagement. He made so many impulsive decisions in the past, he could not let this be another. If he and Adrienne kissed, or more, their relationship—if it even developed into one out of the impending chaos—would be born of mistakes and doubt. Tristan had to put his selfishness aside for once. He cared about Adrienne, more than he cared about anyone still living, and he could not allow her to make a mistake.

He couldn't see her, but he knew his action spoke volumes. He felt the pain in her eyes without experiencing her gaze first hand. It was the second time he burnt her, and it would likely have catastrophic consequences. She squeezed his hand to reassure him that would not be the case. A tear ran down Tristan's face, but he refused to let her see it. When she spoke, her tone was a mixture of sadness and regret.

"Someday," she said softly, "we will be in the same place, Tristan. I know how badly you wanted me tonight. I could feel it. I'm sorry I put you in this position. I'll go now."

Tristan desperately wanted to speak, but kept his head in his hands, staring at the floor. Words, which he always put so much faith in, hung soundless on his lips. He felt her moving away, and she took his hand for a moment.

Tristan held onto her until physics disallowed their contact. His eyes were still fixed on the floor when he heard the door shut behind her. The unspoken words still ringing in his head:

Please, don't go.

Chapter Thirty-One

Tristan called Amy the next day, as promised, but feigned illness. He didn't feel like talking to her about her engagement when he had allowed his happiness to walk out his door the night before. Amy bought his lie and offered to come over and nurse him, but he told her to stay away in case it was contagious. He promised to get together with her as soon as he felt better. They said their goodbyes and Tristan plopped down at his computer and called up Facebook to see what was happening with everyone else. He welcomed drama from someone else's life to make him feel better about his own.

Alec—Doesn't know who he wants to win the Title.

Uninteresting.

Amy—So Happy!

Tristan stifled the urge to throw up on his keyboard and kept looking.

Emma—Had an amazing night with my boy (<3)

What the hell?

What boy? Since when did Emma have a boy? Who was this boy, and where did he come from? Why didn't Tristan know about him? He wanted to call his sister and interrogate her, but he calmed himself down. Her name indicated that she was happy, and that would just piss Tristan off more. He was in no state to talk to anyone, especially family members who could become emotional punching bags. Was he the only person who was miserable?

He continued searching the news feed for a fellow downer.

Adrienne—You're Everything.

Sweet Fuck. Ok, so maybe scanning his Facebook was a bad idea. The last thing he needed to see was Adrienne's mushy sentiments about her relationship. Tristan pushed the power button like he was trying to put his finger through it. He dropped his head onto the desk with a *thud*.

For as long as he could remember, Tristan had difficulty prioritizing emotions. He had strong feelings for Adrienne that he couldn't act on. That was probably the biggest obstacle, but it also had the easiest solution. She was taken and that was that. He couldn't believe his baby sister had a boyfriend—even though she *was* in grade twelve—and he hadn't known about it. Maybe his parents hadn't known either? He would just have to talk to Emma and see what was going on. Finally, he hated that Amy was engaged. He had been working on a whole set of feelings concerning her for the last couple months. He didn't know whether or not they could get together because of Deanna, or because of their friendship, but now it didn't matter because she was betrothed.

Tristan had no problem when Amy started dating Bryan; dating was fine, but an engagement? Three months was *not* long enough to know if you wanted to spend your life with someone or not. Tristan was fairly sure that it wasn't jealousy that bothered him most, but her poor decision-making. He picked up the phone and told Amy he was on his way over.

Amy hugged him as he entered her box-sized dorm room. There were pictures everywhere, most were of her and Bryan, but he saw a few of himself and Deanna too. He sat down on her bed and she splashed down next to him. She put her feet on his lap and laid down anxiously awaiting the conversation. Tristan took a deep breath, checked over his 'speech' and began.

"Amy, I'm happy if you are happy," *So cliché*. "but I think that you may be moving too fast here…"

Nothing like jumping in head first jackass!

Amy's features hardened, and she frowned at him. Tristan struggled to explain himself.

"…I mean, why do you need to be engaged? Or married? If you are happy with him that's awesome, but why can't you do that dating for a while?"

It was obviously not what Amy had expected and she pulled her feet off him and sat cross legged on the bed. She shook her head slightly.

"You sure know how to rain on a girl's parade, Tristan."

He was panicking. Amy continued sternly.

"I love Bryan. If you love someone, why not marry them?" she said, sounding convinced.

Tristan stared at her. She sounded like someone in preschool.

"Did you love, Ryan? How about that guy you dated from out of province before him?"

She frowned. "That was different."

"How so?" Tristan's passion was taking over. "I have been *in love* too Amy. We both know things can change. I'm not saying not to marry him, eventually. I'm just saying don't marry him so fast!"

She was angry, but he couldn't really understand why. "I already got this lecture from my parents Tristan! I thought that I could count on my friends support, but I guess not."

"Amy for God's sake, please listen. I'm not trying to—"

"I should have known better, though. It's obvious you are jealous, Tristan. You had your chance with me and every other girl on campus. Don't take it out on me because you are commitment phobic."

That stung.

Tristan took off his hat and ran his hand over his bald head. He glanced at Amy and her eyes were misted with tears.

"This isn't about me, Amy."

"Oh Tristan," she said. Her anger was fierce. "This isn't one of your movies, this is real life. Don't feed me that bullshit. This is as much about you as it is about me. Ever since D died you have hated relationships and anyone who was happy in one. I just figured I would be an exception, after all we've been through."

That really wasn't it. Tristan knew it would come off that way, but he had tried to avoid this. He tried to be honest.

"I think I should go—"

"Go ahead, Tristan. Run away, but don't expect me to call."

Tristan felt a little guilty, but he didn't think he deserved the barrage he was getting. He was leaving before he lost his temper too. That wouldn't help matters at all. Tristan looked back at a still irate Amy and left her room. She slammed the door behind him. Tristan needed a drink. He flipped open his phone and called Alec.

They got to the Eagle's Nest at 8PM. Tristan got his normal table, and a few of the other guys they played ball with came and went. The night was going great. Tristan even *watched* the drinking contest for once, and he was keeping his hands to himself. Everyone at Tristan's table was laughing and having a ball until about midnight when he caught a glimpse of Bryan, Amy's fiancé. He was on the dance floor with a girl who was definitely *not* Amy.

From the look of things, Bryan was behaving himself, but Tristan knew about the football team's reputation. They were far from one-woman guys. With one eye on Bryan, and the other on his drink, Tristan got back into the conversation at his table. After twenty minutes or so there was no sign of Amy, and Bryan had left the dance floor with his *friend*—she was sitting on his lap at a table about ten feet away. Tristan had *both* eyes on Bryan now.

Tristan ignored the people talking to him as he zoomed in on Bryan.

Tristan's eyes widened. *There's no way he is ballsy enough to—*

The moment he saw the big bastard kiss his random play-thing, Tristan was out of his chair. His body language must have implied mischief because he heard Alec call his name.

Three Words

"Tristan!"

Tristan ignored his concerned side kick.

He cocked his fist back and belted Bryan in the side of the head.

Bryan stood up and shook his head. He just smiled at Tristan for he knew he had the advantage. *Uh oh*, thought Tristan. Bryan motioned for his boys to move back as a circle was made around the combatants. Tristan clenched his fists. His heart was beating a mile a minute, but he wasn't scared. He knew he would probably lose, but he was going down swinging. There was nothing for the two to say to each other, so they just got down to business.

Bryan came at him swinging, but Tristan was much faster. He was able to move and land a good shot to Bryan's kidney, but it didn't faze the much larger man. Bryan turned back around and swung hard at Tristan's head. Tristan was able to get an arm on it, but it still did damage. Tristan tried to shake the cobwebs, but before he could, he got hit again. This one knocked him to the floor. On one knee, he closed his eyes waiting to be rendered unconscious.

But before the blow came, Tristan heard a sickening smack over the cheers and music. The weight of Bryan's suddenly limp form drove the air from his lungs.

What the…?

Pinned to the floor, Tristan struggled. There was shouting, angry voices, and Bryan's unconscious body was pulled off of him. Tristan was helped to his feet by a familiar face. He tried to hide the shock, and conflicting emotions that gripped him.

There was no time to say thank you, or scream at his long lost friend, because the brawl was all around them.

Chapter Thirty-Two

Tristan had never been in a bar fight before, but he thought he held his own pretty well. Ryan was just the way Tristan remembered him, a bull. The two combatants left with bumps and bruises. On the walk home they sounded like kids remembering a boxing match. Each had their favourite moment of the night, and there was a general air of excitement. Nobody felt the least bit guilty for having a go at the football players.

Ryan stayed the night at Tristan's and they agreed to catch up the next day. To say he was surprised to see his old friend would be an understatement. Ryan didn't seem like an asshole at all. It was a complete metamorphosis from the last time they talked. Ryan was exactly the way Tristan remembered him before he moved to Winchester. He was certainly curious about how Ryan came to appear at the Eagle's Nest, but fatigue was quickly taking over Tristan's senses.

Ryan's phone rang at 9AM the next morning. Tristan woke to hear him talking cordially to whoever was on the other end. The conversation seemed more like business than pleasure. Tristan rolled out of bed with a splitting headache. He couldn't tell if it was the result of a hangover, or post-brawl consequences. He figured it was probably a little of both. He made his way to the bathroom where he pulled out some Advil. He offered some to Ryan who respectfully declined with a slight shake of his head.

Tristan sat at the edge of his bed and smiled at his friend.

"So, why the hell were you at the Eagle's Nest?"

Ryan grinned and took a sip of water.

"I have some things to take care of here. I moved home for the summer. A lot has happened, Tristan."

Ryan informed Tristan that his father had passed around Christmas time. Tristan had no idea and he tried to interrupt to let Ryan know that, but Ryan quieted him by holding up his hand. Ryan reassured him that he held no hard feelings. Of course, Tristan hadn't known because they hadn't spoken in so long. Ryan realized that a lot of the friends he had at Winchester weren't friends at all. They didn't give a damn about how he felt about anything except sports and girls. He hated the atmosphere he built around himself and missed the company of friends who actually cared, especially Tristan.

Ryan was very close to his father and he struggled with school second semester. He almost dropped out because he couldn't cope. As soon as exams were over he moved back to Milton to help out his mother. He sought Tristan out, but Tristan didn't answer his calls. Ryan heard that Tristan was a regular at the Eagle's Nest and decided to try his luck there. He hadn't seen Tristan the first night he went, but lucked out and saw him the next. Tristan smiled at his good fortune. Lucky, or he'd have a broken jaw from Bryan's huge mitt.

"To make a long story short Tristan, I've been an ass. I know I have, and I'm sorry," he said, head lowered.

"It's ok, big fella." Tristan replied earnestly, "I'm just glad you finally came around. We make a great team."

Ryan grinned and gave him a *man hug*. Tristan thought Ryan was even stronger that he had been, which seem scarcely possible. After some sorted conversation, and lots of laughter, Ryan agreed to come in on weekends to hang out and make amends. Over lunch, Tristan told Ryan all about Amy's situation. The information made Ryan look ill. Tristan told his friend that he planned

Three Words

on confronting Amy, and at first, Ryan wanted to go, but Tristan talked sense into him. There was no way Amy would be happy to see Tristan, let alone Ryan.

Tristan didn't bother calling before he went over. Amy probably wouldn't have answered it anyway. He hoped he could make her see reason, but he was also prepared for the nuclear explosion that could take place when she saw him. It took him twenty minutes banging on her door to get an answer. Not a good sign.

Eventually, she cracked the door and peered at him.

"What do you want?" Her tone was not friendly.

"We need to talk," he said. "Really, please let me in."

"Why should I, Tristan? You have more bombs to drop?"

"Actually I do. You really need to let me in Amy."

The look in her eyes changed. They suddenly became more panicked. She opened the door reluctantly, and he walked in.

"What happened to your face, Tristan?"

"I got in a fight," he said hesitantly, "With Bryan and his crew."

"What?" Her eyes gleamed red. She was about to begin an angry tirade when Tristan continued.

"It's not what you think. I saw him with another girl, and I snapped."

Disbelief and confusion marred her pretty face. "You're lying."

Tristan understood the situation was volatile. He proceeded with extreme caution. "Amy, I'm not lying. There must have been a hundred people who saw the same thing I did, especially after I brought it to the pub's attention. I wanted to be the one to tell you before you heard it from someone else."

Tears ran down her face, her resolve broken. "He's my fiancé, Tristan!" She dropped to the floor and Tristan knelt beside her.

"I know Amy, I'm sorry." He didn't know what else to say—*I told you so*, probably wouldn't have helped.

He tried to hug her a few times, but she kept pushing him away. "I know you Tristan," she sobbed, "you love that you were right about him. No wonder he didn't call me! I didn't even know he was at the bar." This time she let him hold her. He rocked her like a baby for what seemed like forever. When she finally stopped crying she looked at him.

"Tell me you won," she sad, sniffling.

"I did, but I had some help." He couldn't hide his grin. "I have some more news, but you may want to wait to hear it."

"What's the difference, Tristan? The sky has already fallen on me today. Just tell me."

Here it goes.

"Ryan helped me. He's back."

Amy stared at him blankly for about thirty seconds. When she finally reacted, Tristan couldn't tell if she was going to throw up, or pass out. He hoped that is was the latter. She stood up slowly with one arm stretched out for him to hold on to. She took two steps toward the door and collapsed in his arms.

"Tristan," she managed to say, "anything else?"

He grabbed her hand. Her morbid humour actually made him feel better about things. Once he had her situated, he squeezed her hand and told her to call if she needed anything. He asked if she had a message for Ryan, but she just glared at him in response. Tristan left as Amy was giving Bryan the tongue lashing of a lifetime over the phone. The only words he could identify clearly were, 'fuck,' 'prick,' and 'asshole.' Despite being the bearer of bad news, he couldn't help but smile.

Ryan turned pale when Tristan told him what happened. He was petrified to speak to her when she was already angry. He knew he had to face her wrath sooner or later, but figured it was best if he waited a while—maybe forever. They both felt for Amy, but they saw the events as a blessing in disguise. Better to find out what a jackass Bryan was sooner than later.

Ryan wanted to know all about Tristan's exploits since he got to Saint Agnus. Some things he had heard about, like his career ending injury and man whoring, but he wanted to know the good things. Tristan filled him in the best he could on the last three years of his life. Ryan listened intently until Adrienne came up. As soon as Tristan said her name, Ryan looked uncomfortable.

"You don't like Adrienne?" Tristan asked. "You always did before. You thought she was hot if nothing else."

"No, I like her Tristan. It's nothing really."

"Come one man, I know you better than that. I really like this girl, is there something I should know?"

Ryan's hesitation didn't help Tristan anxiety. Ryan was staring at the floor.

Tristan laughed nervously, "Come on man—"

Ryan's phone was on the night stand and started vibrating. Ryan jumped to answer it but the name of the caller was easy to see.

Adrienne Axley.

What the fuck?

Ryan swallowed hard. His eyes met Tristan's reluctantly.

"Ryan?"

"She didn't want you to find out. She didn't even want us talking, it scared her so bad, it's why I had to find you. I had to tell you—"

"Find out what for fuck sakes!?" Tristan felt like he was going to spontaneously combust. He was losing patience. Ryan turned off his phone and sat on the couch.

"I have to tell you something, Tristan. And you aren't going to like it."

Chapter Thirty-Three

Tristan threw Ryan out in a passionate rage. He didn't care how rational his anger was or if it was even warranted; all he knew was that Ryan had to go. If what he told him was true—and he had no reason to doubt that it wasn't—Tristan was yet again foiled when it came to love. Tristan had to get answers as to why he was cursed. Maybe his ancestors pissed off some witches, or maybe he was in a coma and this was all a figment of his imagination, but something was seriously wrong when it came to Tristan Cage and the opposite sex.

The issue was too personal to talk to the guys about, and Tristan wasn't prepared to sully Adrienne's name. He couldn't talk to Amy about it—no way—and he just sent Ryan away. He needed to talk to someone. He called Rachel and asked her to come over on the double. She must have been able to sense the desperation in his voice because she told him she'd be over on her lunch break. She showed up promptly at noon to find Tristan motionless on his couch. She took her shoes off and rushed to sit next to him.

"Tristan, obviously you are far from ok. What is going on?"

Tristan wondered where to start. He couldn't find a suitable place, so he just let it out.

"My former best friend, who is now my best friend again slept with the girl I thought I could love while he wasn't my best friend. He got this girl pregnant and he broke up with his girlfriend, who was also a dear friend, because he didn't know what they were going to do about the baby. Once they decided to abort it, both their lives were flipped upside down. One rebounded to a complete asshole for comfort while the other became an asshole himself. To make matters worse, I had already been semi-involved with this girl at one point, and they both seemed to forget about my existence during the event and in trying to cover it up afterward."

Rachel stared at him like he had a terminal disease. "Ryan got Adrienne pregnant?"

It was amazing how girls could decipher and condense even the most complex emotional catastrophes. Tristan nodded. He was shocked at how bluntly she put it, but was too depressed to show any emotion. Rachel took his hand.

"Yes. He did. Over two years ago. At least he had the courage to tell me, Adrienne wanted to keep it from me forever."

"Well, were they together?"

"No," Tristan said. "It was a drunken one night stand. Obviously I didn't matter much to either of them. All it took was a little booze to make my memory disappear."

Rachel frowned at his cynicism. "Tristan, you hadn't spoken to Adrienne since the funeral which was when? December that year?"

"Yeah, so?" Tristan didn't like where this was going.

"Well, when did this happen?" she asked, urging him carefully.

"November of first year apparently."

She nodded her head as if her secret question had been answered. "Tristan, Adrienne hadn't heard from you in almost a year. She had no reason to believe that *you* hadn't forgotten *her*. Besides, your sexcapades were hot news as well."

Tristan hadn't thought about that. A year was a long time to wait for someone, especially if you hadn't been given a time frame for how long you'd be waiting. Tristan dropped his head. As angry as he was, he couldn't find any flaws in Rachel's argument.

"And Ryan," Rachel said, "always had a thing for Adrienne. That doesn't excuse him from making a mistake, as he was still with Amy, but he was the one who faced his demons and told you. That must have been really hard."

Rachel's compassion for the two heartbreakers made Tristan fidget, but again, she had a point. Ryan had been jittery, nervous, even scared when he was telling Tristan what happened. He was under specific instructions *not* to tell Tristan under any circumstances, but did the right thing by being honest. Tristan cupped his hand and dragged it over his face. Ryan did a very grown up thing by risking his rekindled friendship for honesty.

Rachel's Oprah moment continued. "And as far as the abortion goes, they obviously didn't mean to get pregnant, it was an accident and their choice to make. The abortion you can't be angry about because it's nobody's business but theirs."

Had Rachel always been this smart?

"I'm not excusing any of the pain you are feeling Tristan, it is brutal for sure, but I just don't think anger is the right emotion. Anger will do nothing but make this situation worse. If you want to hurt, hurt. But don't withdraw your feelings for Adrienne based on this. It wouldn't be fair. Does Amy know any of this?"

Tristan shook his head.

"That is probably best, especially with what she is going through already. She is the one who could justify anger. Ryan cheated on her. This whole thing brought an end to her relationship while she was miles away. Amy will be livid over this. Some things are better left unsaid."

Rachel leaned back on the couch like she had expended mass amounts of energy. Tristan peered at her out of the corner of his eye. He obviously made the right phone call. As much as he wanted to be pissed, he couldn't be if he wanted to be a decent guy. He would have to talk to Adrienne about everything, civilly, and apologize to Ryan for throwing him out.

Rachel hugged Tristan and gave him a quick kiss on the cheek. "Wanna come over for drinks this weekend? Kyle and I both have some time off."

"Sure." Tristan was still pouting, but she left it alone.

"Ok babe. See you then, I have to get back to work."

And just like that, Rachel was gone as quickly as she came. – *Poof*– like a fairy-god-friend.

The first call he made was to Ryan who sounded relieved to hear from him. He assured Tristan that there were no hard feelings for kicking him out. He joked that he had to get home anyway. Tristan was glad that things went so smoothly with Ryan because he had a nasty feeling that his next call would be much more difficult.

As he dialled Adrienne's number he reminded himself of all the points Rachel had made in her favour. Tristan was just as much to blame for the way he was feeling as she was. He also told himself that going through an abortion must have been more painful than words, and he didn't want to make it seem like he didn't care about that.

Adrienne picked up on the first quarter of a ring. It was like she was sitting next to the phone.

"Tristan, Oh my god I can explain—" She sounded so desperate.

"Hold on, Adrienne. I think we should do this in person. I'm not mad. I was, but I'm not anymore. I just think we should do this face to face."

There was a long pause. He thought he could hear her crying.

"Ok, Tristan. When do you want to get together?"

"Is tonight ok?" he breathed.

"Just tell me when to be there."

Adrienne agreed to meet him at seven. Tristan showered and mentally prepared himself for what was to come. He spent the minutes waiting for Adrienne playing online video games to keep his mind busy. He didn't want his classic over-analysis to infect him. When the door buzzer sounded, he jumped.

Adrienne looked fantastic, stunning. She hugged him close when she came in and Tristan felt conflicting emotions. He couldn't get the images of her and Ryan out of his mind. Jealousy was nasty, but it was a lot worse when you had an imagination as active as Tristan's.

They sat facing one another on the couch and Adrienne started to cry right away. Tristan tried to calm her down, but it was no use. He would just have to wait for her to compose herself. Adrienne was proud, and it didn't take her long. Moments later she was poised and in control of her emotions.

"It was a mistake Tristan. A horrible mistake. I was angry with you for cutting me out of your life, and I had other stuff going on too. I'm sorry."

Tristan felt her sincerity, but also her desperation. He could tell she cared about him very much.

"I know. I was a huge prick, we all know that. What I don't understand is how this all happened. I am close to very few people these days, and it seems like all of them are affected by this." He paused, then said, "But I was only interested in dating one of them."

Adrienne's lower lip quivered when he said the last part.

"I have been living with the guilt for a long time, Tristan, long before we started talking again. I'll always wonder who that child would have been. I'll always wonder if I committed a crime that can't be forgiven. Despite the mess of feelings, Tristan, the thing that scares me most is how it affects you and me."

Tristan tried to keep cool, but he couldn't. Tears were threatening to show themselves in his deep green eyes. "It scares me too." He closed his eyes hard to clear the blurry mess they had become.

Valiantly, Adrienne continued, "I've been with Randy going on three years Tristan. He is a great guy, but something is missing" She paused, "He caught me at a vulnerable moment, and I haven't been able to break away from him. Every day I wish he was you Tristan. I have always loved you."

Her hand gripped his, pleading with him to reconsider what she knew was coming, but it wasn't to be.

Tristan wanted desperately to seize the chance, the moment he'd been waiting for, but he simply couldn't do it. It wasn't right.

"Adrienne. This can't happen, especially now. I will never turn my back on you again, but I will not be the reason your relationship ends. If you decide to end things with Randy it needs to be on your terms, for your reasons, and then you need to heal. Three years is a long time. I also need to figure out how I feel about all of this. It hurts that you didn't tell me, you had lots of time and opportunity. I understand that you were scared, but Ryan was too. If it had of been you that told me, things might be easier."

The grip on his hand got tighter and Adrienne was shaking her head.

"The way you look at me, Adrienne, the way we are together, the way you make me feel is amazing, but it is not our time. I don't know if it ever will be." He paused.

Tristan tried to speak again, to fill the void, but she kissed him, long and hard. He didn't want it to end. He knew when it did, their lips may never touch again.

When she released him. She whispered three words to him he wouldn't soon forget. "You're my everything." As he watched her leave, his face a mess of tears and revelation, Tristan realized that her Facebook status was referring to him, not Randy, the entire time.

Chapter Thirty-Four

At the end of June, Matt Staunton and Lacey Connor, old friends of Tristan's, were getting married. Everyone was invited, and it was a guaranteed good time. Amy and Ryan still hadn't talked, and they were both invited. Adrienne was invited as were Rachel, Tristan, and Emma. The wedding would be held in Sageview, at Lacey's parents. A good ol' fashion Barn Party disguised as a wedding. Tristan grimaced as he thought about the group of invites. The barn party could quickly turn into a barn burning.

Tristan's fears worsened when he got his formal invitation. "Tristan Cage and Guest." That probably meant that all the invitations were labeled as such, which then meant that if everyone chose to attend they could have dates with them as well. *Randy would definitely be attending with Adrienne.* The prospects were a nightmare, but Tristan couldn't skip his friends' wedding.

He talked to Ryan about it, and he was nervous too. He didn't think he would take a date, so as to not make things more awkward with Amy.

"I can't take a date man. I'll be lucky if she talks to me anyways."

"What if *she* brings a date?"

Ryan's face dropped, "Oh my god what if she *does* bring a date? I can't look like I couldn't get a date."

Tristan shrugged. "I really think that's a chance you're going to have to take."

Ryan shook his head, "Has she said anything to you about me?"

Tristan chuckled, "Only that she's glad you're alive, but that's as much as she cares to know about you."

"Shit, man, that's harsh," he said, dejected.

"Amy is harsh," Tristan replied matter-of-factly, "you of all people should know that."

"Why do you think I'm so fucking scared of this wedding?"

Tristan started to laugh and Ryan scowled at him. The scowl just made Tristan laugh harder and soon Ryan joined in. They were both in impossible situations; all they could do was laugh.

Tristan didn't know if he should take a date either. Adrienne would have to take Randy, they were together, and that was what couples did. They went to weddings and cheesy family gatherings. They did shit together. It made Tristan green with envy. Tristan certainly didn't want to sit and look at them be couple-y all night. Randy must know about him, unless Adrienne hadn't told him anything, and that would just make things more awkward. Not to mention that he would be with Ryan, who Randy *had* to know about. The list of possible complications was too long to comprehend. It was a good thing he had a new plan for decision making.

He stared at the coin in his hand. *Heads*, he took a date; *tails*, he went solo. He said a silent prayer before flipping the coin into the air. He watched its slow motion rotations in anticipation. It landed gently in the palm of his hand. Tristan closed his eyes as he slapped the coin onto the top of his left hand.

Heads.

—

Callie was overjoyed at the invitation. Her enthusiasm actually helped get Tristan excited over the event for the first time. She told him she was going dress shopping and wanted recommendations. Tristan told her anything blue. She looked incredible in blue.

The day of the wedding came at warp speed, and Tristan hadn't heard from Adrienne. He didn't know if she was going or if she would be taking Randy. Amy and Ryan spoke briefly so that there wouldn't be any unpleasant surprises at someone else's wedding. Amy told Ryan, in no uncertain terms, to keep his distance until she was prepared to deal with him. Ryan didn't argue. He knew Amy better than most.

Ryan, Tristan, Amy, and Callie all spent the night before the wedding at Tristan's. Amy didn't like the idea of being under the same roof as Ryan so soon, but Tristan assured her they could sleep on separate floors, and could even eat in separate rooms. The Cage's had two bathrooms so they wouldn't even have to get ready together. Amy accepted these terms and held Tristan to every letter.

Callie was more excited to be invited to Tristan's parents than she was about the wedding. He wanted to tell her it wasn't a *meet the parents* moment, but didn't want to burst her bubble. Ryan kept giving Tristan all kinds of winks, nudges, and grins when Callie would say things like, "What a nice view up on this hill!" or, "Tristan your house is gorgeous!" Tristan lived on a mound more so than a hill, and the only thing you could see were the trees in the front yard. As far as his beautiful home went, it was average at best. It was a bungalow with a finished basement. Callie was simply the most biased person on the planet.

The four visitors spent the night before the wedding in the basement, watching TV and playing board games. There would be enough drinking tomorrow at the wedding—they all knew that— and decided to have a quiet night before the storm.

Emma introduced her boyfriend, Austin, to everyone nervously. Tristan gave him the standard big brother treatment— gruff responses and inappropriate questions. Emma scowled at him, and Amy elbowed him in the ribs, but he didn't care. This Austin character was going to know who was boss. Tristan had to admit, however, that Austin seemed like a nice young man. He was definitely handsome and apparently he was into sports. Once Tristan got over his protective instincts there was hope for a positive relationship between the two.

Once the introductions were over, Emma dragged Austin upstairs away from the firing squad. Tristan snickered to himself and Ryan gave him a high five. Amy rolled her eyes disgustedly at the immature exchange and went back to reading her book. Callie was on the other couch parallel to them looking at baby pictures of Tristan with Patty. Tristan hadn't noticed and was mortified at his infantile nakedness. It was obvious his mother was reading too much into his relationship with Callie.

"Uhhh Mom. Do you think we could put that away?" Tristan's tone was more than suggestive.

"Oh nooo Tristan! You were so cute!" Callie was beaming. It was almost enough to settle Tristan down. *Almost.*

"Ok, time for a movie. Goodnight mom." Tristan picked his mother up by the arm and forced her up the stairs despite her halfhearted protests.

"Goodnight kids," she called when she got to the top.

"Goodnight," they yelled in unison.

Callie grinned at him and plopped herself down on his lap. "I think your mother likes me."

"She's not the only one," Ryan said as he pointed his thumb at Tristan. Callie giggled and Tristan glared at Ryan from an angle Callie couldn't see. Tristan did care about Callie, but he certainly wasn't over Adrienne and wasn't ready to put himself out there quite yet.

Cameron was a pretty conservative guy, hence the guys and girls could not share sleeping accommodations. Amy would be sleeping on the floor in Emma's room, Callie in Tristan's room, and the boys would all be on the couches in the basement. Since there were only two couches, poor Austin was relegated to the floor. Tristan enjoyed his reluctant acceptance of his position in the pecking order. Ryan added a nice touch just before they went to sleep when he threatened to beat the hell out of the kid if he snored.

Tristan found Callie helping Patty with breakfast the next morning. The two acted like they had known each other for years. He ignored the scene and went to the fridge for some juice. It shouldn't have surprised him that there was already a glass waiting for him in Callie's outstretched hand. Tristan took the glass and shuddered. Things were moving way too fast and they weren't even dating. He looked over his shoulder and saw his mother grinning stupidly at him. People had way too much fun at Tristan's expense.

Ryan dragged himself up the stairs as Tristan polished off his glass of juice.

"Good morning, girls!" He stretched like a bear who had just came out of hibernation.

"Ryan, put a shirt on, you will make Tristan feel bad." Patty joked.

"Ha ha, Mom." Tristan growled. Ryan flexed a bit and winked at the two women. Callie followed him with an impressed look in her eye. Tristan felt a pang of jealousy. "*Dick*" He muttered when Ryan sat next to him. Ryan just smiled.

Amy was the next to rise and only replied to Tristan's good morning. Ryan's efforts received the death stare. She joined Patty and Callie at the counter to help make breakfast.

After eating, the boys cleaned up to allow the girls to start getting ready. With four girls, and two bathrooms, they knew they would be waiting a while. Callie winked at Tristan as she was headed to the shower. She hiked her towel up a bit and blew him a kiss when she thought nobody was looking. Ryan caught a glimpse and shook his head in disgust.

"You are such a lucky bastard. I have no idea how you do it. Chicks are supposed to hate bald guys. You look like a serial killer."

Tristan smiled confidently as he passed the next plate to Ryan. "Muscles aren't everything my friend."

"She's just so hot. They are always hot." Ryan sounded like a child who didn't get the toy he wanted for Christmas.

"Yeah she's smokin'" Austin chimed in.

Tristan and Ryan both turned to glare at him. Austin got the point as he hung his head and went back to stacking dishes.

Amy and Emma got ready downstairs. The two had always gotten along well. The plan was to switch locations (Amy and Ryan) once she was showered and dressed. She could do her hair in Emma's room while Ryan quarantined himself in the basement. Tristan got a huge kick out of the intricacy and planning that went into her avoidance of Ryan. His gigantic sidekick was a good sport though, Tristan thought he could sense some feelings lingering between them, but he dared not voice his opinion.

When the showers stopped running Tristan and Ryan parted ways to get ready themselves. Tristan replaced Callie in the upstairs bathroom, and Ryan cautiously replaced Amy in the downstairs bathroom. Austin and Emma volunteered to go last. Tristan couldn't help but wonder about Adrienne when he had some time to himself. His own stupidity bothered him sometimes. He had an amazing girl in his house, who was really into him and would do anything to make him happy, yet his mind and heart belonged elsewhere. He let the warm water cascade over his body in hopes that it would wash away false hopes and replace them with more rational ones.

Tristan was putting the finishing touches on his suit (black pants, baby blue shirt and tie) when he heard a soft knock at his bedroom door. He took one last glance in his body length mirror and swung the door open. The girl in front of him reminded him more of Cinderella than Callie. Her long blonde hair was up, and the remaining ringlets added class to her look. The blue dress she promised to find fit her just tightly enough to be sexy. Her long legs, tanned and smooth, shone. Tristan checked his mouth for drool.

She gave him a playful shove. "We match."

"You look, I mean, wow." Tristan's inability to formulate a cohesive sentence made Callie smile.

"You don't look so bad yourself, mister." She fixed his collar slightly. "I just came for my shoes. They are in the bag by your bed."

Tristan stood to the side to let her by. She brushed against him purposely. She smelled almost better than she looked. She left Tristan with a playful smile to help the other girls with their preparations.

Ryan passed her in the hall with eye balls bulging and mouth agape. He was tying his tie when he started to speak. "Holy shit, dude, she looks like a supermodel, or a playboy bunny. Either way, are you going to sleep with her? Please tell me you are."

Tristan grinned. "Ryan, Callie and I have been sleeping together for almost a year."

Ryan's jaw dropped to the point where Tristan thought it would detach from his face. "That girl? *That* girl let you sleep with her? No strings attached?"

"Well, something like that. It got complicated so we had to—"

"How many times? What have you guys done? Tristan, you have to tell me."

"No way dude!" Tristan shoved him. "I'm not being the subject of any of your wet dreams. This is gross."

"I don't care if you're there as long as she's there too. God *damn*, Tristan."

Tristan just shook his head and finished getting dressed. He had to admit, Callie was more than fine—she looked angelic—but he still couldn't get rid of Adrienne's constant presence in his gut. Whenever he found himself entertaining romantic, instead of sexual, thoughts of Callie, he was trumped by the spell Adrienne already put him under.

God Tristan, Adrienne is spoken for end of story.

Patty yelled for everyone to gather in front of her willow tree for pictures before they left. Tristan laughed as Amy warned Ryan to stay as far away as he could. Ryan put his hands in front of him to indicate that he didn't want to argue and did as she asked. Cameron got back just in time to set the camera and join the picture. The eight of them managed to create a stunning snap shot.

Ryan was taking his car with Tristan, Amy, and Callie as passengers. Tristan was made to sit up front and he started to think that Amy's grudge was being taken too far. He hoped the two of them could get straightened out at some point so that the whole group could function properly. He started to feel more like the parent instead of the friend.

The air conditioning in Ryan's old Ford Taurus was broken, and it was a hot June day. Matt and Lacey chose the perfect day for their wedding. As for the four in the car, clothing was becoming a burden. Tristan cursed his dress clothes as they were probably the hottest possible garments he could find himself in. The sweat was starting to roll off his bald head. He saw Callie in the side mirror behind him. She was sweating too. He could see the gleam of sweat on her chest and it made his mind wander.

Tristan noticed Ryan using the rearview to steal glimpses of Amy. She looked ravishing in her own right. Her long black hair hung freely over her green dress. Her contacts replaced her glasses and her figure was on full display. Tristan knew his friend; Ryan definitely still wanted her. Unfortunately, Amy didn't look in his direction a single time since they got into the car. In fact, she had spoken to everyone *but* him on their drive to Sageview.

As they approached Lacey's farm, it wasn't hard to tell there was a wedding being held. Small town weddings were like fairs. Everyone was involved. There were tassels, flowers, and pompoms on all mailboxes starting a kilometre from the farm. The atmosphere in the car changed from indifferent, to a general sense of awe. The driveway was lined with flowers and decorations of white, gold, and black. Tristan smiled at the addition of Sageview High's colours to celebrate the marriage of high school sweethearts.

There were cars lined up a fair distance from the house, so Ryan parked where he could and the four walked the rest of the way

Three Words

taking in the sights. The farm had successfully been transformed into a real life fairy tale. Caterers were scurrying around, and there were well dressed people coming and going. Tristan knew Lacey's family was rich, but the spectacle was really impressive. Callie tugged on his arm and pointed out into the field behind the Connor's house. There was a huge white gazebo, freshly built, that Tristan couldn't help but appreciate. It looked like a castle on the horizon.

Tristan hadn't realized it, as he was too busy gawking at the beautiful wedding preparations, but Ryan and Amy were walking side by side, without hostilities. Tristan made a mental note to bring any girl who wanted to kill him in the future to a wedding. Apparently it eased tension and buried hatchets.

Callie was a city girl and had expressed humour when Tristan told her the wedding was taking place on a farm. She seemed skeptical, but was too nice to be openly disrespectful of the idea. If there was any doubt in her mind before, there was none now. She interlocked her arm with his and leaned close to him.

"It's beautiful," she whispered.

All Tristan could do was nod. Someone flagged them down to direct them to their seats. They walked on the freshly mowed grass flanked by white pillars to the enormous gazebo. Tristan saw Matt standing at the back next to the priest. He waved and Tristan waved back. As Tristan motioned for Callie to step past him and take her seat, Matt gave him a subtle thumbs up. He wondered momentarily if he was mentally challenged for not putting a ring on Callie's finger, every other guy seemed to be ready to throw themselves on swords for her.

Amy took the aisle seat, presumably to escape from Ryan if she had to, with Ryan next to her followed by Tristan and Callie. Rows were only four seats wide, but they extended a long way. The gazebo was almost the size of a house. Tristan mentally rephrased his question from earlier in the day. What do *poor people* do if it rains on their outdoor wedding? Tristan noticed that Callie had

Kleenex stuffed in her purse. He rolled his eyes. Girls were so emotional at weddings.

When Pachelbel's Canon began, Tristan smiled. Lacey had always been a fantastic musician, and she loved classical music.

The bridesmaids were dressed in pink and led the way. The flower girl was adorable, as usual, and the ring bearer was actually the dog they bought together—a pug named Bruno. When Lacey finally came into view, Tristan experienced a montage of emotional activity. Lacey's tears of happiness began before she took the first step towards her husband to be. Tristan was shocked at how beautiful she looked. Her brown hair was mostly covered by her veil, but she wore a shimmery white wedding dress without straps. The train was long and elegant. He also felt guilty. He sat next to a wonderful girl who gripped his hand in anticipation, but his mind thought only of someone else. He quickly scanned the room for Adrienne but couldn't find her.

Tristan's eyes watered and Callie squeezed his hand. He looked at her and smiled. There was no reason for her to know where his tears really came from. Lacey stopped and the guests were seated. The priest began, "Dearly Beloved…"

The priest went through the traditional spiel until it was time for vows. Tristan cringed when he realized that they had written their own vows. The ol' heart strings were going to get yanked even more.

Matt went first, "Lacey…" He had to pause and compose himself after the first word. Sobs could be heard amongst the guests, the loudest to his left and right. Callie and Amy were both a mess of tears. Out of the corner of his eye he saw Ryan reach for Amy's hand. Tristan held his breath and waited for the backlash, but to his surprise, she took his hand willingly. She looked at him and mouthed three words that were easy to make out, *Fucking hate you.*

Ryan grinned and mouthed back, *I hate you too, bitch.*

Tristan could see the muscles flex in their hands as they squeezed. Tristan rolled his eyes.

Those two are unbelievable.

Matt finished his vows and Tristan was impressed. He found them more funny than sad, as a guy's feelings tend to be, but they were certainly sentimental. Lacey was next.

"Kevin…"

Her hand shot up to her mouth at lightning speed. The air was sucked out of the Gazebo by the collective gasps of the guests. Matt stared at her, stunned, and the priest looked like he needed a drink. Callie looked at Tristan and Tristan looked at Ryan. Ryan tried to look at Amy but she had her face buried in her free hand. Everyone waited for her to speak again.

"Matt…"

Matt stopped her and the muffled demand could barely be heard, "Kevin, tell me you didn't say Kevin."

Lacey turned and ran from the Gazebo. Tristan was dumbfounded, and he had no idea what to do. He felt horrible for Matt and embarrassed for him at the same time. He didn't want to move or even breathe.

Just then, Lacey came trotting back in with a huge smile on her face. Matt was grinning too. The guests were murmuring with one another, and Callie gave Tristan an inquisitive look. Tristan shrugged, he had no sweet clue what was going on. As she made her way back to the altar Matt grabbed the mike, "Gotcha."

A chorus of cheers and jeers erupted as people laughed and cried. Matt always did have a sick sense of humour. Tristan and Ryan breathed a sigh of relief and sunk down in their chairs. Amy finished her vows and the two shared a long passionate kiss. Tristan was still in shock, he was upset mostly because he could not pull the same goof at his wedding.

When the ceremony ended, Matt's father formally invited everyone to the reception, but Tristan really only heard two words: Open Bar.

Amy and Ryan hadn't released each other's hands since the ceremony. Tristan made faces until he had their attention. Ryan smiled triumphantly and Amy gave him a shot in the ribs. Her eyes said, *don't push it*. The group spent the hour waiting for the reception mingling with other guests. Tristan introduced Callie to everyone he could, and she was immediately accepted. Girls who looked like Callie didn't get rejected often. She was the biggest hit with most of the older men at the wedding, she promised out five or six dances before the music even started.

The meal was fantastic, Tristan expected no less after the impressive ceremony. There was a choice of three entrees and Tristan chose the steak. Men always chose steak. There were many speeches given over dinner, and many kisses demanded from the bride and groom. Dinner lasted about an hour and then tables were cleared away for what was being called a dance—though everyone knew it was actually a party. Once the bar opened up and the music came on, the atmosphere of the wedding became very collegiate.

The bride and groom danced the first slow song to a Lifehouse tune. Tristan thought the song suited them, but it also made him think of Adrienne again. He looked for her a second time with no luck. He had asked around about her earlier, but nobody knew if she planned on coming to the reception or not. When the wedding dance ended, and the hip-hop music came on, Tristan felt more at home. Many of the older folk left after they saw the new couple dance their first dance.

Tristan finally got to talk with Matt and Lacey, but it didn't last long. He was hauled, quite forcefully, onto the dance floor by an inspired Callie.

"I love this song!"

The pace was fast, and Tristan had no dance skills whatsoever, but he didn't care. Dancing with Callie didn't take much effort, she did most of the work. He realized that how she danced had a lot in common with how she moved in bed. Tristan's mind wandered to more vivid places while his body tried hard not to make an ass of itself. Callie let her hair down, literally, and her blonde mane slashed through the air as she danced. She wouldn't let Tristan get away either, every time he thought about going to sit down she rubbed her body against his in a way that would turn a man to stone.

When the next song started everyone recognized the romantic high school classic, *Closing Time*. The song began and Tristan pulled Callie close to him. The expression on her face changed from electric enthusiasm to surprised submission. She put her arms around his neck and he let his hands slide onto her lower back. Hardly any of them knew how to really dance. They just spun in a circle holding on to each other. Nobody cared. It was the closeness they valued, the chance to share romantic moments. Tristan looked over quickly at Ryan and Amy. She was so much shorter than his six foot five frame, and her head rested gently on his chest. Ryan gave Tristan a quick smile and went back into his own little world with Amy.

Callie looked at Tristan. Her eyes blazed with affection for him. Her blue dress glittered in the dim DJ lighting. Tristan was being swept away again, he could feel it. It wasn't just her beauty, but her entire being that entrapped him. Tristan always knew that certain moments made people more susceptible to romantic feelings, but the setting was movie-like, storybook-like. He pulled her closer. The music fuelled him on and he knew every word.

Tristan could feel Callie's anticipation. Her chest heaved with the power of her breaths.

Tristan talked enough in his life. The time for talk was over. He was tired of and waiting when opportunity was staring him in the face. Perhaps all he longed for, all he suffered, had led to this precise moment.

Maybe it was supposed to be Callie all along.

Tristan kissed Callie hard. It was not desire, not selfishness, not passion that drove him, but something else. Callie separated herself long enough to repeat three words she spoke earlier that year. This time, they were not falling on deaf ears.

"I love you."

Tristan smiled, and kissed her again. They spent the rest of the song twirling in each other's arms.

The Last Three Words
(Three Years Later)

Chapter Thirty-Five

Tristan stood at the altar. The breeze coming off the water smelt of ocean. The sun was high in the Mexican sky, and the sea was a transparent greenish blue. The altar was on a platform specifically designed for weddings. It was approximately five feet off of the sandy beach, suspended by hundreds of metal pillars. It was completely portable, the perfect contraption to support the fifty odd guests including the bride and groom. The priest grinned at him, and Tristan ignored the old man. He gazed out into the ocean, daydreaming.

The guests were all chatting and fanning themselves. Tristan figured that was the price a person paid for a scenic wedding on the Mayan Riviera. He felt like he was baking in his tux. Beads of sweat formed on his shaved head. He dabbed his forehead with his sleeve to get rid of some of the moisture before it could roll into his eyes. He caught a glimpse of the remaining members of the wedding party forming at the other end of the platform.

Tristan sent his love to Deanna, he knew she'd have loved to be there. Tristan could see her in one of the blue bridesmaid dresses. He pictured the smile on her face and her wonderful aura. He shook his head to clear the thoughts away. He always thought of Deanna at weddings; he had for years, and it always made him more sad than happy. He couldn't help but picture her as the bride and him as the groom. It never failed.

The wedding march began and the bridesmaids walked forward. His sister, Emma, was first. She looked amazing. *She's really grown up,* Tristan thought. She was no longer the shy little girl Tristan remembered. She smiled at him and he returned her gesture.

Next came Amy's sister, Jackie—she was ten years older than Amy but the spit and image of her nonetheless—and finally was Suzanna, Amy's best friend from university. The three of them looked downright fantastic, but they were nothing compared to the bride. Tristan had seen Amy in almost every way imaginable. He saw her happy, sad, drunk, sick, pissed off, and elated; but nothing, no combination of things, could describe how she looked on her wedding day. Amy was too proud to cry on her walk to the altar, and she held her head high.

Her black hair fell freely, save for one small braid that ran across the peak of her hairline and down the left side of her face. Her dress was traditional white, trainless, and relatively plain, but she made it seem like a one of a kind. Her joy and anticipation radiated from her and infected everyone at the ceremony. Ryan stood proudly at his side. His eyes were fixed on his bride to be. A tear ran down the side of the big man's face. Tristan grinned. Even the biggest and strongest were no match for matters of the heart.

Tristan panicked for a moment, as he had done multiple times that day, and checked his pockets for the thousandth time, and for the thousandth time, he found the rings safe and sound where he placed them the night before. Tristan sighed, and put them into his right hand. He patted Ryan on the shoulder to give him encouragement, and Ryan gave no indication that he had even felt it. Ryan was living a dream, and not even the best man was powerful enough to snap him out of it.

Amy's resolve wavered when she saw the tears in the huge man's yellow eyes. He towered over her, but it had never intimidated her. She looked at home in his shadow, safe and confident. The two joined hands, and the ceremony began. Despite all of

Three Words

Tristan's misgivings when it came to love and weddings, even he could not deny the power of what he was witnessing.

It was a bumpy ride through their vows. Amy's pride lost to her joy and she was sobbing openly. Ryan was the world's largest baby, but he would be well looked after. Before the priest allowed them to kiss, Tristan caught Ryan's own addition to his vows. He looked her dead in the face and mouthed, I love you bitch. Her brilliant smile lit up all of Mexico as she grabbed a handful of hair and yanked his head down for a rather raunchy embrace.

Mr. and Mrs. Carlyle sauntered off to their Sea-doo which pulled a buoy that said "Just Married" in neon letters. They weren't going far—the resort was only half a mile away—but they had to put their own touch on things. The guests clapped as they splashed away and Tristan walked with his sister back to the resort.

Tristan only made it a few steps with Emma before Austin scooped her up and carried her off. Tristan grimaced at the act and didn't want to think about where they could be going. He paused to wait for Ryan's mother. He would be her escort back to the resort. It was suiting as they were probably the only two dateless guests at the wedding. She smiled at him and graciously accepted his outstretched arm.

Once the head table was ready to go, there was still thirty minutes until the new couple got back from their photo shoot. Tristan needed some air, so he walked out onto the balcony. He could hear guests mingling in the hall patiently waiting for the reception to start. Tristan leaned on the railing and looked out into the horizon. The sun was taking on an orange colour as it sunk toward the skyline. He felt around in his pocket for the last ring in his possession. He studied the small diamond meticulously wondering if it was cursed. Nobody, except for he and Ryan, knew about the existence of the ill-fated trinket.

Tristan found the irony in his life morbidly entertaining. The ring that fumbled its way through his fingertips never graced the finger of the one it was meant for—in fact, he didn't even propose.

He figured he was making a mistake when he bought the ring, but refused to listen to reason. Tristan's two and a half year relationship was founded on lies, and the charade could not be kept up forever. Callie left him for someone else three months before the Carlyle wedding.

He held no ill will for Callie, her biological make up was not something she could help. At first, Tristan was embarrassed to tell people his girlfriend left him for another woman, but there was some solace in that, there was nothing he could have done differently. They got along wonderfully the times they were together, but there was always something missing. Tristan scoffed at that thought as he stared at the half carat in his hand. There was something missing besides the fact he wasn't a woman.

Callie seemed so into him that he figured his run of doomed relationships was at an end. Callie loved him, she claimed to love him still, but Tristan understood why they had to break up. He was angry at the time, and his first question had been quite obviously, "How could you have slept with me for so long and not know you were a lesbian?"

Tristan always knew Callie was too good to be true. The looks of a supermodel combined with honesty, sincerity, compassion, selflessness and ambition were more than any man deserved. Tristan was convinced that God was female.

The Carlyle's rained on his reverie. He had lost track of time and the reception was starting. Ryan galloped out like a five year old on Christmas morning and dragged him in.

"Come on Tristan! Everyone is eager to hear the best man's speech! You know, since he's a big shot writer and all."

Tristan smiled at the compliment, but knew it was far from the truth. Tristan was a sportswriter. He had simply combined his love of basketball with his love of writing and history. It made sense to him, but he was still stuck writing about local university basketball games. It paid the bills, but it didn't do much more than

Three Words

that. Tristan hoped he would be much more successful someday. One thing was for sure, he had a killer speech written.

Tristan picked up his pace when he realized that everyone was waiting for him. He demanded the right to speak on the couple as the best man, and as someone who had known them both since the beginning of their relationship. Ryan looked giddy and nervous all at the same time. Amy glared playfully at him as a warning. He ignored her warning. He stood at the podium next to the head table where the wedding party sat. He flipped open the piece of paper he had been carrying around all day long.

He cleared his throat, "Herm Herm."

He got a smattering of applause before he even started. He raised his hand to ask for silence. Tristan felt a rush of power, like Caesar about to give a rallying speech to his troops.

"Ladies and Gentlemen, most of you know me already, those of you who don't know me, obviously don't read too much."

There was scattered laughter.

"It is my job as the best man to help celebrate this marriage by bringing you all up to speed on how these two lovebirds met. I do not want to delay everyone's procession to the bar, so I have written it in poem form. Fear not, it is very easy to follow."

Ryan grinned at him and Amy hid her face behind her hands. After a quick wink to the bride and groom Tristan read loudly and deliberately:

> *One short and one tall,*
> *They don't seem to fit at all.*
> *They come from different sides of a coin,*
> *But still they would join.*
> *One day at a table,*
> *In a high school caf,*
> *Ryan pulled a Clark Gable,*
> *And yanked Miss. Amy into his lap.*

Those attending the wedding from their graduating class gave a cheer at that line, Tristan continued:

> *At first they used each other,*
> *For fun and games.*
> *Both found the other,*
> *Difficult to tame.*
> *They grew together,*
> *Only to grow apart,*
> *But would soon find their way*
> *Back to each other's hearts.*

Tristan paused to look at the newly-weds, and a chorus of *Awwws* rang out from the guests. Tristan raised his hand a second time to let them know his poem wasn't quite done.

> *I never thought I'd see the day,*
> *When screwing up royally would get you laid.*
> *But Ryan Carlyle needed to scratch an itch*
> *And did the job,*
> *by marrying that bitch.*

Some guests gasped, but those who knew the pair roared with laughter. Amy and Ryan were bent over the table with hilarity pains.

> *Just before I sit back down,*
> *Next to the prince and princess with their crowns,*
> *Let me be honest in the end,*
> *There's not a better pair*
> *Than my best friends.*

Tristan bowed like a court jester and smiled at the massive applause he received for his efforts. Whether they were just being polite, or actually liked his speech, it was music to his ears either way. Amy stood and kissed him on the cheek and he got his customary bear hug from Ryan. After the bridesmaids gave their two cents, and the Carlyles had kissed once more, dinner began. Tristan sure was glad they were serving wine right away.

    He had a date with drunken debauchery.

Chapter Thirty-Six

Tristan got back to his apartment four days after the wedding. He kicked his shoes off and threw his sports bag on the floor. He was growing tired of his one room apartment. It was your typical bachelor pad, but he associated it with being a university student, which he no longer was. Everyone else upgraded since they graduated from university, except him. He liked the apartment; he liked the central downtown location. He was close to the gym, the grocery store, and bus stops. That was another thing that irked him, he didn't have a car.

Tristan realized he complained a lot about his finances, but they could have been worse. He was self-sufficient with little debt. His university costs were handled, for the most part, by his academic scholarships. He owed the spillover in student loans, but it was less than ten grand. Tristan could easily walk to *The Sun* offices in fifteen minutes, and by bus it only took five.

He picked up his phone to check for messages. He had quite a few—leaving for a week had its disadvantages. Tristan recalled a time when the majority of messages would have been from girls eager to meet up with him, but times had changed. Tristan was no longer the *ladies' man* he once was. Tristan lost contact with a lot of his female friends during his relationship with Callie. He thought he had all he needed. Unfortunately for him, he had *something extra* that she didn't need.

The majority of the messages were from his editor at the paper. Tristan was supposed to have his analysis of the rival universities done two days ago. Tristan was slightly concerned but annoyed at the same time. He told his boss, Ronald, that he was taking vacation to attend a wedding. Apparently Ronald did not understand the word vacation. Tristan didn't understand why it was so important; he was a sportswriter who didn't even write for the front page of the sports section.

Tristan cursed Ronald's power-tripping personality and moved on to the other missed calls. Most he recognized, his parents—who hadn't been able to make the wedding due to his mother's fear of flying—his sister, who most likely wanted to brag about the fact that her and Austin were staying in Mexico for a second week, Callie—he deleted that one instantly—and Amy. He accessed his voice mail to hear what Amy had to say.

"Trissstan! We love you! It sucks you had to go home early. Just quit your job and work at Ryan's mill—what's that honey? Oh never mind, Ryan says you are too pretty to work with your hands. Hope you got home..."

Amy's message was interrupted by drunken giggles and the message ended. Tristan smiled at the good time his friends were having, but was brutally jealous at the same time. He got two weeks worth of vacation all year. He already used half of it. Tristan took a moment to kick himself in the ass for choosing a profession with so little room for advancement and checked the last message on his phone. The number he didn't recognize. A foreign voice spoke:

"Hello, dis message is for Mistah Tristan Cage. I am calling on behalf of da bank. We would like to—"

Tristan hung up with a shudder. His life was so ordinary, it sickened him. Based on all the movies he watched it would soon be time to be abducted by aliens, swept off his feet, or attacked by giant robots. He waited skeptically for any fantastic event to

take place and shook his head in recognition of his ridiculous daydream. His phone rang, and he rolled his eyes upon answering.
"Hello?"
"Cage? You better tell me you have my article written."
"Ron, I didn't get back until today. You know that."
"What? No, you said you were going on vacation. I didn't realize you were unable to write when you left the country."
Tristan hated him. It seemed like Ron's only purpose was to make Tristan doubt his decision to become a writer.
"Ron, look—"
"No, you look. If I don't have that article by 5PM, you can look for a new job. Maybe they are looking for mediocre sports writers in Mexico."
Tristan laid his head back on the couch and listened to the dial tone for a while. Suddenly Amy's invitation didn't seem like such a bad idea.
Tristan sifted through the papers on his desk to try and find the research he had done on the provinces two hard court powerhouses: Saint Agnus and Winchester. He moved stacks of paper around until he was relatively organized and started to write. The column was only two hundred words, but that made it more difficult for Tristan. He had the most trouble being concise and hated working with limitations. It would take him almost to the deadline to squeeze his information into that small a window.
Tristan had a headache by the time he was finished. He emailed the column to his editor at 4:45. Tristan hated being rushed and hated his boss even more for being a dick on his vacation. Tristan felt a little torn about meeting his deadline. He was happy he wouldn't be losing his job, but also disappointed. Getting fired could have been what the doctor ordered, but now he wouldn't know for at least another week.
After popping a of couple Tylenol and laying down on his bed, his phone rang again. Tristan looked askance at the phone on his desk. He was hesitant to answer it but eventually grabbed it up.

He checked the phone number just to ensure that it wasn't Ronald and then picked up.

"How was the trip?" Alec's halfhearted hello made Tristan smirk. "What are you doing tonight?"

"Well I was planning on recovering. I don't want to go to work tomorrow with jet-lag"

"Don't be such a pansy. We want to play some ball. Interested?"

Tristan wanted to say no, but ever since he was thirteen years old whenever someone mentioned basketball the word no left his vocabulary.

"Yeah, I'm in. What time?"

"Meet us at the gym in fifteen?"

"Yeah, I'll be there."

Tristan rubbed his tired eyes to try and liven himself up, then he He threw on some basketball gear. What better way to celebrate his first day back in the country than playing the game he loved with friends? He couldn't help but answer that question for himself:

A winning lottery ticket, a front page column, and a straight girlfriend would have been nice.

He threw his basketball sneakers over his shoulder and left the apartment with a strong desire to be slightly less ordinary.

Chapter Thirty-Seven

Tristan woke to his vibrating cell phone. With a groan, he rolled over to look at who dared wake him. The name attached to the text message made Tristan groan a second time. The message read:

Tristan. I hope you enjoyed the wedding. I would love to hear from you. Miss you bunches. Callie.

Tristan instinctively clicked the delete button and rolled out of bed. Talking to Callie would only add to his current angst for life. He was dreading the thought of going to work. The sheer volume of the place put him in a bad mood. There were desks everywhere, all strewn with paper, people yelling back and forth, and machines constantly printing, faxing, dialling, or ringing. The life of a writer once seemed so appealing, but lately he started to see it for what it really was: a stressful dead end.

Tristan made it to work with mere seconds to spare. Busses were totally unreliable and hardly ever on time. Tristan was just glad he made it so he didn't have to tell Ronald he was late. He didn't need any more reasons to be on Ronald's black list; constant disagreement, obvious dissatisfaction, public mockery, and failure to meet deadlines were probably enough.

As Tristan walked to his own little island in a sea of others, he eyed the person he hated most at *The Sun*. Julia was a much more assertive journalist than Tristan was, she had attitude, ambition, and absolutely no scruples about selling out to make the boss happy. Everyone else hated Julia, but feared her as well. It was a well-known fact Julia was blowing Ronald to get ahead, and it was working. Tristan thought about exposing the conspiracy many times, but it wasn't fear of Julia that had stopped him, but his conscience. As much as he hated them both, he was not prepared to ruin careers over it. He resented Julia's warp speed ascension to small front page columns, but bit his tongue on the matter.

Julia sat on the corner of his desk and raised an eyebrow.

"What?" Tristan was in no mood for Julia's demoralizing playfulness.

"Tristan, are you cranky today?" She loved to test his patience.

"Cage!" Ronald hollered from his office door.

Tristan glanced up at Julia and she shrugged, "You know he is gunning for you." She pulled her chestnut coloured bangs to the side. "Good luck with that."

Tristan ignored the various comments he received as he passed the other drones en route to Ronald's office. Tristan hated that Ron had the prestige of *Editor* written on his door. The guy was an asshole, yet held such an honourable position. Tristan was suddenly consumed by a desire to write about the correlation between ruthlessness and success, but quelled the desire to lock horns with his rotund adversary.

Ronald sat in his excessively fancy office chair. He leaned back and looked smugly at Tristan. His hands were in his lap, fingertips barely touching one another in a seemingly thoughtful position. Ronald looked like an evil villain. Tristan's eyes next fell upon the half eaten doughnut dripping icing and grease on some poor bastard's writing in the centre of Ronald's desk. Ronald must have noticed, because he smirked at Tristan, oozing contempt. Tristan frowned and followed Ronald's gaze back to the seemingly worthless document on his desk. Tristan felt his blood boil. Upon closer examination, the name at the bottom of the page was clear to see: Tristan Cage.

Three Words

The muscles in his jaw refused to relax. Tristan clenched his fists but said nothing. Instead, he waited for Ronald to speak.

"Well Tristan," Ronald chuckled. His fat jiggled around like a waterbed. Tristan was revolted. "What we have here, under my breakfast, is a surefire piece of crap. Totally unacceptable. It will not be going to print." Ronald grinned. "Obviously."

Tristan did his best to remain calm. "Well, *editor*," Tristan used the word as sarcastically as possible, "I would like a second opinion. It is more than obvious you are biased."

Ronald looked amused. "Second opinion? Cage, I'm the editor. There is no second opinion needed."

Arrogant, power crazed, prick.

"Oh," Ronald continued, "Trevor will be replacing you covering university games. You have proven yourself unreliable. You will now be covering the high school games."

Tristan stood in awe of this man's brutality. Trevor? Trevor was the worst sportswriter on the planet. He didn't even know what a sport was, and had only been at the paper for a year. Ronald was taking his personal vendetta too far. The high school column was only a hundred words, he just cut Tristan's exposure by half and given it to someone with a third of his experience.

Tristan's anger was spinning out of control. Ronald's fat ass reclined with eyebrows raised waiting for a favourable response. He wanted Tristan to get angry, he wanted a reason to fire him. Tristan didn't want to give him the satisfaction, but his temper normally got the best of him in situations like that. There were so many things he urged himself to say, things like, "Whatever you say, you're the boss." Or, "I think you should reconsider, I have written many strong columns, you said so yourself." There were so many reasonable, logical, choices on how to proceed, but Tristan chose something else.

"Everyone knows you are fucking, Julia. Now someone is going to make it slightly more public."

Ronald's face went white. "What?" The tables were turning. Ronald's face changed from pale to crimson. "You have no idea what you are talking—"

Tristan had no interest in a cliché exchange of insults. He already made up his mind. He threw open the office door and screamed at the top of his lungs, "I offered to blow him for a promotion, but apparently only Julia can do that!"

Julia's head spun around, mouth agape. Everyone else responded with gasps, snickers, and whispers. Once Tristan had their attention, his mouth assumed a life of its own.

"Everyone in here is a coward. You all know that Ronald is giving Julia favourable treatment in exchange for sex. It is impossible to get ahead in a place like this. Ronald is a power tripping egomaniac who is too ugly to get any female honourably. There's no way I'm working here a second longer."

Tristan turned to look at a mortified Ronald. "Go get some MacDonald's Ronnie, I quit."

Tristan had yet to consider the ramifications of quitting his job, but he knew it felt fantastic. He walked out of the paper with his head held high. Tristan was tired of seeing the villains win.

By the time Tristan got home, and the adrenaline had worn off, his attitude was slightly less positive. He felt sick to his stomach. He had no job, no income, no prospects, and had just taken two people down with him. Although they weren't innocent, it was not Tristan's place to publicly humiliate them. His conscience was taking over and he couldn't stop it. Tristan's eyes flickered around the room for something to make him feel better. There was nobody there, nobody to talk to. Tristan longed to have Callie back, she had always been amazing in bad situations.

He put his phone on his lap and stared at it. He tried to recognize if he was calling her out of desperation, or if he was actually ready to take the plunge. It had been over three months since he talked to Callie. It may not be the best situation to contact her about. Tristan knew how unpredictable he was, especially when he was hurting, but good sense had never been his strong suit. He picked up the phone and dialled.

Callie assured him that she would be over in a matter of minutes. After they split, she moved to the apartment across the street. Usually Tristan tried to ignore the fact. It was weird, inconvenient, and painful to have her so close by, but that night, it came in handy. Tristan was lying on his bed running through the pros and cons of meeting with Callie when there was a knock at his door.

Tristan took a deep breath before he opened the door. Callie had always been beautiful, but she looked even more so. Tristan wasn't sure if it was because he hadn't seen her in so long, or if it was because she was happier. Tristan tried to expel the thought that being in a relationship with him made her uglier, but it pestered him.

She threw her arms around him and kissed his cheek. He remembered her warmth and pulled her tight.

"Tristan, are you alright?" Callie still cared about him, he could see it in her eyes. They plead with him to talk to her.

"No, Callie. I'm not."

She looked slightly afraid of him, and he couldn't blame her. The last time they spoke hadn't been pretty. Tristan cursed his temper for maiming the people it had. "I'm still angry with you, Callie. But that's not the reason I called."

She relaxed slightly. "Ok."

"I quit my job today, and I didn't leave quietly." Tristan's face screamed guilt.

"Oh God, Tristan, what did you do?"

They sat on the couch and Tristan recounted his story. To his amazement, Callie was laughing. Tristan shook his head at her and threw his arms up in aggravation.

Callie composed herself. "Tristan," She stifled another burst of laughter and touched his arm, "You mean to tell me you are upset about this? That is the best thing I've heard in years." She grinned affectionately and looked him in the eye. "You were happy when you got that job, but not thrilled. You hated it after a couple of months. You didn't like your co-workers, the environment, or your boss. It was clear it wasn't what you were meant to do."

"Yeah but—"

"No buts Tristan! You are so hard on yourself, but you never see what everyone else does. Your heart is huge, Tristan. Sure you have a bad temper, but normally, the people who get it deserve it. Your boss was an asshole, and his relationship was unethical. Sure it wasn't the most professional way to go about exposing it, but neither was their involvement in the first place!" She was laughing again. "You always said you wanted to live your life like a movie, Tristan. I would have to say you took a step in that direction today." She laid her hand gently on his leg. "I think I'll go now, Tristan. This is a good step for us, and I don't want to push my luck."

Tristan held the door for her as she left and turned to look at his empty apartment. He needed out of that place, it defined a part of his life he no longer lived. It was time to move on.

Tristan spent the rest of the night researching university programs for his new life.

Chapter Thirty-Eight

Tristan narrowed things down by morning. He had direction. He was going to win the lottery or come up with a revolutionary invention like tooth floss or Velcro. University was too expensive, and he was too old to go back, at least that was what he thought. Tristan was scared of the unknown, he always had been. He was contemplating informing his parents of his most recent cataclysm when he started daydreaming.

Despair took Tristan by surprise, so he decided to call his parents for a firm reality check. The call went as expected. It had its highs and lows. His parents respected his decision, he was a grown man after all, but raised many of the same questions Tristan had himself. How would he pay his student loans, his rent, or his bills? Basically, nobody knew how he was going to survive. Tristan only realized how horrible his predicament was when his mother suggested moving back home until he was back on his feet. Tristan almost choked on his chewing gum when his mother suggested it. He was twenty-five; there was no way he was moving back home.

Tristan's next call was to Ryan whose first suggestion, predictably, was to come work for him. Tristan appreciated the offer, but was always hesitant when it came to mixing friendship and business. As an employee their friendship may change, and Tristan wasn't willing to gamble with his best friend for a few dollars. Ryan didn't argue and went on to offer other suggestions. They agreed that Tristan was too soft to be a policeman, and not soft enough to teach kindergarten. They also agreed that chicks wouldn't pay to see a bald stripper and Tristan was too proud to model wigs. All in all, the conversations had achieved next to nothing.

It was time for Tristan to get his head out of the clouds and find a career.

Tristan had some realistic options available to him, but none screamed: *that's it, I'm the one!* and that worried him. As much as he loved writing, it was obvious that being a big fancy writer was a lot harder than he first thought. He loved helping people, but had a super weak stomach. That ruled out doctor, paramedic, or *Murse*. He chuckled at the thought of becoming a male nurse, he would never hear the end of it. There were other professionals that helped people though: psychologists, nutritionists, occupational therapists, that kind of thing. There was only one problem: Tristan had no interest in that crap whatsoever.

After hours of searching the internet and wracking his brain, Tristan had only come to one conclusion. He would be attending a local University, preferably Saint Agnus, so he could try and find part-time work and keep his apartment. That made things a bit easier as he could then look at programs specific to Saint Agnus. Tristan was pleased with that at the very least, but decided he needed a break. Subway popped into his mind and he reached for his coat. He didn't have time to finish putting it one when his phone rang.

"Yello?" Tristan was in a much better mood than he had been.

"Tristan! How are you, kid?"

Tristan smiled when he heard Karl's voice. They hadn't talked in quite some time.

"You can hardly call me *kid* anymore Karl," Tristan replied jovially, "I'll be twenty-six in a couple of months."

"Yeah I know, but you'll always be the ballsy kid who tried to steal my daughter."

Tristan chuckled. "We both know it takes two to tango, sir."

"Cut it, you smart ass. I didn't call to get lip." Karl commented sarcastically, "What are you up to anyway?"

"Well," he said, "funny you should ask. I quit my job yesterday."

"It's about time you got out of that shit hole," Karl said gruffly. "I always thought you were smart until you got caught up in that garbage. You are too good for them anyway, Tristan."

Karl always had been skeptical of media, reporters, and anything else government sanctioned. He was old fashioned and steadfast in his belief that each and every government institution was corrupt. Tristan got a kick out of it.

"I'm glad I have your support, but now I'm screwed. I have no idea what I'm going to do."

"Well, my boy, you do whatever you want. It is that simple."

"Not really, Karl." Tristan's voice became much more serious. "I can't afford everything else."

"Money is important Tristan, that is for sure, but don't let it stand in the way of your happiness. If you just find something you enjoy, the rest will work itself out. I promise."

Karl sounded so wise, so aged. Tristan decided then and there that he had to go visit his old friend as soon as possible. The sincerity in Karl's voice made Tristan more grateful than ever for their relationship.

"I know. But still—"

"Are you unsure of what you want? Or do you have no idea at all?"

Tristan plopped back down on the couch. It was obvious Karl was dedicated to discussing this for the long haul.

"I have no idea where to go from here. All I know is that I'll be going back to Saint Agnus."

"Well, I remember I had the same problem when I was your age…"

Tristan braced himself for an elder moment, but allowed Karl his moment in the sun.

"…ahhh never mind. I'll spare you the speech."

Tristan said a silent prayer. He loved Karl, but hated small talk all the same.

"I'll tell you one thing though, all jokes aside."

"Sure Karl, what's on your mind?"

"Well," Karl said, gathering his thoughts, "if there's one thing you are good at, Tristan, it is talking to people. I have never seen anyone handle emotions like you. As long as they are not your own issues to deal with, you don't just give good advice, you are a relative saint. Whatever you choose, you should really consider that trait. You could do some real good in the world, son."

Tristan felt something catch in his throat. After Deanna died, he never heard Karl speak so passionately about anything. Tristan felt honoured by his praise.

"Thanks, Karl. I, well, I'll try."

"Alright kid. Just remember, don't worry about anything but being happy. In the end, it is all we have anyways."

For the rest of the night Tristan replayed the conversation he had with Karl in his mind. Tristan was a firm believer in coincidence over fate, but Karl's call came at an interesting moment. After months of silence, he called to offer his advice at just the right time. Tristan figured D had something to do with it, wherever she was. All he knew was that it inspired him to keep moving forward with hope, rather than desperation.

He turned his attention to youth programs at Saint Agnus. They had some of the best social work degrees in the country. Though teaching might have been the wrong choice for Tristan, counselling teens with issues may be just the right route. He knew he had a very good upbringing, and he knew he was very lucky, but he also knew the trials and tribulations of teenage years. Most of the problems sprung from relationships, but he had also gone to hell and back with Deanna. Tristan knew he would love nothing more than to help struggling kids make better decisions than he had. He may be able to help those worse off than he had ever been.

Three Words

Tristan felt a surge of energy deep inside himself like the world's largest lightbulb had been switched on inside of him. He had heard about revelations, and moments of inspiration, but had never experienced one first hand. He felt rejuvenated, alive, and it all happened within seconds. Tristan looked around the room as though some invisible force was watching him. Tristan finally realized he had a purpose, and that he could do something extraordinary with the time he was given.

Tristan Cage finally had direction.

Chapter Thirty-Nine

Tristan enrolled in summer school that May. He didn't want to wait until September, he already felt like his life was slightly behind everyone else's. Tristan had a little trouble being accepted into a Master's in counselling program without having majored in Psychology. Tristan had a few psych courses, but not nearly enough. Luckily, he was on really good terms with the dean, and graduated Summa Cum Laude. His outstanding academic and volunteer record was enough to take to the dean for special consideration. Tristan went through an interview process to help determine if he was not only qualified, but interested in counselling. He was eventually accepted on the Dean's recommendation. The Dean vouched for him on the grounds that a psychology background was *recommended*, but not necessary. The essential skills of a counsellor would be taught in the Master's program itself.

Tristan's second stint at Saint Agnus was quite different from his first. The party scene no longer appealed to him—not as much anyway. Tristan was much more focused on the task at hand. He had a ton of research to do on different mental and social conditions. The social aspect of the course appealed to him much more than the medical, but everyone had to cover their bases.

Things were going well—better than they had in a long time—until the second week of November. Tuition was due for first semester; a whopping eight grand. The ill-fated letter arrived on a

Thursday. Tristan read the words with astonished denial. The government would not be funding his education because he would be turning twenty-six that calendar year. Tristan was devastated. He had figured out what he wanted, what he needed to do with his life, only to be denied for monetary reasons.

As expected, there was nothing student loans could do to help him. Their hands were tied. Talking to supervisors didn't help at all. The loan wasn't going to happen. Tristan's parents discussed remortgaging their house, but Tristan would have none of it. His parents honestly wanted to get him the money, and they would have, but as much at Tristan wanted to take it, he knew he wouldn't be able to live with himself if he did. His parents already paid thousands to help out with his living expenses during his first degree. It was his sister's turn.

Part-time work would not cover the costs. He had been working at a movie store sporadically to pay rent, but was dependent on that loan for tuition. Most of his time was spent researching for class, he couldn't sacrifice that for tuition, it would have been counterproductive. Tristan refused to ask Ryan—he was too proud for that. Ryan would have loaned him the money in a heartbeat, but Tristan would not ask him. It was hard to admit that his best friend was so successful. Somehow it would make Tristan feel less of a person to show his desperation, even to Ryan.

Tristan sat at his kitchen table with his head in his hands. He found no solutions to his problem, and could see none in sight. Tristan was preparing to admit defeat. He figured he would have to save money and go to school bit by bit. Instead of a year and half, it would probably take four. The thought of being thirty and just starting his career made him feel nauseous. Maybe he could volunteer at a youth shelter or something to tide him over.

The phone rang. It scared the hell out of Tristan who was lost in his angst. Tristan looked at the display and couldn't recognize the number. He assumed it was someone from student loans calling back to reaffirm his hopelessness, but he answered anyway.

"Yeah?"

"Mr. Cage?"

"Yes, this is him. May I ask who is calling?" Tristan said glumly.

"This is financial services at Saint Agnes. You left a message for us earlier?"

"Oh, yeah I did." Tristan knew what was coming.

"Well, unfortunately you do not qualify for in class scholarships due to your Master's status. They are only for undergraduate programs." The woman told him matter-of-factly.

"Yeah I know. I had to try." Tristan tried to remain professional. It was not this poor lady's fault he was going to have to drop out.

"Anything else I can help you with Mr. Cage?"

"Well yeah. I just have another question. How long do I have before my tuition is due?" Tristan hoped he could get an extension. It was better than nothing.

"It is due no later than October first. So two weeks from tomorrow. But yours is already paid in full."

"What? That's impossible." Tristan couldn't catch his breath.

"Yes." The woman sounded surprised at his reaction. "It was paid three days ago."

"But I didn't pay it," Tristan told himself to shut up, but his conscience would not allow it. "I think there is a mistake.

"Mr. Cage, that is highly unlikely. The funds were direct deposited into your account. If there was a mistake it is on the bank's end, and it is your lucky day. As far as we are concerned, you are paid in full."

Tristan could not talk. He couldn't blink. Tristan was so happy he thought it might kill him.

"Hello? Mr. Cage?" A worried voice stammered.

"Thank you." Tristan hung up and leaped into in the air. If anyone saw him they'd have thought he lost his mind. He was running around pumping his fist like he had just won the provincial championship all over again. Then the thought occurred to him. What if it *was* a mistake and they correct it? He would be doubly screwed spending money he didn't have.

His vigour vanished as quickly as it came and he frantically dialled the bank's number.

"Hello. Account number 566051"

"One moment please."

Tristan tapped his foot against the floor neurotically as he waited for a customer service rep. "Hello, Mr. Cage. How may I help you?"

"Hi. I just wanted to check my balance please."

"Certainly. Your balance is forty-three thousand, six hundred and fifty-three dollars and fifty-three cents."

The phone fell from Tristan's hand and shattered. The battery flew off the back of his phone and spun across the tiled floor.

43,000 dollars????

The last time he checked, he had seven hundred. It didn't make any sense! He hadn't won the lottery, nobody died and passed him on anything (to his knowledge) and everyone he knew didn't have that type of money kicking around. His parents must have lied to him, they must have remortgaged the house even when he told them not to.

Tristan skittered across the floor like a man possessed and put his phone back together. He didn't care if it worked. He would run home and ask his parents if he had to at this point. He got a dial tone and his mother answered after two rings.

"Hi sonny!"

"Mom," Tristan was in no mood for niceties. He was flattered but he had been adamant about them not sacrificing their own future for him. "I told you not to mortgage the God damned house."

"What?" She sounded genuinely surprised. Tristan backed off a little.

"Mom, I have forty three thousand dollars in my bank account. I have no idea how it got there. This is the only explanation."

"Tristan, we didn't re-mortgage anything. I have no idea what you are talking about."

"I'll call you back."

Tristan had no idea what was going on. It felt like a dream that could turn into a nightmare at any moment. Tristan wanted to believe that the money was actually his, and that he could continue classes, but doubted the thought every time it came into his mind.

Nobody is that lucky.

He called the bank back and got what sounded like the same agent he had before.

"I'm sorry I hung up on you before. My hand slipped."

The agent chuckled. "It's ok Mr. Cage. How may I assist you?"

Tristan took a deep breath. "The money in my account. I think there has been a mistake. I didn't put it there."

"Oh, wow, what a nice surprise for you, Mr. Cage!" The agent sounded amused, but Tristan was not. "Everyone should be so—"

"How the hell did it get there?!" Tristan cut right to the chase.

"Sorry, Mr. Cage. One moment." Tristan heard typing, silence, then typing again. "It was a direct deposit sir. There is no mistake."

"Deposit from where?"

"A personal account Mr. Cage, from a Mr. Karl Greene."

Chapter Forty

Tristan almost dropped the phone a second time. He hung up on the poor agent without saying another word. There was no way he had the money, especially forty thousand dollars' worth, to *give* to Tristan. Karl wasn't poor, but he was paying out a lot of money to his wife in alimony.

He couldn't accept the money. It was that simple.

Karl picked up on the first ring. "Tristan. Don't say a word. I'm assuming you found out your tuition has been paid, and knowing you, are about to insult me by refusing to accept it. I am going to stop you from making that mistake."

Tristan blinked rapidly in an attempt to comprehend Karl's transformation from friend, to saviour.

"You have been like a son to me all through Deanna's illness and after. I love you like I loved her, and I have no other children. My wife is gone, and the rest of my family is spread out across the country. The money came from Deanna's college fund. You and I both know that she would have wanted you to have it."

Tristan couldn't pick his jaw off of the floor, nor could he stop his eyes from burning at the mention of Deanna's name. Karl spoke with such conviction that Tristan *felt* like his son.

"But. But you need the money. I "

Karl's laugh spoke confidence, "My boy, you have *no idea* what my finances are like. There is plenty where that came from, but if you use what I gave you wisely, you won't need more."

Tristan's astonishment grew. He knew Karl's farm was not overly successful. It was average and Karl made a decent living, but Tristan knew he couldn't have gotten rich from it. He wanted to ask where his stability came from, but knew it would be rude. Good thing Karl seemed to have a knack for guessing his thoughts.

"Tristan, if you must know, I'm rich. Not multi-millionaire rich, but rich enough that I could retire today and never work again and live in comfort."

"But how?" Tristan knew he must sound like a three year old, but he didn't care. The day's events were so astounding, so overwhelming, that he just wanted to soak it up.

"Well, I guess the cat is out of the bag already, eh?" Karl chuckled again. "My father owned a successful real estate business out of province. When he died, he sold the business and split the money between my brother and me. My mother passed years earlier and he knew neither myself, nor my brother, Andy, had any interest in running the business. Fifteen years ago, we inherited a small fortune. I never told anyone in Sageview or Milton because I didn't want the fact that I had money to change the hard working, blue collar reputation I had built. I am proud of my dirty calloused hands, Tristan. I am proud...."

Tristan could only gape at the white wall in front of him. He pressed his toe into the floor until the pressure hurt. He had to be sure this wasn't a dream. He had enough money, not just to pay tuition for the semester, but for the whole year and a half. He would have money left over, that he would return of course.

"I want you to keep it all, Tristan, even if you don't need it. I trust you will honour where it came from, and use it wisely."

Is Karl a guardian Angel? Is he God? That is the third time he knew exactly what was going on.

What do you say to someone who saves your life? Sure Karl hadn't pulled him out of a burning building, he hadn't cured him of a deadly virus, or sewn a limb back on, but he kept Tristan's hopes alive. What were more important than hopes and dreams? In essence, Karl was his saviour. He wanted to cry, to thank him, to fall on his knees and let out his emotion, but he was a man now. He did what men do.

"Thank you, Karl." He whispered. He didn't know what else to say.

"You don't need to thank me, son. And you don't owe me anything. Money is nothing compared to what you gave my little girl. You saved what was left of her life and mine. Now go enjoy some of your new cash, but not too much. Take care."

Tristan could hear the quiver in Karl's voice as he let Tristan go, so Tristan didn't try to stop him. When Tristan looked down at his phone to end the call, one of his own tears splashed onto the keys. Part of him wanted to believe in miracles, but if he believed that, he would resent D's death even more. She deserved a miracle more than he ever would. He chalked it up to Karl's greatness as a human being, nothing more.

Tristan called Ryan, Amy, and Alec and headed to a local restaurant for drinks and merriment. His four companions were just as amazed as he was at his good fortune, but everyone knew him well enough to let the subject die after the story had been told. Tristan's friends knew he was thankful, but also that he felt guilty about accepting the gift. Instead of dwelling, everyone brought their own stories to share with him.

Ryan and Amy enjoyed the rest of their honeymoon on a Caribbean Cruise. Alec got a raise at his job at Smart Tech. Alec was a big wig computer programmer, a regular nerd in sheep's clothing. They had only begun eating when his parents and sister strolled in to join them. Tristan figured they would show up as a surprise. His mother had never been a great liar. When he called to ask them out to dinner she said, "Uhhhh we are too busy, but where are you headed in case we decide to make the trip?" Her attempt at deception was obvious, but Tristan had played along.

Tristan glanced up from his food to take a mental picture of the scene in front of him. Everyone at the table was talking, laughing, and telling stories. They wore smiles and were involved in their own little conversations. Emma sat down next to Amy, and they were chatting about god knows what. Ryan and Cameron were discussing business while he and Alec quizzed each other on the Raptors season yet to begin. His mother was content to enjoy it, and take it all in. She smiled at him and he returned the favour.

—

The next month was one of the most successful of Tristan's young life. He continued to excel in his counselling program and began to rebuild a solid friendship with Callie. She seemed happy in her new relationship, the young lady's name was Stephanie, and she was a successful PR rep for Red Bull. Tristan found it odd discussing homosexual relationship issues, but they helped open his eyes to a breadth of issues he could never comprehend as a heterosexual. He began to value his conversations with Callie even more over time. They helped equip him for some of the conversations he would encounter as a counsellor.

Near the end of October, Tristan's professor assigned a project that would change Tristan's life. The task was to design an original case study that would fuel the topic for their Master's thesis. Tristan was not looking forward to writing an eighty page thesis, but knew it would rear its ugly head eventually. Professor Niering offered to let the case study double as their thesis proposal, as well as a research assignment. By agreeing to take part, they would kill two birds with one stone. The only problem Tristan could think of was that he had no idea how he was going to build his case study, or what he was going to write his thesis on.

Three Words

Tristan had one week to submit his Case Study proposal, then he would have a month to carry it out and study it. He needed test subjects, which meant he needed willing participants, and more importantly, he needed an idea. The idea he came up with could not simply be good, it had to be great. Tristan sat at his computer and stared at his Facebook page praying.

Praying for what?

A sign?

There was no more influential tool for modern teens than the internet. Teens spent hours upon hours playing games, chatting, reading, or surfing the net. Some people even led double lives over the internet. It was used to entertain, but also to escape. As Tristan stared at the Facebook phenomenon, the smattering of personal information flooded his senses. People of all ages plastered their business for all to see—or at least the hundreds of people with whom they were friends to see. People were so desperate for an outlet that they used their most accessible medium, the internet, to get attention. Putting up a message like FML—"Fuck my life"—immediately drew the attention of peers who would ask, "What's wrong?" Facebook, or something like it, was the perfect way to reach hundreds, thousands, of people that needed help.

Tristan began typing frantically to get all his ideas written down before he forgot them. His proposal was done in an hour. Tristan planned to create a website, of his own, that allowed teenagers to discuss relationships issues, their ups and their downs, with a therapist in training—ie him—and with their peers, which was a form of therapy itself. Tristan's website would be a controlled outlet. Easily accessible and anonymous for those who chose to remain so. Tristan was aware of the multitude of challenges he would face. Chat rooms were a notorious red flag for sexual predators, which made a teenage website, specifically about relationships, akin to sending up fireworks for pedophiles. Tristan would have to protect his clients somehow, he just wasn't sure how he could. Tristan also knew that on the internet there was really no way to tell if people were who they said they were, which could also cause problems. Tristan's biggest challenge would be security, followed by accountability. People would have to know who he was, and what he was all about, so that he was not accused of luring teens himself.

Tristan developed a solution to the second issue immediately. He would put a disclaimer, very visible, for all to see before anyone was able to enter his site. It would say that anyone using his website would be a willing participant in a psychological experiment along with any personal information about himself that was required to prove authenticity. Tristan would add his name, age, education and qualifications as well as the purpose of the experiment. By clicking "Ok" before entering the site, it would ensure everyone had read the disclaimer. Tristan reminded himself to run that by his professor before he put it into action.

As far as security for his webpage went, Tristan was at a loss. Fortunately for him, one of his best friends happened to be a genius computer programmer. Alec would be willing to help, and Tristan hoped he would have some ideas on how to make his site secure.

Tristan worked for two hours, but needed to keep going. His brain was in overdrive. He turned his attention to the content of the site; relationships. A sounding board for any teenager who needed advice, needed to vent, or needed to talk to someone who shared similar experiences. The atmosphere would need to be positive, but not corny; educational, not harmful.

Tristan's sketches included links for qualified therapists, help lines and information for more serious issues like addiction and suicide. He had a chat room—he starred that for removal if a procedure could not be put in place to protect the participants—and a place for him to blog about his own life experiences in relationships in order to make people feel comfortable with him. His email contact information was added, as well as space for non-profit educational organizations to advertize. Tristan tried to shut

Three Words

out the knowledge that the internet was enormous, and that it was very possible nobody would ever hear about his site. He hoped that the tendency to Google everything would get him some random hits and grow slowly. He didn't want to promote it.

As Tristan thought, he picked up the phone to call Alec. As it rang, he doodled in his notebook. He wrote both words "love" and "hate" in pencil and looked at the letters. People didn't realize the strength of words, especially words with connotations like the ones on his page. By the time Alec answered the phone, after what seemed like an eternity, Tristan had another revelation.

"Yo, What's up?" Alec chimed cheerfully.

"I need your help man. It's a biggie." Tristan spoke softly his eyes were following his pencil once again moving across the page.

"Anything. You know that. What are we going to do?"

"We're gonna build my website." Tristan replied as if in a trance.

Before he spoke again his eyes looked proudly upon his new creation.

threewords.com

Chapter Forty-One

Alec had to slow Tristan down a few dozen times. Apparently, Tristan forgot that Alec had a full time job, a steady girlfriend, and needed some down time for himself. Tristan hadn't known how large a job it would be to build something like he had in mind. At no point did Alec sound anything but supportive, but he also was unsure of the time frame Tristan expected. He only had a week to get it up and running to meet the deadline. If he were being honest, he wanted the website up and running yesterday. Tristan broke the news to Alec—one week at the most.

Alec didn't sound very positive about the time constraint, but told Tristan that he had built up overtime hours so he could take a couple days off to work on things. Alec warned Tristan not to offer him any money, but was happy to learn there would be money on hand if the website needed it. Alec's solution to the security issue was simplistic, but genius. The site would be password protected. Although it may discourage people from 'dropping in' like Tristan hoped, it gave it a more professional feel, and was much safer for people once they were inside.

The password would only be provided to people who asked for it, and Tristan approved. Tristan was adamant that the website be non profit. That would dodge potentially sticky business issues that Tristan was not interested in. He planned on contacting other non-profit organizations and allowing them to advertize, but nobody else. Tristan also planned on contacting the police to make them aware of his site to see if there was some type of protection they could offer on their end. Better safe than sorry.

Alec slaved day and night for four days straight. The website was up and functional, but it still needed to be fine-tuned and cleaned up. Alec promised to do it over the next week or so. Tristan certainly wasn't going to push him. The site worked perfectly. It didn't look the best yet, but that could be fixed over time.

Alec showed Tristan how to do basic administrative tasks. He installed a program that randomized specific passwords for each client that could not be changed. That person would have a specific signature that allowed Tristan to know exactly who was using his site and when. Passwords would have been pointless if they could be spread around and shared easily. Tristan was also able to spend his time uploading useful documents and writing his introductory blog.

Tristan hadn't realized how difficult it would be to put his experience with Deanna into words, especially words that complete strangers would read, but he needed to earn the trust of his visitors if his experiment was going to work. Tristan poured his heart and soul into his most powerful memories when it came to teenage love. He paused numerous times to compose himself, but soldiered on. He knew that if his website worked, it would allow for an easily accessible, safe, environment for kids to talk about one of their biggest challenges.

When Tristan presented his proposal to professor Niering, he was not disappointed with the results.

"I think you could be onto something here, Cage." The professor stroked his short greying beard. "You avoided legal issues with your disclaimer, as well as your admission that you are just a moderator, not a qualified counsellor. By providing such an accessible—and that is the main thing for kids today, accessibility—by providing a floor for discussion on such a relevant topic, it should yield intriguing results. What are you looking for exactly?"

Tristan anticipated the question for over a week. He had an answer ready to go. "My hypothesis is that kids use the internet so readily because they can remain nameless and have a voice. The fear they have about social ramifications is erased. It is my belief that they will unite and counsel one another through common experiences."

The Professor nodded. He seemed impressed.

"And what will you do?"

"I will be moderating. Ensuring the environment remains safe and secure as well as offering advice, not counselling, based on my personal experiences as well."

"Well, good luck, Cage. I am certainly impressed with the amount of detail that went into this proposal. Even if it doesn't work out, that is the point of experimentation. I look forward to reading about your results."

"Thanks professor." Tristan no longer masked his smile. The truth was, he was proud of himself.

Tristan worked non-stop on threewords.com for over a week. It was time to give himself a break. After he was finished double checking his information, he turned off the computer and kicked up his feet. He hadn't had a beer in a while and decided to have one in celebration of his recent good fortune. The walk to the fridge felt good. He no longer felt guilty about drinking his last lager. He could afford more.

As he wrapped his hand around the neck of the bottle, he remembered something his father once told him: "The only folks who drink alone are bums and alcoholics." Tristan eyed the bottle suspiciously. He was hell bent on drinking it, but apparently he needed to find someone to drink with. He dug his phone out of his pocket and called around. Ryan and Amy were busy being married, and Alec was with his girlfriend. Tristan realized his circle of friends shrunk from what it once was. He toyed with the idea of calling Callie.

What's the worst that could happen?

He still had her number on speed dial and proceeded to press the button that would attempt to reach his homosexual ex-girlfriend. Tristan would have to wait to tell Callie about his new venture, after three rings he got the answering machine. *She is most likely with Stephanie*—Tristan stopped himself, for thinking of Callie and her new lover made him excited—as any typical hormone inspired male—but also jealous. He was not used to the combination.

He sat at the table with his chin on his palm and stared at the bottle of beer. The beer stared back. Tristan refused to relax by himself. He had not reached hermit status. He was a university student again! He could just go out and get loaded at the pub like old times. The thought was appealing, but not appealing enough to convince him. He glanced at the clock. 8:30PM. There was time to catch a late show at the theatre, and it was only two minutes away. Tristan loved movies since he was a kid, but had never loved them enough to attend one by himself.

There was a first time for everything.

He started the lonely trek to the theatre and tried not to think about the fact everyone he knew was busy with their significant others. Tristan suddenly missed Callie more than ever. They saw a ton of movies together, and it was one of things Tristan loved most about her. She always embraced Tristan's nerdy movie fascination. He scuffed his feet as his bitterness festered.

Being alone sucked.

He made his way into the theatre and took his traditional seat at the back. That way he could relax and not worry about hoodlums throwing popcorn or candy. Tristan pulled his touque down low and settled in. He slid down in his seat. He was more comfortable in this position, but it also helped shield him from anyone he might know. Remaining anonymous was important when you went to movies by yourself—or so he had been told.

Tristan was early, as usual, and resorted to playing games on his cell phone. He was enjoying an intense session of Bejeweled when the lights went off and the screen lit up. The theatre filled up and most of the seats were taken, but there were two seats open to his left and right. He figured nobody wanted to sit next to the reclining loser at the back.

The previews had all of his attention until he sensed movement out of the corner of his eye. People closest to the aisle on his right were standing to let someone by. It was too dark to make out anything about the new arrival except that it was a she. Tristan wondered if she'd opt to sit next to the girl two seats away, or next to him. She sat next to the girl. Tristan scolded himself for being so stupid. Of course she sat next to the girl; she was probably part of their group. He was the only one stupid enough to come by himself.

Tristan was mildly disappointed. The girl was attractive for a silhouette. He turned his attention back to the screen. Tristan was just refocusing his attention when a familiar distraction caught his eye. The new girl was standing up—was she leaving? She shifted her position to sit next to Tristan. Why had she moved? Tristan saw a young man coming up the steps to the back of the theatre. Tristan scrunched his nose as he realized she was making room for her boyfriend. Of course she was.

The young man turned and sat two rows ahead of them. Tristan frowned. He turned his head quickly to the side. What if she had seen him going through his procession of facial expressions? He expected her to move again, to escape from the retarded guy at the back, but she didn't seem to notice. She was fixed on the screen like a normal human being. Tristan peered at her out of the corner of his eye. His heart stopped. Tristan felt the sudden urge to vomit or run.

Goddamn the confines of theatre seating!

Sitting next to him was Julia. The same Julia he had publicly humiliated and possibly gotten fired. Tristan slid even lower in his seat to the point where he was almost lying down. She couldn't have recognized him, not yet anyway, or the fireworks would have already started. Tristan propped his elbow on the headrest next to Julia and used his hand to hide his face. How did these things always wind up happening to him? He needed to get out of there. He could turn and walk the other way, but twice as many people would have to move. The other isle was twice the distance as the one to his right. It was worth the risk.

If only Tristan had of noticed the large soda Julia placed in the cup holder attached to the arm rest he could have avoided disaster, but he was too caught up in panic. When he moved to stand up he bumped the large soda just enough to have it rock and splash. Tristan watched in slow motion horror as the liquid made contact with her bare leg. Her arms flew up as she looked at the small mess in her lap. Tristan told himself to run, leap over rows of seating if he had to, but he was frozen.

"I'm *so* sorry!" he whispered. "I was just trying to get out and go to the bathroom."

She glanced up at him with what looked like a smile. "It's alright. Do you have a napkin or something?"

A chorus of *shushes* came at them from the people seated near them. Tristan understood their frustration. He hated movie talkers, but this was an emergency. Without thinking, Tristan pulled his touque off and started dabbing her thigh. He paused after a couple seconds to realize he had not only spilt pop on Julia, but was now rubbing her naked thigh with his touque. In his moment of panic he had also exposed his bald head, perhaps the most defining trait about himself. If Julia hadn't known it was him before, she knew now. Tristan waited for the embarrassed backlash but none came.

He was crouched over her lap and told himself to keep scrubbing or move. Tristan paused as he realized it probably looked like he was staring up her skirt. He turned his head, slowly, to see how irate Julia was. She looked amusedly at him with one raised eyebrow. He could make out the thin line of a grin in the relative darkness.

"You missed a spot. She flicked her eyes downward."

Tristan was suddenly very confused. Either Julia had amnesia or had gone completely insane. He told the entire office that she was blowing her boss and she was hitting on him? It sure seemed that way. Tristan eased himself back into his chair. The movie had started, but that was very far away in his thoughts.

She turned her head to look at him. If Tristan didn't know how much of a skank she was, he'd think her beautiful. Her brown hair was streaked with blonde which complimented her dark skin. The screen flickered from scene to scene shedding a pale light on her face. Tristan didn't know she had a nose ring.

"I bought that Pepsi, mister. You owe me a drink."

Tristan tried to hide his astonishment, but it must have showed.

"Oh, you don't take hints very well. Do you?" She whispered playfully.

"It's not that," Tristan stammered. "It's just that. Well, we hate each other!"

She frowned. "I'm sorry. We just met, and I tend not to hate cute boys who spill a bit of pop on me."

"Julia, really, this is weird." Tristan was losing patience. He was mortified and in no mood for games. Had she followed him there? She was probably toying with him before she stabbed him. Tristan inched away.

She was shaking her head.

"I see." She smiled. "Julia is my twin sister. I'm Robyn."

Tristan stared at the hand held out to him with awe.

Chapter Forty-Two

Robyn Stein was Julia's twin sister, but they shared nothing but their looks in common. Robyn was an accountant who just happened to enjoy long walks on the beach and attending movies solo. Tristan met more than a fellow movie buff that night. Robyn was an avid sports fan who played university soccer out of province. Tristan could tell she was an athlete as soon as he got a good look at her. She was fit; sleek and sexy. Their first date after the movie—Tristan found someone to share a beer with—was the first of many. By Christmas the two were unofficially dating.

Tristan was gun shy about the whole relationship thing and made that clear to Robyn from the beginning. He hadn't gone into detail about his past exploits, but gave her enough information to know they needed to go slow. She was fine with that, but also made it clear to Tristan that she carried no baggage. Her last relationship had been two years prior to meeting Tristan. The two compromised, and dated like teenagers. There were a couple sleepovers and many trips to the theatre, but no meeting families or marriage talk.

Julia hadn't taken the news well when Robyn informed her of Tristan's re-entering of her life. Tristan had been wise and told Robyn what happened up front. He was relieved when she laughed at him. She informed Tristan they were not the average set of twins. Instead of sharing a bond of friendship, they nearly killed each other multiple times. She got along with her sister as a familial formality, nothing more.

Robyn was fascinated with Tristan's research project, which had taken off during their courtship. Threewords.com had gone from internet obscurity to teen safe haven in a matter of weeks. Tristan had been ready to give up hope and call it quits when he started getting consistent hits. By the time his month was up and the project was due, the site was just gaining momentum. Tristan refused to stop working on it simply because his time frame ended. By mid-January Tristan had over 300 registered users with unique passwords and logins. Tristan's clients ranged in age from twelve to eighteen.

Tristan was very successful dealing with the issues he was confronted with. He had a couple red flags for suicidal tendencies and deferred them to the proper authorities, but other than that he took care of things himself. He had private email sessions with many of his clients and seemed to be helping them out. Tristan's greatest success, however, was with the amount the kids were helping each other. The chat rooms were filled with advice and constructive criticism and most people followed website regulations. Any abusers were dealt with swiftly to discourage others. Tristan had no tolerance for put downs, inappropriate suggestions, or random inquiries. His site was for dealing with teen issues. If they wanted to talk about sports or playmates there were plenty of regular chat sites they could access.

Professor Niering was so impressed with Tristan's success that he recommended Tristan for the Henley Award. The award was given to a psychology student who yielded remarkable results in a given study. If Tristan was to receive the award—and he prayed he would—it would go a long way in securing a job. The Henley award was only given to top Masters Students at Saint Agnus.

Robyn thought that Tristan should seek donations to expand his site, but Tristan thought otherwise. He didn't want Threewords to become a media outlet. He wished for it to remain exactly what it was. Tristan planned on expanding, but with his own investments in his own time. He was perfectly fine with the slow expansion the site was undergoing on its own. There were three hundred teens being helped that were slipping between the cracks before Threewords, and Tristan was proud of that.

Tristan's friends and family were astounded with the progress of the website as well. Ryan offered to provide some funds but Tristan reminded him that he was not a charity. Any money Tristan received could not be recognized because he was non-profit. It was better to invest his own money, and only his own, to avoid complications. His parents were so proud. When they first laid eyes on his project they looked at him like a celebrity. Tristan knew he was far from famous, but it was still nice to be recognized.

Things with Threewords—and with Robyn—were moving splendidly into February. Robyn endured Tristan's slow pace for a few months, but started to get antsy. She informed Tristan that she didn't need a title applied to their relationship status, but she did want him to meet her family. Tristan reminded her about the hatred Julia harboured for him, but she brushed that off. She told Tristan if they were going to be together long term, he would have to make up with Julia eventually. Tristan couldn't argue with her line of thinking, besides, it was almost a year since he quit is job at *The Sun*.

Tristan reluctantly agreed to meet Robyn's entire family. He guessed there was more to the situation but was still surprised when Robyn dropped the bomb: They would be attending a wedding, her cousin's wedding, the following weekend. Tristan put on a happy face to accept the news, but inside he was dreading it.

Weddings. Why does it always have to be a wedding? Haven't I been to enough of those already?

Tristan knew weddings were popular ice-breakers in new relationships. They were bubbly and loving and fun, but Tristan saw weddings for what they really were: an excuse for females to fantasize about their own weddings as their unsuspecting boyfriends drank themselves stupid. The conniving female may even get a proposal out of her drunken boyfriend if the mood was right.

The wedding was taking place in Chester, two hours from Sageview. Robyn picked Tristan up in her red Mazda 3. He took a quick look around and was relieved to see that there was nobody with her. He asked about the absence of her other family members and learned they were traveling separately in case the young folks decided to stay the night. There were cabins to rent, and Robyn was adamant they were even more beautiful in the winter.

Tristan and Robyn had a pleasant drive to Chester together. Pleasant was fine, but made Tristan feel old and married. He looked down at his suit. He *looked* married. He glanced nervously at an unsuspecting Robyn as she drove.

She lied to me. This is probably our wedding.

Tristan pushed back in the passenger seat and slid down. Robyn looked over at him playfully, "Sit up Tristan. We're not at the movie theatre. What if we crash?"

Her voice was sweet, and her intentions innocent, but Tristan shuddered. Her concern sounded awfully maternal to him. It would be unfair for him to pick a fight, especially when she had done nothing wrong, so he shoved his concerns far into the depths of his mind and sat up straight. They were almost to the wedding anyway, and where there was a wedding, there was liquid courage.

As they approached the church, Tristan decided to get some much needed background information so he didn't make an ass of himself.

"So, I probably should have asked you before, but who is getting married?"

"I told you Tristan," Robyn looked slightly annoyed, though her annoyance was probably directed at the lack of parking spaces, "my cousin."

"I know that." Tristan figured the fact he was looking for a name would have been obvious, "What's her name?"

Three Words

"Oh, it's a he. His name is Randy." Tristan frowned. Randy; there were lots of Randy's in the world. It was just funny that the last person he encountered with the name Randy had been the one thing that stood between him and the greatest girl alive. Tristan found the irony in the situation cruel. Attending a wedding that symbolized a union he would never have. He rubbed his temple to stop his brain from having a meltdown.

"What's wrong babe?" Robyn put a hand on his arm.

"Oh nothing, really." He smiled to reassure her. "Just had to clear my head."

Robyn had coordinated their wedding outfits and Tristan felt slightly embarrassed as they walked to the chapel. Tristan looked at his orange dress shirt complete with black tie. He was just realizing how ugly it was. Robyn looked stunning in her black and orange dress, but that didn't help matters. They looked like a couple of pumpkins attending a wedding in February. Who got married in February anyway?

The couple took their seats, and Tristan looked around nervously. They were seated on the groom's side of the church and he recognized no one but Julia, who glared menacingly at him as he walked through the door. Tristan and Robyn sat behind her parents in a mid-level pew. There were brief introductions, but "Kenny and Pam" were busy mingling with other relatives. Moments later, Robyn too was engaged in a less than stimulating conversation with some other random person and Tristan found himself staring at the impressively high ceiling.

After a few minutes Tristan's boredom prodded him to search for an alternative means of entertainment. He resorted to people watching with the off chance of seeing something interesting. There was a cute little girl to his left pre-maturely blowing the bubbles she had been given. Tristan smiled at the site and hoped she didn't spill them at an inopportune time. There was an old lady talking freely about bridge strategy and a teenage couple texting at the back. Tristan found it amusing that they were at a wedding with each other and both texting other people—unless they were texting each other…

Tristan's attention was drawn to an attractive young couple who had just come through the main doors.

God that looks like Matt Staunton. Wait, that is Matt! What the hell. Isn't that funny…

Tristan threw an arm up and Matt smiled back at him. Tristan hadn't seen much of the couple since he had attended their wedding three years earlier. Tristan stood up and walked around back to speak with his old friend.

"Tristan! I'm surprised to see you here!"

"Yeah, same here." Tristan waved to Lacey who was speaking with someone else.

"Oh yeah, we weren't going to come, but Lacey and Adrienne were close in high school."

Tristan jerked his head to the side to peer at a nervous looking Matt. Matt couldn't have said Adrienne. There was no way. He must have made a mistake.

Tristan laughed uneasily, "Adrienne? What do you mean? Not Adrienne Axley?"

It was Matt's turn to look uneasy. He looked at the floor then back at Tristan, "Oh my God. You don't know."

Tristan felt his blood pressure rising. At the rate he was going he would have to avoid weddings by the time he was thirty just to stay alive.

"Matt, what are you talking about?" Tristan felt his teeth grind.

"Tristan. I ummm, I really don't know how to tell you this—"

Tristan gripped Matt's sleeve and stared him in the eyes. "Matt, spit it out!"

A few of the guests nearby shot Tristan a glare, but he ignored them. "Matt, seriously, you are freaking me out."

"This is Adrienne's wedding, Tristan."

No…

Three Words

The room started to spin. One of Tristan's hands gripped Matt's shirt sleeve and the other reached out for a nearby pew to balance himself. He felt like he was going to vomit. Adrienne Axley was the love of his life. He never expected her to get married! She wasn't even happy, or at least she hadn't been.

"Matt, tell me you are joking."

Matt looked at him sympathetically, "No Tristan. I'm not. That's why I was so surprised to see you here. Everyone knows you and Adrienne have history."

History? History? We have more than history for fuck sakes.

Tristan didn't know what to do. He knew Adrienne and Randy had been dating for a long time, but he always expected them to break up, he *knew* they would break up. He couldn't have been wrong. If Matt was telling the truth, then Tristan had no more time, no more chances. If Matt was right, Adrienne was soon to be out of his grasp forever.

"Tristan," Matt gently removed Tristan's hand from his arm, "I need to go. I really am sorry."

Tristan watched Matt join his wife and take their seat. Salt in the wound. Tristan had to leave, he had to get out of there. He couldn't breathe. Every second it became harder to function. He looked at the door. Robyn was the last thing on his mind. He could not stay in that church. Tristan rounded the corner only to be stopped by an usher.

"The wedding party is in the foyer, sir. And the bride is en route. Please take your seat."

Fuck this!

Tristan looked at the man in front of him. The poor unsuspecting man. Tristan's fists were clenched tight. Tristan could feel his temperature rising.

"Please move, mister. I need to —"

"Tristan!" He closed his eyes as Robyn grabbed his arm and spun him around. "What are you doing? The wedding is ready to start we need to sit down!"

Tristan was defeated. He couldn't make a scene, not once everyone had seen him with Robyn. He couldn't be the ruination of Adrienne's wedding. He allowed himself to be dragged back to his seat.

"Tristan are you alright? You are pale as a ghost." Robyn felt his forehead and Tristan brushed her hand away.

"I'm fine, just warm."

Tristan no sooner had the words out of his mouth when he saw Randy walking to the altar. Intense jealousy threatened to take over Tristan's free will so he looked at the floor instead.

Tristan could hear the ooohs and ahhhs as the wedding party made their way into the church. He prayed that the wedding march wouldn't start. He prayed that when he looked up the bride would be anyone but *his* Adrienne.

Forget it, Cage. You had your chance. You blew it.

The music started and everyone stood. Tristan felt himself rise and saw the proceedings from outside of his body. A force he was powerless against took control and forced him to watch in tortured silence. He saw her. His eyes burned in awe of her beauty. Her dark brown hair was slightly longer than he remembered. Her bangs were pulled back underneath her veil. Her caramel skin was the perfect contrast to her snow white dress. Her father held her arm as he guided her down the aisle.

As she got closer, Tristan noticed her hand shaking, but he also noticed her tears. He studied her face. He knew Adrienne well.

She was not upset.

She was not scared.

He saw nothing but happiness in her eyes. What was left of his heart shattered. Nothing was more final, nothing more devastating, than seeing how happy she was at that moment.

Tristan was about to turn his gaze away, he could take no more, when her head turned in his direction. Their eyes met. The smile on her face faded to a look of sheer amazement. She looked as if she had seen a ghost. A tear trickled down her face, a tear that no longer seemed a symbol of happiness, but of regret. She paused on her walk, but only briefly. She closed her eyes to quell their treasonous desires, and continued walking.

Adrienne made it to the altar, noticeably shaken, but only Tristan could tell. Only Tristan knew what had happened. The guests took their seats, and Robyn pulled him down by his shirt sleeve. Tristan's eyes were locked on the proceedings. He pleaded with his body to look away, but he could not. His heart felt like it was molten, bleeding fire and flame into his soul. Tristan didn't know if death could be worse than what he was experiencing.

He told himself to hold on. He told himself not to do anything stupid, or crazy. He owed Adrienne more than that, but the pain was too much. He simply could not watch her marry another man. The priest had the first syllable out of his mouth to start the wedding when Tristan stood up. Every guest gasped and looked in his direction. Randy's head spun around and a confused look crossed his face. They had never met. He didn't know who the strange man was standing alone in the crowd.

Adrienne fought to control herself as their eyes met one last time. This time, the tear seared a path down the side of Tristan's face. Adrienne opened her mouth a fraction, but no words escaped her beautiful lips. He wanted to cry out, he wanted to plead with her to marry him instead. He wanted to apologize. He wanted to tell her he loved her.

Tell her you coward. Tell her!

But Tristan left amongst the murmuring guests without saying a word.

Chapter Forty-Three

Tristan took a Greyhound home from Chester. He couldn't face Robyn, and he couldn't watch Adrienne get married. He was relieved when Robyn hadn't chased him out of the church, at least one of them had some sense. He assumed everyone went back to the ceremony like Tristan had never been there in the first place. Tristan stared out the bus window and imagined the aftermath of what he had done. He and Robyn were certainly over, but he planned on explaining himself, if she ever spoke to him again.

Tristan's short-term memory skipped back and forth between images. He saw the pain in Adrienne's eyes one second, and the happiness on her face the next. The mental slide show was unbearable, and Tristan wished there was a power button. The trees made the outside world into a green blur as the bus took him closer to home. Mercifully, he dozed off for the remainder of the drive.

The next sound he heard was the bus driver announcing the stop in Sageview. Tristan was almost two hours from his apartment, but only forty-five minutes from his parents. He started walking from the small Sageview gas Station where the bus dropped him off and made for Karl's. He hoped his old friend would be home, and willing to take in a drifter.

Karl was wise in his years and recognized Tristan wanted nothing more than to go to sleep. Karl asked no questions. He simply showed Tristan to the guest room where he slept so many times. Before Tristan closed his eyes, he finally realized how hard Karl's life must be. Tristan felt alone, but Karl *was* alone. His only child dead and his wife gone shortly after. Karl's aging family members were spread across the country ,and Tristan wasn't sure how much contact he had with them. As he reached to turn out the lamp he swore he would spend the next day with Karl.

Tristan didn't get back to his apartment for three days. He spent one with Karl, one with his parents, and the last with Ryan and Amy. As soon as Tristan told Ryan what happened, Ryan wouldn't let him leave. Ryan was probably the only other person who understood the magnitude of what Tristan experienced. Amy simply gave him a gigantic hug and said no more. What could they say? Tristan didn't expect anyone to say anything. He knew that words could not reverse the passage of time. The only way he could get Adrienne back was with a time machine.

Tristan thought he could handle being by himself once he got back to a computer. He figured he could drown out the guilt and regret by becoming a workaholic. He was wrong. The second Ryan dropped him off and he had nobody to distract him, he was his own worst enemy. Instead of going out, or playing basketball, or calling someone to visit, Tristan endured the silent torture alone. Part of him blamed himself. He deserved what he got for being selfish and stupid for so many years.

Minutes turned into hours, and Tristan suffered. It was almost midnight and he achieved nothing on his website. He spent the time staring at the screen, but his mind was not there. He was focused on something entirely different. Tristan didn't feel like he was in the same room with his body. His psyche was somewhere else, trying to recover what he had lost. Tristan hadn't moved in so long that the sun had gone down and cast the apartment into darkness. He looked across the street at the building Callie now called home. He had yet to visit her due to his pride, or *perhaps* it was fear, either way he had never stepped foot in her apartment.

Three Words

She invited him many times, but never pressured him when he invented a lame excuse.

It was almost midnight and it was likely that Callie was in bed with her lady friend, but good sense was lacking. Tristan put his coat on and walked across the street. He scanned the apartment directory for her name and buzzed number 213. Tristan huddled against the brick wall to escape the chilly winter wind as he waited. He double checked the room number and buzzed again.

She's probably in bed.

Tristan gave up after a few minutes. Lingering outside an ex-girlfriend's apartment didn't help with his pathetic state of mind. He turned his back to walk away when a groggy voice came on the intercom.

"Hello?"

Tristan jogged back to the speaker, "It's me Callie. Sorry, I know it's late."

"Tristan? God, is everything alright?" Somehow Callie sounded genuinely concerned in spite of her obvious fatigue.

"Well, I still have all my teeth and no serious diseases that I know of, if that's what you mean."

"Oh, Tristan." Callie gave a sympathetic sigh that he had grown so accustomed to. "Come on up, but Stephanie is sleeping, so you need to be quiet."

Tristan took the stairs to the second floor and saw Callie peering out her door waiting for him. She shook her head before throwing her arms around his neck. Tristan patted her lower back in a halfhearted return and she ushered him into her pitch black apartment.

"My bedroom door is shut, so we can talk." She pulled her house coat tighter around her waist. Tristan did his best not to stare.

"I'm not even sure why I came here. I just needed to talk to someone I guess."

"Tristan it is so obvious that you aren't ok. What's going on? You know I am here for you." She rested her hand just above his knee. She turned on a small lamp and there was just enough light in the room to make out the concerned expression on her face.

"I made a big mistake, Callie. A really big mistake."

Tristan let it all out. He told Callie all about Adrienne and their history. He told her about Deanna's funeral, the night in his apartment three years ago, and the wedding that day. He told her everything he had been afraid to tell anyone before.

"I always knew there was someone else." she said. She looked sad as she spoke, but not angry. "I'm so sorry you had to see that, Tristan."

"I loved you too, Callie. Just differently, I guess." Tristan worried he hurt her.

She smiled at him as she always had. "I know what you mean, Tristan." Her look became devilish, "I'm the one with the girl in my bed, remember?"

Tristan just stared. She was so kind, forgiving and understanding. Tristan felt honoured to have shared the time with her that he had. She always made him feel confident, strong. When he was with Callie he never doubted himself. She had always believed in him, even in his darkest hours. He squeezed her hand.

"You are something else, girl. You know that?"

She glanced away shyly. "I know you feel hopeless right now *and* alone. God knows I didn't help with that, but I think about you every day, Tristan. I know you will never understand what I did; how could you? But I want you to know that I will always love you. You have a special place in my heart that is irreplaceable. I'm glad you came here tonight, and I hope you come to me every night, if you need a friend."

She pulled him close and they shared an intimate embrace. Tristan felt Callie's affection in her touch and soaked it up. He knew what came next, he had to leave. It was late and she left her partner in bed to talk with an ex-boyfriend until 1AM. Tristan didn't want to strain her relationship, or make her tired for work, so he kissed her cheek and promised to call.

Tristan felt lighter as he walked home. He was suddenly aware that a lot of the anger he directed at Callie after they broke up was really his own guilt. He felt disloyal to Callie because of his feelings for Adrienne. Somehow, during his brief visit, he and Callie forgave each other for their unspoken desires. Realizing these things, Tristan felt no better about the situation with Adrienne, but he did a whole lot better about himself.

Chapter Forty-Four

It was March and Tristan's thesis was due in two months. If he didn't submit it by the first of May he wouldn't be able to graduate until the following October at the fall convocation. Tristan's thoughts were all over the place, but his premise was clear: The influence of Modern Media on Teenage Relationship Dynamics. Tristan had thrown the depression out the window and immediately started researching teenage life before Television and film. As he expected, teen suicide rates were lower, body image issues were virtually unheard of, and predictably, there were lower divorce rates. Tristan new there were many other variables that could affect the rise and fall of statistics, but he was convinced his theory was correct. Movies were designed to entertain and allow people to escape. Tristan was sure they were doing their job far too well. As people escaped they came to long for the types of relationship they saw on screen. As Tristan thought about his own life, he realized teens were not the only ones affected.

The Influence of Modern Media on Relationship Dynamics—scrap the "teen".

Tristan saw the larger picture. The hopes and dreams instilled in young people carried over into adulthood. The hope of finding Prince Charming, or Cinderella, never faded. For many, the only thing that awaited them was disappointment and disillusionment. Tristan was onto something.

He worked constantly on his paper and made major progress by mid-March. He didn't think he'd have any trouble meeting the May first deadline. His clientele had grown to a whopping 800 members on Threewords and any free time he had was spent handing out free advice and policing the site. Tristan's new found obsession with work helped dull the constant thrum of pain inside of him. Adrienne's wedding left a scar reluctant to heal.

He hadn't even known she was getting married! She hadn't told him, in fact, he didn't even know she was engaged. Tristan understood fear, but she should have told him. He thought they shared something special, a bond. Tristan scolded himself whenever he was stupid enough to wander into such thoughts. His own thesis proved his idealistic hopes of finding a soul mate were severely hindered by unrealistic expectations.

He spent a few days in and out of bitter reflection until one morning he awoke to a deafening pounding on his apartment door. He pleaded for the assailant to relax and let him put some pants on before opening. The second he unlocked the door a frantic Callie leaped into his arms sobbing and laughing all at the same time. Tristan was surprised, but laughed along with her.

"Morning, Callie. " His voice was still froggish. "What the hell is going on?"

She pushed herself gently away from him and raised her hand. Her misty eyes gleamed as she said, "I'm engaged!"

Tristan stared in dumbfounded awe at the gigantic rock on Callie's ring finger.

"Oh my God. Congratulations! What. When?"

Callie dragged him to the couch and told him how she and Stephanie had gone to dinner like they did every Friday night. Halfway through dinner Stephanie dropped to one knee and proposed in front of every person at their swanky restaurant.

Tristan smirked at her, "So Stephanie is the man?"

Callie made a fake reaction of surprise and slapped his knee. "Tristan! It's not like that. Don't be such a jerk."

"I'm only playing Callie. I think it's amazing. I'm glad you came over here in person to tell me. It means a lot."

Tristan could see the sheer joy radiating from Callie's entire essence. He had never seen her so happy.

She blushed. "You are the first person I told, Tristan. I haven't even called my dad yet. I want you to be my maid of honour." She had a huge smile on her face.

"Your what? Oh, I don't think so. There *has* to be something else we can call it."

"So you will?" Her eyes were lighting up again.

"I'm not wearing a dress."

She threw her arms around him and laughed in his ear. We aren't wasting any time. We are getting married next month. I know it sounds crazy, but I love her, Tristan. You don't think it's too fast do you?

Of course he did, maybe not the engagement, but the wedding. But who was he? He had more failed relationship attempts than Donald Trump.

"Maybe a little, Callie. But you don't seem to, and that's all that matters. Now go call your dad."

They hugged one last time and Callie was gone in a tornado of bliss. It took Tristan a few moments to absorb what just happened, and realized he had agreed to stand at a lesbian wedding.

Oh well, scratch that off the bucket list.

The next time he saw Callie, he could tell there was bad news. She looked the complete opposite from what she had a week before. Her eyes were puffy, presumably from crying, and she looked dead tired. Her hug was feeble as she greeted him and she walked like a member of the undead to his kitchen table. She sat herself down and looked at him with weary eyes.

"We are having trouble, Tristan."

Tristan was horrified. They had been so happy! Tristan was not prepared to see someone else fall from grace, especially Callie.

"But you two are in love! You can't let—"

"Oh it's not *us* Tristan." Her tone turned bitter. "It's the church, they won't marry us."

Tristan had not seen this coming, he also couldn't understand it. Gay marriage was legal in Canada. There were even couples coming from other countries to have same sex marriages performed. How was it that Canadian citizens could not have a gay marriage *in* Canada?

He voiced his thoughts to Callie, "How is that possible? Gay marriage is legal here."

"Oh I know Tristan." She was having trouble controlling her emotions. "They'll have to marry us eventually, but they are stalling. Steph is Catholic, and they are being difficult about this."

She looked at him and his heart broke. He could tell there was more to the story.

"My father is dying, Tristan. That is why we need to marry so fast. They don't think he will last until summer. Those bastards don't even care. All our papers are tied up legally. I just want him to see me down the aisle."

He knelt beside her and took her hand.

"I'm so sorry Callie. I didn't know."

"I know what you've been through with cancer, Tristan. I didn't want you to have to go through it with me all over again."

Tristan was amazed by her. She kept such a difficult secret to protect him. He hated his selfishness. "Oh my God, Callie. Don't say that. I'm here for you like you are there for me. We'll figure this out. Your dad will see you get married."

She smiled sadly and touched his face. "I wish I could believe you Tristan, but I don't think there's time. I just needed to vent, I need to get home so Steph and I can keep working on this."

She kissed his cheek and wiped it aside with her hand. "You are so cute when you worry, Tristan. Just be there for me, ok? I need you more than you think."

He nodded. "I promise."

Three Words

Tristan was left with an enormous hole in his heart when Callie left. The pain in her eyes was so real, so fierce, that he couldn't get it out of his mind. Tristan understood the rush on the wedding completely and was determined to help somehow. Callie had never been anything but wonderful to him, and he had cut her out of his life needlessly. He needed to make things up to her, as well as be a good *maid of honour*. But how could he, a relative nobody, change the Church's mind? He had no connections, no sway, he was just a student.

It was obvious they needed to stay close to home. Other provinces may have been easier to deal with, but Callie's father was likely too sick to travel. Tristan racked his brain without mercy, and then it hit him. He didn't have to change the law, he just had to make the rules suit the situation. Tristan glanced at his computer.

The miracles of modern technology.

It didn't take Tristan long to find a website that looked promising enough. He made some phone calls and figured out it would take two months to get his certificate. He told the woman on the phone his situation, and that he needed it sooner. She was sympathetic, but firm. The only way he could get it early was if he completed the requirements early. Since he only wanted the basic package, which meant the only thing he'd have authority to do is marry people, it may move slightly faster. She was adamant though; that all studies had to be completed so the website's integrity was not jeopardized. He had never seen himself as a minister, but he was going to get that piece of paper and marry Callie in her own back yard if he had to.

Tristan tied up some loose ends, as well as the three hundred dollar fee, and let the woman go. He walked directly to his dresser and pulled out his blue Superman T-shirt. He was about to do something heroic.

Chapter Forty-Five

Tristan told Callie and Stephanie his plan two days later. He stood awaiting a reaction in their living room as that sat staring at him on the couch. He couldn't tell if they were looking at him like he was crazy, looking right through him, or too shocked for words. He hoped it was the latter. He expected cheers and hugs, maybe even kisses, not silence. He started to fidget.

Suddenly, Callie burst into tears. Tristan had never seen Callie cry until the last couple weeks, but he was growing to expect it. Stephanie took her hand and smiled at Tristan. Callie couldn't speak so she beckoned Tristan over with a wave of her hand. In a dream, being hugged by two lesbians would be erotic, but in real life it was sobering, especially when you were training to be the Minister that married them.

Stephanie didn't seem to care that the wedding would not be formally catholic. They would not have the support of the church, and his training would not include the ability to conduct a full catholic ceremony. Tristan started the discussion on the defensive but Stephanie quieted him quickly. The only thing that mattered to her was getting Callie down the aisle before her father passed away. If her family wanted a catholic wedding, they could always renew their vows, or remarry later on. Tristan looked upon the pretty young lady with new respect. She had a lot in common with Callie.

Tristan put his thesis on the back burner. He had such a jump on it that he could sacrifice a month in order to get ordained. His bible studies were difficult considering he had never read it before. He had to read it two or three times to complete the written requirements. Tristan ignored anyone who called, he simply didn't have the time to talk. He assured friends and family that he would return to the world of the living once his task was finished. Some thought he was losing his mind, others were intrigued. It didn't matter to Tristan however, he was *in the zone*.

When his certificate came there was a huge party thrown. Stephanie made excellent money. She didn't spare any expenses either. There were caterers, free booze, and a whole lot of people in attendance to honour Tristan's accomplishment. He was thankful they didn't make him wear the Minister's costume that Ryan brought for him.

They partied all night long in the common room of the local Delta Hotel. Tristan attempted to get *back in the game* and approached a few girls. He retreated after realizing many of them were gay. He took this as a sign, and cut his losses while the only real damage was Ryan's wild cackle each time he struck out.

"Not even a ladies' man like you can entice a lesbian, Tristan! This is hilarious!"

Callie made her way over to sit next to Tristan.

"Hope you are enjoying yourself," she said playfully. "Thank you, Tristan."

He smiled at her. There was nothing for him to say. He didn't want praise or recognition. He just wanted to see Callie look the way she had the day at his apartment. As he looked at her in radiant glory, he knew he had succeeded. All that was left to do now, was marry the two gals next week.

"Oh, I am. This is amazing, Callie. There must be over a hundred people here. I don't know half of them and the other half are gay."

She threw her head back and laughed. "Look at us, Tristan. I'm so glad we are what we are. I have one more surprise for you."

Tristan wondered why Callie kept looking over his shoulder. He assumed she was checking in on Steph with all those other lesbians around, but when he turned to look, he saw something completely unexpected.

Callie spoke to a completely entranced Tristan. "I called to invite her last week. It was crazy, but the way you described her reaction at the church gave me hope. I took a chance and invited her without telling you, in case I was wrong." Callie leaned closer to him and whispered to him,

"She didn't marry him, Tristan."

Tristan's head whirled around to meet Callie's gaze. She smiled confidently at him. He had no words.

"Go to her." Callie gave him an encouraging flick of the eyes in Adrienne's direction.

Tristan rose to his feet and all sound faded from his senses. Every person in the room vanished from his perception one by one. Their eyes met from across the room. She stood nervously in the entranceway with her hands folded across her midsection. Her black cocktail dress matched her hair in the dim light. The strobe lights produced by the DJ preceded each of Tristan's steps.

Red, Blue, Green, Yellow…

Each step he took seemed to take Adrienne further from him. It was taking forever for him make the thirty foot walk to her. Neither Adrienne nor Tristan looked away from one another. There was tension, but for Tristan, it was overshadowed by passion. He was three steps from her when there was a drastic change in music. He turned his head slightly to see Callie leave the DJ station. She had one last trick up her sleeve.

Tristan's favourite *Lifehouse* song set the mood.

He pushed all of his fears and questions to the side and let whatever was about to happen occur all on its own. He stood before a tear-stained Adrienne.

He couldn't speak, but he didn't need to. He reached out and she took his hand. He felt the eyes on them, but could see nobody else. Her beauty was as captivating as it ever was. He pulled her gently to the middle of the dance floor.

They kissed.

Tristan felt the power of their emotion flow through him like electricity. Tristan was into it, he was lost in the moment—until he couldn't breathe. There was too much saliva being exchanged. He tried to tell Adrienne but she wouldn't let go. Spit was flooding into his mouth faster than he could get rid of it! It was running down his chin.

—

Tristan woke drooling all over his bible. God must have taken offence to Tristan's use of the good book as a pillow and punished him with a vivid dream. Tristan wiped his mouth on his sleeve and let his forehead bang off the desk. As if Adrienne wouldn't have gotten married. He watched her for fuck sakes. The only other option was if she had left Randy at the altar while Tristan was strolling down a country road in Chester.

Tristan rubbed feeling back into his face with his palms as he went to the fridge for a drink of water. Just as he was gulping down the last mouthful a loud bang on his door almost made him choke.

"Just a sec!"

Tristan did a double take. Maybe he hadn't been dreaming after all, maybe it had been a sign. Adrienne was at the door! She hadn't gotten married! She was going to come in and wrap her arms around him and—

Whoa. Slow down!

He calmed his teenage hormone regression and walked to the door.

He felt the ringing in his ears before hearing the audible slap of Robyn's palm on his face.

"Bastard. My sister was right about you."

Tristan rubbed his face and looked left and right as if he expected to get hit again. But Robyn had achieved her objective. Before Tristan had a chance to speak she was on her way down the hall. Tristan didn't bother calling out, or running after her, he knew their relationship was over the second he walked out of that church.

Ouch.

Robyn had made solid contact; he thought he tasted a bit of blood in his mouth. At least he avoided the confrontation for over a month. He made his way back to the fridge, this time for some frozen peas. Peas in his left hand and bible in his right, he sat down to finish what he started a few hours earlier. Tristan looked at the clock.

Midnight.

Ok, finish what I started…

The sting was starting to subside, and he thought his fat lip was shrinking. He knew he deserved what he got, but it didn't help his ego. Here he was, dreaming about a romantic encounter, when in real life all he got was a right hook. Tristan put his book down and allowed his mind to venture off. God had a cruel sense of humour. He knew Adrienne was married. But the possibility—

Jesus!

Another knock on his door. This one much less violent. Tristan muttered a curse as he couldn't help but wonder why his apartment had always been a location for late night meetings. Tristan hesitated on his way to the door. This time he would use the peep hole to avoid another angry mugging.

The tiny hole in the door revealed a menace for sure, but not Robyn.

"Tristan. I'm really drunk and need a place to sleep. Let me in."

Tristan opened the door to allow his younger sister to stumble past him en route to the couch. She was almost there when she turned and collapsed onto his bed. The night was getting better every second. First, a dream he was loath to wake up from, then the wrath of an ex, and now drunken sibling stealing his bed. Things could have been worse. At least he still had his trusty pillow and heart wrenching dreams to look forward to.

—

The tingling in his lifeless arm woke Tristan the next morning. He was face down on the couch pinching his left arm beneath him. He rolled over with a groan and tried to shake some feeling back into his limb. He looked to the right expecting to see his unconscious sister, but Emma was nowhere to be found. She must have gotten up and went back to her own apartment that morning.

After some canned pears for breakfast Tristan sat at his computer to find a brief note from his baby sister,

Thanks Bro. Love you. Xoxo

Tristan shook his head as he moved the note to the side. It must be in the Cage blood to become raging alcoholics during the college years. He opened up his documents to work on one of his many bible study assignments. Tristan just finished emailing his second complete work package to the company issuing his license when he decided to check up on Threewords. He was missing in action for a few days and didn't want youngsters thinking they were being ignored. Tristan grimaced when he logged in; he had over three hundred emails. He took a deep breath and vowed not to leave Threewords alone ever again. He would have to take a break from his studies to clean up his inbox.

About half of the emails were subscription requests, Tristan expected as much. Most of the remaining messages were ongoing issues he had been helping clients deal with over time or updates on how resolved situations were going. It was a regular day at the office when Tristan stumbled across an email that had been left two days before:

Dear Mr. Cage,

I am a little older than your website is designed for, but I have a major problem that I need help with.

I am recently divorced after only a month of marriage. I knew I was making a mistake the day I agreed to marry my ex-husband, but was too scared to admit it to myself. I hurt the man I married, and only realize now that it was all my fault. If I had of been honest with myself, and my feelings, and said what needed to be said long ago, I could have saved his suffering, and my own.

The problem is, I am in love with someone else. I have been in love with this person since high school. He is the most amazing person I have ever known. I haven't spoken with him in a long time…what feels like forever. I can't explain what caused the separation between us. I guess I just chalked it up to life in general, but I need you Tristan Cage. I need your advice, but more, I need you to forgive me.

I will never forget the pain in your eyes that day. For a long time I blamed you for the mistakes I made but no more. I write to you now seeking advice. Is it too late to tell you I love you?

Because I do. I love you Tristan. If you can ever forgive me for denying it these last few years, I will be waiting.

Yours,

Adrienne

Tristan had to re-read the message four times before he accepted its authenticity. He breathed heavily and his hands were shaking. Adrienne's marriage only lasted a month. He had every reason to believe she was lost, confused, but he spent so much time waiting for the right moment that he missed out on so many good ones. Tristan was tired of waiting. It was time to take a chance on Adrienne Axley. He picked up the phone and dialled the number he still had memorized.

He just hoped it hadn't changed.

Chapter Forty-Six

"We're sorry, the number you have dialled is not in service"

He rolled his eyes. *Figures.*

He didn't panic, which surprised him. He simply turned back to his computer and hit the bolded "Reply" button.

> *Adrienne,*
>
> *I love you too. My number is the same.*

As emotionally charged as Tristan was, he had other responsibilities. He threw caution to the wind and hoped that Adrienne would get his message in good time. As much as he longed to talk to her, to be with her again, Callie needed him too. Tristan planned on finishing his studies in the next two weeks, which meant eight hour days at the least. He picked up his bible, took a deep breath, and forced himself to concentrate.

Ryan stopped by two days later to see if Tristan was still alive. One of the perks to owning your own company was making your own vacation time. Ryan told Tristan there was no better reason to take time off than to visit his friend. Tristan stuck his finger in his mouth to indicate Ryan's over the top sentiment was sickening.

Tristan and Ryan talked over beers for an hour. When Tristan spilled his guts over the week's events Ryan was shaking his head.

"Ok, so in the past couple of months you started dating Robyn only to leave her alone at the wedding where you witnessed the love of your life pledging her love for someone else, only to find out she has since been divorced and had her confess her undying love for you. Not to mention you are doing warp speed training in order to be able to marry your hot lesbian ex before her father dies. That's boring."

Tristan chuckled. Ryan's morbid humour was a welcome addition.

"Yeah, you have been spending too much time with Amy. You make it all sound crazy!"

"Well," Ryan said, raising his eyebrows and taking a swig of beer, "It is crazy, but I expect nothing less from you."

"I expect you and Amy to be at the wedding for moral support. Callie said to invite you guys. I know that's pretty informal, but she has a lot going on."

"Oh yeah. We'll be there for sure Tristan. You know that. You know, one of these times it will be your wedding we are attending." Ryan smirked at him.

"Yeah, not anytime soon. I'm in no rush to shackle myself to potential disaster like the rest of you idiots." Tristan took a drink of his own. "Besides, Adrienne hasn't called me yet. It's been two days."

"And the fact that it bothers you so much, Tristan, is exactly why I hear wedding bells."

"Whatever, Jackass. Have another beer."

Tristan endured Ryan's teasing, but there was truth in it. Each random sound from an electronic device made him check his phone in a frenzy. The beep of the microwave, sound effects on TV, even the buzzer for his apartment made him reach for his pocket. Tristan was on edge, but in a way he never felt before. The anticipation was energizing, but the fear was debilitating.

Ryan's jovial demeanour faded after a few moments of silence. He didn't look sad, or angry, just more thoughtful than he had before. Tristan knew Ryan had something to say, he expected all along that he hadn't come all the way to see Tristan for a couple of beers.

"Alright. Spill it. We've known each other a long time, and I know you aren't saying something. Is it about Adrienne again? Do you know something? Tell me. I can handle it."

Ryan raised his hand to quiet Tristan. "Would you relax, it has nothing to do with Adrienne. And it's not bad news. I'm just not as good as you at the mushy stuff."

"What? You love me?" Tristan laughed. Ryan looked so serious. "I already know that. You don't have to—"

"Amy's pregnant."

Tristan's jaw dropped and Ryan smiled.

"Oh my God. This has been the craziest month ever! Congratulations!"

"I know." Ryan was laughing freely now, his nervousness gone. "That's why I was having trouble telling you. You already had so much on your plate."

"Well, I'm not the one who has to live with a pregnant Amy. Talk about walking on eggshells."

Ryan's smile faded, "Oh I know. I already set up the garage into a 'man cave' in case I need to escape—or get thrown out." He paused, "There's one more thing Tristan," Ryan raised his glass. "We want you to be the godfather if you accept."

Speechless, Tristan could only nod. There was no way he would turn down the request. He raised his glass in return as the men toasted the growth of Ryan's family.

Ryan left Tristan to solitary confinement at 4PM. Family men had to be home for dinner, and those without families had minister training to keep them busy, but Tristan had a hard time focusing. He couldn't get his mind off of Adrienne, and the fact he was going to be a godparent. He knew he was growing up, but for the first time he felt grown up. He had direction, career options, love,

341

and a growing family. Everything was falling into place, and it was hard not to think about. If only Adrienne would call.

The phone rang. Tristan yanked it out of his pocket like it was on fire.

"Hello?"

"Tristan, I'm pregnant."

Amy's blunt nature never failed to make him laugh. "I know you fool! Ryan was here all day. He just told me."

"That bastard! He told me he was going baby shopping! Wait until he gets back here."

"Amy relax! Go easy on him. He just wanted to do it in person. We go way back, you know."

Amy sighed. "I know, but he could have just told me! He's such an idiot sometimes." Her harsh words could not hide the affection in her voice whenever she talked about him. "So has he asked you then?"

"Yes. And Yes. I would be honoured."

"Ohhh Tristan! I'm so excited. You will be the perfect godparent. Now we just need to find you a girl."

Tristan spent the next half hour re-telling the same stories he told Ryan. She was ecstatic when she heard about Adrienne and went up one side of Tristan and down the other for not hunting for her at that very moment. According to Amy, he was a dumbass for letting her go in the first place. It was about time Tristan *got his shit together* and under no circumstances was he to go near any *little boys* when he was ordained. Tristan listened happily to Amy's uncensored humour until Ryan got home. He knew as soon as Ryan came in the door because Amy's muffled curses could be heard.

"Ok Tristan. Dinner time here, and Ryan has some explaining to do. See you soon. Love you!"

Tristan hung up with Ryan's cries for help in the background.

For someone who hated being interrupted, Tristan enjoyed the day's distractions. Good news abounded and Tristan stared down at his phone. One phone call would make the day so much better, but he knew it probably wouldn't happen. He was on his way back to his computer desk when he realized Ryan hadn't closed the door all the way. Tristan made his way over to shut, and lock it, when he heard footsteps.

"Can I come in? Or did you rush to close the door because you saw me coming?"

Tristan recognized Adrienne's voice right away and yanked the door open. She stood nervously with her hand on the door frame. She swallowed hard when their eyes met.

"Why call when I know where you live?" She said cautiously.

Tristan had instant amnesia. Everything that happened up to that point simply receded to the back of his mind. His right hand ran through her hair and came to rest on the back of her neck. Her deep brown eyes shut as he pushed his lips into hers. A groan of instinctual need escaped her lips as she succumbed to his need.

The two stumbled backward. Tristan's back made solid contact with the still open door. He put his hands under her thighs and lifted her in the air pushing her into the closet door ahead of him. She moaned with anticipation and ran her nails down his back. Tristan allowed the door to swing shut on its own. It wouldn't lock, but he didn't care. He carried Adrienne to the kitchen where he dropped her onto the kitchen table.

Their heavy breathing and sounds of ecstasy were the only sounds audible in the apartment. Adrienne pulled Tristan's shirt over his head impatiently as he worked on her belt. Her legs were wrapped around his waist. Adrienne paused to look at him once she had his shirt off and ran her hand down his chest and over his still chiseled abs. She flipped her hair to the side and kissed Tristan's bare chest as he hauled her belt through the remaining loops.

Adrienne pulled her own shirt off and Tristan pressed his lips against her neck. She let out a stifled moan as he ran his teeth lightly across her collar bone. He made his way to her bra strap which he moved out of the way with his mouth. Adrienne threw her head back as he pulled her tighter to him.

Tristan picked her up once again and carried her to his bed. Passionate fury gave way to intimacy as he laid her gently down. Tristan heard fabric moving over skin as Adrienne shifted her lower body beneath him. They kissed again, this time with more feeling than the last. Tristan felt her nails dig into his back as he shifted his position above her. The last thing Tristan remembered before losing himself was his whispered name on her lips.

"Tristan…"

The two lovers spent the entire night making up for lost time.

Chapter Forty-Seven

Tristan sat outside Professor Niering's office, waiting to submit his thesis as he reflected on the month's events. He and Adrienne were moving slowly (as far as relationships went) but still enjoyed all the trimmings. They were being grown up about the whole situation and knew Adrienne needed a little time to heal after her brief stint with marriage. Tristan was successfully ordained but knew he was no real minister. He actually found the whole process a little sketchy. Nobody should be able to have the ability to marry people so easily. Certain couples should never be married.

Adrienne was in awe of Threewords and so proud of Tristan. The memberships had grown to hit four figures and Tristan had started accepting volunteers to help him stay on top of emails and advising. It had been Adrienne's idea that he use students majoring in psychology as volunteers. They would have almost the same qualifications he had, and stood a lot to gain from the experience he was offering. It hadn't taken Tristan long to find willing participants, and even had to run interviews to make his selections. He ended up selecting two fourth year students with extensive psychology and computer science back grounds. Why not kill two birds with one stone?

Callie's wedding was small, but Callie and Stephanie wed in Callie's back yard. They had loved ones, most importantly Callie's father, and an ordained minister. What else did they need? Tristan had been nervous as hell, but Ryan calmed him down with a shot of rum before the ceremony. Alcohol, in moderation, had its uses.

They were lucky to receive a beautiful day for their late April nuptials. It wasn't overly warm, but not cold either. Callie always looked stunning in everything, but yellow made her look like a goddess. Tristan also realized, as he watched his friend have her special moment, that love was not a choice we make, but something that chooses us. It had no perception of race, sex, gender, history or age, only of uniting people. Tristan knew true love was rare, and that many people tried to choose someone to love before allowing love to find them, but that day he witnessed true love at work. The way Callie looked at Stephanie was humbling to any who took in the scene, and there were few who were not moved to tears.

Most of the guests wore light jackets or sweaters. Tristan convinced Adrienne to wear a short skirt and long jacket, something he always fantasized about. It was hard to focus at the reception with her constantly winking at him and moving her eyes to look playfully at the bathroom door. She was a crafty minx, that one; she knew his presence at the head table meant that he couldn't move until the dinner was over. She was working him up on purpose. And he loved it.

The sexual tension built until they got back to his apartment where they could finally make love. They had to pause for a moment when Adrienne pulled Tristan's shirt off to reveal his superman T-shirt. Tristan smiled as he had been waiting for that moment all day. She had spurred him on with a sensual *my hero*.

Callie and Steph tried to give Tristan an enormous gift for all his help. He simply would not accept the whopping check that came to him in a thank you card. He walked it over to return it in person only to receive a heartfelt hug from the two of them. They planned on getting their license sorted out when they got back from a mini honeymoon. Callie's father had bought them a four day cruise and insisted they attend. He didn't want his condition

Three Words

stopping his daughter from enjoying all aspects of her wedding. They hoped that they wouldn't have to remarry and that their marriage could be honoured retroactively once their license was granted. Tristan hoped with all his heart that they were right.

Tristan's reminiscing came to an end when the Professor's office door finally swung open to allow him in.

"So sorry, Tristan. Well, how did it go?"

Tristan handed over his 93 page document proudly.

"See for yourself," he replied confidently.

Professor Niering looked fondly at the cover page. "*The Influence of Modern Media on Relationship Dynamics*. I can't wait to read it."

Tristan had grown even closer with his professor throughout the writing of his thesis. The old man had shown nothing but encouragement to Tristan ever since the project that created Threewords. The professor visited the site often, as he was determined to see Tristan win the Henley award for its creation.

"I hope it is up to your standards Professor, but I have to run. See you at graduation."

"Ahhh yes. To be young again." The professor smiled. "I'm sure it is fantastic, Tristan. See you soon."

Tristan walked briskly past the rows of office doors that defined the administrative building of Saint Agnus. He was late, whatever business the professor was attending to had held him up. His family was on their way in to meet him. It was moving day.

Tristan applied for jobs in February and had little luck. Counselling jobs were hard to come by and didn't pay well in the beginning. Most people suggested that Tristan allow companies to advertise on Threewords removing its non-profit status, but Tristan would not hear of it. As tempting as easy money was, he was not willing to sacrifice the site he had founded with such good intentions.

He reapplied in March to the school boards. He had done some research and realized that guidance counsellors were in demand.

Just before Callie's wedding he had received a job offer from Sageview High School. His knowledge of the community, and having grown up there, in conjunction with his fantastic volunteer work and resume had made him a great candidate. After speaking with the principal and promising to coach the Senior Boys basketball team, the job was his. It wouldn't pay incredible amounts of money, but it was a decent start. Tristan Cage would be an Iron Knight once again. He was elated about the opportunity, and the option to stay close to home—something he didn't think was going to end up happening.

As soon as Tristan got the confirmation from his new boss, Principal Miller, he called Karl. Karl had a huge farmhouse, all to himself a kilometre from the school, and Tristan knew he would love some company. Karl accepted Tristan's pleas for room and board before he finished asking. Karl would not hear of Tristan paying any rent either. According to him, helping out around the house would be enough to earn his keep.

Tristan's parents were proud, and a little sad he wasn't moving home to live with them, but it made more sense to live with Karl. He was much closer to the school and Tristan's parents had each other; Karl had no one. Ryan was excited to have Tristan in Sageview as well, he voiced concerns about Tristan's intentions to move away. Now the big fella was happier than ever, ranting about how they would build a cabin to take his son fishing—he was convinced he would have a boy and there was no telling him otherwise—and to get drunk and stupid where the women couldn't find them. This cabin would have a secret location of course.

Adrienne completely understood the move. Though Karl was Deanna's father, and their history was no secret, Adrienne had grown into a secure and confident woman. She loved everything about Tristan, and she loved his unwavering loyalty more than anything else. Deanna had been gone a long time, and she knew Tristan had dealt with it. She was a little worried about the distance the move would put between them, as she was taking over the lease on Tristan's old apartment. Her job as an accountant tied her to city centres, but once she and Tristan took the next step, they could re-evaluate living arrangements.

When Tristan finally arrived at the apartment, his parents, Ryan, and Adrienne had the majority of the moving finished. Cameron met him at the moving van and immediately started raving about how Ryan had moved the couch and bed all by himself. Tristan grinned at Ryan and the big man shrugged.

"Muscles have to be good for something."

Tristan left his parents to finish packing his meagre belongings safely in the back of the van and took the elevator up to find Adrienne. He found her standing in a bare apartment, save for her stack of boxes in the corner where his table had been. He wrapped his arms around her from behind and she sighed, dropping her head back onto his shoulder.

"It's weird, Tristan. So many memories here. It won't be the same without you."

He spun her around. "What are you talking about? You are moving in! Just more memories to be made."

"I guess." She made a coy expression. "I'm just regretting our decision to move slow, I guess." She smiled. "How did your meeting go?"

"Nice change of subject." He grinned at her. "It went well, but the professor was busy, so I had to wait quite a while."

"Yeah well, that's why we are here to help Tristan. We know how important your paper is." She kissed him on the cheek. "Come on, let's go down and help load the van."

—

Two days before graduation, Tristan got a phone call while he was helping Karl clean out stalls. Professor Niering called to inform him of doubly good news. He had recommended his thesis to a publisher for it had been the best he'd seen in years, and he received the Henley award for outstanding research. Professor Niering was a professional man, but he couldn't hide the pride in his voice as he reported to his top student.

Tristan hung up the phone and ran into the stall to tell Karl the news. Karl simply smiled at him and nodded his head. "I never doubted it, son," was all he had to say. Tristan called Adrienne right away and made plans to meet at his parents' house for a celebration. Tristan didn't care that it was a Wednesday, there would be a party in Milton. He did not yet have a car, so he called Ryan to come pick him up.

Tristan heard Ryan's horn at 6:30. He said his farewells to Karl and told him not to wait up. He grabbed his six pack of Keith's—he wouldn't be going *too* crazy—and headed out the door. He stopped on the porch as he frowned at the downpour ahead of him. Tristan could hardly see Ryan's car through the torrent of rain. He went back inside and grabbed his coat.

He hopped in the passenger seat of Ryan's new Dodge Ram.

"Nice wheels. Red too. You hate red."

"Yeah," Ryan grimaced, "but Amy loves it."

Tristan laughed as they pulled out of Karl's driveway with a muddy splash.

The wind picked up, and it was getting dark. Ryan complained about visibility and the uselessness of high beams. They passed the bridge just outside of Sageview where the speed limit changed from 50 to 80. Ryan accelerated, but slowed quickly as he couldn't see far enough ahead to drive too fast. At 60 kilometres an hour, it would be a long trip on the lifeless country road to Milton.

Tristan asked Ryan if he had any food, he hadn't eaten in all the excitement. Ryan told him there was a sandwich in his lunchbox in the back seat. Tristan unclasped his seat belt and reached behind the seat groping for the plastic box. Tristan's roaming hand couldn't find what he was looking for and he cursed.

"Shit Ryan, where is this thing?"

Three Words

"I'm telling you, it's back there." Ryan was leaning over the wheel attempting to see through the veil of rain.

Tristan turned all the way around with his knees on the seat. He looked down to see the sneaky lunch box nestled safely behind his chair. Apparently he had to work on the flexibility of his arms. He reached down and grabbed it as his stomach growled in anticipation. Tristan swung himself around and sat back down properly with the food in his lap. As he turned his head to thank Ryan, Tristan caught a glimpse of an animal on the road.

"Deer!"

Ryan yanked the wheel, a little too violently, to the left. Tristan was thrown, beltless, into the passenger door. He pressed his left hand into the dash to steady himself while he tried to free his right arm that was pinned against the door. Ryan grunted as he fought to control the careening vehicle. They fishtailed back and forth but the rain on the road made it almost impossible to correct. They were hydroplaning. The back of the truck swung too far out and they rolled. The two men heard nothing but their own screams and screeching metal as their lives were left to fate. Tristan could no longer hold himself in place and was flopping around the truck like a rag doll.

Is this the end?

The truck spun on its roof and slid down a bank. It slammed into a tree without mercy. Tristan was propelled through the windshield. Luckily his forearm made contact first, shattering the glass. His left shoulder glanced off the tree that stopped the truck, but at the velocity at which he was moving, he could not stop the roots and stumps of the forest floor from ripping at his defenceless body. His head hit something hard, and everything went black.

—

Tristan came to in a ball of agony. He tried to move, but everything hurt. He was sure his right arm was badly injured, possibly broken, and a mixture of blood and rain ran over his face. He tried to roll onto his back a second time with moderate success. Tristan fought to remain calm.

Breathe, think. You were in an accident, you need help.

Tristan found his options lacking considering they were at least two kilometres from the nearest home. The truck had rolled down a moderate bank. In this weather, passing traffic probably wouldn't see them unless he or Ryan—

Oh my God, Ryan!

Tristan's surge of adrenaline was enough to get him to his feet, but not to erase the pain in his stomach that dropped him to one knee. Tristan was suddenly aware of an unbearable pain just under his belly button. He looked down to see a large gash on his stomach. Tristan groaned and felt the world spinning. He fought with himself to remain conscious. He needed help, but Ryan might too.

With a growl of exertion he forced himself back to his feet and stumbled the twenty or more feet back to the truck. He looked in terror at the front of Ryan's Dodge which was crushed by the tree it had struck. Tears added to the already impossible task of trying to see. Tristan stooped by the shattered driver side window.

"Ryan! Ryan goddammit. Can you hear me?"

The silence was worse than the carnage around him. The gash on his gut singed his insides as he bent lower.

Fuck that hurts…

Tristan could see Ryan hanging by his seat belt. His eyes were shut, but the only blood he could see was seeping slowly from a scratch on his neck.

"Ryan. Ryan!"

Tristan called his friends name but rocked slowly on one knee.

"Ryan!"

His friend groaned as he started to come to.

Thank god…

Three Words

"Ryan," Tristan gasped through water and pain. "Can you hear me?"

"Tristan. What…what happened?" Ryan grimaced when he tried to move.

"We crashed. It's ok though. I'm going to get you out."

Tristan thought frantically. He certainly couldn't lie on his stomach. He didn't know how he was going to reach inside.

"Tristan," Ryan said in a low voice. "Don't bother. I'm pinned. I…I can't feel my legs."

No.

Ryan had saved him so many times, *been there* for him, used his awesome strength to defend him. It was Tristan's turn. Every bone in his body knew there was no way he could make the two kilometre walk to the nearest house—it was *at least* two kilometres. His only hope was to start walking and flag down a car. Ryan was going to be a father. Tristan couldn't let him die there.

"I'm sorry big guy, but I need to get you help. I have to go for a while, but I swear on my life I'll be back."

"Tristan. No wait. Don't leave me here…"

"Just hold on. Just hold on. Promise me." Tristan's tone was strict, masking his pain.

"I Promise."

Tristan reached down to squeeze his hand. "I'll be back."

It took all of Tristan's strength to get back to his feet. He eyed the hill in front of him with fiery eyes and fought the urge to vomit. With his injured arm propped against the gash that weakened him, he crawled up the bank, struggling for every inch. Tristan gasped when he reached the top, and rocked on his feet

D…

Tristan glanced skyward in the pouring rain.

D…he's hurt. Just get me to that house. Get me to that house…

He had only gone thirty feet and the pain was crippling. He looked down at the truck, only the headlights visible in the rain.

With a growl he forced himself onward.

Tristan limped back toward Sageview. Every step he took he prayed for a car, but none came. The image of Adrienne kept him going. He had to get to that house to save Ryan, but also to make sure he saw her again. Many times Tristan had to drop to a knee in order to catch his breath. He had no idea how far he had to go, he just knew he couldn't stop. He wouldn't let himself stop.

Eventually, he saw the mailbox. It seemed to shine like a beacon of hope. Tristan found renewed strength at the sight of it and rallied his senses. He made it to the front steps and prayed that there were people in the house. As he stepped up he tasted blood in his mouth. He couldn't recall any damage to his face. The blood must have been coming from inside of him. Tristan closed his eyes for a moment. He realized he was hurt much worse than he would admit.

Tristan collapsed on both knees at the front door. With the last of his energy he rang the doorbell. His consciousness was fading and he coughed bits of blood onto the wooden doorstep. He heard the faint echo of footsteps coming towards him. A man, mid-thirties, opened the door.

"Isabel, call 911! Mister, hey what's wrong. Can you talk?"

Tristan pulled meekly on the strangers arm to bring him closer. When he had the man almost nose to nose with him he mustered the last of his energy to say, "Accident, two kilometres west... man trapped..."

Tristan felt the warmth of his own blood pooling beneath him. The man was yelling instructions over his shoulder again, but Tristan was succumbing to the severity of his injuries. The world began to spin until Tristan could see no more.

Chapter Forty-Eight

The heart monitor beeped, and Adrienne Axley slept clutching her lover's hand. It was seventeen hours since the surgery, and the doctors were not optimistic about Tristan's chances. He had lost so much blood. The beeping woke her, as it did every few minutes. She rubbed her eyes and chastised herself for falling asleep. She pulled the chair closer and ran her fingers over Tristan's bald head. She kissed him gently and whispered words of encouragement in his ear.

Adrienne rose, reluctantly, to get some water. She passed through the waiting room that was packed with people sleeping all over one another. Cameron and Patty, Emma and Austin, Karl Greene, Alec, Callie and Stephanie, and a dozen other friends and family all slept restlessly. There were people on the floor and in the chairs. Adrienne tiptoed past them toward the vending machine down the hall. She moved with a purpose, she wanted to get back to Tristan's bedside as soon as possible.

On her way back to Tristan's room, she looked in on Ryan. Amy slept in the chair next to him with her head resting on his shoulder. Her pained expression was evident even while she slept. She had taken the news hardest, needing to be sedated after she laid eyes on her gentle giant. Adrienne had been shocked to see Ryan hurt as well. He always seemed so strong, invincible. His status was up in the air as well. The accident put incredible pressure on his spine causing probable nerve damage. If Ryan lived, it was unlikely he would have the use of his legs.

Adrienne felt a strong desire to check on Tristan. She was only gone a couple of minutes, but paranoia was the only reaction available to her. She opened the door, roughly, hoping the sound would wake her fallen hero. Tristan didn't stir. She walked to his bedside and stared down at him. She ran her fingers lightly over the large bruise consuming the left side of his face. Her hand recoiled like she had been bitten and she covered her mouth. Her eyes burned but she fought the tears. It was not denial, but hope. She would not allow herself to submit to the despair that surrounded her. She closed her eyes and breathed deeply. He was going to live.

The next time she woke, Patty was rubbing her arm affectionately.

"You need to eat, Adrienne. I'll watch him for a bit. Go." Patty gave her an encouraging nudge toward the door.

Adrienne looked over her shoulder at Tristan until she was physically out of the room. She was afraid to see the others. Her hopeful bubble was fragile, and she couldn't afford letting it pop.

Adrienne ate her food alone in the hospital cafeteria. She looked around at the faces that surrounded her. Hospitals were miserable places. So much suffering. She couldn't help but offer the life of every stranger for Tristan's, but knew Tristan would never allow it. Adrienne quelled the less than sunny thoughts that threatened to consume her and went back upstairs. The waiting room was frantic. Everyone was up and talking, and Adrienne felt her heart stop. She felt a mixture of panic and anticipation surging through her. She walked slowly preparing herself for the worst. Surely they would have called her if—

No.

Adrienne didn't have time to enquire about anything. Amy threw her arms around her and she could barely be made out over the sobs. "Ryan…is okaaay." She balled into her shoulder, and Adrienne felt a wave of relief and joy cleanse her fear.

Three Words

"It's a miracle. He just woke up and moved his toe. The doctors checked him right away, they think he'll walk too. They couldn't believe it."

Adrienne took her by the shoulders, "His strength Amy, and yours, healed him. Not miracles, just love."

Amy fought to compose herself. "No. Not Ryan or me. Tristan. Tristan saved him."

The others in the room that were sharing in her joy became silent at the mention of Tristan's name. The thought of his heroism only made things worse. Adrienne handed Amy off to Emma and made a beeline for Tristan's room. She met Cameron on the way.

"Ryan would like to see you. He asked me about Tristan but…" Cameron fought to stay calm, but even his manly resolve was no match for a father's fear of losing his son, "…I couldn't talk about it."

Adrienne put her hand on his arm and nodded her head. She looked in on Tristan, whose condition hadn't changed, and went to see Ryan. The nurse attending him cautioned her not to upset him. His condition was miraculous, but fragile. Adrienne understood.

Adrienne's heart broke when she looked into Ryan's eyes. "Tell me he's alright. Cameron was just here and he could hardly talk."

She took his hand. "He's not good." Ryan's eyes filled with tears. He shook his head before she finished her sentence.

"No. No, don't say that to me." He tried to move but was still too weak.

"Get me the *fuck* out of this bed!" He wailed. Adrienne put her hand on his massive chest, "Shhhh. He's going to be alright. He's—"

"I shouldn't have swerved. I should have just hit the deer." Adrienne fought for composure. His pain was so real it threatened to pull the heart from her chest. "I have always protected him—"

"And this time he protected *you*." Adrienne said firmly. His eyes pleaded with her to lie to him, to wake him from a horrible dream, but if that were possible, she'd wake them all.

"I need to see him."

Adrienne asked the nurse, but she was adamant Ryan was not to be moved. It took three nurses, even without the full use of his legs, to stop him from rolling out of his bed to crawl next door. His fury was desperate; his sadness crippling.

Adrienne sat next to Patty at Tristan's bedside. Tears stained her aging face, but her interior was calm. She pressed the back of her hand to her son's face.

"I wish I could say he looks peaceful, but that would be a lie." Patty spoke as if there was no one else in the room, yet Adrienne knew the words were for her. "Tristan always had so much energy, such a zest for life. How did this happen, Adrienne? He is so young."

"I wish I knew, Mrs. Cage." Adrienne was starting to have trouble being the strong one.

"A parent should never have to see their child like this. It seems so backwards."

Adrienne could only nod and listen. Patty was venting, sounding out her thoughts so they didn't stay pent up inside of her. Adrienne knew tragedy had no conscience; it had no bias in where it struck. Tragedy was tragedy. Adrienne could sit and think of all the reasons in the world for why the accident happened. She could blame Ryan, blame God, blame Tristan for not having his seat belt on, but it would only drive her crazy. All she could do was pray that he woke up.

Patty stopped speaking and stared blankly at her only son. Adrienne suggested she get some rest and Patty nodded without expression. She kissed Tristan's forehead and left the room. Adrienne slid closer to him and opened a magazine. She liked to pretend that everything was as normal as possible. Being curled up in a chair with a magazine was pretty standard, save for the love of her life on his deathbed.

Adrienne knew her denial would be the death of her also. She held on to the hope that he would wake for selfish reasons. She needed Tristan, she had always needed him. Even when she was in other relationships she was happy knowing Tristan was alive, out there, if she needed him. There would be no comforting her if he was gone, and that was too scary a thought to allow. There were more people than just her who needed him too. All those in the waiting room, and even those who had yet to come into being. Adrienne put her hand on her stomach. Perhaps the greatest reason she needed him to live grew inside of her.

She found out she was pregnant two weeks before the accident. She was scared to tell Tristan since they were trying to move slowly. It had been that first night, she was sure of it, when there was so much love in the air. She hated herself for being such a coward. If Tristan died, he would never know he was to be a father, and it would be all her fault.

Nobody knew, she had told no one. The thought of carrying Tristan's child without Tristan made her resent her situation. How could she raise their child without him? She reached out and squeezed his hand imploring him to fight harder. His thumb moved. Adrienne's eyes bulged. His thumb moved again. Was this his brain sending random messages to his limbs or was he actually moving?

"Tristan?" She shook his arm. "Tristan!"

His eyes flickered for a moment, and opened slowly.

Adrienne's breathing sped up. She leaned over the bed and kissed him. "Tristan, oh my God!"

He smiled weakly at her. "Adrienne…"

He closed his eyes again. His breathing was laboured. "I don't feel so well…"

"Tristan don't go back to sleep. Look at me." She gently turned his head towards her. "You need to stay awake now. I…I need to tell you…"

Tristan frowned slightly. She realized she was scaring him. "I…you're going to be a father."

A beautiful state of shock came over Tristan. His eyes watered and he squeezed her hand. She nodded her head.

"I know," she said, "I know baby, so you need to fight ok?"

Tristan's breathing was no longer laboured, it was almost non-existent. Tristan's lips were moving slightly, but no sound was being made. Adrienne leaned closer to him, she didn't notice the declining activity of his heart monitor. "What is it? I'm right here."

Tristan closed his eyes for a moment to gather the last of his strength. When he opened them for the last time he spoke his last three words,

"Marry me, Adrienne."

Her strength wavered and broke. She cried openly now and her tears dripped onto his chest. She couldn't speak, so she just nodded her head in a frantic motion. She smiled at him, and he smiled faintly back. Then he closed his eyes, and his chest no longer moved up and down. The heart monitor rang out in monotone morbidity.

Adrienne shot out of the chair and shook him. "Tristan! Tristan!" Her screams brought nurses running. They grabbed her arms and pulled her toward the door, but she fought them. "Tristan! Don't do this! Tristan!" She did everything she could to break free. "Get your hands off of me!"

The doctor could be heard in the background, "His heart stopped. We need the crash cart STAT."

The last sound Adrienne heard before being thrust into the hallway was the charging of the paddles.

Chapter Forty-Nine

Tristan hurt. He hurt A LOT.
 He didn't know where he was. He didn't know where he'd been.
 His eyes snapped open. Everything around him was chaos. Figures shrouded in medical gear had him wrapped in attention. His hearing came back to him slowly, and he could hear voices, frantic in their pleas for help, for order, or for…
 Adrienne?
 He could hear her now. Plainly. She was screaming his name. "Tristan! Tristan! Let go of me you fucking assholes!"
 Tristan could see, through the press of bodies, Adrienne being held in the doorway by medical staff trying to force her from the room. She caught the slight fluttering of his eyes as he tried to focus.
 He saw comprehension dawn on her, then awe. Her eyes went wide, and he watched her reach for him as his strength failed once more. Darkness took him.

—

 Ryan Carlyle sat hunched in miserable silence. He had always been Tristan's protector, the strong one. How could he have failed him? He glanced up every few seconds to look into the room. No change. The doctors told him he would likely regain the use of his legs with intensive therapy. He had gotten the help he needed in time, because of Tristan.

Another glance. Adrienne still held his hand. No change.

He had sent Amy to sleep. She had been through a lot. Everyone had. No matter how much he blinked he could not stop his eyes from watering. Tristan had spent his whole life being unselfish, and now it had probably cost him his life.

After another quick glance at his motionless friend, Ryan bowed his head on his hands.

—

When he next opened his eyes, things had calmed down considerably. Other than the vicious pain, the room was transformed into something almost serene. He blinked the fatigue out of his eyes and winced as he tried to move. A stabbing pain seared his nerve endings and he quickly realized movement would be a task he would tackle later on. He tried moving his toes with little success. He was just so weak!

As recognition seeped in, he remembered the accident. He remembered his proposal, and he remembered dying. He knew he had died, he felt the last breath leave him. He had accepted it, and had surrendered to it.

Was he dreaming then? No, surely not. The pain was proof enough of that. Had the medical team saved him? It was the only explanation. The miracles of modern medicine, of course, but for some reason Tristan was sure it wasn't the doctors that saved him.

He heard a murmur to his right and realized he was not alone. Adrienne was curled up in a chair next to his bed, her hand linked to his with a delicate interlocking of fingers. He squeezed her hand and she shot upright.

Tears were instantaneous, as was the fierce kiss that accompanied it. Tristan could feel the love, and relief, but also the pain. A groan escaped his lips.

He felt her body tense as she eased herself off of him.

He chuckled. "Did… you… gain… weight?"

The smile his comment brought was a stark contrast to the tracks the tears had left on her weathered features. She kissed him again; much gentler this time.

"Am I dreaming?" she whispered. The words brushed his lips.

"Am I?" he replied, emotion starting to surge to the forefront of his awareness.

"I thought. I thought…" Adrienne's strength failed and she cried openly convulsing with sobs in an attempt to catch her breath.

Tristan closed his eyes. Oddly, the pain started to diminish, and he held her close.

—

Ryan came to as Amy shook him frantically. It must have been a combination of the drugs and the pain because it took him a minute to focus. He took one look at her and his heart dropped. Her face was blank, her mouth agape.

They had said it was only a matter of time, before his heart gave out. It had worked too hard, for too long. Ryan could feel his own heart beat faster and he shook his head in denial. He couldn't look at her. He wanted to be held, he wanted to be left alone, he wanted a time machine.

He felt Amy grab his face. She looked him in the eye, her look changed from one of shock to…to…

Amazement?

Ryan frowned as Amy could no longer keep the smile from her face. He didn't understand. She moved to the side and tilted his head gently upward to look into Tristan's room.

Where the impossible was taking place. Tristan was not only alive, but making out.

The nerve of the bastard.

"Amy, go get Cam. Get Patty and Emma, get everybody. I knew that huge heart of his could handle it."

—

Adrienne tried to compose herself as quickly as she could, but she could not stop her heart from racing.

They said he'd never wake up. They said his brain was dead. His brain maybe, but not his heart. Not his heart.

She heard the door open and saw Ryan wheel frantically into the room. He took the other side of the bed and gripped Tristan's hand. She watched as Tristan beamed.

"I saved *your* life. What do you think of that?"

"I think the only reason you woke up was to take Adrienne to La Senza," Ryan joked with minimal composure.

"Wait a second, you knew about that?" She asked feigning surprise.

Tristan gave a meek shrug, "I was more thinking a jewelry store."

Epilogue

Tristan stood at the altar. The breeze coming off the water smelt of salt. The sun was high in the Nova Scotian sky, and the sea was a deep blue. The altar was on a platform specifically designed for weddings. It was approximately five feet off of the sandy beach suspended by hundreds of metal pillars. It was completely portable, the perfect contraption to support the fifty odd guests including the bride and groom. The minister grinned at him and Tristan ignored the old woman. He gazed out into the ocean, daydreaming.

He had come a long way. A month in a coma, another two months of recovery, and that was the easy part.

Wedding planning was a nightmare.

He and Adrienne decided to have the wedding as soon as possible instead of waiting for the baby. They both discovered a new appreciation for time, and the fragility of it. They were assured three months along would not pose a problem to their wedding plans. Tristan was unsure if he had what it took to be a good father and was just as scared as he was excited, but knew he had the support available to him should he need it.

Tristan scanned the group of loved ones in front of him. Patty smiled at him, a mix of pride and good humour. Cameron was a teary mess and the wedding hadn't even started. He had never seen his father cry; until the last three months. His baby sister,

Emma, was wiping something off Austin's face, which earned her a scowl from him. Tristan grinned.

Callie and Stephanie sat in the second row. Callie had a Kleenex box in her lap and was already ripping the tissue from it. Stephanie took her hand and gave it a supportive squeeze while offering Tristan a wink.

Karl Greene was next to Steph and Callie and he looked at Tristan with steady pride. They spoke the night before and agreed that Deanna would be happy for him. Alec and the basketball crew made up the back few rows. Rachel Smith sat in the back, and gave him a cute little wave. Matt and Lacey sat next to Rachel hand in hand. Matt smirked at him, and Tristan was suddenly afraid. Matt wouldn't prank him at his own wedding…

Would he?

He glanced back to the front row where his family sat. Amy was mouthing words to Ryan. Tristan thought he caught a few F bombs, Ryan just smiled.

Tristan looked at his best man. Ryan knew how to wear a suit. He had yet to shed the use of the cane, but he liked to joke that it made him look *elegant* and *classy*. Tristan constantly reminded him the word he was looking word was crippled.

Ryan smiled at him, offering silent support.

Tristan made sure to pace his breathing. He knew Adrienne was the love of his life, but all of the eyes on him made him nervous. He shifted his feet. What took brides so long?

He took a moment to thank the last guest in attendance. To do so, he moved his eyes skyward. He knew the beautiful day was his wedding gift from her. He also thanked her for his life. If there were angels, she was queen among them.

I love you, D. Thank you.

Mere moments later, the music started. The wedding march numbed him to his surroundings. He caught a glimpse of his bride ascending the stairs to walk the isle. His knees weakened.

Three Words

Stunning, breathtaking, phenomenal—Tristan searched his vocabulary for a word that fit. Radiant? He couldn't form coherent thoughts, he could barely breathe. His wife to be was the most beautiful woman on the planet. Ryan must have sensed his mild heart attack. The big man leaned over, "You are a lucky bastard, I don't know how you do it."

The attempt at normalcy brought a smile to Tristan's face, but every step Adrienne took sent the wind from his lungs in anticipation.

This is it.

She wore no veil, and her hair was down. She was as Tristan requested, simply Adrienne. Her caramel skin was even more beautiful in contrast with her white wedding dress. She wore it strapless, and with only a modest train. She shed no tears, and when her deep brown eyes met his, she beamed.

"Tristan Cage, don't you ever cry for me. You are the most amazing man I have ever known, if anyone should be in awe, it is me."

Speechless, Tristan took her hand.

Silence reigned, only the sound of whipping wind and birds competed with the minister's soft voice. Tristan knew she was speaking, but couldn't really hear the words. He stood, staring at his wife, his future.

The first, and last, three words he heard were from Adrienne's lips.

Baby, I do.

Tristan Cage was married, in front of all those he loved. And when they kissed to make it official, an angel smiled.

About the Author

Matt Turner was born and raised in Dutch Settlement, Nova Scotia where he graduated from Saint Mary's University with a History/English major. He currently lives in Alberta with his wife and dog. A High School English teacher by day and Basketball enthusiast by night, Matt penned his debut novel, Three Words, in 2010.

CPSIA information can be obtained at www.ICGtesting.com
Printed in the USA
LVOW080342251012

304315LV00001B/3/P